T0374419

# Love Me

# Love Me

## CATHERINE M. CLIFTON

EDITED BY:
MALLARY BUNDY, MELISSA COPELAND, AND LINZY CLIFTON JR.

# LOVE ME

This is a work of fiction. All of the characters, names, incidents, organizations, and dialogue in this novel are either the products of the author's imagination or are used fictitiously.

iUniverse books may be ordered through booksellers or by contacting:

iUniverse
1663 Liberty Drive
Bloomington, IN 47403
www.iuniverse.com
844-349-9409

ISBN: 978-1-4697-6671-3 (sc)
ISBN: 978-1-4697-6673-7 (hc)
ISBN: 978-1-4697-6672-0 (e)

Print information available on the last page.

iUniverse rev. date:  10/11/2020

# Contents

## Part III—Discovering Self-Love

# Part I

A Little Necessary Evil

Have you ever asked the questions,
Why me, Lord? Why me?
And waited for an answer?
Sometimes life will put us through the
ringer just to get our attention.
With all the complications we have to
endure in life, it's sad that something bad
has to happen in order for something
good to take effect.
These are the things
I've labeled as God's
Necessary Evils.

# Prologue

What happened? I struggled to remember. I tried to lift myself up and look around, but the pain was too overwhelming. The swelling on my face pinned my eyelids shut making it nearly impossible to see. I scanned the room but there was no one in sight. Wincing, I tried to make out where I was. The half-lit room was empty. Static hummed nearby, and was that...music? Perhaps from a radio. It couldn't be far. I tried to sit up. I touched my head and then I saw it. Blood, still warm, oozed from my body. Suddenly, the pain in my face fell away and my eyes went wide. I called out.

"Help!" I assumed no one could hear my faint voice over the roaring television.

"Help..."

Lying in a puddle of my own blood, I felt as though this was the end. The end to a life that was filled with nothing but hurt, lies, and betrayal—all misguided by love. Love can drive some people to do some very bad things, like betray the one person they claim they care for. Love is a crazy thing; and for me, it might have cost me everything. Lying curled up in a ball and hardly breathing, all I could think about was who would do this to me. Who would want to see me hurt like this? Tears ran down my face as the names of people I knew and loved ran through my mind. I couldn't believe any of them would want to see me like this. Resentment filled my heart as I reminisced about the events that led up to this tragic day in my life.

# Chapter 1

ༀ

# Who's the Oldest?

It was a hot Friday morning, and I was running late to class as usual. The Florida heat was beating me down as I struggled to make it out of the house on time. I dashed out the door to my car, wearing a pair of my favorite jogging pants, and a plain white tee. I clinched my backpack, with a bagel and cream cheese in one hand, and keys in the other. I tried to make it to Mr. Taylor's class on time. He taught Psychology, a class I hated being late for. Being able to recognize different personalities and trying to understand human behavior was exciting, and I wanted to learn all about it. I shared the same class with my boyfriend, Damien Fletcher, whom I had been dating for the past four years. Considering he was just as smart as I was, I knew he had taken some notes. I pulled into the parking lot, finished off my bagel, and wiped away any excess crumbs from my face. I wanted to make sure I looked half-way decent before entering class. As I was about to step out of the car, I looked down at my feet, and realized I had run out of the house wearing my bedroom slippers.

"Man…well, it's too late to go back home."

I got out of the car and headed for Mr. Taylor's classroom. Now, what most people didn't understand about me was the fact that I really didn't care what they thought about me, as long as they didn't say it to my face. I slipped into the classroom and sat towards the back, looking around trying to see if I could find Damien.

I'm not sure how we hooked up, but we were as opposite as opposites could be. He was very well known and had the looks and brains to match. He was adored by the ladies, but he was only interested in one person…me, Rhonda Brown. All types of women threw themselves at Damien, but the ones who I always seemed to get a laugh out of, were the dressy and flashy types who wore name-brand clothes and high-heeled shoes. To me, it felt as though they were dressing for the club instead of class. But it was their right to wear whatever they wanted, do whatever they wanted, and say whatever they wanted. However, when it came to Damien, he was off limits. Whenever girls would approach him, I wouldn't say a word. I would just give him a subtle look to let him know that I was watching. I had nothing to worry about, because as fine as Damien was, I was the only person who had his heart and I knew he wouldn't do anything to jeopardize our relationship. The bell rang. Class was over. I stood by the door waiting for Damien to exit the classroom.

"Hey, so what did I miss?" We began to walk towards the courtyard.

"Nothing much. I got notes if you need them." Damien handed me his notebook.

"Thanks." I took the notebook and placed it in my backpack.

"So, what happened this morning?"

"Nothing. Just running a little late. That's all."

"Was it really nothing, or was it Caroline?"

Damien knew I was late because of Caroline, but I wasn't in the mood for any confrontation.

"I couldn't leave until she came home. You know that." I turned away from Damien and started to walk off in the opposite direction. Arguing about my sister was a lose-lose situation, and there were so many other things on my mind besides Caroline. She was battling her own demons, and it was up to me to give her space, and to make sure she was okay.

"Wait! Wait!" Damien shouted. I made it to the center of the courtyard as Damien tried to catch up with me.

"Look, I'm sorry. I know you care about your sister, but she's a grown woman, and you're not her mother. You shouldn't have to babysit her. She's the oldest, remember?" Damien was trying his best to make eye contact, but I knew if I looked into his eyes, I would give in.

"You're right! She is the oldest, but she's also problematic. Or did you forget that? I don't want to wake up one morning and discover she never made it in. So, if I have to watch her night after night to ensure she's safe, then so be it. I'll watch. If I have to stay at home until she comes in, then fine. At least I know she's home safe. I don't do these things because I want to, I do them because I have to. She's the only family I have left."

I walked over to a big oak tree in the middle of the courtyard. I took a quick breather in the shade, hoping it would cool me off. I didn't want to be mad at Damien, but I hated talking about Caroline. He was constantly hounding me about a situation that wasn't going to change any time soon.

"Then get her to stop. Put her in rehab. Do something other than what you're doing now because it's dangerous."

"I know the streets can be crazy, but I'm totally capable of taking care of myself."

"Really? So, tell me…what are you going to do when you go out one night and Caroline is being attacked? Jump out and defend her honor? You're her little sister, Rhonda, not her bodyguard. If something were to happen to you and I wasn't there, then…" Damien paused.

"Nothing's going to happen to me. Besides, I don't go out alone. I have protection." I smiled thinking about the gun I bought from a crackhead off the streets.

"Oh, so you're a gangster now? Come on, Rhonda. Move in with me. That way, if you have to go out at night, you won't be alone." Damien pleaded with me, and I knew he meant well; but there was no way I was moving in with him.

"It's a sweet offer, but you know I can't leave Caroline. Not now. Maybe one day in the future when she's better." Caroline was ruining my so-called love life, but what else could I do? I couldn't trust her to be alone.

"In the future?" A smirk emerged across Damien's face. "Are you sure we're going to have a future together? Because right now all I see is you and Caroline. Where am I in this picture? Or was I ever in it to begin with?" I could sense the frustration in Damien's voice.

"You're there! You get me with the good and the bad, remember? I know it's a lot to ask, but give me some time. Let me get Caroline situated, and once she's clean and off the streets, I'm all yours. But until that happens, I can't leave her at home alone. I won't!"

I was hoping Damien would've been a little more understanding, but I knew it was hard to ask any man to put his life on hold while hoping for a miracle, because when it came to Caroline, it was going to take a miracle to get her clean.

I remembered how Caroline used to be, before going off to college. She was the girl all the guys wanted to be with, and all the girls wanted to be. She had thick bushy hair, a flawless smile with the prettiest white teeth, and a body to die for. Growing up, all the girls wanted to look just like Caroline—including me. Caroline had it all and she knew it—the looks, the boys, and on top of that, she was smart. She had everything going for her, and then six years ago out the blue everything changed. The sister I knew and respected ceased to exist.

"Okay. One day you'll see it's just not worth it. You care more for a person who doesn't give a damn about themself, but one day you'll see that Caroline is only good for one thing, and that's bringing you down."

Damien began to head back towards class. I wanted to call out to him, but my pride wouldn't let me. If that's how he felt, then it was best he left. I stood up from under the oak tree and started to walk towards my car. Damien killed the mood with his qualms and moralities, so finishing class today was definitely out of the question. He knew his words hurt me even though they needed to be said. Irritated about everything, I had to get away. So, I decided to head to work early to try and clear my head.

Moments later, I pulled up at Justine's Antique Doll shop, and headed inside. Making dolls had become my passion, and the types of dolls I made were very unique. I only prepared special orders for big-time clients, and these weren't your regular every day clients. Statuses ranged from CEOs to high-ranking officials. If Rachel only knew how much money I was really making, she would probably pass out and die. However, through creative thinking, I found a way to really make these dolls fly off the shelves, by inserting something I knew would sell. And what's something all of these rich business men are in the market for? Drugs. Hard to obtain, yet highly profitable. When I learned how to lace the dolls with cocaine, that's when the money started flooding in. And I wasn't going to work with anything less than the best quality. My product was pure, uncut and the real deal. Who would've thought that a straight-A student would get involved with the drug cartel, but since the death of my parents, there were a lot of things I had to do that I didn't like?

For instance, I had to take on adult responsibilities at a young age to keep from losing my parents' house. I don't know what Caroline did with their insurance money, but we were broke. She never contributed enough money to help pay for anything, so in return, I had to rely on some of her questionable friends for help. At first, I was hesitant about having any dealings with the cartel—until times became so unbearable, that I was left with no other options. I figured Caroline's friends would eventually rat me out, but since the money was so good, they never said a word. The better I became at my art, the less people I had to interact with. As time progressed, I soon became my own boss. I had my own unique connections for obtaining the drugs, and I had to make sure the cocaine was hidden so well that no one—not even the best drug dogs in the world—would be able to detect its scent. When it was all said and done, kilos of uncut cocaine were now picture-perfect vintage dolls. I had made so much money from selling dolls that I never had to work or attend school again, but they had become such great covers, that I decided to keep the ruse going.

Selling my dolls seemed easy compared to making them. I worked from home, which turned out to be a challenge because Caroline was always there. So, I decided to only work at night whenever she was away. Damien always assumed I was out keeping an eye on Caroline, when in reality I was at home making dolls. I loved my sister, but she knew how to take care of herself.

So far no one knew of my side job, and that's the way I wanted to keep it. If Caroline ever figured out there were drugs in the house, then I could only imagine what would happen next. That's why I decided to sell the dolls out of the shop. My best friend Rachel owned the shop. Her grandmother left it to her in her will, and Rachel's mother, Justine had been trying to convince Rachel to sign over ownership to her, but Rachel wasn't hearing it. She loved that shop and had no intentions on giving it to anyone—including her mother. I didn't want Justine to take over any more than Rachel did. Justine was too controlling and too nosey. One day she almost caught me while I was writing up one of my transactions in the back. The money I made from one of my sales was sitting on the counter. I was so busy that I forgot to put the cash away. Luckily, Rachel called Justine up front, which was the only thing that saved me, because there was no way I could've explained how or why I had so much cash lying around.

And it was a lot of cash. One doll, depending on the size, could run a buyer up to half a million dollars. However, for record-keeping purposes, I claimed I sold the dolls for about forty-five dollars. As for the actual profits, I hid them well. I was the queen of offshore accounts. If I was ever caught, I wouldn't sweat it, because my money was hidden so well. It would've been next to impossible for anyone to figure out the name on the account, much less the account numbers.

At one point, I decided to quit the drug game since I no longer needed the extra money, but the offers continued to roll in, and who was I to say no? Money like that could change someone's life, and since Rachel and her family were so good to me, I would leave everything to her in case something ever happened to me. I didn't want anything to happen to her, and the fact that she was a single parent was the main reason I kept her out of my operation. Rachel had been my best friend since junior high and we always looked out for each other. When my parents died, her grandmother offered me a job at the shop. That's how I learned my craft. I learned a lot about drugs while attending college. You would be amazed at what was taught on and off campus in relation to narcotics. I didn't consider myself a pusher but rather an artist. That's why no one was ever suspicious of my clients. Middle aged white men and women would come in to pick up their orders, and some even bought in their kids to make the front look real.

"Hey, Rhonda, why are you here so early?" Rachel stood behind the register reading a magazine.

"I wasn't in the mood for class today. So, I decided to come in early to help you out. Besides, Caroline is at the house and you know I'm not trying to deal with her right now." I walked behind the counter to join Rachel with a magazine.

"So how is she doing, considering she just got out of rehab?"

"I don't know. She's never at home. When I'm coming in, she's going out. I try to talk to her, but all she wants to do is fight. Like it's my fault she's the way she is."

It seemed as though Caroline had become the topic of the day. Thanks to her I may never have a normal life, but it was good to know that everyone else was so worried about poor little Caroline.

"Well after your parents died, Caroline took it hard."

"No! Don't blame this on my parent's death. This is all Caroline. She chose to do drugs and start hooking. They were my parents too, but you don't see me out there trying to destroy myself."

It was as if our parent's death had become a way for Caroline to justify how she was living her life. Damien was right about one thing; Caroline was the oldest, and she was supposed to have looked out for me, but instead I was left to defend and support myself. So, the one person I didn't feel sorry for was Caroline.

"Why are you so hard on Caroline? She's your sister. Hell, she's the only family you have left. So why do you talk about her in such a cold way?" Rachel closed her magazine and turned to face me.

"Because all day long I have to defend Caroline's actions to everyone out there, and I'm tired of it. I love her and I hate her at the same time. She was supposed to have been there for me, but instead she abandoned me, and now I'm supposed to feel sorry for her? Well I don't." Why we were still talking about Caroline was beyond me.

"Look, Rhonda, I know you love Caroline because I see the hurt in your eyes every time you talk about her. I know you, and there's more going on than you're willing to share. I swear all I'm trying to do is help you." I knew Rachel meant well, but she didn't know Caroline. Not like I did. "You know what happened to her. I would think you would cut her some slack." Rachel was going on and on about Caroline, and I knew she was referring to the fact that Caroline was raped, and of course that's an absolutely horrific thing to happen to anyone, but I was tired of Caroline continuing to make me feel bad about myself because of something she went through. Caroline use to be the best sister in the world, but after the rape, the fun-loving sister I once had returned home completely changed.

"Yes. I know! That's the point. I know. Everyone knows. She was raped and I get that, but she uses it as an excuse to do whatever she wants. I've tried to help her countless times, and she won't even try. All she does is fight with me on everything, and I'm sick and tired of it."

The love I once had for Caroline was now replaced with hate. If she ever loved me as her sister, then she would pop out of the trance she walked around in, and truly see me. I wanted to love her, but she made it so hard for me to even try.

"It's got be hard for her to deal with what she's been through. I know if I would've gone through what she went through, I don't know if I would've made it. So why can't you ease up some, and just be there for her? She's your sister, and maybe she needs you more than you realize."

I couldn't understand why everyone was fighting me on this subject. My relationship with Caroline was mine to deal with and no one else's.

"If it was only that simple, but there's nothing simple about Caroline. I love her, she knows it, and she uses it against me. She's conniving, selfish, and the older sister I once grew up with was no longer there. I would give anything to have the old Caroline back, but she's in a place where I can't reach her. So, until she decides to get it together, she'll remain a stranger to me."

I had a lot of my dreams crushed because of Caroline, and I blamed her for a lot of the drama I endured in my life. Selling drugs was probably something I would have never thought about doing, but because of Caroline, it became my last alternative, and I hated her for it. Everyone else wanted to view her with their blinders on, but not me. She may have fooled some people, but I saw Caroline for who she really was—a big disappointment.

# Chapter 2

## The Blow Out

It was late and I dreaded going home because I knew Caroline would be there. I walked into the house and it was a mess. The living room was a wreck as well as the kitchen. I walked into Caroline's bedroom, and there she was prepping in front of the mirror, as if she was getting ready for another night out.

"I can't believe you! I've been gone all day, and you've done absolutely nothing to this house. It stinks and it's a mess!"

What was it going to take for Caroline to get it? I was tired when I got home, and the last thing I wanted to do was to deal with an adult who behaved like a child. The only thing she seemed to be good at was prostituting and getting high.

"If it irritates you so much then you can clean it up...because it's not bothering me."

What was irritating me was *her*. She had the nerve to be smoking a cigarette inside the house, which she knew drove me crazy. She would do these things just to get under my skin. Caroline thought if she drove me crazy enough that I would eventually move out and leave her the house, but that wasn't going to happen.

"I would be surprised if anything bothered you. You know they say the dead can't sense anything?" I picked up some of Caroline's dirty clothes and started to throw them at her. "Can you smell that? That's your funk stinking up the house. This house stinks! You stink!"

I continued to throw clothes at Caroline and before I knew it, she was chasing after me. I tried to close my bedroom door, but Caroline busted through the door, and pinned me down on the bed.

"Look…I don't know what your problem is, but I suggest you chill out. I've got somewhere to be and you're making me late. So, stop being a brat, and leave me the hell alone!" Caroline released me and then it was on. I jumped on her back ready to take her down.

"I hate you! You make me sick!"

I had Caroline by the hair, and she was elbowing me in the chest. Her blows hurt, but I refused to let go of her hair. Every time she would hit me in the chest, I would knee her in the face. Before long, we both were tired, and I decided to let go of her hair.

"You trick! Look at my nose."

Caroline's nose was bleeding very heavily. Part of me felt bad, and the other part of me felt as though she deserved it. We were never like this before, and now we couldn't stand each other.

"You came after me, remember." I lifted up my shirt, and looked at the bruises on my chest. She was going to pay for what she had done.

"You're crazy, you know that? You come home starting with me and now look at my nose. You need help." Caroline was in the bathroom trying to stop her nose from bleeding.

"Are you still high? You go out night after night, and then come home high as a kite every morning. You don't cook, you don't clean, and you barely help me with the bills. All you are is wasted space. I swear, if you weren't my sister, I would've kicked you out a long time ago." I headed to the kitchen to find something cold to put on my chest. It was on fire and so was I.

"You would've kicked me out? Are you serious? Mom and Dad left this house to both of us. You don't have any authority to put me out, today or any other day." Caroline walked towards me, and then she threw her bloody rag at me. She was so nasty and it drove me insane.

"You want to talk to me about authority? How about I call your probation officer, and then you can see just how much authority I have. I know you have drugs in your system, and now would be a good time for a test. What do you think? Should I give her a call?" I wanted to show Caroline that she didn't have the upper hand in this situation.

"Go ahead and call. Maybe then you'll get what you want. Me out of your life." Caroline paused and looked around the house. "Mom and Dad would be so proud of us." Caroline walked back to her room and closed the door. What she said shouldn't have hurt, but it did. She knew I didn't want her to go away, but I did want her to get clean. I guess it was the price I had to pay for the type of work I did. Karma! I went upstairs to apologize, and before I could knock on the door, I could hear Caroline in her room crying. I hated her because I never really knew how to feel about her. She would drive me crazy, but at the end of the day, she was still my sister. I knocked on the door and let myself in.

"Hey. I just wanted to say..." By the time I opened the door, all I could see was Caroline sitting at her desk, hitting the pipe! "Are you crazy? You're lighting up in the house? Come on, Caroline!"

That was the last straw. Caroline had officially crossed the line. She smiled at me, with tears running down her cheeks, as she blew smoke in my face.

"This is what you wanted, right...well now I'm officially high. So, go ahead and make your call. I'm not going anywhere. Go ahead, Rhonda. Make the call." I took the pipe from Caroline and broke it on the floor.

"You are so sad, and I actually had the nerve to feel sorry for you. What was I thinking? How can you feel sorry for a dope fiend, when they don't feel anything for themself?" As I turned to face the door, Caroline jumped up out of her chair and grabbed hold of my arm.

"You think I don't feel. I feel! Every day I feel! I can't even close my eyes without thinking about everything that has happened to me. You stand there and you judge me, but you don't know the half of what I've been through. You sit on your high horse and have the nerve to look down on me. Get out! Just get out!" Caroline tried to push me out of her room, but I was determined to stand my ground. Every time she pushed; I would push back even harder.

"You're a drug addict, and yet you don't want anyone to judge you? Are you serious? How about this…why don't you try being clean for once. Try going to rehab and this time making it work. Do something other than selling your body and coming home high, because I'm sick and tired of it!" Caroline finally stopped pushing. She eased her way over to her bed and decided to lie down.

"Just get out. I can't fight with you anymore."

I was about to say something else, but I decided to keep it to myself. What I was looking at was a sad sight. Caroline had fallen so far in my eyes, and there was nothing she could've said to make me understand why she was doing this to herself. I looked at her and I walked out of the room.

Now what was I going to do? I couldn't work with Caroline in the house, so I decided to get up with Damien. Within the hour he was at the house, and I was more than ready to leave.

I walked by Caroline's room, and she was still passed out on the bed. I made my way to Damien's car and we drove off.

"So, where do you want to go?" I didn't have a clue as to where I wanted to go. My chest was hurting, I was tired, and all I wanted to do was sleep.

"Can we go back to your place? I'm tired and I'm frustrated, and I just want some peace and quiet if that's all right with you."

I looked over at Damien while he was driving, and all I could think about was how he was so perfect for me. He was the calm to the hell I had to put up with on a daily basis. It was days like this that made me want to give it all up and just sit back and make real synthetic dolls.

"My place? Are you sure about that? I mean you seemed as though you wanted to cut my head off earlier today." I hated how I would mistreat Damien. I blamed Caroline for a lot of it, but for the most part I blamed myself.

"Yes, I'm sure. I was wrong for the way I treated you today. You were right. I needed to wake up and realize that you can't help someone who's not willing to help themself." Damien grabbed my hand and smiled.

"So, are you staying the night or are you just waiting it out until you think Caroline is gone?" I knew Damien wanted me to stay, and this time I wasn't going to disappoint.

"I'm staying." I leaned over and gave Damien a kiss on the cheek as we stopped in front of his place.

"What was that for?" Damien turned the car off and shifted all his attention towards me.

"I wasn't fair in the way I treated you today; you didn't deserve that. I had a lot of things going on in my head, and I took them out on you, and for that I'm sorry."

Damien escorted me into his apartment, which he always kept clean. To some he would be considered a neat freak. His apartment was decorated with high-end furniture and mainstream art. His place looked, felt, and smelled like home. I headed straight for the bedroom and collapsed across the bed. It felt good being in a drama-free environment, and for once, I was truly considering if I should call it quits and move in with Damien for good. He loved me. Plus, I wouldn't have to deal with Caroline, and I could finally get out of the drug game. Damien crawled onto the bed and embraced me in his arms. He held tightly, and my body was able to relax and feel at ease.

"I love you. You know that, right?"

"I know."

Damien was the one person who loved me, flaws and all, and I was too afraid to give him all of me. He released me from his grip and gave me a passionate kiss.

"I love you so much. I wish you didn't ever have to leave."

Damien didn't know how bad I truly wanted to make that happen. I looked into his eyes, and realized just how much I needed him. Damien's hand accidently bumped my chest, and the pain from the bruising made me cry out. Startled, Damien eased back as he began to examine me.

"What happened? What did I do?" I reassured him that it was nothing he had done, and then I showed him the bruises on my chest I had received from Caroline. "Who did this to you? How did this happen?" To me, the question wasn't who, but why? Why was I allowing these things to happen to me if I didn't have to?

"I did. I started with Caroline when I got home and this was the end result." I pulled off my shirt, and turned onto my stomach, hoping that the pressure would take away from some of the pain.

"Why do you stay there? I've told you several times that you could move in with me, but you continue to turn me down. What is it going to take for you to leave the house of horrors?"

I wanted to leave so badly, but I didn't know where to begin. I couldn't see bringing my lifestyle into Damien's world. I couldn't! The only way I could move in was if I gave up making dolls and I was able to walk away from Caroline-for good. The thought of both options scared the life out of me, but something had to be done. I couldn't keep living on this rollercoaster ride I called life, especially if I expected Damien to remain in it.

"I'll stay." Damien was so busy ranting that he didn't hear me. "I said, I'm staying. I'm yours." I didn't have a clue as to how I was going to make it happen, but being with Damien just felt right.

"Are you serious? Don't play with me, Rhonda. You're going to move in?" Damien seemed so excited; I just prayed that I had enough strength to follow through.

"Yes. I think it's time. I'm going to settle things with Caroline, and then it's just you and me." I knew in my mind I was saying exactly what Damien wanted to hear, but doubt was already clouding my judgment, and the first move wasn't even made.

"Things are going to work out, and then you're going to wonder why you didn't move in with me earlier!"

I really wanted things to work out, but I needed to figure out a way to complete my last doll. I had a lot of drugs stashed around my parent's house, and I couldn't leave them unattended-not with Caroline living there. My mind started to wonder about so many things that I almost forgot where I was, until I started to feel Damien's hands all over my body. His touch was so gentle, and he made sure he was cautious around all my bruises. He ran his fingers up and down the spine of my back, and then he kissed me all over until I couldn't take anymore. Our body chemistry was perfect together. I wasn't certain about a lot of things, but being with Damien was the one thing I felt sure of.

# Chapter 3

# A Move Set into Motion

I was sitting at work trying to figure out how I was going to make this move happen. I needed to finish my last doll, but I wasn't sure if I was ready to leave Caroline at home alone. She was unstable and on top of that, an addict. I was deep in thought when a gravelly voice broke my concentration. It was Officer Tate—or plain old Jacob in my eyes. He was the father of Rachel's little boy Jacob Jr., but we all called him JJ. Jacob was a nice guy but he wasn't happy in his marriage to Stacy, who was Caroline's best friend. Stacy and Caroline met their freshman year in college, and they were inseparable ever since. Stacy had pasty, freckled skin and overly bleached hair which made Caroline's curvy caramel features look goddess-like in comparison. If I cared anything for Stacy, I would've told her that her husband had a baby by another woman, but I never did. I always blamed Stacy for what happened to Caroline, and knowing that her husband was happy with someone else was the type of retribution I was comfortable with. As for Jacob, I wasn't sure when him and Rachel hooked up. It just happened out the blue. One day, Rachel went off to college and the next thing I knew, she was back home with a newborn baby, and just my luck, a cop for a boyfriend. Karma!

"Hey. Is Rachel around?" Jacob was making his usual rounds which enabled him to spend some time with Rachel and JJ. I was so caught up in my own thoughts that I had become unaware of everything that was going on around me. I didn't have a clue as to where Rachel was, but I was good at stalling.

"I'm not sure. Let me check."

I went into the back of the store to see if I could find Rachel. The fact that she was messing around with a cop should've stopped me from selling my dolls a long time ago, but it didn't. I never considered Jacob a threat, because he was always distracted by Rachel and JJ whenever he came around. The truth of the matter was, he never paid any attention to me or what I was doing. I could've been selling drugs directly in his face, and he wouldn't have noticed. I looked around and I discovered a note from Rachel sitting on the counter. She had stepped out to pick up JJ from daycare. I headed back towards the front of the store to show Jacob the note, but before I could speak, I noticed him checking out the dolls on the shelf. I dismissed him until I noticed how much attention Jacob was giving to each doll. He was examining them as if he was looking for something in particular. Maybe I was wrong. Was I so arrogant to not consider that maybe Jacob had figured out what was really going on in the shop? It seems as though I had quit my doll-making scheme at just the right time. Whatever drugs Jacob thought he was going to find, weren't located at the shop, and his desperate attempt to seize a laced doll was going to lead him down a path to nowhere.

"You know, I don't think JJ would choose a bisque doll over his nerf collection."

I walked in from the back of the store with the note in my hand. I smiled, trying my best to play it cool.

"Oh, I was just looking. It's amazing how you guys are able to make them look so life-like." Jacob put the doll back on the shelf, and turned his attention back towards me.

"Well, I found this in the back." I showed Jacob the note hoping that it would be enough to get him to leave. "Rachel went to the daycare to pick up JJ."

"Alright. Well just let her know I stopped by." Good, he was leaving, and I could get back to my thoughts.

"I will. See you later." As I was about to turn my attention to something else, Jacob stopped. What did he want now?

"By the way, how's Caroline? I saw her in lockup a couple weeks ago. Did rehab do her any good?"

First, it was the dolls and now it's Caroline. Where was Rachel when I needed her?

"She's...well what can I say? It's Caroline. She's trying in her own way." Which I knew was a bunch of bull. Caroline wasn't trying to do anything but get high. I wish she had someone in her life who would help her get back on the right track, but who would that be? Caroline had no one but me, and now I was considering leaving her as well.

"Well, let her know that I wish her well." Jacob put his hat on as he headed towards the door.

"I will, and I'll be sure to let Rachel know that you stopped by."

Jacob left and I let out a sigh of relief. What was I going to do with the extra drugs? Even if I was capable of completing the last doll, how was I going to sell it? If the cops were watching the shop, then there was no way I could sell a doll out of it, and then there was the issue of Caroline. How was I going to break the news to her that I was moving out? She pretended as if she wanted the house to herself, but I knew Caroline, and she hated being alone. So, in order for me to move out, I needed someone else to move in; but who? Stacy was married, and Rachel had a kid, which made it impossible for her to live in a house with a drug addict. I was going to have to dig deep, and pray that I could find someone who didn't mind being roommates with Caroline. As for my last client, I was going to have to find a way to deliver the doll or it was game over—especially if

Jacob decided he wanted to come by the house one day and start snooping around.

Time passed and I finally got up the nerve to go home. Sooner or later, I was going to have to face Caroline with the truth. As I approached the house, I noticed it was quiet. Usually when I returned home, Caroline had something blaring off in the background, but today was different. I didn't hear anything as I walked through the front door. Something was definitely wrong. All kinds of thoughts ran through my head and then it clicked. The drugs! She couldn't have! I knew I hid them well, but I've never stayed out all night, not since I bought drugs into the house. Caroline would've had plenty of time to snoop if she felt like it. I raced to my bedroom. I fumbled with the handle as I tried to open the door. My room was ransacked. My stomach dropped. A layer of sweat formed on my brow as I leaped to check under my mattress and the baseboards in my closet. No! This couldn't be happening. There was over one hundred thousand dollars' worth of drugs in my room alone. I went into our parent's room and I let out a sigh of relief. It hadn't been touched. I went into the closet and the rest of the drugs were safe. I headed back to my room contemplating how much of the drugs Caroline actually found. She was off God knows where with a lot of uncut cocaine. If she didn't know what she was doing, she could kill herself. The dangers of my lifestyle were coming full circle. If Caroline was to die then it would be my fault. I kept the one demon she couldn't fight concealed in our home. My mind raced as I sorted through my things, and then out of nowhere, I heard the front door slam. I hurried downstairs and there she stood, out of breath and half dressed with sweat dripping down her face, while holding a large pillowcase, which I assumed was my stash.

"Caroline."

"The one and only."

"Where have you been?"

I kept an eye on Caroline, but more importantly, my stash.

"You want to know where I've been. Now that's funny, but you know what? I'll tell you. I've been walking around all day trying to sell this, but no one would take it. It seems as though no one knows how to break it down." I looked at Caroline, and I couldn't tell if she was high or not. I reached out for the sash but she pulled it back.

"Where did you get that from?" I tried to make my move again, but Caroline wouldn't let me get close.

"Oh, you know exactly where I got it from. Everyone has been asking me all day long where this came from." Curiosity took over and I just prayed that Caroline didn't slip up and say my name.

"And what did you say?" Caroline had me and she knew it. She was going to milk this for everything its worth.

"I don't know. That depends on whether or not you can help me out." And so, it began. Whatever Caroline had brewing in her head, she could hang it up. There was no way I was making a deal with her.

"Help you with what? What do you want?"

The only thing I had on my mind was retrieving my stash. If I had to fight it out of her hands then so be it, but one way or another I was getting my stash back.

"I want..." Caroline's hands were shaking and she seemed excited. "I want you to tell me why you had this in your room."

Tears began to stream down her face. I didn't know what to make of it. Was Caroline trying to show me that she cared, or was it a trick?

"It's not mine. I was holding it for someone else. Now give it back."

I held out my hand signaling for the bag, but Caroline didn't budge. Her hands gripped the pillowcase even tighter.

"Why are you lying to me? You think because I get high that I'm stupid? What are you doing with this in our house, and I want the truth, Rhonda?"

Caroline had some nerve. She tried her best to sell my stash all day, and now she wanted to know where I got it from. She couldn't be serious.

"The truth? You want the truth? You're so funny. The truth is that it's none of your business. All you need to know is that it's not mine, and I need it back." I reached out for the pillowcase and Caroline pushed me back. "Don't touch me! You ransacked my room in search of what? You stumbled across something that didn't belong to you, and then you had the nerve to try and sell it! Did you even think about what would happen to me if you did? How would I pay that back? As usual, you were only thinking about one person, and that's yourself. Was that the truth you were looking for?"

Caroline took the stash and threw it at me. She was wrong and she knew it, but she came after me hoping that I would tell her what? I picked up the pillowcase and headed towards my bedroom.

"Why are you doing this? That stuff can destroy you. Look at me! Can't you see how it's destroyed my life?" I stopped in my steps. Caroline was right. Drugs had destroyed her life, but she chose to use them. I didn't.

"Yes. I see. But you made that choice. No one but you decided to use drugs, and now you want to give me a lecture about not using them. Really! You know what...I'm moving out."

There was no subtle way to ease the blow. I was leaving and that was that. Caroline was going to have to find a way to deal with it, because I was tired of dealing with her.

"You're moving out?" Caroline appeared shocked, as if she thought I would never move out, but she had just proven to me why I should've left a long time ago.

"Yes. I'm moving in with Damien. We both know that it's time for me to go. I'll try and find you a roommate, but I can't live here with you anymore." I thought it was going to be hard for me to tell Caroline that I was leaving, but with her most recent stunts, it just made it easier for me to get it off my chest.

"Damien? Are those his drugs? Did he turn you on to this?" Caroline was reaching. There was no way Damien was involved in drugs, but she was going to believe whatever crazy thought entered her head.

"Damien? No! Damien doesn't do drugs, and you know that. Don't play crazy, Caroline. They're not mine and they're not Damien's. Satisfied?" I went to my room to try and clean it the best I could. Then I was leaving. I had witnessed enough drama for one day.

"No, I'm not. And you're not leaving!" I turned around, because I thought my ears were deceiving me.

"I'm not leaving? Who are you to tell me anything? I'm leaving and there's nothing you can do about it."

I grabbed my suitcase and started packing. The quicker I got out the house the better. Once Caroline had left for the night, I would return back to retrieve the rest of the drugs.

"You heard me right, and if you think I'm playing then try me. You're not going anywhere." Caroline had lost her mind if she thought for one minute, I was going to listen to her.

"And why's that? How do you think you're going to keep me here? By kidnapping me? I'm leaving! Now move out of my way." I tried to walk pass Caroline, but she blocked the doorway.

"I just love it when the tables are turned. Don't you?" Caroline started smiling as if she knew something I didn't.

"What are you talking about? Are you still high? Damien will be here soon, and I need to finish packing." Caroline walked into my bedroom, grabbed my suitcase off the bed, and threw it on the floor.

"I told you that you weren't going anywhere. You see, I have all the power in this situation, and this time you're going to listen to me." I knew Caroline was right, but I wasn't about to let on that she was.

"Or what? What are you going to do if I don't listen to you?" Caroline walked over to the telephone and picked it up.

"I'll call the cops, and see what they have to say about all the drugs that are stashed away in this house. Then I'll call Damien and let him know that he's about to shack up with a drug dealer." Caroline started smiling as if she had me, but I was willing to call her bluff.

"Call. Go right ahead, and I'll be sure to let everyone know that those are your drugs, and not mine. You see, I'm the straight-A student with no priors. So, who do you think they're going to believe; me or you?"

Caroline stepped back, hesitating, as if she was unsure of what her next move should be. One thing I knew for sure, I couldn't allow her to call the cops. If they thought for one minute there were drugs in the house, I would be finished. They were already snooping around the doll shop, and it doesn't take a genius to put two and two together.

"Well I'll take my chances seeing who they believe. I'm calling the cops." Caroline picked up the phone and I waited to see if she was serious. She started to dial, and without thinking, I yanked the cord out of the wall.

"You're not calling anyone. Don't you get it? If they think for one minute those are your drugs, then you are off to jail, and for a long time. Are you willing to take that chance just to get back at me? Think about it, Caroline, before you do something, we'll both regret."

I was willing to reason with Caroline, as long as it kept her from involving the cops. The last thing I needed was for everything to fall apart. Especially, when I was trying to go the straight and narrow.

"See, I may be a lot of things, but I'm not stupid. You don't want me to call the police, and I get it. You're hiding drugs in the house. Very understandable. But the way you're acting...tells me that it's something more. Something big. So, in order to keep me from ever making that phone call, you're going to inform Damien immediately that you're not moving in with him."

I couldn't believe it. Caroline called my bluff. I needed a way out and I didn't have one. There had to be something I could do in order to get Caroline to change her mind, because she didn't want me to stay any more than I did.

"Why? Why do you want me to stay here? All we do is argue and fight over everything. So, tell me Caroline, why are you so dead set on keeping me trapped in this hell hole that you call home, because it hasn't been that for me in a long time."

"You're my sister and I need you; that's all to it. So, you have to stay." That was a nice try, but I wasn't buying it. Yes, it was true that Caroline needed help, but she didn't need my help.

"You're not fooling anyone. You found some drugs in the house, and now you think what? That by keeping me here you may get a chance to score? Well, I hate to burst your bubble, but there will be no more drugs coming in or out of this house. That was the last of it. So, tell me again, Caroline, why do you really want me to stay?"

She was going to have to come up with something better than "I need you," because that wasn't going to fly.

"I don't care about the drugs. What I care about is you. Apparently, I don't know my own sister, and before things get too far out of control, I just need a chance to make them right. No matter which way you look at it, you're in the drug game, and I'm not cool with that. My life may be screwed up, but I be damn if you screw yours up as well. Now, I may have failed you in the past, but I'm not about to let that happen again."

Why? Why was she doing this to me? Time I'm ready to move on with my life, she wanted to care. Well she was too late, because at that particular moment, I didn't want nor need her help.

"I can't believe you. Now you wanna care. Unbelievable! You were getting high in your room just the other day, and now you want to lecture me about using drugs! This is my life! You were raped and I get that. Then Mom and Dad died, and you decided to throw your life away. It wasn't our fault they died; it was an accident, and it wasn't your fault you were raped, but you can't see past that. They're dead, and it's like you died with them, because you're not even here."

I knew I had gone too far, but I didn't know what it was going to take in order for Caroline to see that she was throwing her life away. I didn't want to hurt her, but she needed a reality check.

"It's my fault! All of it! There are things you don't know about. Let me rephrase that. There are a lot of things you don't know about!" Tears were streaming down Caroline's face. My mind was racing. That was not the reaction I was expecting—at all. What was she talking about? What didn't I know?

"Your fault? How was it your fault?" Caroline started to walk off, but she had opened a bag of worms that needed to be addressed.

"No. I can't talk about it. Just know that you can't leave. I don't care what you think about me, but you're not moving out of this house."

Whatever Caroline was hiding was eating away at her, and I needed to figure out what it was. She was good at keeping secrets, but this one I knew she wanted to share.

"You either tell me what you're hiding or I'm gone. Now what's going on? What aren't you telling me?"

Caroline turned around, and I could see the intensity in her eyes. I hadn't seen her look like that in a long time. Whatever she was hiding had to be big.

"You're not going anywhere...and if you try anything stupid, then I'll call the cops, and have them tear this house apart, just in case I didn't find all the drugs."

"Stop avoiding the question, Caroline, and tell me! What are you hiding?"

"I'm not hiding anything. What happened in the past is just that! In the past. So, leave it alone. Now what you can do is, clean up your room, unpack your suitcase, and stop asking me questions; because I'm not playing...you're not leaving this house."

I couldn't believe it. I was stuck, and I didn't know what to do. I couldn't chance the cops getting involved, and now I've discovered Caroline was hiding something from me. Time was running out and Damien was on his way. The tables were truly turned, and now I had to figure out a way to tell Damien that I wasn't moving in. Not just yet. I hated Caroline for what she was doing to me. She may have won this round but the fight was far from over.

# Chapter 4

# Chipping Away at the Truth

I was running out of time, and if I didn't uncover the truth soon, then I was going to lose everything I had worked so hard for. I tried to explain to Damien that I needed a few more days before I could officially move in, but I could sense the doubtfulness that lingered in his eyes. I needed a plan and I needed one yesterday. If I was going to figure out the truth, then I needed to speak with someone from Caroline's past, and Stacy was the perfect candidate. Whatever Caroline was hiding, I knew for a fact that Stacy would know something about it.

I headed over to Stacy's law firm hoping that I would be able to get something out of her. I wished Caroline wouldn't have dropped out of college, because she would've been a great lawyer. I observed Stacy, and I hated the fact she was living the life Caroline was robbed of. Now she spends all of her free time either representing Caroline in and out of court, or bailing her out of jail. I entered Stacy's office and it was immaculate, and seeing her in her perfect suit working the perfect job just made me hate her even more.

"Rhonda. It's been a long time. So, what brings you by? Caroline in trouble again?"

Agh! I couldn't stand her. The first thing she thinks when she sees me is that there's something wrong with Caroline. The quicker I get my answers, the faster I could get the hell out of her office.

"No. She's not in trouble…literally. But she is in trouble." I knew that would catch her attention. Stacy had been trying to fix Caroline ever since the rape.

"What do you mean? In trouble how?"

I didn't know how to approach Stacy about Caroline, because I couldn't stand the sight of her, but I needed answers, which meant I had to look past my disgust for her and proceed with my line of questioning.

"Well, just the other day we got into another heated argument, and I told Caroline she couldn't blame herself for being raped, and that she shouldn't beat herself up over our parent's death, because it was an accident—but she did. She kept saying how it was all her fault. Why would she say that? Why would she blame herself?"

Stacy's entire demeanor changed. Yet again, I had hit a subject no one wanted to talk about. Now I was certain there was something going on, and I wasn't going to stop prying until I was able to expose the truth.

"What all did she tell you?" Was she deaf? If Caroline had told me anything at all, I wouldn't be in her office having this conversation.

"Nothing. That's why I'm here. I need to know what happened to make Caroline blame herself for everything that has happened. I know about the rape, and our parent's car wreck. So, what is it that she's not telling me?"

I was hoping that Stacy would be truthful with me, because if not, then I was going to have to play dirty. One way or another I was going to get the truth.

"I can't tell you. If Caroline didn't tell you, then obviously she doesn't want you to know. She's only doing this to protect you."

Really. She was going to play this game with me. Then fine. Let's play.

"She doesn't want me to know? Now that's amusing considering how she's your best friend, and yet she's keeping secrets from you as well. Huh. It's funny how that works. You see, Caroline's secret is destroying her life, and until she faces it, she's going to continue on this downward spiral that no one is trying to help her get off of. Now, I'm not here to play games with you; all I want is the truth. I just want to know what happened to my sister to cause her to blame herself for actions that were out of her control."

Stacy sat in her chair in silence. Whether she decided to tell me anything or not, she was now curious as to what Caroline was keeping from her.

"I can't tell you much, but if you want to uncover the truth, then you need to talk with Brad Parsons. He can tell you whatever you need to know." Here we go again. Now Stacy was sending me on a wild goose chase.

"No! I'm not going to start some witch hunt with the hopes of stumbling across the truth. Someone out there who knows the truth is sitting directly across from me. Now why can't you tell me what's going on? What are you so afraid of?"

Stacy was starting to irritate me, and she was about to push me to expose Jacob's secret life.

"I can't play these games with you, Rhonda." Playing games! Was she serious? Now I was frustrated and upset.

"Does it look like I'm playing games with you? Because of you my sister is a walking train wreck. She told me you begged her to go to that party, but then you left her there alone. Who leaves their friend alone at a frat party? Who was so self-absorbed with themselves that they never came back to check up on their so-called best friend? That was you."

"Look, Rhonda…"

"No! You look. Caroline had a lot going for herself, and you took that away from her. You were her friend. You should have stayed or at least walked her home that night, but you didn't. Her life is destroyed because of you!"

I couldn't believe how upset I had gotten. Tears were streaming down my face, and my heart was racing. The love I had suppressed for Caroline came pouring out, and I couldn't stop it. The reality I didn't want to face was hitting me head on. I loved my sister, and I wanted her back. I wanted the truth and someone was going to give it to me.

"I didn't destroy her life. She did that all on her own."

Now I was seeing red. I couldn't believe the words that were coming out of Stacy's mouth.

"Really?"

Before I knew it, I was over Stacy's desk with my hands wrapped around her neck. My sister's life was ruined, and she was too conceited to accept her part of the blame. Some of Stacy's coworkers busted into her office to pull us apart. She had started a war that she wasn't prepared to win. One of the guys asked Stacy if she wanted to call the cops, but she fanned them away. As they walked out, I tried to compose myself and gather up my things. I figured I wasn't about to get anything else out of Stacy, so it was in my best interest to move on to someone else from Caroline's past. Besides, I was drawing unwanted attention to myself, and that was something I did not need.

"Look Rhonda...I get it. You're upset, but trying to hurt me isn't going to help Caroline. I'm sorry! I know you don't believe me, but I do blame myself every day for what happed to her, but I can't change the past and neither can you. The truth is out there but I can't give it to you, but if you keep digging into the past then you're going to stumble across some things that you're not fully equipped to handle just yet."

I had already stumbled across someone who I thought was my sister's friend, but soon discovered she was nothing but a fraud. I guess if I was to accomplish anything then I needed to find Brad

Parsons, but I couldn't leave without giving Stacy a present since she was so helpful in hindering me from the truth.

"Well, I understand you can't say anything and I respect that. You and Jacob have always been there for me and Caroline, and so I want to apologize for the way I've behaved today. I wish you, Jacob, and JJ the best and I promise you won't hear from me ever again."

A look of confusion came across Stacy's face. My work was done, and I had set in place the perfect exit.

"JJ? Who's JJ?" I continued to wander out of the door as if I was a deaf mute. If she wanted to play games then I was willing to play along too.

"Who's JJ? Don't play with me, Rhonda. If you know something then tell me."

If she wanted answers then she was going to have to talk to her husband, because I was done talking with her. Stacy was yelling down the hall, but I continued walking as if I didn't hear her. Her coworkers began exiting their office, with confusion and disbelief plastered across their faces, while instant chatter and whispers filled the air. I opened a door I had promised to keep closed, but I was done with keeping everyone's secret, especially when secrets were being kept from me. If Brad Parsons was the one holding the key then I needed to find him and fast, because once Stacy confronts Jacob about JJ, then I was going to have to deal with a very pissed off Rachel. I was burning bridges I knew I needed, but I had to do whatever it took to get Caroline back. My sister was killing herself slowly and I needed to know why.

# Chapter 5

### ❧

# Some Secrets Are Not
# Meant to Be Shared

It was hot, I was tired, and I was in no mood for going to work, but I couldn't afford to start changing my routine. If someone was watching me, then I needed to keep on pretending as though nothing had changed. Caroline had me trapped, Damien was pissed off, and to top it all off I had to face Rachel about JJ.

When I entered the store, I noticed there was no one at the front counter. Something wasn't right, and I was afraid Stacy had already confronted Jacob about JJ. I looked around the store, and there was no one in sight. I went into the back to stow away my belongings, and that's when I ran into an unexpected guest.

"Who in the hell are you? And what are you doing back here?" My heart was racing, and this idiot had scared me half to death. He better have a good explanation for being in the back of the store, or I was calling the cops, which was the only sane thing I could do to keep from shooting him.

"It's okay. I'm Prez Ramirez."

"That's nice to know but what are you doing back here?"

"I work here."

He worked here? When did Rachel hire someone new? I was definitely uneasy now. If Rachel had hired Prez, then there was a good possibility that I was probably fired. Me and my big mouth! I should have never said anything to Stacy about JJ.

"You work here? When did that happen?"

"A couple days ago...and who are you?"

I looked at Prez, trying to figure out who he was, and why was he here. Our workload wasn't heavy enough to require any additional help. So, something was definitely up.

"Where's Rachel? Is she here today?"

"Yes. She stepped out, but she told me she would be back in a few minutes. Do you need me to call her?"

"No. I don't need you to call anyone. So, what did she hire you for?"

"Just to help out doing a few odd jobs here and there, but you never told me who you were. I'm not supposed to let anyone back here." Was he serious?

"I'm Rhonda. I work here."

"Oh, yes Rhonda. You're one of the doll makers. Rachel told me you're one of the best."

I couldn't have felt any worse...I revealed JJ to Stacy, while Rachel was secretly giving me praise.

"I do have a gift, I must admit, but not to be rude, since there's no one here, do you mind watching the front counter? I have a doll I'm working on, and I really need to have it completed by the end of the week."

"Sure, I don't mind."

Prez left, and headed towards the front to cover the counter. As my heart was slowly calming down, I was finally able to check him out. He was not bad looking at all. Cute, as a matter of fact. He looked as though he was a mixture of Latino and Black and he had a nice body as well. I watched as his kind; honey-colored eyes searched for a button on the register. My gaze followed the curve of his back downwards and my mouth went dry taking in an eyeful of his thick...whoa. I had to snap out of it. I immediately felt guilty for even thinking that. Damien was so good to me. He didn't deserve my wandering eye.

I pulled out my laptop and started to search the web. There had to be something listed on Brad Parsons, but why couldn't I find it? Why wasn't he popping up on any of the websites? I continued searching. Then out of nowhere I heard the back door close. Rachel walked into the room, and eased down into a chair beside mine with tears in her eyes. My heart immediately fell to my feet. What had I done to my best friend?

"Rachel. Are you alright?"

"No! And don't pretend you don't know what's going on."

"I don't know what you're talking about. What's wrong?"

Rachel turned my chair around to face hers. I could sense whatever it was she had to say was going to be intense. As she stared into my eyes, I tried to figure out what was going on inside her head.

"You told Stacy! I made it very clear that you were to never mention JJ's name around her, or something bad would happen... right?"

"Yes."

"So why did you tell her? I don't know what your reasons were, but you told her. Do you know what you have done?"

"Look. I didn't tell her anything. She came at me with a lot of useless mumble jumble, regarding things I could care less about. All I wanted was the truth about my sister, but then she had the nerve to try and go all self-righteous on me and...."

"And what? You thought that gave you the right to expose my secret that I asked you to keep. Do you know what you have done? Oh my God!"

Rachel was crying uncontrollably, and I didn't know what to do. I was afraid that my friendship with Rachel was in serious jeopardy.

"You may have cost me my son! Why did you have to say anything?"

"Wait a minute. What are you talking about? How could I have cost you JJ? I didn't say anything to Stacy about him. All I did was mention his name. So, what's going on?"

"No! It's apparent you can't keep a secret. So why would I tell you anything else? I trusted you, Rhonda! How could you?"

"You can't trust me? Are you serious? For five years I have kept this secret to myself, and neither you nor Jacob has had the decency to tell me why. I mean…does he ever plan on leaving Stacy? Who knows? I don't. So, don't sit up on your high horse being angry at me about something I seem to know absolutely nothing about."

Rachel looked as though she wanted to inform me of what was going on, but before she could, Prez walked into the room and interrupted our conversation.

"I heard yelling. Is everything okay?"

I looked at Rachel and started to walk off. I knew I was wrong for the part I played in exposing her secret but I was tired of people giving me half-truths.

"I don't know. Why don't you ask your boss! She's good about keeping people in the loop."

"Rhonda, please."

"Oh, and by the way. Who is he? That's right. You didn't tell me anything about him either."

"Prez, could you give us a minute alone? I need to talk with Rhonda in private."

"Sure." Prez closed the door and headed back up front.

"Look, there are a lot of things you don't know about, and it was kept that way in order to protect you. I still can't tell you everything because this affects more than just you. So, if you don't want to open Pandora's Box, then I suggest you stop digging."

"See, now you're starting to sound just like Stacy. I don't know what it is that everyone knows except me, but I'm going to figure it out, because one thing I don't like is secrets being kept from me."

"Look, you need to stop or you're going to ruin a lot of people's lives in the process."

Ruin lives…now I was getting frustrated. All I was hearing was the same old thing over and over again—the talk of other people's lives being ruined while my life was slowly going up in smoke. I didn't want to hear it anymore.

"Let me see…Caroline is strung out on drugs, and she's prostituting on the side. You're messing around with a married man, and on top of that you had his kid. My boyfriend is on the verge of leaving me, and to make matters worse, my sister is holding me hostage in my own home. So, tell me again, whose life am I going to ruin, because it seems as though we have all done a great job of that on our own."

"You're right. We all have messed up, but I promise you, Rhonda, there is more to the story then what you know. I beg you to stop. Please! Just leave it alone."

"Are you not listening to me? My life is already ruined. So how is uncovering the truth about what happened to Caroline going to destroy so many lives? She's a mess. You've seen her, and you expect me to stop searching for the truth? You're my best friend, and I thought you would have understood my reasoning behind all of this, but you don't. Why's that?"

"Damn it, Rhonda! Why won't you listen? Can't you see that this is bigger than you and me? So please…just let it go."

"If this is so big, then tell me, how is it that you're involved and I'm not? Caroline's my sister, but you seemed to know more about what happened to her than me. Why's that?"

"I wish I could tell you but I can't. All you have done is complicate things in a way that you couldn't understand. Please, if you ever loved me and JJ, then stop digging."

I was hurt. Everyone I knew was keeping secrets from me, and yet I didn't know? First it was Caroline, followed by Stacy, and now Rachel. I didn't know whose lives would be affected by me uncovering the truth, and at that present moment, I didn't care. I was tired of people lying to me, especially when all I wanted was the truth.

"I do love you guys, and you of all people should know that. But this…this is affecting Caroline. She's sick, Rachel. What am I supposed to do? Turn a blind eye to my sister, all because some secrets may come out? Well I can't do that. Caroline needs help. So, why can't you understand that?"

Rachel and I both were in the back of the store crying our eyes out. Whatever this secret was, it was affecting more than just Caroline.

"Rhonda. Please…don't. Don't do this. I'm begging you. Just let it go. I'll help you get Caroline back on the right track, but this… this has to stop. So please just leave it alone."

Rachel was terrified of me looking into the past, and as much as I wanted to reassure her that I would stop, I couldn't. If I took care of everyone but my sister, then what kind of sister would I be?

"I love you, Rachel…and you know I wouldn't do anything to hurt you or JJ, but this is my sister! Our parents are gone, and Caroline is struggling with some inner demons she can't seem to shake. Now, if I was to come home one day and something bad had happened to her, then no matter what I may have felt for her in the past, I would truly blame myself if I didn't do what was needed in order to get my sister back in her right mind. She's sick. That's all I know, and I'm trying my best to do whatever I can to help her. So, I'm sorry, but I've got to figure out what happened to Caroline."

I was about to walk out, and part of me wanted to stop and call the whole thing off, but I couldn't. I felt as though I was hurting so many people, but in reality, Caroline was the one who was truly hurting the most, and that's why I had to continue on with my investigation into her past.

"He's not biologically mine! So please stop. Stop before you cause me to lose my son."

I slowly turned around in shock.

"What are you talking about? JJ is your son."

"Yes, he's mine but I didn't give birth to him."

"What are you talking about? I saw when you brought him home. He was a baby. You introduced me to Jacob, and told me you met him while you were away at college. What's going on, Rachel?"

"I didn't have JJ. I'm his mother in every way that counts, but biologically, he's not mine."

"So, all of these years you've had me covering up a lie? Why? I don't see the point in it." I paused and began to think. Nothing was adding up. "I don't get it. Why would you get mad if I told Stacy about JJ, if he's not yours? It doesn't make any sense."

Rachel seemed terrified. I needed to figure out what was eating away at her that would make her so afraid to tell me the truth?

"He's not mine, but Jacob is his father. That's why."

"So, you're helping your boyfriend lie about a child that he had with another woman? Okay. So, what am I missing here?"

"Come on, Rhonda. Don't make me tell you. Just let it go."

"No! I want you to tell me what's going on. What aren't you telling me? Who's, JJ's mother and why are you covering for her? Most importantly, why don't you want me to know…?"

Then it clicked. But it couldn't be. No. There was no way.

"No…No! I see your wheels turning. Rhonda! No."

"Caroline? Is she? Is Caroline, JJ's mother? Tell me! Is JJ my nephew?"

"Rhonda…Please!" Rachel was crying uncontrollably. I had guessed right. My sister had a baby I didn't know anything about, and from a cop, no less. But when? The only times Caroline was away was when she was locked up or in rehab.

"I'm right, aren't I? Caroline is JJ's mother! Tell me, Rachel. I want to hear you say it. Is Caroline, JJ's mother?"

"Yes! Yes, she's JJ's mother. Please, Rhonda. Don't say anything."

"Hush. Don't…just don't." My brain was going fifty miles per hour. How could I have missed it? This whole time I've been babysitting and watching over my own nephew. "Caroline has a child! How? When? When did this happen?"

I couldn't wrap my mind around the fact that Caroline had a child and Rachel, someone whom I've loved like a sister, had been lying to me for years. How could she? How could she betray me like this?

"If I tell you, will you promise not to say anything?"

"Rachel!"

"I'm not telling you anything unless you promise me. I'm serious, Rhonda. Promise me."

"Fine. I promise I won't say anything. Now tell me. How did you come about raising my nephew without me knowing about it?"

"Before JJ was born, I was approached by Jacob, and he told me that he needed my help. He revealed to me that Caroline was pregnant, and most importantly she didn't want you to know."

"How could she? I've been taking care of her for all these years, and yet she chose to keep me in the dark." I was starting to get upset.

"No. It's wasn't like that. She was only looking out for you."

"How? By lying to me?"

"She was afraid, Rhonda. She couldn't risk Stacy finding out about the baby and on top of that she didn't trust herself. That's why Jacob had her locked away in rehab—to ensure she didn't use during her pregnancy. After the baby was born, they approached me about adopting JJ."

"I can't believe her. How could she give our family away without talking things over with me first? All we have left is each other, and she would keep something like this from me!"

"You were making plans to go off to college, and she didn't want to burden you with having to take care of someone else."

"JJ wouldn't have been a problem. He's blood, and she felt as though she couldn't trust me with the truth."

"No…Caroline loves you. Think about it, Rhonda. If Caroline would have told you she was pregnant, how do you think you would have reacted? You might not even be in college right now if she would have decided to tell you the truth about JJ."

"You don't know that! You don't know what I would have done, or how I would have reacted. All you did was conspire with my sister to lie to me. How could you? Who were you to decide what was best for me?"

"Rhonda..."

"Don't. Just tell me. Why did they choose you to adopt JJ?"

"Because of you! Don't you get it? Caroline didn't want to ruin your life by burdening you with a baby. So, when you started working at the shop, Caroline figured since I wasn't going anywhere, that it would be easy for you to be a part of JJ's life. So, I pretended as if I was going off to college to set things in motion."

"Okay so you and my sister conspired to lie to me for years. I have a nephew and Caroline is his mother. So...Jacob and Caroline. I don't get it? How does that work? I thought he was with you."

"We're just friends. He's in love with Caroline, and if Stacy was to ever discover the truth, then she would take JJ away from me just to prove a point. Can you image Stacy raising JJ as her own? It would kill Caroline, and you know it."

As hurt as I was, I couldn't imagine JJ being raised by Stacy. It made me sick to even think about it.

"I don't get it. If Jacob loves Caroline so much then why wouldn't he leave Stacy to help me take care of her? I mean, he's letting her kill herself slowly. That's not love."

"Think, Rhonda! Think! If Stacy ever discovered Caroline had a baby by her husband, then she would do everything in her power to finish destroying her. I know for a fact that you can't stand Stacy, so think...think about what you're doing. If you want to help Caroline then leave me and JJ out of it. Throw Stacy off of our scent. Do whatever you can to protect your nephew."

I didn't want anything to happen to JJ, so I was willing to play along for a while.

"Fine. I'll leave you guys out of it, but I still need to find Brad Parsons. I've tried searching the web, and there's nothing. It's like after college he just fell off the face of the earth. I don't know what happened, but I need his help. He knows what happened to Caroline back in college, and he's the only person who can tell me the truth about what really happened to her."

"If I give you a piece of the puzzle, will you promise to hurry up with your little investigation, before you get us all caught?

"Sure. So, what do you have?"

"I overheard Caroline talking about Brad once. He changed his name. That's why you can't find him. His new name is Brad Stevens, and he's a doctor up in Clearwater, but you didn't hear that from me."

"Clearwater."

One thing was certain: my life was full of nothing but lies. There were so many secrets going around, I didn't know who or what to believe. I hated being so cynical, considering I had a few secrets of my own, but what I couldn't get over was the fact that Jacob was in love with Caroline, and they had a son together...JJ. If Stacy ever discovered the truth, she would hurt Caroline just for the hell of it. A lot of people have blamed Stacy for what happened to Caroline, including me, and the last thing I would want to happen is for the tables to be turned. Stacy and Rachel had pieces to the puzzle, but did they both have the same piece, or did one know more than the other? Those were the clues I needed to figure out, before I ended up doing more harm than good.

# Chapter 6

## ❧
## Deal or Let Go

Time had passed, and I needed to make my next move, but I was in the dark about how to make that happen. As I struggled to come up with a plan, I couldn't get over how and why Caroline wouldn't get her life together, knowing that she had a son. I wanted to say something to her about JJ, but I had promised Rachel that I wouldn't stir up any more trouble. So, my next move was to find a way to approach Brad Parsons, aka Brad Stevens, about Caroline. He was a psychologist up in Clearwater—a profession I would have loved to pursue if I lived a legit life. Since I was heading out to Clearwater, I decided it would be in my best interest to unload my last doll there. Evidently, the cops were watching the shop, so it only made sense to move my merchandise to a new location for my final sell. If my client wanted the doll as badly as he claimed, then they would meet me in Clearwater to get it.

I also wanted to come clean with Damien about everything that was happening in my life, but I needed to keep him out of the loop and for good reason. If the cops ever suspected Damien as an accomplice in my schemes, then he could go away for a long time, and I couldn't risk that. I needed to keep him as far away from the truth as possible, and as much as I cared about Damien, that didn't stop our relationship from falling apart. I truly loved him, but in our case, was love enough? I had broken his heart so many times I was surprised he still wanted to be with me. I wanted to invite him along to Clearwater, but there was no way I could explain the doll or the money, so it was in my best interest if Damien stayed behind. It was sad that Damien and I were moving further apart, but on the contrary, Prez and I were moving closer together. It wasn't as if we were trying to make things happen, they just did. We would have lunch together and his hand would accidently brush up against mine, or we would hang out after work at coffee shops while immersed in intense movie debates, and to top it all off, I was teaching Prez the craft of making dolls in my spare time. Damien noticed the amount of time we were spending together, and he wasn't comfortable with that at all. So, to make peace, I decided to surprise Damien with a romantic dinner for two over at his place. I informed Caroline that I would return home in the morning, but I had to keep a close eye on her as well. She was starting to notice changes in my behavior, and I didn't want to slip up and say anything out of the ordinary that would let on that I knew about JJ. So, I decided to keep my distance, and it worked.

At Damien's, I decided to change into a very sexy cream dress, and I was also sporting a new pair of high heels. Something you would never catch me wearing, but in this case, Damien deserved it for putting up with me. It was the only way I could show him that I was truly grateful for having him in my life. Dinner was ready, the candles were lit, and still no Damien. I called his cell, but it continued to go to voicemail. What was really going on? It wasn't like Damien to be out late. Time passed, and my dinner and surprise were both ruined. I decided to pack up and call it a night.

As I was leaving, I heard the house phone ring. I was going to answer, but I didn't recognize the number, so I let it go to voicemail.

A female voice came across the speaker, "Hey you, I had a good time. I hope you did too. If so. Maybe we can do this again."

I couldn't think straight. My chest burned. I didn't know if I was going to puke or faint. My world was closing in around me. Was I overreacting? I heard the voice. He had dinner with another woman—there was no denying it. I could hear my shaky breaths and see my hands tremble as if they didn't even belong to me. I tried to slow my breathing. I knew I had to be overreacting. Damien wouldn't do this to me. But I had been pushing him away. And I hadn't been completely faithful myself. So why was I so angry? All I could see was his ugly, disgusting, cheating face. The rage burned in me all over again. How...how could he do this to me? I knew there were plenty women out there who would love to cater to him 24/7. As for me, I had damaged my relationship with Damien and even though I was hurt, I was a big girl, and maybe the time had come for us to part ways.

As I was about to leave, Damien walked in. I didn't know how to react. There were no words for how I was feeling. Part of me was sad and wanted to crawl into a hole and never come out, while the other part of me wanted to scratch his eyes out right here and now. I could tell he was caught off guard as well. His body language was all over the place.

"Hey! What are you doing here?"

"Nothing. I thought I would surprise you, but lucky me...I was the one who was surprised."

"If you would have told me you were coming over, then I would have made plans to stay home."

"Then it wouldn't have been a surprise."

"Come on, Rhonda."

"No. It's okay. You have your life and I have mine. You didn't know. So, we're good. I was just leaving."

I reached for my bag but Damien stopped me.

"Hey, wait a minute. Where are you going? You're all dressed up, and I'm supposed to just let you walk out like that?"

"Yes."

"Rhonda, what's wrong?"

"It's nothing. I wanted us to have a nice time together, and like always I ruined it. So…."

"You haven't ruined anything. Look at you. You're wearing heels! Come on."

Damien was good at making me laugh, but I didn't want to laugh, I wanted to be mad. He had strange women calling his house and I wasn't cool with that at all.

"Stop making me laugh. I'm trying to be mad right now."

"Why? I don't like it when you're mad, so what's wrong?"

I didn't want to sound like the jealous girlfriend, but what could I do? I heard the message. Was I supposed to ignore what I heard? So instead of saying anything, I walked over to the answering machine, and I hit play.

"I don't get it? Is there some secret message on there that I'm supposed to know about?"

"I don't know. You tell me."

The messages continued to play, and then the message from the mysterious woman played, and Damien looked at me as if nothing was wrong.

"So, is that what has you all hot and bothered?"

"Really? We're going to play this game now?"

"She's no one."

"She's no one now, but just a few hours ago she was someone who seemed to have had all of your attention. Hell, you couldn't even answer your cell."

"Like I said, she's no one, and besides, my phone was off."

"Oh! So, your phone was off, and you're out with another woman while I'm sitting here looking like a fool, but I'm supposed to feel okay, because she's no one."

"Why are you trying to make this into something, when it's not? I told you it was nothing, but you are free to believe what you want."

"And I will. Bye, Damien."

I didn't know how he expected me to react, but this wasn't going to work. It was one thing to have to deal with chicks being in his face all day long at school, but to have to deal with this at his home? I wasn't for it. Maybe we needed a break, or just some time apart, but whatever we needed, we needed it fast.

"That's right! Leave. All you seem to be good at is walking away. So just go."

"Are you serious? You're going to turn this around on me? You have strange women calling your house all times of the night, and you're the one out with God knows who, doing God knows what, but you have the nerve to catch an attitude with me, all because I want to leave. You're kidding me, right?"

"Oh, come on, Rhonda! Let's play fair, shall we? Lately, whenever I come by your job, you seem to be out with Prez. Is he your new man now? Because you never have any time for me? At first, your excuse was Caroline, and now you don't even have one. You're just not available."

"Prez. Really! I'm not with Prez; I thought I was with you. Besides, Prez and I are just friends. That's it! He doesn't want anything from me, and he's not pressuring me into anything either, but one thing is certain. He's not calling my phone all times of the night, but can you say the same? No. You can't."

"Let's face it, Rhonda. You don't want to be in this relationship. You've come up with excuse after excuse to not be here, but if you truly loved me then you would stay."

"It's not that simple and you know it."

"It is that simple."

"Really? So, to hell with my sister? She doesn't matter, as long as I'm with you, then everything is good?"

"Rhonda…"

"No! I get it. Caroline is just a crackhead gone wrong. If anything was to happen to her, then it would be a service to us all. Right? Good-bye, Damien."

"Rhonda. Wait."

Damien reached out for me but I pulled back. I was so tired of him hurting me, because of my family.

"Don't. I'm sorry. You know I wouldn't do anything to hurt you. Please. I'm sorry."

"I'm sorry too. Bye."

My heart was breaking. Damien may have said some hurtful things to me in the past, but this was the deal-breaker. I had too much on my mind, and all I needed was for someone to be there for me and to not want anything from me. I loved Damien, but it was time to let go.

Driving home, I felt as if I lost everything. All the secrets, all the lies, and above all, I didn't know who I could trust. I may have been keeping my own secrets, but at least they wouldn't hurt anyone but me. Tomorrow, I was driving to Clearwater, and one way or another I was going to discover a way to get Brad to talk. Once I unloaded my last doll, everything was going to change. I was moving out—whether Caroline liked it or not and as far away as possible. I needed a new start, in a new place, and I had the means to make it happen. I was going to miss Rachel, JJ, and even Caroline in my own twisted way, but it was time to move on.

As I was driving home, I passed by the doll shop, and noticed the lights were still on inside the building. It was late, and there was no reason for anyone to be inside the shop that time of night. Curiosity took over, and before I knew it, I was creeping inside the shop trying to play detective. I could hear footsteps coming from the back, and though part of me wanted to check it out, the other half of me wanted to run out and call the cops. I held my purse close, with gun in hand, and before I could decide on what to do next, Prez came walking out from the back.

"Man! You scared me!" I let out a sigh of relief.

"Scared you?"

"It's late. What are you doing here?"

I eased my gun back down in my purse. I didn't want Prez jumping to any conclusions.

"What am I doing here? What are you doing here and all dressed up?"

"I saw the lights on and I decided to come in. So why are you still here?"

"Nothing—I mean…I was just heading out."

"No, I'm serious. It's really late and you're still at the shop. You didn't think that would draw some kind of attention? So, I'll ask you again. Why are you still here?"

"It's like I said before. No reason."

No reason. I wasn't buying it, so I decided to see for myself just what Prez had been up to. As I began to head towards the back of the shop, he stopped me.

"What? What is it that you don't want me to see?"

"It's nothing. So, let it go."

I breezed by Prez and opened the door. I looked around the room and, to my surprise, there was a doll sitting on the counter. I didn't know what to make of it. We had progressed in our steps but not enough for him to be creating on his own.

"What are you doing?" I picked up the doll and examined it. If I was able to get a good look, then I could figure out what Prez had been up to.

"I told you it was nothing. I wanted to surprise you, but things didn't go as planned." The doll looked semi-complete. The arms were half in and the legs were nowhere in sight.

Okay, what was I missing? I was trying my best to surprise Damien with a romantic dinner, while Prez was at the shop trying to create a surprise for me.

"It's nice. At least you tried."

"Yeah, but I didn't try hard enough."

Prez took the doll and threw it in the trash.

"Wait. It's salvageable."

"No, it needed a lot of work…but anyway you never answered my question. Why are you so dressed up? Had a hot date?"

"No. All I had was a dose of reality...anyway it's late, and I'm about to head out. So just make sure you lock up, and I'll see you later."

"Wait. So, you're all dressed up and you're about to head home?"

"That's the plan. I mean where else can I go? It's late and everything is closed."

"Come with me."

Prez grabbed my hand and gently pulled me to the front of the shop. He turned on the radio and dimmed the lights.

"What are you up to?"

"You look nice, and from what I can tell, your night did not go as planned, so just be quiet and enjoy the music."

I couldn't help but smile. It felt good to have someone do something nice for me, for a change. I felt Prez's hands around my waist guiding me to move with the rhythm and for the first time, I allowed myself to look at him. Really look at him. His eyes were kind and I felt like I could trust him with anything. The way he looked at me filled my stomach with butterflies. For a moment, the shop, the dolls, my growing tower of problems—they all fell away. I laid my head on his chest and we danced and talked the night away. But as pleasing as my night was, I felt guilty for being with Prez even though things were rocky between me and Damien.

"Okay we've got to stop. I've got to get some sleep tonight."

"Sure, I understand. Well, I hope you enjoyed yourself tonight."

"I did...and thank you."

"Don't thank me. All I was doing was helping out a friend."

"You're sweet. If I..."

"If you what?"

"Nothing. I was just thinking out loud. Thanks again."

I made my way over to switch off the lights, and when I turned around, I walked directly into a kiss. I didn't know how it happened, but I enjoyed it. From the way he caressed the side of my face, to the hint of peppermint I tasted on his lips. I was wrong for what I was feeling, but it felt so right.

"What are we doing?"

"Shush…."

"I can't."

Prez didn't say a word. He continued kissing me as if I had said nothing. He held me ever so slightly in his arms, as he eased my body in closer towards his. I wanted to fight what I was feeling, but I couldn't. I was kissing Prez. I should've been thinking about how I was hurting Damien, but I felt as though Damien had made his choice. He wanted to do his own thing and now I was doing mine.

"Goodnight." Prez whispered in my ear as he headed towards the door.

I hope Prez didn't think he could start a fire without having to put it out. As he escorted me out the door, he walked over to his car and I walked towards mine. I didn't know what I was thinking, but I ended up following Prez back to his place. I didn't hide the fact that I was following him, as I pulled up behind his car into the driveway. Prez got out of his car as I sat in mine, unsure of what I was doing. He leaned on his car as he waited for me to exit mine. As I approached him, I really didn't know what to say.

"I don't know why I'm here but…"

Before I could finish what, I was saying, Prez leaned over and gave me another kiss. He embraced me in his arms, and before I knew it, he had me pinned up against his car. Our kiss was more passionate then the one at the shop, and all it did was make me want him even more. Before I knew it, we were inside his house ripping off each other's clothes.

One thing was certain: Prez's apartment looked like a bachelor's pad. From the moment I entered his place, it screamed "man cave". He had dark leather furniture, the basic television sitting on a crate, and there were no paintings hanging on the wall. There were clothes scattered all over the place, and his bedroom was a mess. I was amazed that he was able to find anything, much less a light. He turned on the light switch long enough to rake everything off his bed, and then they were off again. I could easily tell his place needed a little TLC, but he made no excuse for how it looked. He just focused all of his attention onto me. I couldn't believe what was happening. My mind was in a daze. Was I really doing this? Prez and I were now beyond just being friends. We were having sex, and as guilty as I felt, it was definitely what my body needed. Even though it was wrong of me to compare the two, Prez was much more aggressive in bed than Damien. He didn't say much. He just took what he wanted and I loved it. I laid in the bed, mystified over what was happening. I couldn't get over how I was just at Damien's, and now I was in bed with Prez. I guess in my own demented way, this act was a way to seal the deal of me and Damien being officially over.

# Chapter 7

## Breaking Down the Wall

Morning had arrived, and I needed a way to sneak out of Prez's apartment without waking him up. I had mixed feelings about what happened, and there was no way I could address any questions regarding our most recent encounter. I thought it would be best if I left before Prez woke up. As I eased out of bed, I fell onto the floor. Afraid that the thump had awakened Prez, I looked up and, to my surprise, he was still asleep. I put on my clothes and quietly left the house. I drove home in deep thought trying to figure out what had just happened. I slept with Prez. I knew in my mind I wanted my relationship with Damien to be over with, but no matter how I looked at it, I was still in love with him. None of it mattered anyway. I was going away to Clearwater and I wasn't coming back. My life carried too much baggage at home, and there was nothing else I could do for Caroline to get her to turn her life around.

I pulled up in the driveway and walked into the house. Caroline was sitting in the living room, like an angry parent, waiting for her child to return home from a late date. I didn't know what her problem was, because I remember telling her that I would return home in the morning.

"What's up?"

"I don't know. You tell me."

"Look, I told you I would be back in the morning, so chill out. You're not my mother. You're barely my sister."

"I'm barely your sister..."

I knew I had tapped a nerve. I could see Caroline getting upset, but I didn't care. Today was the day I was breaking free of her prison.

"You told me you were going over to Damien's...right?"

"Yeah...and..."

"Damien has been calling the house all night looking for you. So, where have you been, and why are you lying to me?"

"If you must know, I was at Damien's, and then we had a big fight last night, no thanks to you. I went and got a room, because I didn't feel like coming home and seeing your face. It can be disappointing at times."

"You little..."

"What? Say it. You kept me a prisoner in my own home which may have cost me my boyfriend. So, thank you Caroline! Thank you, very much."

"Don't blame me for this. You were the one out there playing doughboy, not me. All I was trying to do was protect you."

"Well you picked the wrong time to want to play big sister, because right now I don't want, nor do I need your help."

"Why do you feel as though you have to fight me on everything? All I'm trying to do is help you, so why can't you see that?"

"You know those drugs must have really done a number on your head, because I've been trying to help you for years, and all you've done is fight with me on everything. You didn't take care of me or yourself. You didn't pay any bills, you didn't feed me, you didn't care anything about me, and so I had to learn how to take care of myself. So please forgive me for being a dope dealer, but what else could I do when there was no one else to take care of me? Tell me! What was I supposed to do? Live in the cold, starve, or worst of all, die? Is that your version of helping me?"

"I'm sorry alright, I'm sorry. I know I haven't been there for you like I should've been, but I'm trying. The day I found those drugs in your room, I began to realize that I couldn't allow my self-pity to ruin your life. I wanted to let you in on what's going on in my life, but it would've been wrong of me to do so. Besides, I'm afraid if you would've known the truth about everything, then I would have lost you forever."

"Why do you do this to me? I was happy! I was with Damien, and I was done with the drugs, but you couldn't see that. You chose to see what you wanted to see, and now I've lost my boyfriend, and I've done something so stupid that I can't take back. Now, I don't know what this secret is that you're carrying around, but how bad could it be? I mean look at us? Tell me, Caroline…just how worse off could we get?"

I figured Caroline wanted to tell me about Jacob and JJ, but I already knew, and I was over it. If she decided to tell me the truth, I would act surprised, and then I would reassure her that, everything was going to be okay. After that I was packing my bags, and heading off to Clearwater. I knew for a fact Caroline wasn't going to tell me the truth, but I was optimistic that Brad would spill if I could guilt him into it. I would show him some pictures of Caroline, and then I would explain to him how she turned out. Hopefully that would be enough to get him to share what he knows.

"Just promise me you won't overreact."

"Fine. So, what is it, Caroline? What's this big secret?"

Caroline was shaking again. Whatever it was, it was big. She could barely compose herself to form words.

"It's about Mom and Dad."

Mom and Dad. I wasn't expecting that.

"What about Mom and Dad?"

"Well they're…it's complicated."

"Complicated how? What is it, Caroline? Spit it out."

"Oh, Rhonda…" Caroline's voice was shaky. She started to cry but I wasn't in the mood for it.

"No! Kill the crying. What is it? What about Mom and Dad?"

"They're not dead!"

I heard the words but they didn't register. My parents couldn't be alive. I went to their funeral. I wondered if Caroline was high again, because what she was saying didn't make any sense.

"What are you talking about? They're dead! We were at their funeral."

"No. They're not dead. They're in jail."

"Stop lying! Why are you doing this? They are dead! You hear me? Dead!"

"See? That's why I didn't want to tell you. I knew you wouldn't be able to handle it."

"No! You're the one who can't handle reality. Our parents are dead, and you need to find a way to deal with it."

"My life fell apart the day our parents decided to get their own form of justice. Dad couldn't deal with the fact that the cops were going to let one of the rapists go free and…"

"Back up. So, you're serious? Our parents are alive and you didn't tell me."

"I'm so sorry, but I couldn't. Everything that has gone wrong in your life has been because of me, and that's why I didn't want to say anything. I've been trying to find a way to get them out, but I haven't had any luck."

I sat down because I couldn't believe what I was hearing. Our parents were alive, but they were locked away in prison. Why the funeral? Why the cover-up? None of it made any sense. It was hard for me to deal with the fact that JJ was my nephew, but now I had to somehow swallow the fact that my parents were alive, and in jail of all places.

"What did they do? No…let me rephrase that. What did you do to make our parents throw their lives away?"

"Rhonda."

"No, Caroline! What did you do? You have destroyed so many lives including your own! So, what did you do? Why are our parents in jail?"

"Calm down and I'll tell you."

My blood was boiling. I wanted the truth, but I wasn't sure if I wanted to hear it.

"Back in college when I was…, the cops arrested the three guys who were involved, but the truth of the matter is there were actually four. I told Dad, and he insisted the cops bring the fourth guy to justice, and since I was in and out of consciousness during part of the…you know, I was afraid it could've been this guy I had a crush on, but I wouldn't allow myself to believe it."

"And why not? What made him so special?" After the incident my parents became very protective of Caroline and they never involved me in her case. They thought they were protecting me but all it did was leave a lot of unanswered questions. Caroline was, understandably, never ready to share any of the details of what all happened that night and I eventually gave up asking about it.

"I don't know. It was something about the way he treated me leading up to that night at the party. I just couldn't see him doing something like that to me. Anyway, time passed and no one would roll over on the fourth guy involved. Finally, Dad threatened that if nothing was done, then he was filing a suit against the school, and that he would make it a public disaster for them and anyone else who was involved in the cover-up. The school didn't want to taint their reputation with a scandal, so they decided to threaten the other boys' families by going to the press if they didn't talk."

"Why weren't they in the news in the first place? Considering what they did to you…how could they keep something like that from the press?"

"The rape went to the news, but the name of the school, and the boys who were involved didn't. Oh, it was a cover-up if anything, but the parents of the other boys involved didn't want their family names being dragged through the mud, so they had to give up the fourth person involved."

"So, who was it? Who was the fourth person?"

"Greg Parsons."

"Greg Parsons?"

"Remember the guy I told you I had a crush on? His name was Brad Parsons, and Greg was his older brother. He was also at the party that night. Come to find out, he was watching me and Brad the entire night. Brad tried to make out with me but I turned him down. I wanted to, but I was saving myself for the right guy, and if he was Mr. Right then it would have happened, but not at a frat party in some stranger's bedroom."

I couldn't believe it. Caroline was a virgin before the rape. With all the boyfriends she had in high school, I figured she lost her virginity a long time ago, but I was wrong.

"So, Brad must have told Greg about what happened, and Greg got upset."

"Upset? But why would he get upset? You weren't making out with him."

"I know, but he felt as though I was acting as if I was too good for Brad. At first, I thought that it was because of the color of my skin, but come to find out, it was deeper than that. Greg was a spoiled rich kid and he was used to getting what he wanted. He figured if Brad wanted me then he should have me, but things didn't work out that way."

"So, by turning Brad down, it was like an insult to Greg?"

"Right. I made him look bad in front of his friends, and on top of that, his baby brother. So, to teach me a lesson, Greg and a couple of his frat brothers got together, and they beat and...raped me all night long."

Tears were gushing down Caroline's face. I knew it had to be hard for her to talk about that night. It probably felt like she was reliving the attack all over again.

"They took something away from me…something I can never get back. I know you look at me in disappointment whenever you see me walking the streets at night, but no matter how smart I am mentally, in some way I'm still trying to hold on to that moment that was taken away from me."

My heart was breaking for my sister. All I could think about was how she was beaten and…I tried to ensure her that everything was going to be okay. The moment I hugged Caroline she broke down in an uncontrollable cry. Tears flowed from my eyes as my heart shattered for my sister all over again. All the love I held back for her came pouring out. How could they? How could they do those things to my sister?

"It's going to be okay. If nothing else, you have me." I needed Caroline to finish her story, so I tried my best to calm her down. "So, are you okay?"

"Yes. I'm fine."

"So, what happened? Did they arrest Greg?"

"No. He never made it to jail."

"You're kidding me, right?"

"No. His parents got some big-time lawyer to come in, and he was able to get the charges dropped."

"I don't get it? He "raped" you. As a matter of fact, he was the ringleader behind the entire thing. So how could they just let him go?"

"Because money can do that. Dad became enraged, and he claimed he wasn't going to stop until he got some form of justice."

"So, what did he do?"

"He went over to confront the Parsons, and things got heated. I begged Dad to leave, but he wouldn't listen to me. Mom couldn't talk him down either. Brad grabbed me by the arm, insisting that we leave, and that's when Dad snapped. He punched Brad in the face for just touching me. Before I knew it, Greg came into the room with a loaded gun warning us to leave. So, Dad being Dad walked up on the gun, and dared Greg to pull the trigger. He told him that one way or another he was going to jail, and if it had to be his blood to send him there, then so be it. We could easily see that Greg was afraid to pull the trigger. So, dad reached out to grab the gun, and before we knew it him and Greg were tussling. We were all yelling at them to stop and then…"

"And then what? What happened?" I couldn't believe they kept all of this from me.

"The gun went off. I started screaming and I ran over towards Dad. When I pulled them apart, Greg fell to the floor. Blood was everywhere. The Parsons freaked out and called the police. Dad didn't know what to do, so while the Parsons were attending to Greg, we slipped out the front door. Dad was freaking out, because, yes, he wanted Greg to pay for what he had done to me, but he didn't want him to die. While we were driving away, Mom was trying her best to calm Dad down, and then all of a sudden Dad lost control of the car, and that's when we wrecked."

"So, the wreck was real…but they didn't die."

"Yes, and when I woke up, I was in the hospital, and Mom and Dad were nowhere in sight. I begged for someone to tell me what was going on, but no one would give me any answers. After a while, an officer came into my room to explain everything that had happened. Mom and Dad were brought in for their injuries, and then they were hauled off to jail."

"So why did they arrest Mom? She didn't do anything wrong."

"The Parsons' lawyer was a sneaky little bastard. He put Mom as an accessory to murder, because she drove Dad over to the Parsons knowing that he was unstable—so, they say. I tried to fight it tooth and nail, but I didn't have the money or the means to pursue it. Stacy has been trying to help me get their case overturned, but as of now we still haven't had any luck."

"So why didn't they arrest you? You were there too."

"Because I was Greg's victim, and no matter which way they would have tried to spin that in court, it wasn't going to come out pretty. So, they left me out of it."

"So, Mom and Dad were arrested for killing Greg, but what I don't understand is, why the funeral? Why fake their deaths?"

"Because it's what Mom and Dad wanted."

I was shocked. I couldn't believe what I was hearing.

"You're lying. They wouldn't do this to me."

"They didn't want to, but after they received a life's sentence for Greg's death, they didn't want you visiting them in jail. And you were all I had left…I didn't want to lose you as well. So, I lied to you and everyone else about what really happened."

"But why would you lie to me? I'm your sister. How could you keep something like this from me?"

"Because I was afraid if I would have told you the truth, then you would have blamed me and left. Back then, and even now, all we do is fight, and I didn't want this to be the deal-breaker; so, I lied to you. I know it was a selfish thing to do, but I was in a very dark place back then, and I didn't want to be alone, so lying to you was the only thing that made sense."

"Caroline, you told me our parents were dead! You were so worried about being alone that you forgot to think about me. At least you had them in your life. I had no one. You would mentally check out on me religiously, and in return I was left all alone to defend myself. So, you're right about one thing. You were selfish, and I don't know if I could ever forgive you for this."

"I know you're hurting and I'm sorry. I didn't mean for things to turn out this way, but—"

"No. Don't go there. See, this is your M.O. You always have good intentions, followed by bad results. I know you meant well, but this time you took things too far." My mind was trying to process everything I had heard. "So, tell me something. How did you do it, because you couldn't have pulled this off by yourself? Tell me, Caroline, who helped you cover this up?"

"What makes you think I needed any help?"

"Caroline, please. I know you. So, who helped you?"

"Who always helps me when I'm in trouble?"

"Stacy."

"And there you go. Her and Jacob both decided to help me with the cover-up. Stacy had a friend who worked in communications, and he was able to erase any and everything online that dealt with our parent's arrest."

"So that explains all of the roadblocks I kept running into online."

"Yes. It was as if the arrest never happened. As for Jacob, he was friends with the guy who ran the funeral home. So, as a favor he was willing to go the full length to make the entire thing seem believable, and it worked. No one was ever the wiser."

"I still don't believe this. I know Mom and Dad didn't want me to know they were in jail but they were okay with you faking their deaths?"

"In a way, yes. I told them a couple of months after I did it. They were surprised at how elaborate my plan was, but they understood my reasoning behind it. You're my sister, and I didn't want my mistakes to drive you away. I get that I'm a mess, but you have always been there for me, and I don't know if I could've made it this far if you weren't a part of my life. I really did need your help, Rhonda, and to be completely honest, I still need your help. That's why I didn't want you to move out."

Listening to Caroline explain herself was heartbreaking. I knew she meant well, but she went about it the wrong way. I thought about Brad, and I decided I would still go to Clearwater, but now with a new purpose. My plans to leave home were now halted, and my focus was back on Caroline. I guess my breakup with Damien was for the best, because I was going to do everything within my power to help save my sister. Even if that meant saving her from herself.

"I want to hate you right now, but I can't. So be honest with me. Is there anything else I should know about?"

Since Caroline was all about telling the truth, I wanted to see if she was going to be honest with me about JJ.

"No. That's it."

"Really. So, you're going to keep lying to me about JJ?"

A surprised look came across Caroline's face. I didn't want to stir up any more problems, but since we were all about the truth, then I wanted to hear it.

"How do you know?"

"I backed Rachel into a corner until she had no choice but to tell me the truth. So, I'm waiting on you to explain to me why you kept my nephew a secret from me."

"Look at me, Rhonda. Do I look like the motherly type to you? I couldn't even take care of you, and you were old enough to see about yourself, so how would I look bringing JJ into this kind of environment?"

"He's blood, Caroline. Why didn't you give him to me? I would've moved out and raised him. I would've done everything within my power to keep us together as a family."

"And I don't doubt that, but you were doing so well in school, and I didn't want to mess that up for you. Now look...you'll be graduating college soon, and Mom and Dad will be so proud. Besides, Rachel wasn't going anywhere, and Jacob always made sure JJ had everything he needed."

"What he needed was his mother. His real mother! You. So why wouldn't you get clean? If for no one other than JJ. He's your son."

Caroline became emotional as tears welled up in her eyes.

"I know he is...but that doesn't mean I can take care of him. Besides, it's not like I don't see him. Rachel brings him by on my good days, and I'm able to spend as much time with him as I want. You know in the beginning I must admit, it did hurt when I would hear him call Rachel mommy...but I've learned to be okay with it, because I know he's happy. I finally get what Mom meant by necessary evils. It was wrong of me to give up JJ, but if you look at the whole picture then you'll see that he's with someone we trust, we can see him every day, and most importantly he's happy. So, if he's happy then I'm happy."

"You know I love Rachel. She's my best friend, but JJ is your son. I have some money stashed away, and if I help you get clean, would you petition to get him back? I may be approaching graduation, but you and I both know I'm not going anywhere anytime soon."

"He's happy, Rhonda. How would I look taking him away from the only mother he knows?"

"How do you think he's going to feel once he's older, and he realizes you never came back for him? If you were to get him back now, then yes, he would be upset, but he's young and eventually he'll get over it, but one thing is certain. You're his mother, and I want you to use that to get better." I paused because there was something of greater importance still weighing on my mind. "But you know, there's still something I just don't understand."

"And what's that?"

"If Jacob loves you so much, then why wouldn't he help you better?"

"Jacob isn't the problem; it's me. He's tried countless times to help me, and all I've done is given him grief about it."

"But why? Don't you want to get better?"

"Of course, I do, but it's not that easy. I'm having an affair with my best friend's husband, and even though I blame Stacy for what happened to me in college, she's still my best friend. She's done a lot for me over the years, and the last thing I would want to do is hurt her any more than I've already have. She can't have kids. You know that?"

"No. I didn't know."

"So, can you image how she would feel if she found out about JJ? I can't do that to her. I won't. Jacob loves me, and I get that, but that's as far as it goes."

"Why are you doing this to yourself? He loves you."

"And you think I don't know that, but what kind of family could we have been? A crackhead, married to a cop, raising a kid. No. It wouldn't have worked out, and you know it."

"Don't you think Stacy deserves to be with someone who at least loves her? Jacob is in love with you. You had his child. How do you think Stacy is going to feel once the truth finally comes out? Because you know it'll come out. She's going to be hurt whether it's now or later."

"I know, but when the time comes, I'm going to be a mother to JJ, and I'll be with Jacob, but until then, why don't we leave things the way they are. I'll work on getting clean, and you work on finishing school. Deal?"

"What about JJ?"

"Deal?"

"Fine. Deal."

I walked away but not discouraged. Things were going to change. I headed towards my bedroom and began to pack.

"But I do have to go out of town for a couple of days to take care of some unfinished business. Nothing serious."

"You sure about that?"

"Yes. I'll be back in a few days, but you keep doing whatever it is that you're doing, because you look better. You seem better too."

Caroline began to smile. She walked over towards me and gave me a big hug, and I immediately hugged her back.

"Thanks. I love you, Rhonda."

Tears began to form in my eyes and I couldn't stop them from flowing. It felt nice to have a small part of my sister back. I vowed from that moment on to do whatever needed to be done in order to get my family back on track.

# Chapter 8

❧

# Infiltrators in Clearwater

I was feeling better about going to Clearwater. I didn't know how things were going to turn out, but I was optimistic. My buyer was in place, and I had made an appointment to see "Brad Parsons aka, Brad Stevens." I didn't know what I was going to say to him. All I knew was that I needed his help. I practiced for hours as to what I would say, but nothing sounded right. How do you approach someone whose brother was accidently killed by your father? My appointment was approaching nonetheless, and I needed to pull myself together in order for my plan to work. I had a lot riding on this meeting, and I couldn't allow myself to screw it up.

As I was driving along the highway, I noticed an unmarked car with a missing left mirror following close behind me, but I chose to ignore it, due to the many random thoughts I had running though my head. Once I arrived at Brad's practice, I sat nervously in the lobby, anticipating the various outcomes. Moments later, Brad's receptionist called me into his office, and there he sat: the perpetrator behind a lot of my family's drama. I could see why

Caroline was crazy about him in college. He was very handsome—another blonde-hair, blue-eyed devil.

I scheduled myself as a new patient who was suffering from depression and anxiety disorder.

"Hi. So how are you today?"

"I'm good."

"That's good to hear." Brad glanced at a file in hand then back at me. I see that you're new so, I'll let you begin."

"Where do I start? Um…I stress a lot…primarily because of my sister."

"Okay. So, tell me a little bit about your sister."

"Well, she's a mess, and I don't know how to help her. She's been through a lot in her life, and I don't see any way in reaching her."

"And how is your sister's life affecting yours?"

I wasn't keen on how to answer. I came to Clearwater looking for answers regarding my parents' arrest, not to expose some hidden secrets I didn't know about myself.

"Her life only complicates mine, and I spend the majority of my time taking care of her, which leaves no time for myself."

"And does that upset you?"

"Yes. To a degree. I know she needs help, but she's also destroying my life in the process."

"In what way?"

"Her dependency affects my decision-making, and it's putting a strain on my so-called love life. I've had relationships fail due to commitment issues, because I'm always taking care of her."

"Is your sister aware of her actions?"

"Oh yes. She knows exactly what she's doing. She would guilt me into taking care of her, and like a fool, I would always give in."

"You mentioned guilt. So, explain to me: why do you allow your sister to manipulate you?"

"It's simple, because deep down I do love her, and I want her to get better, but she has to meet me halfway, and she won't."

"Did something traumatic happen to cause her to act out in such a way?"

"You can say that. She was raped back in college, and ever since then, she's never been the same. I feel guilty for wanting to leave her, but I need a life of my own that doesn't include Caroline."

"Caroline..."

"Yes. I want to leave her but I don't know how." Brad looked as though he had seen a ghost. He looked down at his notes and then back at me. "Is something wrong?"

"No. I'm sorry it's just...you seem very familiar. Are you sure your last name is Clark?"

"Clark...Brown. It's all the same. Isn't it, Mr. Parsons?"

"Parsons. I knew it. You two favor so much. So why are you here? What does Caroline want now?"

"She doesn't know I'm here."

"Is that right? So why are you here? Because if it's about your parents then there's nothing I can do? I've told Caroline over and over again that my hands are tied."

"Look, I don't know what you and Caroline may or may not have discussed, but I just found out a couple of days ago that my parents were alive. So, you can see my point as to why I'm here."

"So, you're telling me Caroline lied and told you that your parents were dead."

"Yes. She told me they died in a car wreck years ago, which turned out to be a lie, because...surprise-surprise, they're in jail."

"Why are you here? There's nothing I can do for you?"

"Yes, there is. You can help me."

"Help you how? Your father shot and killed my brother."

"My father didn't shoot anyone. From what I hear, your brother aimed a loaded gun at my father, they tussled, and the gun went off. Sounds like it was an accident to me."

"Well my parents don't see it that way. Their son is dead, and it's because of your father. So, like I said before, there's nothing I can do for you."

"Your brother beat and raped my sister. How can that not affect you? She's tormenting herself, and there's nothing I can do about it!"

"And if I could help you then I would, but there's nothing I can do for you."

"Yes, you can. You can talk to your parents and somehow convince them to free mine."

"My parents are the reason yours are in jail to begin with. They're not going back on their word. They promised your parents would rot in jail, and I believe them. They're not going to help you no matter what I say to them."

"You're a psychologist. So, tell me, Doc. How do you think a woman who had her virginity taken by a couple of punks should feel? Caroline doesn't know how to cope with her rape, and on top of that, she blames herself for our parent's arrest. My sister is a mess, and I blame you and your family for making her that way."

I could tell that my words had affected Brad. He sat at his desk and was silent for a moment.

"She was a virgin?"

"Yeah, and now she's so screwed up in the head that she's out prostituting night after night, because she feels like she has some kind of control over the situation. How sick is that? Your family has destroyed my sister, and now she needs our parents more than anything. There's nothing I can say to get through to her, and to make matters worse, she has a kid who doesn't even know that she's his mother and—"

"Wait…Caroline has a child?"

"Yes. She kept it a secret from everyone. Primarily me. I just recently found out that I have a nephew, and I don't want to lose him all because his mother can't get it together."

"So, you're sure about this? Caroline has a child?"

"Yes. She gave him up at birth because she couldn't take care of him."

"And you know this for a fact?"

"Yes, and why are you so freaked out?"

"I'm not freaking out. A little shocked, maybe. It's just hard to believe that Caroline has a child."

"Welcome to my world."

"So, do you happen to have a picture of him?"

"A picture? Why are you so interested in Caroline's son? I came here looking for help, and all you seemed to be worried about is what my nephew looks like. Why's that? Is there something I should know?"

"No, but this session is over."

"I don't think so. If I leave this room, I'm calling Caroline, and I'm telling her everything."

"No! Don't call her."

"Then tell me. What's so special about JJ?"

"It's crazy."

"What is it?"

"I have a feeling he may be my son."

"Oh, come on. He's not your son. His father's name is Jacob, and I've seen him with JJ since the day he was born. So, tell me the truth. What's so special about my nephew?"

"Did you say Jacob? Oh, I'm certain, JJ as you call him, is my son. After your parents' trial, I felt so bad about everything that happened to Caroline that I cut myself off from my family, and changed my last name. I was in love with Caroline, and I wanted her to be a part of my life. So, we would hook up on occasion, and then one day Caroline found out that she was pregnant. I was thrilled, but I could easily tell that she wasn't. She started coming around less, and then it happened."

"What happened?"

"She called, and informed me of her miscarriage. She stated she couldn't take losing anyone else, and that's when she broke things off between the two of us."

"I don't get it? Why would she keep lying to me? I thought we were getting somewhere the other day, but I was completely wrong."

"No...I think I know why she lied to you."

"Why?"

"She did it because of my parents. If they knew Caroline had a baby, my baby then they would have fought to take him away from her."

"But why? Your family hates us. What could they have possibly wanted with JJ?"

"A grandchild. Now that Greg's gone, I'm their only child, which makes JJ their only grandchild."

"They wouldn't dare."

"Yes, they would, and Caroline probably figured that much. So, I get why she lied."

Brad was right. Maybe Caroline had a good reason for lying to me. The more I thought about it, I began to see where Caroline was coming from. There would be no way in hell I would allow the people who put my parents in jail to raise my child. For someone who was stung out a lot she seemed to be able to put things together pretty well.

"So, what are you going to do? Are you going to continue to destroy my sister's life by mentioning this to your parents, or are you going to do what's right? Because you and I both know that your parents would go after JJ just for the hell of it. So, what's your play, Doc? Can I trust you to keep this to yourself?"

"I don't know. I mean you expect me to pretend as if my son doesn't exist. I don't know if I can do that."

"And why not? He might not even be yours. Who's to say that Jacob isn't JJ's father?"

"Because he's not."

"And how can you be so sure?"

"Because…"

"Because of what?"

"Because Jacob's gay, and he's been covering it up for years."

There was no way that someone as fine as Jacob was gay. He couldn't be.

"Jacob. Gay. Come on! Is that the best you can come up with? Jacob is not gay."

"Oh, but he is. Caroline found out about Jacob shortly after he married Stacy, and from what I know, she never mentioned it to her. She didn't want to taint their friendship, considering Stacy was the only person helping her with your parents' trial, but one thing is certain. Jacob is gay. That's probably the only reason he's been helping Caroline cover up this lie about JJ."

What was really going on? My life was unfolding like a soap opera. Secrets, lies, and affairs. I was afraid of what would happen next. Was I going to discover that Caroline wasn't my sister, but my mother?

"So, Jacob's gay. Man! That's crazy."

"I know. It's a lot to take in."

"That's for sure, but not to get off of the subject. I really need to know what you plan on doing with the information I told you. Because if you're thinking about going after JJ, then don't. Caroline has been through enough, and you taking JJ away from her would only push her over the edge."

"I would never do anything to hurt Caroline, but what am I to do? Ignore the fact that I have a son, or pretend he doesn't exist? Well, I can't do that."

"And I'm not asking you to, but hear me out. JJ is the only good thing Caroline has in her life right now. So, don't take him away from her. She loves him."

"And I understand that, but I'm not walking away from my son. I'll help Caroline in any way that I can, but…"

"But what? You don't get it, do you? I'm the only person out there fighting for Caroline, and I'm tired. The only reason I came here today was to try and right a wrong, but I will not allow your family to continue to destroy mine. If you cared anything about Caroline, then you would've fought for her years ago when she needed you the most."

"I wanted to, but it's complicated."

"Complicated how? Caroline loved you. Do you know how different her life would've been if you would have stuck around? She needed someone like you in her corner years ago to help her get through this mess. So, if you're not going to back down, and I have a funny feeling you won't, then I suggest you start fighting for what's yours, and that's your family. Caroline and JJ."

"What's the point of fighting for Caroline when all she does is push me away?"

"And I get that..." I looked down at Brad's fingers, and he wasn't wearing a wedding band, so he was waiting on something or someone. "But I see you're not married, and I'm not questioning why, but if you ever loved my sister then I beg you not to give up on her."

"I could never give up on Caroline, but…it's complicated. You wouldn't understand."

"You're right. I wouldn't. All I know is that my family fell apart years ago, and everything I thought to be true has turned out to be nothing but a lie. Now I know you loved your brother, but he beat and raped my sister…the woman whom I think you may still be in love with. So, if you want to do a good deed then find a way to help me get my parents out of jail, but if not, then just leave us alone. Don't bring any more drama into our already complicated world."

I got up and left out of Brad's office. I didn't know what bomb I had just set into motion, but I had a feeling it was going to blow up in my face.

There was too much information floating around in my head that I was trying to process all at once. Half of it I couldn't believe, and the other half I didn't want to believe.

It was getting late, and I had to meet with my buyer so I could unload my last doll. As I was circling the coffee shop trying to find somewhere to park, I looked into my rearview mirror, and noticed the same unmarked car with the missing left mirror. It had to be the same one from earlier—how many unmarked, one-mirrored cars could there be in Clearwater? I started to feel uneasy. I couldn't wait to get rid of this doll so my constant paranoia could go with it.

I started to feel uneasy about the entire situation, and I wasn't sure it was smart or even safe for me to make my last drop. I didn't feel comfortable carrying the doll with me, but I didn't feel like I should leave it in the car either. I backed out and continued driving. I circled back, and looked around for the unmarked car. I waited and then I took the backpack out, and hid it somewhere special. I made sure no one was watching, and I headed back towards the coffee shop to finish up my last buy. I knew the buyer was coming in with his wife. She would be wearing a red sundress, and he would have on a pink polo shirt and brown khaki pants.

While I was sitting down waiting, I decided to go to the restroom. When I opened the door, someone rushed me from behind.

"Leave. Get in your car and leave now!"

"What! Get off me."

"Go. Now!"

As I was released, my attacker was already ten feet away by the time I turned to catch a glimpse of him. He was tall, lean, and, from the sliver of his exposed neck, I saw that he was brown-skinned. His giant strides carried him out the door within seconds, but not before he turned to lock eyes with me. Prez. I couldn't read his expression. Why was he here? I blinked and he was already getting in a car—an unmarked, one-mirrored car. Before I could make sense of this, I decided to heed his warning and get the hell out of there. If he was willing to risk scaring the life out of me, it had to be for good reason.

As I exited out the back, I noticed my buyers entering the shop. I hid around the corner, and I watched as the couple waited. Thirty minutes passed, and the guy checked his watch as the woman slowly scanned the room. The longer they waited they appeared confused and upset. An hour passed and they left. Moments later, the unmarked, one-mirrored car that was following me pulled up, and they got inside. Was I being set up? How was Prez involved? I drove away lost, scared, and upset. I didn't know what to do or where to go. Not only was I being watched, but I was being followed as well. My emotions took over as I began to cry out of control. Lies! That's all my life has been for the past couple of years. Lies! I came to Clearwater looking for help, but in the end, I discovered nothing but lies, and deception.

# Chapter 9

## The Cost of My Actions

I laid in bed trying to wrap my head around everything that happened in Clearwater. Some things were hard to grasp, while others were too inconceivable to even think about. All I could do was cry. It was late when I returned home. I wanted to pack up and leave town, but I was afraid of being followed. What would happen to Caroline if I was locked up as well? How would she survive without me? I felt as though I was having a panic attack. I could hear knocking at my bedroom door, but I refused to unlock it. All I wanted to do was drown in my own self-pity. I was starting to see how Caroline felt on some of her bad days. There was pounding at the door. Caroline was yelling for me to come out, but I ignored her. Suddenly the pounding stopped, and I could hear a key unlocking the door. I jumped up to try and stop Caroline from entering the room, but I was too late.

"How could you?"

"What are you talking about?"

"I just got off the phone with Stacy, and she told me Brad's in town. Why's that? Where did you go, Rhonda?"

"I went to Clearwater, if you must know."

"Did you go and see Brad?"

"What do you think?"

"Why would you do that? I told you everything you needed to know, so why would you go and see him? Why?"

"You told me everything." I laughed. I couldn't believe Caroline had the nerve to keep lying to me. "What version of the truth are you talking about?"

"What…"

"You are a **liar**, Caroline. You wouldn't know the truth if it fell off of your tongue by accident."

"What are you talking about?"

"You know the other day I was so excited, because I thought we had made some kind of progress in our relationship. You were being truthful with me, and things were looking up, but little did I know you were still lying to me."

"Rhonda."

"No! Don't 'Rhonda' me! You lied to me! Over and over again, all you did was lie, and that makes me wonder…are you even capable of telling me the truth about anything?"

"Rhonda I'm sorry, I…"

"No, you're not. You lied to me about JJ knowing full well Brad was his father. Why?"

"I wanted to tell you the truth, but I didn't know how."

"It's easy. You open your mouth and you spit it out. It's not that hard, but for you, I may be wrong."

"Rhonda, please. Think about JJ. He's happy. We're able to see him whenever we want, and we know he's okay. What do you know about the Parsons? Nothing. They would turn him against us, and we would never see him again."

"Who do you trust?" I was frustrated and tired of the lies.

"What?"

"No. I want to know; who do you trust? You've been lying to me, Stacy, Rachel—hell, everyone if you look at it. So, who do you trust, because it sure as hell isn't any of us?"

"Trust had nothing to do with this. I was protecting my son. When JJ came into this world, he was a blessing, but I didn't want to destroy his life because of the way I was living mine. So yes, I lied to you and everyone else, but my son was safe and that's all I cared about."

"So does Rachel know that at any time, if Brad decided he wanted to petition for paternity, that he would win, and she would lose custody of JJ? Your intentions were good, but your outcomes are all the same. In the end someone always winds up getting hurt."

"I will not feel guilty for trying to do what was best for my son. I've seen what the Parsons can do, and there's no way I was going to allow them to sink their claws into my child. Let's not forget, they're the reason our parents are still sitting in jail!"

"That may be the case, but did you for one-minute think about Brad? I think for some odd reason he's still in love with you. Maybe if the two of you would've stayed together, then things would've turned out differently. Who knows, JJ could've had two stable parents in his life, instead of this phony arrangement you decided to put together."

"JJ has stable parents."

"Who? Rachel and Jacob? They're not even a real couple."

"But they love JJ. To him, Rachel is his mother and Jacob is his father."

"Jacob...The same Jacob who happens to be gay? Come on, Caroline! Really."

"Jacob's gay..."

Caroline and I turned around, and Stacy was standing in the doorway. I don't think either of us heard her enter the house.

"Stacy, what are you doing here?" Caroline gave me a look. She took a step towards Stacy reaching out her hand, but Stacy pulled back.

"Jacob is not gay! And you of all people shouldn't be spreading rumors."

"Stacy..." Caroline said in somber voice.

"No. Why would Rhonda say something like that?"

I didn't say a word.

"Talk to me, Rhonda. Tell me what's going on?" Stacy was furious.

"I don't know. Why don't you ask Caroline? She's the one with all the answers."

Stacy turned all of her attention back towards Caroline.

"Caroline. What's going on? Is Jacob really gay?"

Caroline clearly didn't want to answer that question. Her silence was slowly eating away at Stacy.

"Why are you here, Stacy?"

"Fine. If that's the way you want to play it then so be it. I'm going to tell you why I'm here, and then you're going to tell me the truth about Jacob."

"Stacy..."

"No. I'm here because Brad just left my office trying to figure out if you had a child. He mentioned the name JJ. The same name Rhonda has mentioned to me once before. Now I don't know what's going on, but I want to know how and why my husband is involved."

Caroline gave me the deadliest stare, and then she turned back around toward Stacy.

"Fine. If the truth is what you want, then I'll give it to you. I got pregnant from Brad five years ago, but I didn't want his parents to know about the baby. So, Jacob agreed to adopt him."

"I don't understand. Why would Jacob go along with this?"

"Do you really want to know?"

"Damn it, Caroline, don't play with me. Just tell me the truth. Why did Jacob agree to adopt your son?"

"Okay! If you want to know then here goes. As you know I find clients in some of the strangest places. Well, there was this cop who wanted me to meet him at a hotel over near Montgomery

Street. So, I did. When we finished, I left the hotel, then I realized I had forgotten my bag inside the room. When I went back to get it, I could overhear two guys in the room arguing. I decided to wait outside until they were finished, and then I would go back into the room and get my bag. The door was cracked open and I was able to see inside the room, and that's when I noticed it was Jacob in the room arguing with another cop. So, I listened in, and discovered the other guy was mad at Jacob because he wouldn't be truthful about who he really was. Something about, 'you're a fake' and 'I wonder if your wife knows'. Well, things got intense and the guy told Jacob he was in love with him. And then he kissed him…and well…Jacob kissed him back."

Caroline averted her eyes and Stacy looked like she was going to be sick.

"I must have made a noise, because Jacob turned around and saw me at the door. At first, I wanted to run but I didn't. They came out of the room, and the other cop made threats towards me and warned me to never speak of what I saw to anyone. After he left, Jacob begged me not to mention any of this to you, and I only agreed to his terms because he promised to help me whenever I was in need. So, whenever I was in a bind, Jacob has always been there, and when I found out I was pregnant with JJ, he volunteered to be one of his adoptive parents. I never meant to hurt you, but what else could I do?"

"So, you allowed me to stay married to Jacob knowing he was gay."

"Stacy, it wasn't that simple."

"My husband is gay, and he's been helping you raise…your child."

"Stacy."

Caroline tried to approach Stacy, but she fanned her off.

"Don't! I have been nothing but a friend to you over the years, and you do this to me."

"I didn't do anything to you. Your husband was the one who wanted this secret kept, not me."

"But you went along with it. If you were ever my friend, then you would've told me the truth. What would have happened if I would've contracted some kind of disease from him? What were you going to say? 'Sorry. I should've told you'? This is my life, Caroline!"

"You're right. This is your life. My life ended the night I was raped! The fact that your husband is gay. Big deal. My father accidently killed a man because he raped me at a frat party that you begged me to go to. *Your* life? *My* life was over years ago."

"That's not fair and you know it."

"Fair! You want to talk fair. Okay then…let's be fair. You're right. I was wrong to keep this from you, but as brave as I wanted to be, the fact remained that Jacob was still a cop, and he could've put me away whenever he wanted to! So, what were my options, Stacy? Tell me…what was I supposed to do?"

"You could've come to me, and the fact that you're still blaming me for your rape says a lot."

"Because you are to blame. My life could've turned out so differently if you would've never invited me to that frat party, but look at me. Look at me, Stacy, and tell me just how were you going to help me? My parents have been sitting in jail for the past six years, and you still haven't been able to do anything for them."

"It's hard when you're fighting against the Parsons, and you of all people should know that, but if you would've come to me, then I would've done everything within my power to help you. Instead you chose to help cover up the fact that the man I'm in love with is gay."

"I needed help that Jacob was willing to provide. So, I'm sorry, Stacy, for thinking about someone else other than myself."

"Okay. I see how you're going to play this. I just want you to remember one thing. How does that saying go that you're always telling me? What goes around comes around. Well I want you to remember that, because you are no friend of mine!"

"Stacy!"

"Leave me alone, and don't ever talk to me again."

Stacy stormed out of the room. Whatever she was about to do wasn't going to be pretty, and I, for one, wasn't waiting around to see what it was. I knew for a fact she was on her way to confront Jacob, and once that happened all hell was going to break loose. Jacob would turn on Caroline, and he might even help Brad take JJ away from her. Next, he would probably turn me over to the cops and hold me—on speculation alone. Yes. I had opened a gate that should've stayed closed. If ever there was a time to leave town, then it was now. I went to my closet, and I started packing as many suitcases as I could find.

"What are you doing?"

"Stacy just left here mad as hell. Now it doesn't take a genius to figure out what could happen next. Jacob is liable to come after the both of us, and there is nothing we can do to stop him."

"He wouldn't."

"Yes, he would. You just blew his secret out the water. Your leverage with him is gone. And JJ—he may be gone as well. So, I'm not sitting around here waiting on Jacob to come and arrest me. I'm leaving, and if you had any sense you would be leaving too."

"And go where?"

"I don't know. Anywhere! But if we stay here, Brad is going to find a way to take JJ away from Rachel—and he will—and you and I both could be joining Mom and Dad upstate. If you love JJ, then I suggest you get him and run."

"This is all your fault. Everything was fine until you had to go and open your big mouth. I can't leave! What am I supposed to do with Mom and Dad's house? And what about JJ? How am I supposed to take him away from Rachel without freaking him out? Damn it, Rhonda. You have ruined everything."

"Me! Really! So, you're putting this on me. I went to Brad looking for help because I was so worried about you, and now you want to try and turn this around on me by telling me this is all my fault. Well grow up, Caroline. This is nobody's fault but your own.

You blackmailed Jacob, you gave up JJ and kept him away from Brad; our parents are in jail because of you! This is your fault. This is all your fault!"

I grabbed my suitcases and walked out of the room.

"That's right. Leave. You stir up this mess and then you leave me here to clean it up."

"This is your mess. You just placed me in the middle of it and never once thought about getting me out of it. I'm still going to find a way to get Mom and Dad out of jail, because someone has to fix this family, because we're way past broken."

"No. You've done enough."

"No. I've just gotten started."

"And where are you going?"

"I don't know, but I can't stay here. I will not be punished like everyone else who has tried to help save you. You need to wake up, and realize these games of yours are hurting everyone, including yourself."

I loaded up my car and left. I had no clue as to where I was going, but I needed to get as far away from Caroline as possible. There was a storm coming, and I wanted to be nowhere near it.

# Chapter 10

## Pouring Salt in An Open Wound

My plan was to drive as far away as possible, but I knew I couldn't do that without saying good-bye to Damien first. No matter what happened in the past, I loved him and nothing was going to change that, but when it came to Prez, my feelings were all over the place. I was falling for him but after the incident at the restaurant I no longer knew what to feel. I pulled into Damien's driveway hoping that he would be home. All I wanted to do was say good-bye and be on my way. I rang the doorbell, but there was no answer. I was going to use my key, but decided not to. I was no longer Damien's girl, so it was best if I left my key and went on my way. Part of me wanted to walk away, but I couldn't. I needed to see him. I had so much to tell him, and maybe then he could understand why I did what I did, and why I was leaving town. I used my key to unlock the door.

As I walked through the house, I didn't see anyone, but I could hear noises coming from the bedroom. I stepped closer to the door and my stomach dropped. Loud moans filled the hallway clearly like there wasn't a whole four walls and a door separating us. I wanted to burst into the room and confront Damien, but who was I to say anything? My heart was aching and there was nothing I could do about it. As I turned to leave, I heard the bedroom door open, but I kept walking.

"Rhonda! Is that you?"

I refused to turn around, and continued walking.

"Rhonda!"

I didn't want to see anything. All I wanted to do was to get out of Damien's house as fast as I could. I tried to speed up, but Damien grabbed me by the arm and turned me around to face him.

"You didn't hear me calling you?"

"I could hear you just fine. I could hear a lot of things to be honest."

"Why are you here?"

"No reason. No reason at all." I reached into my pocket and pulled out Damien's house key. "And here's your key back. I won't need it anymore."

"Rhonda."

"No. I get it. You've moved on. So, I'm good, and I'll see you around."

I headed toward the door, but Damien cut me off.

"Wait. You're not going anywhere. Not until you tell me why you're here."

"Whatever my reasons were, they're pointless now. So, like I said before, I'll see you around."

"Wait. You come into my place unannounced, and then you refuse to tell me why. I don't know what kind of games you're playing but—"

"Me! Playing games. You're hilarious! Anyway…I came here because I'm leaving town, and I wanted to see you before I left, but low and behold I walk in on you having sex with…"

I had no clue who Damien was having sex with. I wanted to leave but had the sudden urge to know who this mystery woman was. As I headed toward his room, Damien made several attempts to stop me, but I forced my way past him and shoved open his bedroom door. When I turned on the lights, I stood in shock as I watched my best friend stumble while trying to get dressed. My emotions took over so quickly that I found myself standing in the doorway, speechless, and embodied with rage. I looked down at my hands as they began to shake. I became afraid of what I would do next. Damien walked into the room, and I could hear him talking, but I couldn't make out anything he was saying. All I could do was look at Rachel. *How could she?* My best friend. How could she do this to me?

"Rhonda. Look."

Was she really talking to me? She had the nerve to form her lips to speak my name.

"Rhonda. Do you hear me? Rhonda." Damien called out to me, but I could barely hear him.

I looked at Damien and then Rachel. I couldn't speak. All I could do was stare. I felt as though my eyes were deceiving me. Somehow, I snapped out of my trance and headed towards my car.

"Rhonda!"

I stormed out of the house, got into my car, and sat there trying not to hyperventilate. I tried to move but I couldn't. I didn't start the ignition, I didn't cry, I didn't do anything but sit in silence. I looked over at my backpack that was sitting in the passenger seat. I reached inside of it and pulled out my gun. I had no idea what I was going to do with it, but I got out of the car and headed back inside the house. Damien and Rachel were talking in the kitchen when I entered the room. Their eyes widened when they saw what I brought with me.

"Rhonda! What are you doing?" Damien cried out.

"Don't. I trusted you, and this is how you repay me? By sleeping with my best friend?"

"Rhonda." Rachel could barely get my name out her mouth. *Why was she still talking to me?* All she was doing was making matters worse for herself. I glanced at the gun in my hand. Was I really doing this? Could I have overreacted? I looked at Rachel then Damien and my anger intensified.

"Shut up! Please just shut up before you make me shoot you." I aimed the gun at Rachel then Damien.

"Rhonda, please. Just calm down." Damien pleaded with me.

"I'm calm. Trust me. I'm calm, because if I wasn't, I would've shot the two of you by now." I looked at them both in disgust. "All I want to know is why."

"Rhonda, baby."

"Damien, you're pushing your luck. All I want to know is why? Why were you sleeping with my best friend, and I want to know now?"

"I don't know why. It just happened."

"It just happened." I turned to face Rachel. "So, you've been keeping tabs on Damien since we've been together. Is that it?"

"No, Rhonda, it's not like that."

"Then how is it? Please, Rachel; explain to me how you ended up in bed with my boyfriend."

"I don't know. He started coming around more than usual. Always talking to me about you, and then out of the blue, things started to get a little tense between the two of us."

"And tonight?"

"Caroline called me and…I don't know. I came by to tell Damien you were leaving town and—"

"So, I decide to leave town and you two decided to hook up. Nice. Very nice."

"Rhonda, it's not like that and you know it."

I looked at Damien and Rachel and the sight of them made me sick. I glanced at my gun and thought about how this would play out. If I shot them, I might feel better for a minute, but it really wasn't worth the consequences. I needed to cool off and be smart about this. I wasn't about to go to jail over these frauds. A tear escaped down my cheek, but not from sadness. I lowered the gun and hastily wiped my face. Rachel let out a small sigh of relief. Deep down I knew the deed was done and there was nothing I could do to change that. The two people I thought the world of betrayed me. I smiled and shook my head at how stupid they looked standing there cowering. I turned and walked out the door.

I got into my car and drove off. I had been lied to, cheated on, and taken advantage of for the last time. Everyone had made a fool of me, and now it was time for things to change. I drove around for a while trying to figure out what to do next. Tears of disappointment streamed down my face as I cried out in frustration. After driving around for a while, I soon felt a sense of calm. Then a somber mood overcame me. I immediately thought about Caroline, and how I exposed her secret to Brad, and left her all alone to deal with the fallout. I was wrong for betraying and abandoning my sister. I quickly turned the car around. I was no longer leaving town...not just yet.

I drove home, and when I got there, I opened the door, and Caroline jumped up in shock as I entered the room.

"What are you doing here? I thought that you were leaving town."

"I changed my mind, and besides you're going to need someone here with you when the walls come tumbling down."

Caroline walked over and hugged me, and I hugged her back. I didn't realize just how much my sister really needed me.

"So, what are we going to do?"

"We're going to start taking care of business."

"Business how?"

"Well as you mentioned before, we need to take care of the house."

"What are we going to do about the house?"

"I'm going by the bank tomorrow to pay off the note."

"You have that kind of money?"

"Yeah. I have that kind of money."

"Okay, but won't that cause some kind of red flag to go off?"

"No. I have a small bank account I've been depositing money into for years. So, we're good. Everything's legit. Next, we need to get in touch with Brad, and work on a plan that involves getting JJ back."

"Wait! Brad. No. I'm not bringing Brad into JJ's life."

"You may not have a choice. What happens if Brad goes after JJ himself and gets custody? He could shut you out of JJ's life completely, and you wouldn't be able to do anything about it."

"What about his parents, Rhonda? You know I couldn't take it if those people were ever a part of JJ's life."

"I know, and that's why it's so important that you play nice. You need to get Brad over here as soon as possible and work something out. Regardless of what you may think about his parents, it's easy to see that he still has feelings for you. So, play on that. Get Brad on your side and work something out so you can stay a part of JJ's life. I just found out I had a nephew, and I'm not ready to lose him."

"You're right. I don't want to lose him either, so I'll do it, but there's no telling how Brad is going to react once he finds out I've kept JJ away from him all these years."

"Just explain to Brad why you did it. Play on his love for you. You can do this. You've been lying to everyone for years, so what's a couple more days?"

"I lied because I had to."

"And as far as I'm concerned, you still do."

"What happened?" asked Caroline.

"What are you talking about?"

"Why the change? At first you were willing to leave town and call it quits, and now you're here fighting for us, trying to make things work. So, what happened?"

"I guess I needed a little inspiration. I didn't welcome it, but I needed it. I'm going to do everything within my power to make this right. We're going to get Mom and Dad out of jail, and we're going to find a way to get JJ back as well. We both have spent our lives protecting other people, and now it's time for that to change. It's time we started looking out for ourselves."

"I don't know what got this fire started inside of you, but I'm glad it happened."

I smiled. I wasn't ready to tell Caroline about what I had just witnessed. Rachel and Damien broke my heart. Plus, I was embarrassed. But none of that mattered. I could tell Caroline's spirit was lifted. My heart was breaking but my sister was smiling—something I haven't seen in a long time. She actually seemed happy. I was ready to set in motion a chain of events that I couldn't take back. I wasn't sure about what I was doing, but my family's survival depended on it. The old Rhonda was gone and a new Rhonda had resurfaced. I wasn't sure about a lot of things, but I was determined to not play the fool ever again.

# Chapter 11

## Facing Down the Enemy

A broken heart can either push you over the edge or ignite a fire inside you that you never knew existed, and I was on fire. Everything I had discussed with Caroline was coming into play. The mortgage was paid in full, and Caroline had convinced Brad to meet with her so they could discuss issues regarding JJ. I quit my job at the doll shop. The cops could watch all they wanted, but there was no way I was going back into that place. Plus, Damien wouldn't stop calling, so I had to change my home and cell number. I wanted nothing else to do with him or Rachel. I needed to get my life together, and this time I was going to do what was right. Stacy was on a war path, and Rachel had no idea Caroline and Brad were in the midst of taking JJ away from her. I knew Jacob wanted me behind bars, and he wasn't going to stop until he got me there. I had no idea what my future held, but for once I was going to make the best of it, even if it was short lived.

I decided it was time for me to go back to school. It was the only front I had left, and I didn't want to compromise it. I headed back to school hoping I could squeeze in some extra credit to help pull up some of my failing grades. As I walked down the sidewalk to the business building, I saw Damien walking towards me. I couldn't stand the sight of him and I didn't want to hear anything he had to say, so I turned around and headed in the opposite direction. Why was I leaving? I hadn't done anything wrong. Trying to avoid Damien was going to drive me insane. If I was going to start over, then I needed to face Damien and move on. I turned around and headed back towards class. As I skimmed the courtyard my heart started racing as I saw a familiar face approaching me. It was Prez. I guess Jacob had made his case and I was off to jail. As he neared me, I couldn't do anything but surrender. I had nowhere else to go.

"Rhonda. I need to talk to you."

I looked at Prez trying to figure out who he was. He didn't carry himself like a dealer but the way he handled me at the restaurant cried out law enforcement. But it didn't matter because in my eyes he was nothing but a liar. Just like Damien.

"So, what are you? NARC? FED? CIA? Who are you, Prez, or is that even your real name?"

"There's so much I wanted to tell you, but I couldn't."

"Prez? So, is that your real name?"

"Come on, Rhonda. This is serious. I need to talk to you."

"And we're talking. So, what do you want? Are you here to take me to jail? I mean that's why you were working at the shop right? To spy on me? To check out my work? Come on, Prez! Just be honest with me."

"Yes. I worked at the shop to keep an eye on you because that was my job."

"Okay, so you did your job. Now I'll ask you again. Are you here to take me to jail?"

"No. That's not why I'm here."

"Then why are you here?"

"I need to talk to you about your case."

"My case. Wow. So, I guess I'm in the big leagues now."

"Rhonda. You're at the top of the FBI hit list. Your dolls have been confiscated all over the world. This is serious."

"Okay, so you're with the FBI. That figures. And I'm at the top of their hit list…no thanks to you, right?"

"Rhonda."

I thought about how things transpired between me and Prez and grew angry all over again.

"So that night I caught you at the shop. You only came on to me so I wouldn't be suspicious about why you were really there? Didn't you?"

"No, Rhonda. It wasn't like that and you know it."

"No! The only thing I know is that I got played. You sleeping with me was just part of the act, wasn't it? You don't care about me. Hell, you probably don't even like me. I was just a mark you had to bring in. Right?"

"Look, I wasn't thinking. I messed up. I allowed myself to get too close and…"

"And nothing. You messed up. I messed up. Hell, we all messed up. So, what do you want from me, because I have a class to go to?"

I looked over and I could see Damien still standing by the front door. Whatever Prez had to say, he needed to say it quick. I had a score I needed to settle, and I was pressed for time.

"The cops are looking to make an arrest. They still don't have enough evidence on you to make it stick. So, if I were you, then I would use that as my cue to leave town."

"And why would I do that?"

"To save yourself."

"From what? Prison? Look Prez, you're a cop, and no matter how you look at it I'm on the other side of the fence. So, whatever happens, happens—whether I want it to or not. So, thanks for the heads up, but I'm a big girl, and I can deal with what's coming my way."

"I don't get it."

"Get what?"

"How can you not care? You could go to prison. Don't you get that?"

"Yes, I get it, but what do you expect me to do? I can't just up and leave town. My sister needs me. So, when the time is right, then I'll leave, but for right now I'm going to take advantage of what time I do have left and enjoy myself, before the walls come tumbling down."

I smiled, because it was all I could do to keep from crying. My livelihood was in jeopardy, and there wasn't anything I could do about it. I wanted to cry, but why? My tears weren't going to change anything. My anger wasn't going to change the fact that I sold drugs. All in all, I understood that I had to pay for my actions—no matter how I felt about the situation.

"I don't want you to give up. I need you to fight this head-on."

"Why? When you're the one who's trying to put me in jail. So why do you even care?"

"Because I do. I wouldn't be here if I didn't."

"Well, you have a strange way of showing it. And besides, I am fighting. Just in my own way. I now understand there are certain things in my life that I have to fight for, and then there are other things I have to learn how to let go. I know in the end I may wind up losing everything, but I realized a long time ago, that's the price you have to pay when you're me."

"Why are you doing this to yourself?"

"Look, I can't do this with you. You've warned me. You've done your part, and now I have to go."

I tried to walk off, but Prez grabbed hold of me and pulled me in for a kiss. It was unexpected, and I didn't know how to react. He was the enemy. He couldn't be trusted, and yet I couldn't force myself to break away.

"You've got to let me go. This isn't going to work and you know it."

"I can't...and that night at the shop wasn't an act. I really do care about you."

"Why are you doing this to me? I don't need this in my life right now, and I don't need you. Just leave me alone and let me be."

"I've tried and I can't."

"Then try harder. I have to go." I tried to walk off but Prez stopped me.

"Please, Rhonda! Don't do this to me. I love you."

"No! No. I can't do this with you. Just leave me alone. There's no way this can work. I may be going to jail. Like you said yourself."

"It still doesn't change how I feel about you. I love you, Rhonda. I've done everything but break the law myself just to protect you. All I can think about is you."

Why now? I couldn't understand why this was happening now. I had a plan. It was a good plan, and I couldn't allow Prez to come in with his "I love you's" and ruin everything. It felt nice. He felt nice, but this time I couldn't think about myself. This time I had to do what was best, and let him go.

"Too bad I don't feel the same way about you. So just leave."

"Why are you lying to me? I could feel it in your kiss. I know you feel the same way as I do."

"What I feel is irrelevant. I'm leaving now, and you're going to let me. My fate is sealed and I'm good with that. So good-bye, Prez."

"Rhonda. Please."

I could hear the shaking in Prez's voice. His emotions were getting the best of him, and me as well. I almost cried when I heard the pain in his voice, but I had to force myself to walk away. As I headed toward the classroom, that's when I noticed Damien had already left. Maybe it was for the best. It gave me some time to try and get my head together.

Later on, that evening when I arrived at home, I noticed a familiar car sitting in the garage. It was Brad's car. I guess Caroline was playing it safe. Making sure Stacy and Rachel wasn't aware of Brad being in town. I walked inside the house, and things must have been going well between the two of them. Caroline had this glow about her, and she seemed happy. It was like seeing the old Caroline again. I knew from that moment on, I was making the right decision, and now it was time to set the rest of my plan into motion.

I kept an eye on Caroline and Brad as I made my way back into the garage. I opened the trunk of Brad's car and removed his spare tire. There awaiting me was my doll I had to ditch up in Clearwater. It was easy to figure out Brad's car. He had MD license plates that read B.S. Dead giveaway, but I knew my doll would come in handy later on, so I decided to keep it. It was too dangerous to keep the doll in the house so I examined it and placed it back in the trunk of Brad's car. I walked back into the house and went to my bedroom. As I sat in silence it gave me a chance to think about everything that happened over the past year. Was I making the right decision? Was I even capable of doing what I had set out to do? Would I get cold feet? There were a lot of thoughts clouding my judgment, but I had to be strong and shake them off. I knew what I had to do, and it was time I completed my plan.

# Chapter 12

### A Minor Set Back

I took a couple of days to think about what I had set out to do. Time was of the essence, and I needed to set my plan into motion before I developed cold feet. It was getting late, and I needed to speak with Stacy before she headed home from work. The beginning of my plan started out with Stacy and it was going to end with her as well. As I made my way towards the building, I noticed the sun was going down, and it was later than I thought. I tried to enter the building but it was locked. I was too late. My plans were now on hold. I couldn't move forward without consulting with Stacy first. As I headed back towards the car, my mind was so preoccupied that I didn't hear the footsteps until they were right behind me. I whipped my head around, but something struck my temple, hard. I fell to the ground as my vision went dark.

When I awoke, I struggled to remember. I tried to lift myself up and look around, but the pain was too overwhelming. The swelling on my face pinned my eyelids shut making it nearly impossible to see. I scanned the room but there was no one in sight. Wincing, I tried to make out where I was. The half-lit room was empty. Static hummed nearby, and was that... music? Perhaps from a radio. It couldn't be far. I tried to sit up. I touched my head and then I saw it. Blood, still warm, oozed from my body. Suddenly, the pain in my face fell away and my eyes went wide. I called out.

"Help!" I assumed no one could hear my faint voice over the roaring television.

"Help..."

I struggled to get up, but my body was in too much pain. Who would want to do this to me? So many names ran through my mind, but I wouldn't allow myself to even fathom the thought of any of them doing this to me. As I laid on the floor, I started to laugh out loud. I had pissed off so many people that it was more like who didn't want to do this to me. My life had been a whirlwind of problems, and there were a lot of things that didn't make sense, and this was one of them. I didn't know if I was raped or not, because my body hurt all over. Finally, someone must have heard me. A guy came running into the room telling me that he had called for help. Part of me was relived, and the other part of me didn't care. If someone I knew could've done this to me, then I was definitely moving forward with my current plans. There was no going back.

The paramedics soon arrived, and I was taken to the hospital where the doctors ran tests, and examined me all over. I was so exhausted that I eventually passed out. It felt as if I had slept for days. When I woke up, to my surprise, Caroline was sitting by my bed. I was so happy to see her.

"Hi. So how are you feeling?"

"Okay, I guess. A few bruises here and there."

"Well, the doctors say you're doing good, and that you should be able to come home within a couple of days."

"That's good to know."

Caroline continued to stare at me. She seemed upset.

"So, what happened?"

"I don't know. I was heading to my car, and before I knew it someone came up and hit me from behind. When I woke up, I was in a strange room, and then I was brought here."

"I'm so sorry...you know I tried to get the doctors to explain to me what happened, but they wouldn't tell me anything. I stressed to them that I was your sister, but they didn't seem to care."

I sat in silence. There was so much I wanted to tell Caroline, but couldn't.

"Rhonda."

"Yeah."

"Are you okay? I mean, are you even listening to me?"

"Yeah. I'm listening."

"So, tell me. Were you...were you raped?"

I could tell the entire incident had taken a toll on Caroline. I could see the pain in her eyes as she gazed over my fragile body. I wanted to lie to her but I knew eventually the truth would come out.

"Yes. I asked the doctors not to tell you anything, because I wanted to be the one to tell you myself."

"Rhonda!" Caroline burst into tears.

"I know...but I felt it was only right if the news came from me. The doctors told me that I was drugged, beaten, and raped."

Caroline became distraught. How could I comfort her, when I didn't understand why any of this was happening myself? My mind was racing. I couldn't even allow myself to think. Whoever did this to me was going to pay. The fact that I was beaten and raped left me enraged.

"Why us? I mean, what did we do in our lives to deserve this? I don't get it. What did we do?"

Caroline became excited. I was numb. I could feel the tears as they rolled down my cheeks, but I couldn't feel any emotions. I was trying my best to cope with reality, but everything seemed so bleak. I felt like I was slipping away into a world of darkness.

"I don't know why, and right now I don't even care."

"How could you say that? You were raped and beaten half to death. You didn't ask for this to happen. So why wouldn't you care?"

"I don't know, Caroline. You tell me. I've been trying for years to convince you of the same thing."

"I know, and I should have realized it then, but I get it now." Caroline grabbed my hands, and even though I knew I was wrong for how I was feeling, I felt like I was allowed to be angry, even if it was just for a minute. "I did everything but get my life together after I was raped, and after Mom and Dad were sent to jail, I allowed myself to check out on life. I was wrong, Rhonda. Don't you get that? Wrong. And the last thing I would want you to do is to follow in my footsteps. I'm going to get my life together, and I'm going to make you and JJ so proud."

I knew Caroline was serious about everything she said. The last thing I wanted was for her to feel any sort of guilt, so I had to change my attitude, my way of thinking, and pull myself together.

"I know you will. So, let's make a new deal. If you promise to get your life together, then I'll promise not to throw mine away."

"I promise."

I tried to smile, but it hurt. I was willing to try for Caroline, but someone was going to pay for what they had done to me.

"I hate this. I hate that something like this had to happen to you. You're just a kid. You didn't deserve this."

"And neither did you. We're going to be fine. We have each other and you have JJ. Remember that. Speaking of, how's that going? What did Brad say?"

"Are you sure you want to talk about that right now?"

"Hey, I'm bed bound for a couple of days, so amuse me."

"Well, I told Brad about what happened with JJ. I explained to him how I didn't feel as though I was fit to raise a child, and how I sure as hell didn't trust any of his family to be around my son."

"So how did he react?"

"He was conflicted and I could tell he was hurt."

"So, he's not going to help you?"

"No. He's going to help. It's one thing if he didn't know he had a son, but now he does. He made it very clear he wanted JJ to be a part of his life. So, right now he's in the process of challenging the adoption."

"You know Rachel is going to fight you on this."

"I know, but there's nothing I can do about it. Brad is JJ's father, and he has the right to challenge the adoption."

"But, do you think he would try and double-cross you?"

"I don't know. He could if he wanted to. I just don't want JJ around his parents. I know that's asking a lot of him, but I don't trust them."

"So, what about you and Brad? I saw you blushing when I walked in the other day. So, I assume he still has feelings for you."

"He does, but I'm afraid he's scared to show his true feelings. I want things to work out, too, but I'm afraid as well."

"Afraid of what?"

"Failing again. I've failed so many times, at so many things, that I don't know if I can take disappointing myself, or anyone else for that matter, ever again."

"You'll do fine. I'm certain. If Brad truly cares about you, then you won't have to worry about doing this yourself. He'll be there to help you."

"I know. I know, but enough about me. Let's talk about you."

"Me? There's nothing else to talk about."

"Really. Then who is Prez?"

"What are you talking about?"

"Some guy named Prez has been here checking on you every couple of hours, since the day you arrived. I'll give him another hour or so and he'll be back. So, who is he?"

"He's no one."

"No one, huh? Well, why does Damien seem so annoyed by him? Every time he comes around Damien gets upset."

"Damien has been here too?"

"Yes. Even Jacob stopped by, and I know that had to be hard for him, considering he can't stand either one of us right now."

"Great. So, everyone has seen me like this."

"What are you talking about? We were worried about you. We could've cared less about how you looked. We just wanted to make sure you were okay."

"I'm not shallow, Caroline. I wasn't talking about my looks. I was referring to looking weak. I'm a fighter, and yet I wound up in the hospital beaten and raped. Do you know how that makes me feel...and to have someone I—" I was too afraid to tell Caroline what I was really thinking. "Just to have people I care about see me like this. It's too much."

"I know you're not weak and so does everyone else. You being here doesn't justify anything. There's a sick bastard out there, and he will be caught. Trust me, none of us, including—Damien could ever think you're weak. He loves you, just as much as I do."

"I wasn't talking about Damien."

"Then who?" Caroline thought for a minute and then it hit. "Prez? Wait a minute! Have you fallen for this guy?"

"I don't know. I may have. It's just... he makes me feel so strange."

"Strange how?"

"I can't explain it. It's complicated."

"So why haven't I ever met him? Who is he?"

"Because you're complicated as well." Caroline laughed. I think we both needed something to smile about. "But as far as Prez goes— he was a surprise that came too late."

"Why do you say it like that?"

"Because there is no future for us. He's a cop, Caroline. More like the Feds to be exact."

"Feds. So, does he know about...?"

"He knows everything."

"And yet, he still wants to be with you. That's saying a lot."

I laughed because Caroline was right. For Prez to know as much as he did about me, and still want me, made me fall for him even more. I loved him and I was finally able to admit that much to myself, but that was all I could do. There wouldn't ever be a Rhonda and Prez, and I had accepted that.

"Why are you making me laugh? You know it hurts."

"I know but you needed it."

"Well, whatever happens just know that I love you."

"I love you too."

For the longest, I prayed for this day, but I hated that it took my downfall in order for it to happen. Caroline was turning over a new leaf while my world was slowing falling apart. My life wasn't going as planned, therefore I needed to hurry my plan along, before there was no plan to set into motion.

# Chapter 13

Bringing My Plan to Light

I sat in the hospital thinking about everything the doctors had explained to me, and I felt disgusted. My heart was heavy as I was stuck wrestling with the truth. The more I thought about it the sicker I felt. All I wanted to do was close my eyes and avoid the entire situation. I was beaten and raped, and though I thought that would've been the worst part of my ordeal, it wasn't. The doctors had informed me that I was pregnant. What was I going to do with a baby? A baby wasn't part of the plan. I didn't want to think about it. If I allowed my mind to falter, then my plan would surely crumble.

Damien and Prez tried to visit me while I was hospitalized, but I denied them both visitation. My condition was distressing enough without having to explain to them that I was pregnant, and that one of them was the father. The good news was that it couldn't be my attacker's baby because it had only been two days since the incident and I was six weeks into my pregnancy. I could only pray the doctors didn't slip up and mention anything regarding the baby to anyone. With everything that was going on in my life, being pregnant couldn't have come at a worst time.

One thing was certain, I needed to speak with Stacy. She was the only person who could set my plan in motion. I wanted to call her, but I didn't know what to say. Thanks to me and Caroline, Stacy discovered her husband was gay, and that her best friend had been betraying her for years. I needed to find a way to set my fears aside in order to make the call. I tried calling her several times, but with each call I kept hanging up the phone. There had to be a way for me to get in touch with her, without having to call her myself. Then it hit. I had one of the nurse's make the call for me. I knew that it was a coward move, but I didn't know what else to do. I didn't want to prolong my plan any longer.

After a couple of hours, Stacy finally arrived. I didn't know how she would react, but she was the only one who could help me.

"I know I'm the last person you want to see right now, but I need your help."

Stacy stood in the doorway then quietly made her way into the room. She continued to look at me. Staring at me with her cold, dead eyes. I didn't know what to do, or how to react. I waited for her to go off on me, but there was nothing. Just a cold blank stare.

"I understand if you don't want to help me. I'm sorry for wasting your time."

Then out of nowhere, Stacy burst into tears. I didn't know what to make of it. My body was sore all over, and it wasn't as if I could get up and run out. I was trapped in a room with a woman scorned, with no way to defend myself.

"I'm sorry. I'm so sorry." Stacy kept repeating over and over again. I was in shock. I didn't know what to make of it.

"Sorry for what? You didn't do this to me."

"But I blamed you and Caroline for a lot of my problems. It wasn't your fault Jacob is gay, and yet I blamed you for it. I knew Caroline was trapped in a tough situation, but I chose to blame her as well. I just hated I was in the dark about so many things."

Finally, I wasn't alone. Someone other than me knew how it felt to be kept in the dark. I just prayed Stacy's compassion lasted long enough for me to explain my plan to her.

"Don't feel bad. I was in the dark about a lot of things as well. Everyone thought they were protecting me, but you see how well that turned out." I was afraid to go any further, but I knew I had to. "The reason I asked you here is because I need a favor."

"You need a favor. Okay. What is it?"

"If I tell you something, will you promise not to flip out on me, and allow me to finish?"

"You sound serious. What is it?"

"You're not going to flip out right?"

"No. I'm not going to flip out. So, what is it?"

"I'm in a whole lot of trouble."

"Trouble how?"

I wanted to explain everything to Stacy, but part of me still didn't trust her. Not completely. But in order for my plan to come together, I had to put my fears aside and tell her everything, or there wasn't going to be a plan.

"The cops are looking to make an arrest."

"They know who did this to you?"

"No. They're looking to arrest me."

"But why? I don't understand. You were attacked. So why are they looking to arrest you?"

"Because the arrest doesn't have anything to do with the rape. The cops are looking to lock me up...because I sold drugs."

The room became silent as Stacy started to pace back and forth.

"Are you messing with me?"

"No. I'm dead serious. Around the time when I thought my parents had died, I found myself left with no options. Caroline was always strung out, and then the bank was threatening to evict us from the house. So, I needed a plan, and before long I was selling drugs."

"I don't get it. You're a straight-A student. You're smarter than this. Selling drugs is something you just don't do. Come on, Rhonda!" Stacy was in disbelief. "Okay. So, explain this to me... when did you find the time to do something like that? I mean you were always at school or at work."

"See, that's where it gets tricky. Remember back in the day when Rachel's grandmother gave me a job at the shop?"

"Yeah. I remember. You were so excited about having a job."

"I know. It was my first real job and we were strapped for cash. I didn't want to make any mistakes, so I made sure I watched everything that everyone did, because I wanted my dolls to be perfect, and they were."

"Okay so what does that have to do with anything?"

"It has everything to do with it. I became so good at it, that I learned how to make my dolls out of cocaine, and then I started selling them out of the shop."

"Rhonda!"

Even though I didn't like Stacy, I still felt as though I had disappointed her.

"I know. Trust me, I know, but it gets worse. The Feds are onto me."

"Rhonda. The Feds! I can't go up against them. What do you expect me to do?"

"I don't want you to go up against them. I want you to cut me a deal with the district attorney. I have prior knowledge that they don't have that much evidence on me, but I know if I turned myself in voluntarily then maybe I could work out some kind of deal."

"I don't know if that's a good idea. You're playing a very dangerous game, and it could backfire."

"If I sit around and wait for them to gather more and more evidence against me, then I'm going to lose the upper hand in this situation. Please. I know there's something you can do."

"Are you sure you want to do this?"

"No, but what other choice do I have?"

"I understand. So, is there anything else I should know about?"

I thought about lying to, Stacy, but I knew I needed to be completely honest with her. My life was about to change, and I needed to put things in order before everything fell apart.

"Yes. I'm pregnant."

"You're what! When did this happen?"

"I'm assuming before the rape, considering how far along I am."

"You're about to have a baby. Are you sure you want to go through with this? Because once I make that phone call, there's no going back?"

"I have to. I would prefer to spend part of my life with my child, rather than getting caught later on, and never having that option at all."

"Does Caroline know?"

"No. She doesn't know. As of now, the only people who know are me and you, and that's how I would like to keep it."

"So, are you sure about this? I mean really sure."

"Yes. Help me with this and I'll forever be in your debt. I can pay you whatever you want. Just please do this for me."

"No. Don't worry about anything. This one is on me. Let me see what I can do, and then I'll get back in touch with you. Sounds good?"

"Yes…and thank you."

I began to cry. My life would never be the same. I didn't know if Caroline would ever forgive me for what I was about to do, but this was something that needed to be done. I was making plans for the baby as well. I needed that peace of mind. My plan was now set into motion and there was no going back. There were going to be several roadblocks ahead that I was going to have to force my way through, but I just prayed that in the end I was making the right decision.

# Chapter 14

## Dealing with The Aftermath

Something was definitely up. The cops had been to the hospital to question me about the rape, but there was no information shared in return. I had to make a decision based on what I wanted the most. Did I want to find out who beat and raped me, or did I want to start and complete my plan. Something private was taken from me, but something significant was taken away from my family. Maybe one day in the future I would discover who did this heinous act against me, but for now I couldn't stray from my current plans.

It was my release date and Caroline was nowhere in sight. I waited and waited, but she never arrived. Time passed, and finally one of the nurses came in to inform me that my escort had arrived. As she rolled me out of the room, there stood Prez waiting by the nurse's desk.

"What are you doing here?"

"I told your sister I would bring you home today."

"Why?"

"Because I need to talk to you."

"What is there to talk about? I thought we've been through this already."

"It's about your case."

"My case...which one?" It was sad that I was a criminal and a victim at the same time. I know the cops didn't see that one coming.

"Your rape."

Prez escorted me to his car, and although I was hesitant about getting in, I needed to know what information he had.

"So, what news do you have?"

"The cops have a suspect in custody."

"Already! Who?"

"It was your sister who helped bring him in."

"Okay! So, who is it? Tell me."

"It was Jacob."

"Jacob? As in Jacob Tate? But why? Are you sure?"

"Yes. When your sister discovered where they found your body, she was certain she knew who it was."

"Where did they find me?"

"In a hotel off of Montgomery Street. It was like Jacob wanted to be caught. He left you in the same room Caroline claims she caught him in years ago."

"Jacob beat and raped me? Jacob!" All these years I never viewed Jacob as a threat, and low and behold he was the one who had committed such a cruel act against me. "I don't get it."

"You don't get what?"

"Take me to see Jacob. I need to know why."

"Rhonda. I don't think that's a good idea."

"I need to see Jacob now!"

Prez drove me to the police department where they were holding Jacob in custody. I could tell he didn't want to go through with my request, but I wasn't going to back off until I was able to speak with Jacob in person. Prez escorted me into a holding room, where I sat and waited until an officer brought Jacob in. I could feel the tension in the room—mostly from the cops who were looking at me like they wished I was the one in the hot seat and not Jacob.

"Prez, can you give us some privacy?"

"I'm not leaving you alone with him."

"Then leave another officer. I don't care who. I just need you out of the room. Please." The things I needed to say to Jacob I couldn't say in front of Prez.

"Rhonda."

"Please. For me."

Prez didn't want to leave, but he eventually backed off, and walked out of the room. Jacob and I sat in silence for a while before I decided to speak.

"So, it was you." Jacob didn't say a word. "Why? I knew you were mad at me but…"

"Mad! Mad couldn't describe how I was feeling."

"Jacob. You beat and raped me. Regardless of what happened in the past, I didn't do anything to you to deserve this."

Tears fell from Jacob's eyes. I could see he was hurting, but I didn't care. He hurt me, and he took something from me that wasn't his to have.

"Are you sure about that?"

"And what is that supposed to mean?"

"You did this to yourself."

"I did this to myself?"

If I had my gun I would've been in jail for murder. I couldn't believe Jacob had the nerve to tell me that I did this to myself! Really. He wanted to come at me like that.

"Yes! You wouldn't leave things alone. You kept digging and digging trying to figure out what happened in the past. You destroyed everything."

"I was digging because of my sister. You were there when they brought her in after she was raped. You saw what was done to her."

Jacob wouldn't say a word.

"You saw how badly my sister was beaten and raped, and yet you were able to do the same thing to me. Caroline was destroyed after that, and someone else lost their life in the process. To make matters worse, both of my parents were put in jail, all because someone else thought it was their right to try and teach my sister a lesson. So, was that your plan? Were you trying to teach me a lesson?"

"No. I just wanted you to experience how it felt to have something taken away from you that was private."

"I didn't tell your secret and neither did Caroline. Your wife stumbled upon the truth, and it was hers to do with as she pleased. You beat and raped me over something that had nothing to do with me! You left me unconscious and barely alive in a hotel room, all because you couldn't deal with the fact that your wife found out you were gay!"

"I'm not gay! My wife didn't suspect anything until you and your sister decided to open your big mouths!"

"Are you for real? Caroline has kept your secret for years. Even I didn't know until recently."

"And I'm supposed to believe that?"

"Believe what you want, but what you fail to realize is the fact that your sexuality wasn't our secret to tell. Caroline and I didn't care if you were gay or not. Besides, you were taking care of my nephew, and he loves you. So, what reason would I have to hurt you?"

"I don't know."

"You don't know because you were wrong."

"I wasn't thinking. I love JJ. I wouldn't do anything to hurt him."

"No. The only person you love is yourself. You couldn't see past that fact that someone knew your secret. Someone who you loved and cared about knew."

"She calls me a fraud. She even threatened to tell my squad if I didn't agree to a quick divorce. I love Stacy! I've never slept or had sex with any guy. I'm not gay!"

"You're still missing my point. We didn't tell your secret. I could care less if you were gay or not, but how do you think this is going to affect JJ? Did you for one-minute think about him?"

"You don't get it."

"You're right. I don't! Everyone was so worried about me uncovering Caroline's past, because of their own hidden secrets, that no one ever stood back to look at how it was affecting her. No one has stood up for my sister in years, and the day I decided to say enough is enough, I have to endure the wrath of Jacob. So, you're right. I don't get it."

"I saw what Caroline had gone through, and I hated what was done to her. I saw the hurt and pain in her eyes after the rape. When Stacy demanded a divorce and threatened to out me, in some kind of way I sorta felt like I was going through it, too."

"So, I'm supposed to feel your pain because of what?"

"You set all of this in motion; giving Stacy hints about JJ, saying I was gay, and telling Brad that he had a son."

"Brad. So, you knew?"

"Oh yes. I knew. I saw the papers where he was contesting the adoption."

"Whether we like it or not, Brad is JJ's real father."

"I'm his father! The Parsons are nothing but poison. How could you betray your sister? How could you betray your parents?"

"I didn't betray anyone. Everyone has been lying to me for years. You took it upon yourself to hurt me in the worst way possible, all because you couldn't handle the truth. I never played the victim and I'm not about to start. You beat and raped me. Fine. I have to live with that. My parents are in jail. Fine. I have to live with that as well. My sister is a tormented and misguided soul. Fine. The fact that I could've lost my baby because of you; I find that very hard to live with!"

I was so emotional. I wanted to keep the pregnancy a secret, but Jacob had set my emotions on a rampage.

"Baby? What baby?"

"My baby. The doctor discovered a lot of things when they performed my rape kit. So, my life is what it is. I can live with that, but can you live with what you did to me?"

Tears continued to gush from Jacob's eyes. I knew the news about the baby was tearing him apart.

"I'm sorry. I'm so sorry. I didn't want to hurt you. I was in pain, and I wanted you to feel the same pain I was feeling. I was so angry. I just...."

"Your pain. I've been in pain for the past six years. Have you not paid any attention to my life? It's a mess. Pain is all I've known for a while now, and all you have done is add on another little piece to my already screwed up life."

"Rhonda. I'm so..."

Before I knew it Prez had stormed into the room, and started to beat up on Jacob. The guards had to rush in and pull them apart.

"How could you hurt someone like that? How!" Prez was fired up and it was almost hypnotic.

"I messed up! I know that. I'm so sorry, Rhonda. I'm so sorry."

"Don't talk to her. Don't." Prez was still upset. One of the guards had to pull him outside the room in order to calm him down.

"Tell JJ I'm sorry. Please."

"Come on, Prez. Let's go." I could no longer look at Jacob. Just the sight of him made me sick. Prez escorted me out of the room and back to his car. Once we made it to the car, Prez grabbed hold of me and held me tightly in his arms. I wanted to cry so badly, but I wouldn't allow myself to look weak. Not again. I didn't know what to make of the situation. Prez didn't say anything. He just held me in his arms. When he finally released me, I got into his car and I didn't say a word. During the ride home we sat in silence. I didn't know what to say. Prez pulled up into the driveway, and before he turned off the ignition, he grabbed my hands and looked into my eyes.

"Are you alright?" I could tell Prez was perplexed by what I had said to Jacob earlier.

"I'm fine."

"And the baby?"

"So, you overheard?"

"Yes." I didn't want Prez to know about the baby. In truth, I didn't want anyone to know.

"The baby's fine."

"Rhonda. You know what I'm getting at."

"I know...but." I knew exactly what Prez was inquiring, but I wasn't sure if I was ready to give such an answer.

"But what?"

"I don't know. I just don't feel like talking about it right now."

"Come on, Rhonda. Don't do this."

"Don't do what? Look! You're the only person besides Jacob who knows that I'm pregnant, and that's the way I would like to keep it."

"What about the father? Shouldn't he know?"

"He already does."

I looked into Prez's eyes, and I didn't know what else to say. He was the father, and I knew that would destroy Damien. All the times I made love to Damien, not once did I have a pregnancy scare, but one night with Prez and my whole world changed.

"So, if me and Jacob are the only two who know then..."

I wanted to tell Prez but part of me didn't. He was a cop. I could lie and say that it was Jacob's baby, but what good would that do?

"Then you must be the father."

"I'm the father. Are you sure about that?"

"Am I sure...whatever." I felt offended. Why would I lie about something like that? I wanted to but I didn't. I got out of the car mad as hell and headed towards the house.

"Wait. I didn't mean it like that."

"Then how did you mean it? You honestly think I would lie about something like that? Well I didn't. I'm pregnant, and yes with your baby. So, why is that so hard to believe?"

"Rhonda."

I didn't answer. I couldn't believe he would question me on something like that.

"Rhonda, look at me." Prez grabbed hold of me and held me close in his arms.

"I'm sorry, I didn't mean to upset you. I just wanted to be sure you said the right name. That's all. We were only together once. And..."

"And that's all it took. I know it seems crazy but that's life. We slept together once, and I got pregnant. Now if you need more proof, then I'll be willing to do a paternity test for you."

"No. You don't have to do that."

"Yes, I do. I want to put your mind at ease, so that you're able to raise this child without suspicion. So just say when and where, and I'll be there."

Prez leaned over and kissed me.

"We don't need a paternity test. I trust you." Prez kissed me once again, and I started breaking down slowly.

"I love you." I said it so fast that I couldn't take it back, but considering everything I had been through, was it wrong of me to allow myself a little bit of happiness even if I knew it wasn't going to last?

"You love me?" Prez held me tightly in his arms. I didn't think he would ever let me go.

"Spend the night with me." I didn't know what I was thinking, but for some reason I didn't want Prez to leave.

"What? But."

"I can't...well you know...but that's not what I want. All I want is your company if that's alright with you."

Prez smiled with approval.

"That's fine with me."

Prez walked me inside of the house where Caroline, Damien, JJ, and even Brad were waiting.

"You're home! Surprise, sort of. What took you so long?" Caroline walked over and hugged me.

"I had to make a quick stop. That's all."

"So how do you feel?"

"I feel fine. I heard that you solved the case, so thank you."

"I would do anything for you. You know that."

I looked at Damien and the sight of him no longer bothered me. With all that had happened, I needed to learn how to value myself and treasure those who truly loved me.

"Rhonda, I just want you to know that I'm sorry and that…" Damien and his apologies. I didn't care to hear them.

"No. Stop."

"No. Let me finish. I hurt you and I'm sorry."

"This isn't the time." Prez tried to persuade Damien to stop.

"No. It's okay. I accept your apology. Now if you'll excuse me." I tried to walk past Damien, but he stopped me.

"Hey, man. Don't!" Prez was definitely in protective mode. He stepped in to ensure there was no contact between me and Damien.

"And who are you supposed to be? This is between me and Rhonda." Damien tried to break past Prez, but Prez held his ground.

"No, it's not. The day you slept with my best friend, you ended things."

"He what!" I forgot Caroline didn't know.

"It was a mistake and I'm sorry. You know I love you." Damien was committed to getting me back, but my love for him had faded. All I wanted to do was rest.

"Really. You want to do this now! I just got home from the hospital, and you want to come at me with this."

"No. This is not what I had planned, but I don't know what else to do. When I heard you were in the hospital, I freaked. I hated when you would go out at night, and now look. Look at what happened, and I wasn't there. I wasn't there to protect you."

"There was nothing you could've done. Jacob had it out for me, and he wasn't going to stop until he made me pay. Well, I've paid the price and now I'm trying to move on. Without you."

"Rhonda." I could tell the entire situation was eating away at Damien, but I couldn't be with him even if I wanted to. He betrayed me with my best friend. There was no going back to him.

"Damien, please. I've moved on and so have you…"

"With who? Him?" Damien was furious at the sight of Prez. "We have a history together. You don't even know this guy. How could you throw all of that away for him?"

"Are you serious? You threw our relationship away the day you slept with Rachel."

"Rhonda, you're starting to get upset." Prez tried to calm me down, but I was already livid.

"Why are you still talking to her?" Damien tried to make his stand against Prez.

"Damien, stop. This isn't his fault. Besides, Prez has always been there for me when I needed him. So just leave him alone."

"When you needed him…it's always about you and your needs."

"And what is that supposed to mean?"

"You're angry with me for sleeping with Rachel, but you slept with Prez way before I ever touched her."

"I what?"

"Damien, you need to leave. Now!" Caroline was upset and Brad was holding her back.

"No. Not until she hears this. The night you tried to surprise me. You left upset. I called and called, but you never answered. So, I went out looking for you, and guess where I found you? At the shop with this fool." Damien glanced at Prez in disgust.

"Hey this isn't cool. She just got home." Brad tried to step in but Damien wouldn't let up.

"No. She needs to hear this. She wants to lay blame, then let's. Just so you know, I followed you after that, too. So, I—"

"You what? You were spying on me?"

"No. I was trying to find you, so I could apologize, but you. You're quick. You seem to move on very fast. The next thing I know you and Prez were back at his place, and I saw him kiss you. You slept with him that night. Didn't you?"

Everyone in the room became quiet. There was no hiding the truth.

"Yes."

"Do you love him?"

I looked at Damien, and even though I was afraid to tell him the truth, I knew it had to be done.

"Yes."

Damien averted his eyes and started to walk off.

"Don't. Don't do this." Damien was wrong for what he had done, but so was I. I had lost so much, and the last thing I wanted to do was to lose him as a friend.

"You made your choice."

"And so did you, but you're still my friend. So please. Don't do this."

"Friends? Come on, Rhonda. I don't know how to be just friends with you. I love you, and you know that."

"I know, but still…you've been a part of my life for years, and I…I can't lose you. I can be mad and I can hate you, but I can't lose your friendship."

I could feel Prez ease away, but I grabbed his hand and pulled him close. Damien walked over and kissed me on my forehead.

"I understand, but it's going to take some time."

"I know."

Damien walked out of the house, and I tried to wipe my tears away in secret. I glanced at everyone as I headed towards my bedroom. I needed a minute to be alone. Prez waited downstairs as Caroline made her way up to my room.

"Are you okay?"

"Yeah I'm fine. Just a lot to take in. That's all."

"I can't believe he did that, and today of all days."

"It's okay. He had to say what was on his heart. When a man is burdened you let him speak."

"But, Rhonda."

"No. It's okay. Anyway, I see Brad's here. So, what's going on?"

"Well, it was going to be a surprise but…"

"But what? What's going on?"

"Brad got custody of JJ."

"He what? How did Rachel react?"

"She didn't take it well at all but she had to let him go."

"So, what's going to happen to JJ? He's moving to Clearwater with Brad?"

"We're moving to Clearwater."

I was in shock. I couldn't believe my ears. Caroline was moving out, and with Brad of all people.

"You're moving to Clearwater, but why?"

"It's the only way I can keep an eye on JJ. I know Brad is going to have a soft spot in his heart for his parents, and if they are to be around my child, then I need to be there with him."

"And Brad?"

"He wants to give it a shot as a family."

I was so happy for Caroline. She was finally getting a second chance. I could only pray that she was truly happy.

"I'm so happy for you." I started to cry. As soon as I was getting my sister back, she was leaving me, yet again.

"Don't cry. You're going to make it harder for me to leave."

"So, when are you leaving?"

"Tomorrow."

"Tomorrow! Why so soon?"

"Well to be honest, Brad and I had been discussing this for a while, but I didn't want to spring this on you, not until I knew you were okay."

"I understand, but don't worry, I'm fine. I have Prez. So, I'm good." I hugged Caroline. "I'm so happy for you."

"I love you so much."

"I love you too."

I wanted to tell Caroline about the pregnancy, but I couldn't ruin her happiness. If Caroline knew I was pregnant, she could feel reluctant about leaving with Brad, and I didn't want that. So, I decided to keep it to myself. I felt as though I was turning into Caroline with the decisions I was making regarding my future.

Karma! Caroline and I walked back downstairs and we celebrated my return home, and her departure to Clearwater. Things were finally looking up, and I wanted to enjoy every minute of it, before it all faded away.

That night I slept in Prez's arms thinking about everything that had happened, and how it all played out. He reassured me that everything would be alright, but I knew differently. My life was about to change, but I couldn't allow my fear to alter my current plans. I had made a promise to myself that no matter what, I wouldn't back down.

# Chapter 15

### ✤

# Freeing Myself

I t was time to complete my plan. I was up early. I needed to set things in motion before I developed cold feet. I got dressed, and I left Prez and Caroline a note for them to read when they woke up. Hopefully by then my plan would have been completed. As I walked out of the house, part of me didn't want to leave, but I knew I had to go. I loved Prez, but I had to put my love for him aside and press on. As I headed towards Stacy's office, I decided to take a slight detour over to Rachel's. Once I arrived at her apartment, I knocked on the door, and, surprisingly, she let me in.

"What are you doing here?"

"I needed to see you."

"Why? I thought you were done with me and Damien."

"You're right…what the two of you did to me was wrong, but you're still my best friend."

"Your best friend?" I could see the relief and the warmth in Rachel's eyes.

"Yes."

"So, how are you feeling?"

"My shoulder still hurts but the doctors said it could be a few weeks before it completely heals, other than that, I'm okay. How about you?"

"Not too good. You know Brad got custody of JJ."

"Yeah. I heard. So how are you coping?"

"I'm not going to lie. It's hard! I know in my mind, JJ isn't my biological son, but I've raised him since birth. I'm the only mother he's ever known, and now he's gone. I know I had to let him go, but I didn't think it would hurt this much."

"I know it's hard, but at least you have the option of visiting JJ. If Caroline wouldn't have worked things out with Brad, then she would've lost him as well. Brad made it very clear he wasn't going to stop until he got custody of JJ."

"And I understand that but I'm his mother in every way that counts. I love him, and even though I know he's with his "real parents" it still doesn't take away the pain."

"I know, but you'll always have me."

"Thanks, Rhonda…so tell me. Why are you over here so early? What's going on?"

"Nothing. I just wanted to see you, that's all."

"You just wanted to see me. Okay."

"But I can't stay. I just wanted you to know that I love you, and you'll always be my best friend."

"Why are you talking like that?"

"Like what?"

"Like you're going somewhere and not coming back."

"It's nothing. I just wanted you to know. That's all."

As I prepared to leave, I gave Rachel a huge hug good-bye. I left before I accidentally confirmed her suspicions. I rushed to Stacy's office, and when I arrived, she was waiting and ready to begin.

"So, are you sure about this?"

"Yes. If the district attorney is willing to take the deal, then yes, I'm sure. I just pray I'm not railroaded in the process."

"Did you ever tell Caroline what you were up to?"

"No. I didn't tell anyone. I just need to do this before I change my mind."

"Before we leave, I just want you to know why I'm doing this. In the beginning, I was so angry at you and Caroline for keeping Jacob's secret that I hated you for it, but after you were attacked, it was like reliving Caroline's rape all over again. I knew right then I needed to move past what I was feeling, and just be there for you guys."

"Thanks. I couldn't have made this happen without your help."

"Don't thank me just yet. Let's wait and see what happens."

Stacy escorted me to the police department where the district attorney was anxiously awaiting to take me into custody.

"So, is everything in order?" The DA looked over at Stacy as she handed him an array of files and documents.

"Everything is there. The sales, the drugs, and the doll." Stacy handed the DA the last doll I hid in the back of Brad's trunk. I brought it in to use as evidence against myself.

"Alright. Well here we go."

I stood in a daze as an officer read me my rights. I sat in lockup, and then finally it happened. I watched in amazement as my parents were released from jail. As they were transporting me out, they were bringing my parents in. Tears escaped my eyes as I saw them for the first time in over six years. They were alive and in the flesh. Seeing them in real life was almost too overwhelming. It all felt like a dream. I wanted to call out to them, but I didn't. I was overjoyed with happiness. My plan was complete.

Stacy kept her word and came through like she promised. She taught me how to play the district attorney's hand. If he really wanted me, then he had to comply with my demands. I would only turn myself in under one condition, and that was if the DA was able to get my parents released from jail. I had my last doll and some left-over drugs, which could be used as evidence. The DA was more than willing to jump at the chance to finally have me in custody. They released my parents from jail and I received 20 years in prison.

There was no going back. Karma was finally staring me in the face, and all I could do was accept it and move on.

I knew that if I told anyone about my plan, then I would either break or talk myself out of it. I loved Prez, but I knew I had to let him go. I hated the thought of giving birth in prison, but I knew that Prez would be a great father, and that one day in the future he'll understand the reasonings behind the choices that I made. I loved Damien, but he was better off without me. Regardless of what happened in the past, Rachel would always be my best friend, and Caroline…well Caroline was finally back.

## Letter to Caroline

Dear Caroline,

I love you so much. For years I have waited for the old Caroline to return, and now you're back. I hate that I have to leave you now, but know that I was doing what I considered to be right. My doughboy lifestyle had finally caught up to me, and to ensure they wouldn't include you in my selfless scheme I'm turning myself in. If the cops wanted me then, I wanted something back in return. The drugs I had gave me leverage, and that kind of control allowed me to be able to get Mom and Dad released. Our parents are coming home. I wish that I could be there to witness such a joyous day, but you and JJ can enjoy it for me. None of this is your fault. I committed a crime and now I must pay for it. Tell Mom and Dad I love them and that I'm sorry. I don't know how long I'll be away, but know that you are the best sister in the world. Flaws and all. Take care and stay on the right course.

I love you.
Rhonda

———

*Letter to Prez*

Dear Prez,

What can I say? You turned out to be the man of my dreams, and I'm so glad that we met. At first, I was afraid to let you in, but I'm glad that I did. You knew the true me, and yet you allowed yourself to love me anyway. I knew it had to be hard for you to even think about being with me knowing that I was a criminal, but you did. I know deep in my heart I was wrong for what I had done, and that's why it was up to me to make things right. I'm a big believer in Karma, and I know that if I didn't do what was right, then things would never turn out the way they were supposed to for me or my family. Once Caroline discovers what I've done she's going to need some reassurance that I'm okay. I have known for a while the cops were after me, so to right a wrong I'm turning myself in, and hopefully something good will come out of it. My parents will be released and will be returning home from prison. I just need you to know that I love you so much. Our baby is going to need stability in its life, and I know you can provide that. I had Stacy to run a paternity test, and you should have those results back as soon as possible. Hopefully that will be enough to put your mind at ease about raising this baby as your own. It was hard for me to do this, but I couldn't love you and live a lie. I was a criminal and you stood for justice. I couldn't ask you to break the law just to protect me, so please forgive me for leaving. Whatever you do, please make sure our baby knows who I am. Please! But most importantly know that I love you with all my heart.

Rhonda

I was only six months into my incarceration and I felt as though I wasn't going to make it. The pregnancy was the only thing that saved me from the terrors that transpired through the night. The inmates were horrible, but some of the guards were even worse. I denied visitation from everyone except Prez. There was no way I could stop him from coming even if I wanted to. He was the law, but there was no way I could face Caroline, much less my parents. I sacrificed my freedom in order to make things right, and no matter what I would have told them they wouldn't have understood my reasoning behind what I did. But when it came to Prez, it was a different story. In the beginning our visits weren't too bad. I would get emotional on the inside, but I wouldn't allow myself to break. I didn't want Prez to think I was weak. I wanted to show him that I could take care of myself, but as I progressed in my pregnancy, it became impossible to keep a brave face.

During one of our visits, Prez was so busy talking, that he didn't notice I wasn't paying him any attention. All I could do was stare at him. He was so handsome. I loved him, and I missed him so much. I would feel the baby kick and move around, and it tore me up inside to know that I would miss out on so much of its life. Eventually, I couldn't keep it together anymore, and I broke down crying. I didn't mean for it to happen, it just did. I couldn't stop the tears from coming. All I could think about was how much I was going to miss my baby once it was born. Everyone's life was coming together while mine was falling apart. I was so embarrassed by the way I acted that I got up and walked out of the visitation room. I could hear Prez calling my name through the phone, but I continued to walk away. I went back to my cell and continued to cry. What did I do? Did I really think things through before I acted? Now I was facing the truth. My child was going to grow up without me, because I thought I could fix everyone else problems but my own.

The next day I sat in my cell thinking about the sex of the baby. I sat in silence contemplating different boy and girl names. I had become attached to the baby and detached from my current reality. I knew it was going to kill me to let go once the baby was born, but my mind wasn't ready to deal with that reality. The guard interrupted my train of thought to escort me to my scheduled OB appointment. While I waited for the doctor to arrive, the curtain slowly opened, and there stood Prez. I was so surprised to see him that I started to cry again. Either I was turning into a punk or the pregnancy was getting the best of me. Prez closed the curtains, walked over, and gave me the most passionate kiss I had embraced in a long time. I held on to him with force too afraid to let go. I continued to cry in Prez's chest like a weeping child. He tried his best to calm me down.

"What are you doing here?"

"I came to see you and the baby. After what happened yesterday there was no way I could leave here again. Not without my family."

"Wait. What are you saying?"

"What I'm saying is that you're coming home."

Was I hearing him, right?

"Home, but how?"

"I had a bigger fish in custody, and the DA had to decide on whom he wanted more. You or him."

"Are you serious? You really got me out of here?"

"Yes, I did. So, you're going home and with a clean record."

"I don't get it. Why would he let me go?"

"Let's just say I know how to deal, too, but in a legit way."

All I could do was smile. I was going home. I received 20 years in prison—I had to deal with that. I only served half a year and I almost couldn't handle that. Having a boyfriend who worked for the FBI, Karma! I didn't know how my future would to turn out, but in the end, I finally understood what my mom was talking about. Sometimes life does require a little necessary evil in order for you to get your life right.

# Part II

# The Numbing Effect

The thoughts of the mind can elude the heart.
Leave your state of mind stripped
and your world torn apart.
The truth about love
most people don't want to hear.
For it can disguise itself as resentment,
pleasure,
and sometimes fear.
It can drag you through the mud
and leave you in the rain.
It can be the best thing you ever had
and can complement itself with a wedding ring.
For the emotions of the heart can lead to a
lot of mistakes
Remember that in life, there's a thin line
between love and hate.

# Prologue

No one told me it would feel like this. I grabbed my chest as I tried to soothe my heart. The pain was so unbearable that I could barely breathe. I didn't know what to do. I stood alone in silence. My face was burning hot. My hands were shaking, and for the life of me, I couldn't stop crying.

"What did I do? What did I do?"

So much had happened so fast that none of it seemed real. I tried to move but I couldn't. My thoughts had me paralyzed.

"What did I do? Oh God what did I do?"

All I could do was stare at the blood on the floor. There was no way I could fix this. I allowed my emotions to overcome me, and now my life was spinning out of control. I could hear Olivia upstairs crying, but I couldn't move. I knew she needed me, but fear and shock had a hold of me, which made it impossible for me to think straight.

"I'm coming, baby, I'm coming." I mumbled to myself. With every blink, a tear fell. At that moment nothing seemed real. All I could think about was how was I going to fix this...but I knew I couldn't. The situation was no longer in my control. I thought my life was getting better, but then Karma had a way of rearing its ugly head. The distress in Olivia's cries grew louder and louder. She knew something was wrong. With all of the yelling and screaming that had taken place, she had a right to be alarmed.

"Mommy's coming."

I looked down. There was blood on my hands. I began to wipe it on my shirt, as I slowly stepped over the body that was lying on the floor, then I headed upstairs. I walked into Olivia's room, and as soon as she saw me, she stopped crying. She knew her mother and I loved her with all of my heart. I picked her up and positioned myself in the rocking chair that sat beside her crib. I sat in denial, trying my best to phase out everything that was going on around me, but nothing worked. I held back my tears as I tried to rock Olivia to sleep. What was I going to do? I couldn't go back to jail. I couldn't go on the run. Not with a baby. I had no idea what my next move would be. I sat and prayed that these events were nothing more than a bad dream, but the sirens outside my window brought that dream to a reality. Love can make or break anyone, and as for me it took me to my breaking point. I closed my eyes as I thought about the events that led up to this tragic day in my life.

# Chapter 16

⁂

# Coming to A Realization

There was a pile of paperwork stacked upon my desk, and the only thing I could think about was the lunch date I had planned with Prez. I always enjoyed the time we would spend together, and Prez was good about keeping my spirits up whenever I thought about home. It was hard not to think about my family, especially when the Bureau would keep Prez away on various time-sensitive cases, but that never stopped him from putting his family first. That's why our lunch dates were so important, and today was extra special, because Prez was coming home from an assignment, and I hadn't seen him in over two months. I understood what his job entailed, and that's why I never complained about the length of time when he was away. I, on the other hand, landed a job in the medical lab at Washington Hospital Center in Washington, DC. It turned out to be a great job. No one knew about my past, and that was the way I wanted to keep it.

I continued to watch the clock, but time wasn't moving fast enough. My boss, Mr. Wyatt, had volunteered my services to the medical lab, since majority of his technicians were out of town on business. I didn't have any problems running the lab, but I worked in research, and working in the lab only prolonged my case studies. I had been on my feet all morning, and I was tired, excited, and way overdue for a break. As time began to wind down, I gathered up my things to leave, when out of nowhere I was approached by Mr. Wyatt.

"Rhonda, good, I caught you in time. I need you to do me a big favor before you leave."

I looked at the clock, and Mr. Wyatt couldn't have come at a worse time. Whatever he wanted, it had to wait, because I didn't want to miss my lunch date with Prez.

"Sure, Mr. Wyatt, what can I do for you?"

"The judge sent over a DNA test that needs to be processed as soon as possible."

"Sure, not a problem. I'll get Jennings to put a rush on it, and when it's completed, I'll let you know."

"No, you don't seem to understand. I need you to run it. You're the best technician I have in this office, and I can't risk any mistakes. The judge is putting a lot of pressure on me to get this back today, and even though he wants it done fast, I need it done right."

I stared at the clock, and there was no way I could run the test, and meet up with Prez at the same time. I looked at Mr. Wyatt, and I couldn't disappoint him. He was always there for me whenever Prez was away, and most of all, he was a great supervisor. So, it was settled. My lunch date with Prez was off.

"Am I keeping you from something?"

"No. Don't worry about it. I'll call you when the results are in."

"Thanks. I knew I could count on you."

I really wanted to see Prez, but work stood in the way. I tried to call and let him know that I wouldn't be able to make it to our lunch date, but he never answered his phone. I proceeded on with the DNA testing. It didn't take as long as I thought it would to run the test. As I looked over the results, I noticed something was off. So, just to be safe I ran the test again, and yet the results were the same. I didn't have time to try and figure out what was wrong, so I made a copy of the results, and I gave the original copies to Mr. Wyatt. I rushed out hoping to catch Prez. Once I made it our usual rendezvous spot, there was no one in sight. Before I knew it, a half hour had passed, and that's when I decided to head back to work. My entire day was centered around my reunion with Prez, but because of some foolish test, I had missed my chance to reunite with him.

The work day was finally over, and I couldn't get out of the lab fast enough. I stopped by the daycare on the way home to pick up Olivia. She was so precious, and every time I looked at her, she reminded me so much of Prez. She was the only good thing that made DC seem somewhat normal. When I arrived at the house, I was hoping Prez would be there, but he wasn't. Disappointed, I tried calling his cell once again, but like before, there was no answer. I didn't know what was going on. I knew I had my days right. I just prayed nothing was wrong. I went ahead and cooked dinner just in case Prez decided to show up later on. Time passed, and Olivia was starting to get restless. I headed upstairs for our nightly ritual. She loved bath time. After we were done, I dressed her for bed and began to rock her to sleep. As I held Olivia in my arms, I looked into her eyes, and it made me think about the test results I had concealed in my purse. Once she was asleep, I laid her down in her crib, and I took the papers out of my purse and began to review them. Everything seemed typical, but there were a couple of markers that seemed a bit off. Unsure about the reading, I went into the closet and pulled out a lock box. I opened it up and removed an envelope that was addressed to Prez. In the letter was a copy of the DNA test results I had performed on Olivia before I was sent off to prison. It was going on two years since the test was performed, but the results shouldn't have been that different to read compared to the new tests that were given today. I compared my test results to the test that was performed earlier today, and I noticed that it wasn't the new test that was incorrect; it was mine. There were too many mismatches between the DNA, which meant the paternity index value and the combined parentage index were wrong. I never caught it before, because it had been years since I last ran a DNA test. Working in the lab, I was so used to seeing numbers and deciphering codes that it never crossed my mind to recheck my own paternity test. I had always assumed it was correct. My results showed Prez as being the father, and considering the time frame around the pregnancy, he had to be the father. So, what was I missing? I couldn't think straight. Could someone have made a mistake? But how? Olivia favored Prez so much. He had to be her father. My mind was racing and I needed answers. As I was packing up Olivia's diaper bag, I heard a noise coming from downstairs.

"Prez." I whispered to myself. I put away the lock box, hid all the papers in my purse, and raced downstairs. Prez was standing in the living room surrounded by all of his luggage. All I could do was smile. I was so excited to see him. I felt like a kid on Christmas day.

"Hi." I pushed his luggage out of the way. "I missed you." I leaned in, and before I knew it, Prez grabbed hold of me, and gave me the most intense kiss.

"I missed you too…" Prez continued kissing me as if he had no intentions of stopping. "So, where's Olivia?"

"She's asleep." Prez mouth and hands were all over me, and for the most part I didn't want him to stop. "I just laid her down."

"Good." Prez picked me up and took me upstairs.

"What's gotten into you?"

"Nothing. I can't miss my wife?"

"I don't know. Did you?" I laughed. I loved teasing Prez and he knew it.

"How about I show you!"

Prez made love to me, and whatever thoughts were on my mind were no longer there. All of my attention was on him. He was usually aggressive whenever we made love, but tonight was different. There was more passion than force between the two of us, which only intensified the desire we had for each other.

I laid in Prez's arms trying my best to block out any thoughts pertaining to the paternity test. We were happy together, and I wanted us to stay that way.

"So, what did you do while I was gone?"

"Absolutely nothing."

"Nothing. Are you serious?"

"Yep. Mr. Wyatt has been leaning on me hard, and now he has me running the lab as well. So, in my off time, I would try and spend as much time with Olivia as I could, and after that the day was usually gone."

"So, that's all you did while I was away. Work and see about Olivia?"

"For the most part, yeah.

"I wish you would get out of the house more, and make some new friends. You do have a life you know."

"I know, but Livy and I are okay. I don't have to hide anything from her, and plus she doesn't ask any questions, but if I tried to go out and make new friends, then I would have to lie about my past, and pretend to be someone I'm not, and that's just too much work."

"See, you're making excuses again. You need to get out of the house and live a little."

"And I will now that you're back."

"But what happens when I'm gone again? You need a life, Rhonda, outside of work and seeing about Olivia. You're using them as a crutch so you won't have to face reality."

"And what reality is that? I'm all alone up here. I have no friends, because I don't trust anyone…and my family…"

My family. It was going on two years since I last spoke with anyone in my family. While I was locked away in prison, I had six months to think about all the choices I made leading up to my incarceration. I was so adamant about putting everyone needs above my own, that I left myself out in the cold. I decided from that point on that I was going to start taking care of Rhonda first, and then everyone else.

Following my release from prison, I gave birth to a beautiful baby girl. Prez proposed to me, and then we were married shortly after. We moved to DC because of Prez's job with the Bureau. I didn't mind the move, since it allowed me to be as far away from my family as possible. There were a lot of things I was willing to do in order to start over, but there was one thing I couldn't bring myself to do and that was face my family. I told myself after I gave birth that we would move back to Florida, but it never happened. I haven't spoken to anyone, including Caroline, since my incarceration. No one knew I was free, and I wasn't ready to tell anyone—not just yet. I didn't know what I was waiting on. Olivia was almost two, and I knew it was time for me to return home and face my family. Whenever I would ask questions regarding home, Prez would always tell me that if I wanted to know anything, then I needed to go home and visit.

"What about your family?"

"Nothing. I was just rambling. Besides, me and Olivia, we're fine. I don't need anyone else in my life right now other than you."

"You're wrong, Rhonda. You need your family. So, what's stopping you from going home if…"

"Why are you so adamant about me returning home? Are you keeping something from me?"

"I'm not keeping anything from you, but I do think you should go home and visit with your family. You went to jail so your parents could be free, so I'm sure they would love to see you."

I knew Prez was right, but so much happened in the past and I didn't know how I was going to face my parents, and to be completely honest, I didn't know if I wanted to face them.

"I'm sure they know by now that I use to sell drugs. So, tell me Prez, how am I supposed to look them in the eye after everything I've done? And my father…"

I started to get emotional. My father was headstrong and he always tried to instill the best in me. My mother, on the other hand, was the voice of reasoning. She would always try to persuade my father to give in just a little bit whenever I couldn't have my way. I had disappointed them both. There was no way I could return home and confront them. Not after what I did.

"I'm sure they would understand. Take a couple of weeks off and we'll go down together."

"I don't know. So much has happened."

"I know, but just think about it."

I had so much on my mind: the DNA test and now the thought of returning home. I closed my eyes and prayed that a good night's rest would help me to decide on what to do next.

My life wasn't perfect, but I was trying my best to make up for all of my past mistakes. My parents had always raised me to do what was right, yet I sold drugs as a means of survival. Even though I blamed Caroline for a lot of my drawbacks, the truth of the matter was, the only person I could truly blame was myself. By no means did I plan on selling drugs, and the concept of going to jail had never crossed my mind. I didn't ask to be raped, and the idea of marriage had always frightened me. In no way could I have imagined having a baby, but soon I discovered how quickly life could easily change everything. When it came to Olivia, she ultimately transformed my life. There wasn't anything I wouldn't do for her. Becoming a mother gave me an insight into a whirlwind of emotions I never knew I had before. I now understood the severity of my parents' reactions towards the mistreatment of their children. I just prayed they were more forgiving towards me than I was of Caroline when she was forced to confront all of her secrets.

# Chapter 17

### ✿

# The Unexpected

The next morning when I woke up, I discovered the letters I received while in prison lying next to me in bed. I guess Prez figured if I was going to keep questioning myself about going home, then I should at least know what I was getting myself into, which only made sense, considering I had cut myself off from anyone associated with my past. For the most part, I blamed them all for my downfall, which made it very hard for me to forgive and forget. I grabbed all of the letters and began to sort through them by date. I noticed letters from Caroline, Rachel, and maybe one or two from Damien, but what threw me for a loop was that I didn't receive one letter from my parents. They knew I was locked up, yet they chose not to write me. I could hear Olivia over the intercom, and she was still asleep, which gave me some time to start reading through some of the letters. It was a lot of "how could you," "I miss you," and "I can't wait to see you again, letters, but then I came across one letter from Caroline that left me speechless. In the letter she explained the wellbeing of her and JJ, and then she went on to state how she was trying her best to make things work between her and Brad. Then

150

she went on to say how she needed me to do her a favor. Caroline
wanted me to see if I could get Prez to speak on Jacob's behalf at
his trial. Was she serious? Did she forget that Jacob beat and raped
me? I could've lost Olivia, and she wanted me to help that monster
get released. I didn't know what to think. I was furious. I took
the letters and I shoved them in my purse, and that's when I came
across the DNA tests that were left in there from the night before.
I took the tests and I ripped them up. Regardless of what the truth
was, I didn't want to know. I had enough changes in my life, and I
wasn't ready for any new ones. I could hear Olivia over the intercom
making noises. She was up. As I walked to her room, I couldn't
help but think *what if.* There were so many variables involved that
the slightest mistake could ruin everything. As I picked up Olivia,
all I could do was stare into her eyes. Was Prez really her father, or
could there have been a possibility that it was Damian all along? I
couldn't bear to think such thoughts. I dressed Olivia and then we
headed downstairs. To our surprise, Prez was in the kitchen cooking
breakfast.

"Say surprise!" I walked over towards Prez with Olivia in my
arms.

"Well, good morning to my two lovely ladies." Prez gave me a
kiss on the cheek, and then he took Olivia from my arms and began
to play with her. They looked so happy together. "How's my girl!"
Olivia was so happy to see him. "Daddy missed you. Yes, I did. Yes,
I did."

I started to feel sick. There was no way I could hurt Prez, not
intentionally. I needed to figure out the truth. It was the only way I
could put my mind at ease.

"Hey. Are you okay?"

"Yeah I'm good."

"You sure?"

"I'm sure...so tell me something. What happened to you
yesterday? I waited for you, but you never showed."

"I'm sorry about that. Debriefing took longer than expected. But trust me, getting home to you guys was the only thing on my mind."

"Well that's good to know. I'm just glad you're home. We really missed you."

"I missed you guys as well. It feels so good to be home." Prez glanced over at Olivia. "And she's getting so big. I didn't think I was gone that long."

"Tell your daddy you're a growing baby!" The older Olivia got the more she resembled the both of us, which made it hard for me to understand what was going on with my DNA results. "And oh, by the way I got the letters you left for me. And…"

"And what? Did you read any of them?"

"Yes. I read some, and you know what's strange?"

"What's that?"

"I didn't receive one letter from my parents. Why didn't they write me?"

"Maybe they didn't know what to say."

"Maybe. But let's be honest. I was arrested on drug charges. They probably wanted nothing to do with me."

"Why would you say that? They love you. I've talked with your father numerous times, and he never gave me that impression."

"Wait a minute. You've spoken to my father. When?"

"Last time was about two weeks ago. He calls me twice a month and I let him know that you're okay. He's worried about you. That's why I'm always pushing for you to go home and visit. Your parents deserve to know that you're out, and that you're okay. Besides…don't you think it's about time they knew about Olivia?"

I was in shock. All I could hear was Prez's voice on a loop while I tried to process what he said. 'I've spoken to your father numerous times.' I felt blindsided.

"You've been talking with my father and you didn't tell me."

"Because whenever I would mention anything to you about your family you would go off. So, I kept it to myself. Trust me, I was going to tell you, but I could never tell when the time was right with you.

You can be so moody sometimes." Prez placed Olivia in her high chair and fixed our plates. I didn't know how to react. "Look I'm sorry for not telling you, but I didn't want to keep upsetting you. I know how you feel about your parents and…"

Prez was right. Maybe I'm overreacting. I took a breath.

"No. Stop. It's okay. You didn't do anything wrong. Besides, I know how I can get sometimes, so you get a free pass on this one."

"Why, thank you…" Prez placed a plate of homemade waffles topped with fruit and a side of bacon in front of me. "Now eat up. I worked hard on this meal."

"Did you really?" I started to look around the room.

"What are you looking for?"

"The box."

"What box?"

"The one the waffles came in."

"Ha. Ha." We both started to laugh. I loved the time we would spend together. We were a family, and that was the only thing that mattered.

"So, have you thought about it anymore?"

"Thought about what?"

"Going home to visit your family."

"Yeah, and you're right. I do need to go home and visit. So, I'm going to call Mr. Wyatt today, and let him know that I need some time off, and then we'll be good to go."

"So, you're really doing this?"

"Yes. It's now or never. I've got to stop running away from the past and face it head-on. Even if I don't want to."

"Don't worry, I'll be with you every step of the way."

I smiled. I just hoped that Prez was ready to meet the real Robert and Patricia Brown.

All of my paperwork was in order and we were ready to go. Once we touched down in Florida, we headed towards my parents' house. It had been almost two years since I last saw them, even though they didn't see me in the police department that day. I didn't know what to say. I was so nervous. As we pulled up to the house, it felt like I was having an out of body experience.

"Are you okay?"

"No, but I have to do this."

"If you need me, I can go with you."

"No. Just stay here. I need to talk with them first, before I tell them about you and Olivia."

"Alright, but if you're not back in 10 minutes then we're coming in."

I took a deep breath. They were my parents. So why was I so afraid? I was more afraid of them then I was of the police.

"Wish me luck."

I walked to the door. I stood there for a minute before I finally pressed the doorbell. I waited and pressed it again, but there was no answer. Finally, I was forced to pull out my set of keys. As I tried to open the door, my key wouldn't turn. They must have changed the locks. As I was about to walk away a middle-aged white woman answered the door.

"Yes. Can I help you?"

"Oh...I...I was looking for...my parents. Robert and Patricia Brown...they live here."

"Oh, the Browns...yes, they sold me this house a couple months ago. They didn't tell you?"

"No, they didn't. I'm sorry to have disturbed you." I walked back to the car hurt and confused.

"So, what was that all about?"

"My parents. They sold the house. I don't understand why they would sell it, considering the house was paid for. It doesn't make any sense."

"So, they sold the house and moved away, and you don't have any idea as to where they could've gone off to?"

"No. Not a clue. I don't know where they are."

"Well, don't worry, we'll find them. Let me make a couple of calls and see what I can do."

I sat and waited as Prez made some calls to the Bureau. I couldn't wrap my head around my parents selling the house. Maybe they wanted to get away, or maybe they just needed a new start, but whatever their reasons were, they were kept from me.

"Believe it or not, I found them."

"Okay, so, where are they? Where did they go?"

"You ready for this?"

"Yeah. Where are they?"

"They're in Clearwater."

Clearwater? Why would they move to Clearwater? Then it hit me. Caroline. She was living in Clearwater with Brad.

"Yep. So, what do you want to do?"

"Take me to Clearwater. I need to find out what's going on."

Within a couple of hours, we were in Clearwater. As Prez pulled up to the house, my butterflies returned.

"Okay, remember if you're not back within 10 minutes then I'm coming in."

"Okay." I tried to psych myself up to get out of the car. "Let's try this again." I got out of the car and walked towards the house. I stood at the door trying to figure out what to say. I took another deep breath and then I rang the doorbell. When the door opened, to my surprise it was my mother.

"Mom…" The sight of my mother made me gasp. Her hair was longer, her body was toned and muscular, and her skin was radiant and glowing—but as soon as she saw me the smile on her face vanished. She looked at me and slammed the door in my face. What just happened? I rang the doorbell again. And again. Nothing. No one came to the door. Finally, I started to hammer on the door with my fist.

"Mom! I know you're in there. Mom!" Finally, the door opened. It was my father. "Dad."

"Rhonda. Is that you?"

"Dad…"

My father picked me up in a hug and twirled me around.

"I can't believe it's you. Come in. Come in."

I walked into the house and it felt like home even though it wasn't our old house.

"I'm still in shock. I can't believe you're here. How? When did you get out?"

"I was released over a year ago. I wanted to tell you but..." I started to get emotional. My father was alive and standing before me. "It's you. It's really you, and you're standing here. You don't know how much I've missed you."

"Come here, baby girl."

I walked over towards my father, and he grabbed hold of me and gave me another big hug. All I could do was cry.

"I missed you so much."

"I missed you too, baby. So how have you been?"

"I've been good. A lot has happened and…"

"Wait…wait. Let me get your mother. Patricia. Patricia."

"I doubt she would like to see me."

"And why would you say that?"

"Because when she answered the door, she slammed it in my face. Now what's that all about?"

"She did what! Patricia."

My mother walked into the room. Even though she slammed the door in my face, I was still excited to see her.

"Yes, Robert."

"You don't see your daughter standing here?"

"I see her."

"Patricia!"

"What, Robert? What do you want me to say? 'Oh, Rhonda, it's so good to see you, and, oh, by the way, thanks for getting us out of jail'…but wait. How were you able to do that? That's right. By selling drugs. She's a convicted drug dealer, Robert."

"Tell me something I don't know, but regardless of what she's done, she's still our daughter."

"No, Dad, it's okay. The truth of the matter is, yes, I sold drugs, and I'm not proud of what I did, but I've paid for my crimes. So, shouldn't that be enough?"

"Enough? Did she say 'enough'?"

"Calm down, Pat. She's been through a lot as well."

"A lot! She didn't serve six years in prison for being accused of something she didn't do. I did. She didn't come home, and realize that her whole world had been completely changed. That was me."

My mother got up in my face.

"Do you know what happened to us when we got out of prison?"

"No…I don't."

"People were giving us strange stares, and at first, I thought it was because everyone had presumed, we were dead. But oh no, that wasn't the case. It was because our youngest daughter was on the front page of the daily paper: 'Rhonda Brown convicted on drug charges.' Do you know how embarrassing that was for us?"

"So, is that why you guys sold the house? Because you were embarrassed? I was lied to for over six years, and all you were worried about was being embarrassed?"

"No, we sold the house because we found out you had paid it off."

"And what was wrong with that?"

"How else did you pay it off? With drug money, of course. People would've criticized us for living there. So, we had to move."

"Dad. Are you hearing this? If you would've written me when I was locked up, then you would've known that I didn't pay off the house with drug money."

"Then how else did you pay if off, because you sure as hell didn't have any money saved."

"But I did. I made so much money from selling my dolls that I never had to touch any of my paychecks I made while working at the doll shop. So, I started depositing them into a bank account. Later on, I found out about our college funds. Since we weren't using any of the money, I was told I could pay a penalty and withdraw all of it. You know, since everyone thought you guys were dead, I could do that. So, I took the money and placed it into the account as well. You guys only had a few years left on the house, so I saved until I had enough to pay it off. So, you sold your house for nothing."

"And we're supposed to believe that?"

"You know what mom; you can believe whatever you want. I don't have time for this."

I was about to walk out until my father stopped me.

"No. Don't leave. If anyone is grateful, then it's me. So, thank you. That was another nice thing you did for us."

"Are you serious, Robert?" My mother was livid.

"Pat!"

"No! Why are you so mad at me? Tell me! I deserve to know the truth, because this…this isn't you. This isn't my mother."

"You're right. I'm not your mother, because I couldn't have raised such a stupid child."

Tears fell from my eyes. Whoever this woman was, she wasn't my mother.

"Pat, that's enough! Granted, Rhonda had made some mistakes in the past, but that doesn't give you the right to treat her like this. None of us are perfect. Don't forget you've made mistakes made as well."

"No. Let's not forget about the mistakes you've made!"

"Well, I see this is everyone's fault but hers." I turned to walk away, and my mother grabbed me by the arm.

"You listen here. I didn't ask to go to jail!"

"And neither did I, but unlike you I found a way to make it work, instead of blaming everyone else for my problems. You can't deal with the fact that I had to sell drugs. Well get over it, because I did, and you know what's really killing me right now? Is the fact that neither of you ever asked me why. Why did I do it?"

"It doesn't matter why you did it. What matters is that you went through with it."

"That's right. Blame me. I can take it, but Caroline couldn't. She was an addict! You get that? An addict. She couldn't see about me or herself, but you wouldn't know anything about that, now would you? You weren't left to defend and support yourself. That was me. So, don't try and judge me like you knew what type of hell I went though, because you don't."

And before I knew it my mother hauled off and slapped me. I was in shock.

"Don't ever refer to your sister as an addict! She's been through enough, no thanks to you."

"No thanks to me! Are you serious? Wait…so that's it. That's why you're so mad at me. You're blaming me for Caroline's addiction! I can't believe you! For you to even think that I would ever give drugs to my own sister lets me know that you're right about one thing. You're not my mother."

I turned to walk away.

"Rhonda, don't. She's just upset. That's all."

I turned to face my father.

"Is that right…so tell me dad? Do you feel the same way she does?"

"Rhonda…" His facial expression said it all.

"You can't even lie to me with a straight face."

I stormed out of the house, and I left the front door wide open. I didn't care about anything at that point. The fact that my parents think I would give drugs to my own sister had filled me with rage.

"Rhonda." My father rushed to the door, but I had already made it to the car. I had nothing else to say to them.

"I'm ready to leave now!"

"What happened?" Prez seemed confused by everything that was happening.

"Can we please leave? Now!"

My father made his way over to the car, but Prez pulled off.

"So, are you going to tell me what happened?"

"Nothing happened. Nothing at all."

"Rhonda."

"I don't want to talk about it right now. Just give me some time. Okay?"

"Okay."

We checked into a hotel, and once Prez opened the door, I dropped everything to the floor.

"Are you okay?"

"Yes. I'm fine. Just give me a minute."

I headed straight for the bathroom and locked the door. I turned on the water and I grabbed a towel from the rack. I just prayed the noise was loud enough to muffle my cries. I was on the floor bawling like a baby. My parents had broken my heart. Eight years ago, when I had received the news about their death, the hurt and the pain I had experienced then was nothing compared to the heartache I was feeling at that moment.

"Rhonda, are you okay?"

"Yes, I'm fine." I continued to cry. "I'll be done in a minute."

"Okay. Well, Livy and I are going to head out and see if we can find us something to eat. We'll be back soon."

"Okay."

Once I heard the door close, I lost control. I was so angry. How could my parents even consider the thought of me giving drugs to my own sister? I loved Caroline. Granted she treated me like crap in the past, but the fact remained that I would do anything for her. My parents on the other hand could hate me, doubt me, and go as far as disown me; but I was to the point where I didn't care anymore. I had survived without them for eight years, and I was certain I could go another eight years without them as well. They made it very clear how they felt about me, and in my eyes they had only one daughter…and that was Caroline.

# Chapter 18

## The Homecoming

O nce morning had arrived, I was more than ready to leave. I couldn't get back to DC fast enough. The ranting of my parent's voices kept playing over and over again in my head. To them, I was an embarrassment. I was nothing more than a convicted criminal. Not their daughter. The faster I got out of town the better, but no matter how fast I moved, I wasn't moving fast enough. Prez was in the bathroom getting dressed, and I used that as my time to finish packing. Once Prez was done, he walked out of the bathroom and noticed that I had Olivia in my arms, packed and ready to go.

"So, what's going on? Are we supposed to be leaving?"

"Yes. I don't know what I was thinking coming back here. I'm just ready to go."

"You're ready to leave…but we just got here."

"I know but this was a mistake. So, can we please go home?"

"Home. Okay so what happened? Ever since we left your parent's house yesterday you've been on edge. So, what did they say to you, and don't lie to me?"

"I don't want to talk about it. I just want to go home."

Prez took Olivia from my arms, and then he grabbed hold of my hands.

"I'll take you wherever you want to go, but I need you to talk to me. You're good at shutting people out, but I'm not just anyone. I'm your husband and I can't help you if you don't talk to me." Prez was right. He was my husband and I was supposed to be able to lean on him during hard times, but it was never easy for me to share my pain with anyone. Including him. "Come on, Rhonda. Tell me. What happened?"

"My parents. They think I'm the one who hooked Caroline on drugs. Me! Of all people. Granted I was convicted on drug charges, but that doesn't make me a monster. I love my sister. I would never give her drugs, but my parents…they didn't want to hear it. In their eyes it's my fault. Everything's my fault."

"No, it's not and you know it. Did you explain to them your situation, and that it wasn't you who hooked Caroline on drugs?"

"Yes, but they didn't want to hear it. All they were worried about was their precious Caroline."

"And what about your father? I just find it hard to believe that he would say something like that about you. I mean he sounded so worried about you whenever we spoke over the phone."

"Well technically he didn't say it; my mother did, but that doesn't excuse the look he had on his face when she said it. It's like they were in cahoots together, and I was the outcast."

"I don't think you should give up on them; not right away. I mean, give them some time to process everything that has happened, and…"

"Time. It's been almost two years. They've had plenty of time to figure this out, and they have. I'm their scapegoat. If something goes wrong, then blame Rhonda. I'm the easy way out."

"Don't do this to yourself. They love you. They're just hurting."

"And so am I! My sister lied to me for over six years before I uncovered the truth. She was a strung-out drug addict who was no help to me, or anyone else for that matter. I was forced to survive on my own by any means necessary; and I did."

"And no one is blaming you for that."

"You're wrong. Everyone is blaming me, and that's the problem. You see, I've had time to think about everything that has happened too, and you know what I've come to realize?"

"What's that?"

"That I was the only one who was willing to do a selfless act, for a bunch of selfish people. Well, I'm done with putting everyone else's needs above my own. You and Olivia are the only ones who matter to me, and no one else. Now can we please go home?"

Prez grabbed our luggage and we headed out. As we were driving to the airport, I noticed we were heading in the wrong direction.

"Hey where are we going?"

"I need to make an important stop before we leave."

Before I knew it, we were in an upscale neighborhood, surrounded by big houses and extravagant cars.

"And who lives here?"

"A friend."

We pulled up to a cottage-style Tutor home. It was a gorgeous house and it had money written all over it.

"Give me one minute and then we can go.

I watched Prez walk towards the house, but instead of going through the front door he went through the side gate, and headed towards the back of the house. I had no clue as to what he was up to. I sat in the car and I watched Olivia as she slept. There was something calming in watching a baby sleep. Before I knew it, Prez was making his way back to the car.

"So, you're good? We can leave now?"

"No, not just yet."

"Why's that?"

"Because I need you to get out and come with me."

"Get out. Why?"

"Just come with me."

Prez grabbed Olivia and escorted us to the gate.

"What is this all about?"

"You just have to wait and see."

Prez opened the door, and as soon as we walked through it, all I heard was "surprise!" Caroline rushed me with the biggest bear hug imaginable.

"Rhonda! It's you. It's really you."

"Caroline."

I didn't know how to feel. I was so torn with my feelings that I was left in shock. Caroline's embrace was so needed and unexpected that all I could do was hug her back. No matter what my parents may have said to me, I loved my sister, and I couldn't allow them to taint my feelings towards her.

"I can't believe you're out." I stared at Caroline and she looked good. "And wait, I have a surprise for you."

I looked around and I saw Brad and JJ standing by the pool. JJ was so handsome. I missed my nephew.

"Is that JJ? He's gotten so big."

"Yes, and he's dying to see you…but first."

Caroline walked me into the kitchen and there sat Rachel.

"Rachel!"

"Rhonda!"

I was so happy to see Rachel, but from the moment I laid eyes on her, I could easily tell she was using. From the noticeable weight lost to her bloodshot eyes, and tell-tell body odor. Caroline was an addict for six years, so I knew one when I saw one.

"So, what have you been up to? I heard you got out over a year ago. So why haven't you called?"

"I had a lot on my mind. Trying to figure out how to start over without everyone judging me."

"I can understand that, but you look good. You look really good, and I see you're still with Prez." Rachel stared at Prez through the sliding glass door.

"Yeah what's up with that? How come you were able to tell Prez you were out before you were able to tell me? I'm your sister; I thought you would've told me first." Caroline leaned up against the counter with a serious look on her face.

"Well let's see. Prez was the reason I was released from prison, so he would've known before you anyway."

"Prez got you out? But how?" said Caroline.

"I don't know how it happened. All I know is that I did six months in, and then out of nowhere Prez came in and told me I was going home."

"Well I don't care how you got out, I'm just glad you're out. That's all that matters. And..." Before Caroline could finish speaking, she caught a glimpse of my hand. She immediately grabbed it and gawked at the rings on my finger. "Wait a minute. What's this? Was there something else you forgot to tell me?"

"Why no...why would you ever think that?"

We all laughed considering our past history of keeping secrets from each other.

"Come on, Miss Brown. Fill me in and don't leave anything out." Caroline insisted.

"You mean 'Mrs. Castillo', thank you very much."

Everyone in the room went crazy with excitement. Rachel seemed genuinely happy for me as she jumped up and gave me a huge bear hug and Caroline commenced to covering me with kisses.

"Mrs. Castillo! Wait a minute, I thought Prez's last name was Ramirez." Caroline suggested.

"I did too, but come to find out that was his cover name. I guess that's what happens when you fool around with someone who works for the FBI."

"I can't believe you! Mrs. Castillo. This is too much. Why didn't you call and tell me? What about Mom and Dad? What did they have to say?"

My whole demeanor changed. Mentioning their names had immediately killed my mood.

"What? What did I say?"

"Nothing. It's just, we're not talking. That's all."

"You're not talking? What happened? Dad didn't mention any of this when he called me yesterday."

"I don't know. For some reason they think I'm the reason you were strung out on dope. Like I would ever give you drugs. Now why would they think that?"

"Come on, Rhonda, let's not do this today. We're celebrating your homecoming. It's supposed to be a happy day today. So, let's not spoil it with talks of the past."

Caroline was right. It was supposed to be a happy occasion, but our parents had left a sour taste in my mouth that wouldn't go away. In the end, I wasn't asking for much. All I wanted was the truth.

"You're right. Let's not spoil it, but we will talk later."

"Okay. Later it is."

"Rhonda, I'm sorry, but I may have already ruined your party." Rachel had an uneasy look on her face

"Ruined it how?" I replied.

"I was so excited when Caroline called and told me that you were out, that I called and told Damien as well."

"You what!" Caroline and I looked at each other in disbelief.

"Wait. That's not the worst part. I also invited him to the party."

"Rachel. What were you thinking?"

"I wasn't. I was just trying to get you two back together. My mistake, but I'm sure once Damien discovers you're married, then he'll leave."

I looked outside at Prez playing with Olivia. I still hadn't told anyone about her, and I sure as hell didn't want Damien to see her. In case there was an error behind my DNA test, I didn't want Damien making any speculations about Olivia being his child.

"What are you looking at?" Caroline followed my eyes straight to Prez. He was by the pool playing around with Olivia. "You really do love him, don't you?"

"Wouldn't have married him if I didn't. With Prez I was able to notice the difference between being in love, and knowing that I was loved. That's what made him so different."

Rachel walked over towards me and Caroline.

"I'm sorry. I wouldn't have invited Damien if I would've known you were married. I wasn't trying to cause any problems. It's just... he really wanted to see you."

"Don't worry about it. I'll deal with Damien when he gets here."

Prez waved at me and then he picked up Olivia and headed towards the house.

"Hey by the way, who's the little girl Prez is carrying? She's so cute." Caroline stared at Olivia through the window.

"That would be our daughter, Olivia."

"You're *what*? You had a baby? All this time I thought Prez was playing with some random kid by the pool."

Caroline and Rachel both stared at me in shock.

"Yes. I wanted to tell you before I went away to prison, but I didn't know what to say. So, I didn't say anything. Everything just happened so fast."

"Okay, I get a lot has happened, but you could've called or wrote me. We're sisters. That's supposed to mean something."

"And it does. Trust me, I wasn't trying to keep it a secret from you, but in all honesty, I just wasn't ready to tell anyone." Prez opened the door and walked towards me with Olivia.

"Hello, ladies. She was having a fit so here you go." Prez handed me Olivia. "Just a big fat momma's baby."

"Stop picking on her. She's just a little irritable right now. That's all."

"Oh, Rhonda, she is too precious...and you say her name is Olivia?" Rachel was too busy trying to pinch Olivia's cheeks.

"Yes. Olivia Caroline Castillo."

"You named her after me..." Caroline began to tear up.

"Yes. Regardless of what we've been through, you're right about one thing. We are sisters and that's supposed to mean something."

"So, have you guys had a chance to catch up?" Prez looked at me with a sneaky smirk on his face.

"Yes, and thank you for this. I really needed it."

"Don't thank me. Thank Caroline."

"Yeah, once Dad told me you were out, he gave me Prez's number and I set everything up. Rachel drove up last minute just to be here."

"Thanks, guys. This was really nice."

Olivia was starting to get fussy. She needed a diaper change.

"Oh, somebody needs to be changed."

"Okay pass her back." Prez insisted.

"Are you sure? I can change her."

"This is your party, and I want you to enjoy yourself. So, don't worry about Livy, I'll take care of her."

"You sure?"

"Yes. Now go."

Caroline, Rachel, and I headed out back to mingle. I zoned in on JJ and I started to tease him about his height. He was growing like a weed and he actually seemed happy. I could see the hurt in Rachel's eyes every time she looked at him. I needed to figure out what was going on with her, and more importantly why she was using. Brad, on the other hand, was too busy filling me in on all of the trips they had recently been on. Everything was going great and then my heart started to race. The moment I was dreading had finally arrived. Damien showed up. He was still handsome as ever. He was the only guy I knew who could take a preppy style and make it look good. I looked around for Prez, but he was nowhere in sight. I started to get nervous as Damien approached me.

"Rhonda."

"Damien Fletcher."

Everyone started to scatter, and Damien and I were left alone to talk.

"Can I?" Damien leaned in to give me a hug. Lord help me. He smelled so good. "You look good."

"And so do you."

"I hope you don't mind me being here. Rachel called me and I... well I wanted to see you."

"No. You're fine. So how have you been?"

"I've been good. Working. Trying to stay busy."

"Same here. Working my dream job. Becoming a true lab rat."

"That's good to hear. I still can't believe you're out. I remember when I read in the paper about what happened. I was in shock. Rhonda Brown. Arrested on drug charges. And all I could say to myself was, "Not my Rhonda." Why didn't you tell me you needed help? If you needed money that bad you knew I would've given it to you."

"I know, but it wasn't your responsibility to take care of me and my sister. Hell, to be honest it wasn't mine either, but I did what I had to do in order to survive. I'm not proud of it, but there's nothing I can do to take it back."

"So, the drugs, were they the reason you never moved in with me?"

"That among other things. The timing was never right."

"You sure it was just about timing and nothing else?"

"Yes, I'm sure. You knew how I felt about you, and..."

"And what?"

"Nothing. You know what, it was good seeing you, but I have to get back to my other guests..."

I began to walk away, but Damien grabbed me by the hand.

"Rhonda, don't. I miss you." Damien went to release my hand and that's when he noticed the wedding ring on my finger. "Wait a minute. You're married?"

There was no way to hide the obvious.

"Yes."

"But why, Rhonda? Why?"

"Why what?"

"Why would you do this to me? We were supposed to have worked things out, and gotten back together. Not go off and marry other people. Why didn't you wait for me? I waited for you."

"Because all we did was hurt each other. I'm not right for you and you know it. I'm happy, and I hope you'll find the same kind of happiness one day, but it won't be with me."

I turned, and Prez was walking out the house with Olivia in his arms. He spotted me talking with Damien. Damien looked up and saw Prez with Olivia.

"You married the cop? Are you serious? What did you do? Marry him out of gratitude? Come on, Rhonda. You don't love him and you know it."

"Don't try and tell me how I feel, because at one point in time I loved you with all of my heart, and you took that love and you spit on it by sleeping with my best friend. I trusted you and you betrayed that trust…and for what? An easy lay? So, don't talk to me about love, because you don't know what real love is."

We must have gotten loud. Everyone had turned around and was staring at us. Rachel looked at me and began to walk off.

"Rachel, don't." I started to chase after her and I stopped her outside the back gate. I knew she was already in enough pain, and I didn't want to cause her anymore. "Rachel, don't leave. I'm sorry. I didn't mean to bring up the past."

"No. I understand. You still hold some sort of resentment towards me, and there's nothing I can do or say to make you understand how truly sorry I really am."

"I know you're sorry, but you broke my heart. Back then, I was in love with Damien, and we were going to move in together and start this new life, and then bam! Everything blew up in my face. You knew how I felt about him, and yet you allowed yourself to sleep with him anyway. Why?"

"I don't know why? It just happened…"

"And that's the root of our problem. You knew by sleeping with Damien it would hurt me, and yet you went through with it anyway…"

"And I'm sorry. I don't know what else to say, but I'm truly sorry. If I could go back in time and change what happened then I would, but I can't. So, I'm putting myself out here; can you ever forgive me or not?"

My friend was hurting, and I was allowing the past to be a part of that hurt. I was married, and there was no reason for me to allow what happened in the past between me and Damien to affect my friendship with Rachel here and now.

"Listen to me. You're my friend. My best friend. What you did... yes it hurt. We both know it did, but I love you, and it wouldn't feel right if you weren't a part of my life. So, let's turn the tables here. Can you please forgive me for acting like such an idiot? I love you and nothing is going to ever change that."

Rachel was in tears. She walked over and hugged me. There was so much going on with her, and I hated seeing her this way. I looked up and Prez had made his way over towards us.

"Are you guys okay?"

"Yes. We're fine." I pushed Rachel's hair out of her face and wiped her tears away. "We're good, right?"

"Yeah. We're good."

I looked at Prez and noticed he didn't have Olivia with him.

"Hey, where's Olivia?"

"She's with your sister." I looked over and Caroline was holding Olivia, and Damien was playing with her. I thought I was going to pass out. I just prayed Damien didn't ask any questions about her. Rachel walked off and Prez and I were left alone. "So, what was that about?"

"Nothing. Just hashing out the past."

"And did that past happen to involve Damien?"

"Yes, but it wasn't like that. I'm still working through a lot of stuff that happened to me...and yes, some things still hurt more than others."

"So, what are you saying? You still have feelings for him?"

"No, that's not what I'm saying. Look let's just drop the subject. I'm with you. I'm married to you, and you're the only one I want to be with. Okay?"

"If there's something still there then…"

"There's nothing there. Trust me. Let's just try and enjoy the party."

As we walked through the gate, Damien approached me and Prez.

"Don't worry, I'm leaving…and I'm sorry for ruining your party." Damien then turned towards Prez. "And congratulations. I wish you both the best."

"You didn't ruin anything, and it was good seeing you."

Damien walked away and Caroline walked over with Olivia. I waited until Damien was gone before I took Olivia back.

"Hey. Did you have fun with Auntie Caroline?" I asked Olivia then I turned to face Caroline. "Thanks for watching her, and hey… can we talk…in private?"

"Yeah, sure." I grabbed Caroline's hand and turned towards Prez. "Hey, I'll be back in a few minutes. Okay."

"Take your time."

We walked away from the pool and headed towards the house.

"So, what's up?"

"Let me ask you one question. While you were holding Olivia, did Damien happen to mention anything out the way to you about her?"

"No why?"

"I was just wondering." I felt at ease. No questions equal less confusion.

"But he did mention how she favored his father."

"He said what?"

"Yeah. He was playing with her, and he said that it was odd how she favored his father so much."

"But you didn't mention I was her mother, right?"

"No. Why? Could Damien be Olivia's father?"

"No…and don't ever say that out loud again. Prez is Olivia's father, but I don't want Damien getting any ideas in his head that she might be his."

"And you're sure Prez is the father."

"Yes. I had Stacy to do a paternity test. Why?"

"No reason. Just making sure you're sure."

"I'm sure. Anyway, have you heard from Stacy lately?"

"Yes, I spoke to her about a week ago."

"You got her number? I need to speak to her."

"You sure everything is okay?"

"Yes. I'm good."

I was nowhere near being good. My paternity test bought up a lot of unanswered questions, and to make matters worse, Damien was now comparing my child to his father. I needed to speak with Stacy before any more comparisons could be made. Seeing Damien again only proved that there were still some old feelings lingering around for him, but none of it mattered because I was in love with Prez. Prez made me feel loved and I needed that. My return to DC was now on hold. Rachel's wellbeing was weighing on my mind, and Caroline's letter regarding Jacob's release was a serious issue that needed to be addressed. My life was good. I had a child who was healthy and a husband who loved me, so why was I willing to jeopardize everything for the truth?

# Chapter 19

### ⁕
# Nothing but The Truth

Caroline insisted we stay at her place while we were in town visiting. I was fine with the idea considering there were a lot of things we needed to catch up on. I was also debating on whether or not I wanted to know the truth regarding Olivia's paternity. What if Damien was Olivia's real father? I was scared to even think about what that would do to my relationship with Prez. No matter what Damien may have thought about him, I really did love my husband, and I would do anything for him, even if that meant lying.

The next morning during breakfast, Prez insisted I spend some quality time alone with Caroline in order for us to play catch up. He stated he would watch Olivia for the day and suggested I get out and enjoy myself. Prez then gathered up Olivia's things and prepared to head out. Brad decided to follow suit, and he took JJ along with him. Caroline and I were left alone in the kitchen to finish cleaning up.

"So, it seems as though the house is ours for the day." said Caroline.

"Yeah it seems that way."

"You know I still can't believe you got married before me. So, tell me little sis…how's married life treating you?"

"It's good. Prez's job keeps him away a lot, but he's good at making up for it."

"Well, he seems like he really loves you and Olivia, and I'm glad to see that you're finally happy." Caroline seemed sincere.

"Me too. I see you and Brad aren't doing too bad yourself. Love the house."

"I figured you would. I told Brad about how when we were younger, we would talk about what type of guys we would marry, and what type of houses we would live in one day. I remembered how much you loved Tutor style homes, so when I saw this one, I knew it had to be mine.

"You remembered that, huh? Well you would be amazed to know that Prez and I bought a colonial style home up in DC, because I distinctly remember that style house as being one of your favorites."

"You're kidding me, right?"

"Nope. You have my home and I have yours. Figures. We were always more alike than we were willing to admit."

"Isn't that the truth? You know I went to bed thinking about you last night."

"Why's that?" I was curious to know where this conversation was heading.

"I thought about how you looked when you saw Damien yesterday. You still have feelings for him, don't you?"

"No, and why do you keep saying that?"

"Because, I could still hear the hurt in your voice when you lit into him yesterday about sleeping with Rachel."

"And that's all it was. Hurt. Besides, I've moved on with Prez and I'm happy now. Just like you've moved on with Brad."

"I may have moved on with Brad, but no one said anything about me being happy."

"What are you talking about?"

"I know you got the letters I wrote you when you were locked up, right?"

"Yes. I just recently read a couple of them."

"So, that means you've probably read the letter I wrote to you regarding Jacob's release."

"I did."

"And…"

"And what? What do you want me to say? You seriously think I would ask Prez to speak on behalf of the monster who beat and raped me? You're kidding me, right?"

"Rhonda. Look, I need you to do this for me. Please. You know I wouldn't ask you to do this unless it was important."

"Are you serious? There's no way in the world I would ask Prez to do that. Really, Caroline? And why would you want him released? So, he could get another go at trying to kill me? Hell no!"

"Look, Rhonda, you don't know everything…"

"You're right. I don't…and I don't wish to know either. Jacob is a sick human being, and I'll never forgive him for what he did to me."

"I love him. Please!"

I thought I was going to be nauseous. There was no way in the world my sister was in love with that sick bastard.

"Why are you saying that? Is Stacy blackmailing you? What does she have on you now, because there's no way in hell you're in love with that rapist?"

"But I am…"

"Why, and did it happen to slip your mind that he's gay?"

"He's not gay."

I felt like my ears were deceiving me. First Jacob's gay and now he's not. What was really going on?

"But him and the officer…at the hotel…why would you lie about something like that?"

"Because I was left with no other options. One thing I didn't lie to Rachel about was the love Jacob and I shared for each other, but Stacy played a big role in us never being together. I couldn't chance her knowing about us while she was working on Mom and Dad's case. So, I revised a plan to lie and say that Jacob was gay. Yes, I know. It wasn't one of my brightest ideas, but nevertheless it was a plan. I told Brad Jacob was gay so he wouldn't be suspicious about our relationship, and it worked. Years passed and Jacob decided he would use my lie to get him out of his marriage with Stacy. He figured Stacy would divorce him and not blame me, but things didn't go as planned. Brad found out about JJ, and there went our plan..."

"So, you and Jacob really did have a relationship together?"

"Yes, but once Brad decided to challenge the adoption, I was left with no other choice but to work things out with him. Jacob became irate because I wouldn't run away with him, but there was no way I could leave my son—not with the Parsons. So, I chose Brad over him, and that's when he snapped."

"So, you talked to him on the day that he attacked me?"

"Yes, but I couldn't foresee his reaction."

"You knew he was unstable, and yet you didn't think to call or warn me. You set him off, and you did nothing to protect me!"

"No! Don't go blaming your rape on me. I couldn't control Jacob any more than you could. I didn't know how he was going to react until it was too late."

"So, tell me something. How did you know about the room they found me in if you never caught Jacob in there with another guy?"

"Because the room they found you in was where Jacob and I would meet whenever we wanted to spend time together."

"Hold up! So, if all of this is true about Jacob not being gay, and you two were actual lovers, then why didn't he ever try and stop you from self-destructing? You were out there selling yourself and getting high, and he chose to do nothing about it. What kind of love is that?"

"Because in the beginning I fought against anyone who tried to help me. Including Jacob. So, whenever I would go out, he would watch over me. He even threatened to arrest me on more than

one occasion to keep me from walking the streets at night, and I
continued to screw up. It wasn't his fault I wouldn't change. I was a
junkie, and junkies make wrong decisions. Regardless of my choices,
Jacob has always been there for me, and now it's time I returned the
favor. I need your help, Rhonda. I'm not trying to hurt you, but I
love him."

"You love him…" I didn't know what to think.

"Yes."

"I don't get how you can love a man who beat and raped your
own sister. It doesn't make any sense. What's wrong with you?"

"I don't expect you to understand, because I don't quite
understand it myself. All I know is that I love him, and nothing
about that has changed."

"Then you'll have to love him from prison, because I'm not
helping you."

"Come on, Rhonda, don't do this. If it wasn't for me, then you
would've never known that it was Jacob who beat and raped you.
Do you know how hard it was for me to turn him in? But you're my
sister and I decided to put you first because I love you, but you have
to also understand that I love Jacob as well. So, I'm asking you to
please…help me."

"Okay, say I was to help you, and Jacob was released from prison.
Then tell me something Caroline, what were you going to do with
JJ? Leave him here with Brad while you skipped town with Jacob?
Is that your plan? I mean have you even thought this thing all the
way through?"

"Yes. I have. I was going to ask Brad for joint custody of JJ. I
don't want to hurt him, but I'm not in love with him. So, trust me,
Rhonda, I've thought long and hard about this, and yes, the lifestyle
I have here is nice, but my heart is with Jacob."

"So, you're willing to give up everything for a man who's volatile,
who apparently has no respect for your family, and for what? Love?
Well guess what, Caroline? Love is way overrated. I was deeply in
love with Damien, but somehow, I was able to grow more and more

in love with Prez. Do I still have feelings for Damien? Yes! But do I want to make a life with him? No. Sometimes you have to look at the big picture and try to figure out what's more important. The love you have or the one you crave."

Caroline was in tears. I knew firsthand how much love could really hurt, but she needed to wake up. Her son needed a stable home. Not a set of dysfunctional parents.

"You're right, but I feel like I'm part of the reason why Jacob's in jail. Even if I don't go to him, would you still ask Prez to speak on his behalf?"

"Listen to yourself. You know damn well if Jacob was released today, you would go running back to him. It hasn't been two years since JJ was taken away from Rachel, and yet you're willing to make new changes in his life once again. Don't you think he needs some kind of stability right now? I mean are you even capable of thinking about someone else other than yourself? He's your son."

"And you think I don't know that? I love JJ, but I didn't ask to be his mother. You guilted me into this. Telling me to do what was right and that I would be a good mother. This isn't me, Rhonda, and you know it. Playing Susie Homemaker. I feel like I'm going crazy. I can't do this, and I don't get how you're able to do it either."

"I'm able to do it because I love my family. I look at Olivia and I'm thankful every day that I have her. You try being locked away and having no one to love, and no one to love you back. You'll change your tone really quick. You may not be in love with Brad right now, but I know in time you could fall back in love with him, because when it comes to JJ, you've got to be willing to compromise."

"And what if I can't fall back in love with Brad? Then what? I stay in this house and go crazy."

"I don't know, Caroline...you can do whatever you want to do. You work on trying to get Jacob released. You sign over custody of your son to Brad. You do whatever you like, but just keep me out of it."

I walked off in disgust. Some people take for granted the life they are blessed with, then try to justify to others as to why they don't want it anymore.

"Rhonda!" I continued to walk away. "Rhonda. I know you hear me." Caroline grabbed me by the arm and stopped me.

"What do you want?"

"I want you to stop judging me. You pretend to have it all together, but I saw your face yesterday when thought Damien knew about Olivia. You were afraid. So, tell me, little sister, is Prez really Olivia's father or is it Damien?"

"Okay, just because your life is full of drama, doesn't mean mines has to be as well. Prez is Olivia's father, and I have a paternity test to prove it. So, for the last time…let it go."

"That's right. You did say you had a paternity test done, which only proves one thing."

"And what's that?"

"You doubted yourself. You didn't know who Olivia's real father was. Did you?"

"For the love of God. I only had the test done because I was going to prison. You do understand that, right? I wanted Prez to know for certain that Olivia was his child."

"Okay. So, say I buy that. Then what are you so worried about? I know you, Rhonda. Something has you on edge. You're so quick to judge me and my problems, yet you're holding something back, and I want to know what it is."

"Why? So, you can try and blackmail me with it? No thank you. I'll deal with my problems, my way."

"That's right. Judge me, but keep all of your secrets to yourself."

I needed to see Stacy. I knew if I asked Caroline for her number, it would only stir up more problems. I couldn't leave on my own, because Prez had the rental. I was going to need Caroline's car, but how could I get it without making her suspicious?

"Look, I don't have time for this. There's nothing going on. Prez and I are fine, Olivia is our child, and there is nothing for you to worry about."

"Okay. I'll leave it alone, but you have to promise not to repeat anything I said to you today."

"Don't worry, Caroline. The last thing I would want you to do is ruin your happiness…"

"Ha, ha. Whatever. Look, I'm sorry, okay? You're here to spend time with me, and all I've done is burden you with my problems. So, let's start over. It's a beautiful day out. So, what do you want to do today? The guys are gone, and we have the rest of the day to ourselves."

I could use going to see Rachel as an excuse to see Stacy.

"Well, Rachel looked really down yesterday, and I wanted to know if you had any current pictures of JJ, I could take her. Maybe that would help cheer her up."

"Rachel looking down. Come on, Rhonda. You're playing with me, right? You and I both know Rachel was high as a kite yesterday."

In that instance, Caroline confirmed my worst fears. Rachel was using. I knew it. I just didn't want to believe it, but something had to have happened in order for Rachel to give up on herself and start using drugs.

"I figured, but why? Rachel's a smart girl. She has her own business, and…"

"*Had* her own business. Justine took that away once she found out Rachel was using."

"Do you know what happened to her?"

"No, but I've heard stories. None I wish to repeat."

"I can't do this. Can I borrow your car? I promise I'll bring it back in one piece, but I need to go and see Rachel. Please."

"If I let you use my car, then I'll be stuck here all day by myself with nothing to do. That's not happening. So, I'm coming with you."

I didn't want to take Caroline with me, but what other choice did I have. I called Prez to let him know that we were driving down to Tallahassee to check up on Rachel. He reassured me to take my time and to drive safe. I loved the fact he was always considerate of my feelings, and that he worried about my safety. The trip I was making with Caroline was definitely one for the books. We both had our own agenda for going back to Tallahassee. I was going in search of the truth, and Caroline was only following her heart. Regardless of our reasons, one thing I had come to learn was no matter how good our intentions were, bad things could easily happen.

# Chapter 20

# The Actions of Our Pain

Within a couple of hours, we made it to Rachel's apartment. So many thoughts ran through my head as to why my friend was truly hurting. But whatever her reasons were, I only wanted to hear them from one person in particular, and that was her. Caroline and I got out of the car and rang the doorbell. No one answered. I rang it once more, and finally Rachel answered the door. She looked a mess. We must have taken her by surprise, because she was shocked to see us.

"Rhonda...Caroline. What are you doing here?" Rachel was trying to compose herself by straightening her wrinkled shirt and running her hands through her matted hair.

"I came by to check on you, and from what I can see, I made a good call."

"Why's that? I'm good. There's nothing to worry about."

"Rachel, please. I lived with Caroline for years, so don't try and play me for a fool. So, can we come in?"

Rachel glanced over her shoulder hesitating, then nodded awkwardly as she opened the door.

"Sure, why not?"

As we walked in the apartment, I looked around the room and Rachel's place was a mess. There was hardly any furniture in the house, and there were clothes scattered all over the place. Dime bags and crack vials were everywhere, and there were dishes piled up in the sink, but most of all, it smelled. It felt like Caroline all over again.

"Oh my God, Rachel. What have you been doing?" I was afraid to sit down anywhere.

"Apparently nothing. Girl you nasty." I was shocked by Caroline's comment, considering she hardly had any room to talk.

"Caroline!"

"Well she is." Caroline blurted out

"Like you were any better." I insisted.

"I was never this nasty."

"No. You were worse. You just didn't notice it, because I was always around to clean up your mess." Rachel arms were folded, her body began to fidget, and she couldn't stop biting her nails. I could tell she didn't want us to be there.

"Well, Rachel, seeing you like this has definitely reaffirmed my decision to never do drugs again because you look a hot mess."

Caroline could be so incentive sometimes, but in that moment, I knew exactly what she was trying to do. She was looking for a way out, and she wanted me to give it to her. Knowing Caroline, she probably had only one thing on her mind, and that was going to see Jacob.

"Okay, Caroline, that's enough. How about you go and visit someone. Anyone. I don't care. Just leave. Besides, me and Rachel, we have some catching up to do."

"That's fine with me. I'll be back soon."

"Bye!" I closed the door and I looked over at Rachel. She was wiping away the tears from her eyes. "Hey…are you okay?"

"Yes. It's just hard hearing the truth. That's all."

"So, what happened?"

"I don't know. So much happened after you left."

"Like what? I don't get why you're using drugs? My arrest alone should've been enough to scare you away from them."

"That would've been the smart thing to do, but in my case your arrest was part of the reason I started using."

"You're joking, right? You're trying to blame me for your addiction."

"And why not? Granted, you weren't the only reason I started using, but it was an array of things that you were a part of that made me break."

"Like what?"

"Like when we fell out because of Damien. I was so hurt because I thought I had lost my best friend, and then there was the custody issue regarding JJ. When he was taken away from me, that's when I started to crack. I was so hurt. So, when you came by to see me, I just knew everything was going to be okay. I figured I would at least have you to lean on for support, but the next thing I knew you were being hauled off to jail. I tried to be strong and get myself together, but I couldn't. I was in too much pain."

"Pain! You want to talk about pain?" I had to calm myself down. I was allowing Rachel to upset me. I was supposed to be there to help her not to push her over the edge. "No. I'm not going to do this with you. I wasn't the one who put the needle in your arm, that was all you. Let's not forget you caused me just as much pain as I caused you. Besides, if you were hurting so bad, then why didn't you ever tell me about it?"

"I tired. I went to see you when you were locked up, but you didn't have me listed on your visitation sheet. So, I couldn't talk to you. I wrote you, but you never wrote me back."

I started to think about all the choices I had made, and how I didn't list anyone on my visitation sheet. I never thought about how it would affect the people in my life.

"I'm sorry. That was my fault. I was so ashamed of what I had done, that when they locked me up, I didn't want to see or hear from anyone. Besides, I didn't want anyone to know that I was pregnant. The entire situation was stressful enough."

"You could've talked to me. I would've understood. But no. You chose to shut me out when I needed you the most. I didn't know what was going on, or why you were being arrested. There were so many questions I wanted to ask you, but I couldn't."

"Well, you have your chance now. So, what do you want to know?"

"Did you really sell drugs out of my shop? The cops came by and raided it after you were arrested. I didn't know what they were looking for, and that's when they told me that you were trafficking drugs in and out of my store. I didn't know what to think. I had such mixed feelings about the entire thing. So, did you do it? Did you really sell drugs out of my shop?"

"Yes." Without hesitation, Rachel slapped me. I didn't know what was up with the slapping, but if one more person was to lay a hand on me then I was going to jail for manslaughter.

"I'm sorry. I didn't mean to do that."

"No. I deserved it. I should've told you what was going on, but I didn't."

"But why out of my shop? That was my livelihood, Rhonda."

"Because your store was the perfect front. I was able to mold my dolls out of cocaine, and no one was ever the wiser. I didn't tell you, because I figured if I was ever arrested then the cops couldn't use anything you had to say against me, because you weren't knowledgeable of anything I was doing."

"Well you're right about that, because I didn't know what was going on. As time passed, I tried to cope with my emotions, but I couldn't. Finally, I couldn't take it anymore. So, I went to talk with a friend, and she told me how she understood my pain. She also gave me, you know…something to take the edge off. She told me it would help numb my pain, and it did."

"Come on, Rachel. Why? You're smarter than that."

"Yeah, this coming from the drug dealer."

"Touché. I'll give you that one, but come on. No true friend would ever give you drugs."

"I hear what you're saying, but you weren't here. You don't understand the hell I was going through. I needed them."

"No. You wanted them. I watched Caroline for years, and she was only able to get clean when she wanted better for herself. As long as she wallowed in self-pity, then she stayed high, but you're my best friend, and I can't lose you to this addiction. So, if I have to take you to rehab myself, then I will, because I need you to get better."

Rachel smiled slightly, but she couldn't hide the hurt in her eyes. Not from me. I wished I could take away her pain but I knew there was nothing I could do. The repercussions of my actions had caught up to me once again. Karma.

"You're right. I need to get better."

"You know I'm right."

"So, tell me something. How were you able to work around all that dope without ever being tempted to use it yourself?"

"Because I had something more powerful then temptation. I had hate."

"Hate. How's that?"

"When you see someone, who's strung out they usually don't have any control over themselves. No matter what they want to do, the drugs always seem to overpower their thoughts. Well, Caroline was my drug. The hate I had for her was enough, that I didn't need anything else."

"So right now, if you were still in the drug game, could you be able to resist temptation, since you and Caroline are on good terms now?"

"Well things are different now. I have Olivia. She's my drug now, and there's nothing I wouldn't do for her. If I'm not around to raise her, then who would she have to depend on? My parents? I don't think so. Caroline? Not a chance. So that only leaves me, which means I have to stay in my right mind…for her."

"I wish I was strong like you."

"What are you talking about? You are strong. You're one of the strongest people I know. So why are you doubting yourself?"

"I don't know, Rhonda. I'm just tired. I'm tired of being sad all the time. I'm tired of the pain and I just want it all to go away."

"Okay, look at me." Rachel turned to face me. "My parents. They hate me right now, because I dealt drugs. Damien is hurt because I married Prez, and Caroline...well, we go back and forth all the time. If anyone should be strung out it should be me. My life has been full of ups and downs, but I have always believed that no matter what we go through in life, things will somehow get better. They have to, because you're my girl."

"You know. I'm so glad you're back and I promise, if I ever feel overwhelmed again, I'm calling you."

"That's right. Call me. Don't call this so-called friend of yours, who thought giving you drugs was the right thing to do. By the way. Who was this friend? You never told me who it was."

"It doesn't matter. You wouldn't want to know anyway. So..."

"No. You're wrong. I do want to know, because if I could put my hands on the person responsible for this, then I would."

"See, that's why I'm not telling you."

"Okay. Keep it a secret, but I will find out."

"Why? Tell me, why do you want to know?"

"Because you're my friend and we're supposed to take care of each other. What this person did to you was cruel and selfish, and one way or another I will find out who it is."

"And what are you going to do once you discover who it is? You can't criticize someone for giving me drugs especially when you used to sell them."

"And you're right, but I still want to know who it is." Rachel got up as if she was uncomfortable. "Why are you protecting this person? Come on, Rachel. Just tell me who gave you the drugs."

"I can't. So just drop it."

"Oh no. Now I really want to know who it is. Tell me, Rachel. Who got you hooked?"

"Stop it, Rhonda."

"No! Not until you tell me who it is!"

"No. We're not playing this game again. I'm not telling anything."

I looked on the coffee table and I saw Rachel's cell phone. I grabbed the phone, and I started to look through her recent call log.

"No. Give me that."

"I will if you tell me who it is. If not, then I'll call every number on this list, and I'll ask them if they ever sold you drugs."

"You wouldn't!"

"Try me." Rachel looked torn. I knew she didn't want to tell me who it was, but I needed to know. "Tell me, Rachel...who gave you the drugs? Trust me, I'm only doing this to help you."

"Fine. It was Stacy. Stacy gave me the drugs."

"Stacy. But why? Are you sure?"

"Yes. I'm sure. Now give me back my phone." I gave Rachel her phone, but then I was left with a dilemma. I needed to know what was up with my test, but I also needed to know why Stacy would hook Rachel on drugs. "So, what are you going to do? Cause more drama?"

"You would like that wouldn't you? Then it'll give you another reason to get high, right."

"Whatever."

"No, it's not whatever. So, what are you going to do? Are you going to check into rehab?"

"I don't know."

"What you mean you don't know? You need help, Rachel. Look around you. This has to stop."

"And it will. I just need some time."

"No. You've had enough time. If you want to get better then you have to make a move, now. How about you ride back with me and Caroline, and we can check with Brad to see if he would be able to get you into one of the rehab clinics in Clearwater."

"I don't know, Rhonda. What about my apartment?"

We both looked around.

"How about we start by cleaning it up first and then go from there."

"Okay."

Rachel and I cleaned her apartment from top to bottom. When we were done, we both were tired and sweaty.

"Oh man, you owe me. I wasn't planning on doing any kind of manual labor when I came here."

"You. Neither did I."

"Well it looks good."

"It does. Thanks."

"Okay, now that I've helped you. I need a favor."

"Sure. What you need?"

"Can I borrow your car?"

"Why? What's going on?"

"I need to go and visit a friend without Caroline knowing about it."

"Who, Damien?"

"No, and why does it always have to be Damien? I do have other friends."

"Like who? But you do need to go by and see him."

"And why would I do that? I've moved on."

"You have, but he hasn't. I know you love your husband, but Damien is hurting. I feel like if it wasn't for me, the two of you would still be together. So, please, for me. Just stop by and see him before we leave."

"I'll think about it. So, can I borrow your car? I promise I won't be long, and if Caroline shows up before I get back, just tell her to wait for me. I'll be back soon."

"You're not going to start any problems, are you?"

"I said I wouldn't." Rachel gave me her car keys. "Thanks, and don't forget to start packing while I'm gone. I won't be long. I promise."

"Okay."

I got into the car and I headed for Stacy's house. I promised Rachel I wouldn't stir up any more trouble, and this time I was going to keep my promise. She had been through enough, and I didn't want to be the one to cause her any more pain. Stacy, on the other hand, needed to pay for what she had done to my friend. True enough, we all had hurt each other at one point in time, but there was no excuse for what she had submitted Rachel to. I on the other hand needed to stay focused. My true objective was to discover the truth regarding my paternity test. Having Olivia made me view a lot of things very differently. Even though I wanted Stacy to pay for what she had done to Rachel, I've grown to learn that it wasn't my place to make her pay. My only priority was to make sure Rachel got better, and that my secrets regarding my paternity test stayed hidden.

# Chapter 21

❧

## Setting the Record Straight

On my ride over to Stacy's, I had time to sit and think about what I wanted to say, but I knew once I got there, nothing would come out the way I wanted it to. I arrived at her house and rang the doorbell, and before long Stacy answered the door.

"Rhonda. You're out."

"And hello to you too."

"I'm sorry. Come in." I walked into Stacy's apartment and it was night and day compared to the train wreck I had just left at Rachel's place. Modern furniture, contemporary art, and high-end electronics. Everything seemed so well put together. "You look good. So, when did you get out?"

"Almost two years ago."

"Two years ago...but how?"

"I don't know. Prez worked something out with the district attorney, and the next thing I knew I was being released."

"I'm surprised I never heard anything about it." Stacy had an inquisitive look on her face. "Anyway. You and Prez. I take it you two are still together."

"You can say that."

I showed Stacy my wedding ring.

"Are you kidding me? You got married?"

"Yes. I'm trying my best to turn my life around, but it's hard when people are always judging you, so that's why we decided to move away. I didn't want Olivia growing up around a bunch of insensitive people."

"Olivia. Oh my gosh…your baby."

"Yes. I forgot to tell you. I had a little girl." I pulled out a picture of Olivia and showed it to Stacy. "We named her Olivia. She'll be two this year and she's a handful. I love her so much and there's nothing I wouldn't do for her."

"She is too cute. Well I'm happy for you. You even look happy. So, tell me, what brought you my way?"

"My paternity test." There was no need for me to beat around the bush. I wasn't Stacy's biggest fan at the moment. The quicker she answered my questions, the faster I could leave her apartment. Playing nice with her was starting to irritate me.

"Your paternity test. What about it?"

"Where did you send it for processing?"

"Why? What's going on? Was something wrong with it?"

"You can say that. Someone screwed it up."

"Screwed it up, but how? I sent it to one of the best labs in town."

"And that doesn't change the fact that it was wrong. I didn't want to believe it at first, but just recently I looked at it again and that's when I caught the error. All this time I've had the test I've never once paid any attention to it, and when I do…Bam! I find out that something's wrong with it."

"So, what you want me to do? Send it off again?"

"No. Because someone in that lab did this intentionally, and I need to figure out who, but most importantly why."

"But how do you know it was done intentionally? It could have been an honest mistake."

"An honest mistake is when samples are accidently switched during testing. That's a mistake, but when my indexes are clearly wrong, and yet they seem to add up on my probability results, then that's when we have a problem."

"You talk like you know this stuff."

"I should. I work in a lab, day in and day out. That's why I'm kicking myself for not catching this sooner."

"So, I'll ask you again. What do you want me to do about it?"

"Find out who screwed with my test. Someone in the lab had to do this based on the orders from someone higher up. This wasn't some random mistake. Whoever did this took their time trying to make sure that my test looked legit."

"And what happens if I don't find anything?"

"Trust me. You'll find something."

"So that's it? You want me to investigate your test? You're not the least bit curious about what's going on in my life."

What I wanted to do was lay my hands on her for what she had done to Rachel, but I promised myself I wouldn't cause any more problems.

"I'm sorry. I didn't mean to be rude. I was so zoned in on this test that I completely forgot to ask you how you were doing."

"It's alright. I understand. Now I don't know if Caroline told you or not, but I did meet someone new."

"You did. Who?"

"Well you may know him. Gregory Fletcher…"

"Gregory? Damien's father? How in the hell did that happen? Isn't he a little too old for you?"

"Not the reaction I was looking for, but yes. We're together now and besides, he's not that old. Anyway, after you were arrested Damien called in a favor from his father to see if he could try and get you released."

"But how? We made a deal with the DA. What could he do?"

"Rhonda! Gregory is a rich and very influential man, and besides that…he's a judge."

"A judge? I don't get it. Damien never mentioned to me that his father was a judge. To tell you the truth, he never really talked about his father at all."

"Yeah, they weren't on the best of terms. Gregory told me Damien blamed him for his mother walking out on them years ago, but when he found out you were arrested, he had no other choice but to turn to his father for help."

"This doesn't make any sense. Anyway, why would Gregory agree to help me? As a judge, isn't he bound by some kind of legal or ethical code? Because I know for a fact helping a convicted drug dealer isn't one of them."

"To get back into Damien's good graces, Gregory would've been willing to do anything, included helping you."

I didn't know what to think. Damien was willing to help me even though I had turned my back on him.

"I see there were a lot of things going on behind the scenes that I didn't know about, and that's what I don't get…"

"And what's that?"

"If Gregory was so committed to helping me, then why didn't I hear from him when I was locked up?"

"I don't know. Gregory never got into the details about your case. He's out of town right now, but if you'd like, I can call him and find out."

"No. That's alright. It's not that important."

"Well, you know you can always go and ask Damien. I'm sure he'd be more than happy to explain everything to you."

"I bet he would. Anyway, let me go before Caroline starts to freak and sends out a search party after me."

"Caroline? She's in town?"

"Yes. Why?"

"No reason. I just thought she would've stopped by to see me. That's all."

I didn't need Stacy wondering about Caroline's whereabouts. Even though Stacy had moved on, if she ever figured out that Jacob wasn't really gay, and that he had been seeing Caroline all along, then there would be hell to pay for all of us.

"She's watching Rachel for me. It seems as though my friend has developed a nasty little habit that she needs some help with."

"Oh…I'm sorry to hear that."

I bet she was. Another day, Stacy. Another day.

"Yes. We're taking her back to Clearwater with us. She needs help. So, I'll be on my way, and it was good seeing you."

As I was walking out, I saw a picture of Stacy and Gregory together at an event, and the resemblance of Gregory and Olivia was so uncanny that I almost lost my footing.

"Rhonda, are you alright?"

"Yes, I'm fine. Just a little clumsy. That's all."

"Alright. Well take care and don't forget to call."

"Okay. I won't."

"And tell Caroline I said hi."

I walked back to the car and nothing seemed clear. There were too many similarities between Olivia and Gregory, which wasn't good. I hated to do it, but I needed to see Damien.

It was getting late, so I decided to call Caroline and ask her to phone the guys to let them know that we would be returning home a little bit later than planned. I pulled up to Damien's apartment, and I sat in the car contemplating on whether or not I should go in. Finally, I decided to get out the car and to face Damien head on. There was nothing to fear but the truth, but the truth is what scared the hell out of me. As I stood on the doorsteps, I became hesitant about ringing the doorbell, but I knew that if I didn't face my fears then there would be a lot of unanswered questions floating around in my head, so I put my fears aside, and I rang the doorbell. Within minutes, Damien answered the door.

"Rhonda. What are you doing here?"

"Hi. Can I come in? I really need to talk to you."

"Sure. What's up?"

As soon as I walked into Damien's apartment, I saw nothing had changed. There were a few new pictures of us placed around the house, and seeing them out in the open is what surprised me the most.

"Hey…I was just at Stacy's, and she told me that your father…"

"My father…so you're aware they're dating."

"Yes. It's a little weird, but, hey, that's her choice. Anyway, she also told me that you asked your father to help me when I was locked up. You never mentioned to me that your father was a judge. Why?"

"Because people tend to treat you differently when they know that your father's a judge. Besides, we weren't on the best of terms anyway. We had a falling out a couple of years ago, and I really didn't have that much to say to him or about him, but after you were arrested, I didn't know what else to do. I had no choice but to turn to him for help. He flew down, and Stacy brought him up to speed on your case. We tried to see if there was something we could do to try and get you out, but you kept refusing to see our lawyer."

"What lawyer? No lawyer ever came to see me."

"What are you talking about? You're telling me you never met with Mr. Parcel?"

"No. Never. As a matter of fact, this is the first time I've ever heard his name mentioned."

"Well that's crazy, because every time he went to visit you, he was told you didn't want any new representation."

It was now clear that someone had it out for me, and now more than ever I needed to figure out who this person was, and why were they interfering with my life.

"I'm sorry, Damien, but none of that ever happened. I never met nor heard of a Mr. Parcel, but tell your dad that, I'm grateful for what he tried to do for me…and most of all, thank you. At least you tried to help, and that means a lot."

"Rhonda, you should know by now that there's nothing I wouldn't do for you. Nothing."

"I know, and by the way, I see you have a lot of our old pictures lying around the house. Now it's become quite apparent to me that either you miss me, or you've lost your ever-loving mind."

"Ha! You're funny, but anyway when I saw you the other day…I don't know, it brought back a lot of old memories of us when we use to be together. So, when I got home, I started to rummage through some of our old pictures together, and that's why their sitting out."

"If you say so. I'm not prying. Whatever you do in your spare time is none of my business. Anyway, it was good seeing you again; and I really mean that."

Damien leaned in to give me a hug and then he whispered in my ear.

"It was good seeing you too. I love you, Rhonda."

And without notice Damien tried to kiss me.

"Hey wait. What are you trying to do? You know I'm married, so why are you doing this?"

"Yes. You're married to a guy who we both know you're not in love with. Your home is here with me, not with him."

"Come on, Damien, and we're doing so good."

"How? By lying to ourselves? Come on, Rhonda."

"No. You come on. You honestly think because I was with you for all of those years, that it would've been impossible for me to move on and fall in love with someone else. Well, guess what, Damien? I did. I moved on."

"If that's the case, then why do you sound so upset? What I said shouldn't have bothered you, if it wasn't true."

"I'm not upset. What I am is irritated, because you just don't get it. I love my husband, and I would do anything for him."

"So, you're serious. You're really in love with this guy?"

"Yes, and why is that so hard to believe?"

"Because I know you, Rhonda, and if you were truly over me then you wouldn't be here."

"I'm only here because of…" I had to stop myself. I almost mentioned Olivia's name. True enough, I was looking for answers, but I needed to leave before I said something I would truly regret. "You know what, never mind. I really have to go."

"No. Don't leave. Not yet."

"Come on, Damien. I have to get back. Caroline and Rachel are waiting on me, and besides, we have a long ride ahead of us. So, goodnight."

"Fine. Run away, but you can't hide from the truth." I tried to walk past Damien, but he stopped me. "Wait. Before you go, I need you to do me one favor."

"And what's that."

"Kiss me."

"Damien." I turned to walk away.

"No, I'm serious. I don't know when I'll ever see you again, so come on. For old times' sake. No pulling away. No holding back. Just one kiss."

There was no way I was going to kiss Damien. I loved Prez true enough, and I didn't believe in playing with fire. Damien and I shared a past together, and that alone was a recipe for disaster.

"No. I'm not playing this game with you. So, let me go."

"Not without a kiss first."

"I'm not going to kiss you. Now move." Damien had me pinned up against the wall. I felt flushed. He took his hand and ran it down the spine of my back. "Don't."

"Rhonda, please. I haven't seen you in almost two years, and when I do, the first thing I'm hit with is the fact that you're married. So please don't do this to me. Just one kiss. One kiss, and I'll leave you alone. I promise."

"Damien. I..."

Damien ran his lips across mine. I didn't know how to feel. I wanted to break free, but against my better judgment I allowed the kiss to happen. Damien was right. There was definitely something still there, but I was wrong for what I was allowing to happen and I needed for it to stop.

"Stop! What we're doing is wrong. If I was your wife, you would be hurt right now if I was doing this behind your back with Prez. So, come on. Let's not disrespect my husband any further. I have to go."

"I'm sorry, but no matter what, remember I love you."

Damien stepped aside, and I was finally able to walk away. As I passed by the coffee table in the living room, I noticed a bunch of pictures scattered all over the tabletop, but what caught my eye was a picture of Olivia sitting on the top of the pile.

"Hey, what's going on in here?"

"Oh, it's nothing. Just reminiscing. That's all."

Damien tried to hide the picture of Olivia, but he was too late. I had already seen it.

"Reminiscing. Really! So, what's up with this?" I pushed Damien's hand away from the picture, and then I grabbed it off of the coffee table. It looked as though Damien had taken a picture of Olivia while at the party.

"It's nothing."

"Nothing. Really. Then why do you have a picture of my daughter…"

Shoot. I slipped up. I promised myself I wouldn't mention Olivia around Damien, but he was up to no good, and I needed to know why.

"Your daughter?"

"I meant Olivia."

"No. No. You said your daughter. I knew it. I looked into her eyes, and I saw myself through and through. I didn't ask any questions about her because I had a feeling you were her mother. Her face stayed on my mind, and something told me not to let it go, and I'm glad I didn't."

"Don't get excited. She's not yours."

"And I'm supposed to believe you. Look at me, Rhonda, and tell me that little girl isn't mine."

"She's not yours Damien. I can see how she favors your father, but she favors her father as well, who happens to be Prez; not you."

"I don't believe you."

"Then don't!"

"Come on Rhonda. Don't play me like this."

"I'm not playing you, I'm not lying to you, and I'm not leading you on in any way, and you know why? Because Prez is Olivia's biological father, and just to be sure, I had a DNA test ran on her, and it confirmed what I've been telling you all along. That you're not her father. Prez is."

"Then it's wrong."

"No. You're wrong. You just want it to be something that it's not. She's not yours, and I'm sorry, but I have to go."

"Rhonda!"

"Just let it go, Damien. Please."

I raced to the car and I headed back to Rachel's as fast as I could. My suspicion was right. Damien was on to me about Olivia. I needed to find a way to beat him to the punch before he discovered the one thing, I didn't want him to know: that there was an error on Olivia's DNA test. That little bit of evidence was enough to turn my whole world upside down. I loved my family, and I would do anything for them, but one thing was certain. Nothing was as it seemed.

# Chapter 22

❦

# Don't Lie to Me

Caroline and I talked with Brad to see if he was able to get Rachel into a local rehab clinic. I hated seeing my friend so tormented, but she knew it was for her own good. I promised to be with her every step of the way during her in processing. After Rachel was admitted into rehab, I headed back to Caroline's. Prez and I were in the process of packing when I started to zone out. So many thoughts were running through my head that I didn't know where to begin in my search for the truth. I was staring off into space when Prez grabbed hold of my hand.

"Hey. Are you alright?"

"Yeah, I'm fine. I'm just trying to wrap my head around everything that has happened. That's all."

"I know it's a lot to deal with, but everything is going to be alright. Okay."

"Okay. So, are you ready to go?"

"Yes. Wait a minute. What about Olivia? You have all of her things?"

"Yes. I don't know what Caroline was thinking when she bought all this stuff. Shoes, clothes, toys…I had to buy an extra suitcase just so we could carry it all back."

"Hey, don't be hard on her. She's just excited about having a niece. I'm sure you were the same way when you found out about JJ."

"Yeah, five years later but, hey, the past is the past, right? So where is Olivia anyway?"

"She's with Caroline."

"Alright. Well, I'm all done. You ready to go?"

"Ready."

We headed downstairs and, to my surprise, my father was there, and Caroline was standing beside him with Olivia in her arms.

"Dad. What are you doing here?"

"I heard you were leaving today, and I couldn't allow you to go without saying good-bye first."

I was stunned. I didn't know what to think. I looked around for my mother, but I didn't see her. "So, I guess mom didn't come with you."

"She couldn't make it. You know your mother."

"No. I use to know my mother, but anyway. I'm glad you're here."

"You know I couldn't miss seeing you off, and, about the other day, I'm sorry. Your mother has been through a lot, and well, just give her some time."

"I would if I knew what I was giving her time for, but I don't. She had it in for me the moment I returned home, and no one has yet to tell me why."

"Sit down." I placed my luggage in a corner, and I sat down on the couch beside my father. "Can you guys give us a moment alone?" Caroline and Prez left the room, and they took Olivia with them. "Okay, when Caroline would go and visit with your mother in prison, it wasn't hard for her to figure out that Caroline was using. She never said anything to Caroline about it; she just hoped and prayed that Caroline would eventually kick her habit. Then, soon after our release, we were informed of your arrest. Your mother was so hurt, and she felt as though you were the one responsible for Caroline's addiction."

"But I wasn't."

"I know, but it didn't help matters any when Caroline relapsed over a year ago. Brad found her in their bathroom stoned out of her mind."

"What? She never mentioned any of this to me."

"And why would she? She was ashamed, Rhonda. We were so afraid that we had lost her, that your mother became enraged. She went to Caroline, and took her to rehab herself. Your mother was so committed to getting Caroline better that she stayed with her every step of the way until she was clean, but in return, she blamed you for all of Caroline's shortcomings."

I was in tears. I hated what happened to Caroline, but what hurt the most was the fact that my mother blamed me for it.

"I would never hurt Caroline. Never. Grated she put me through all sorts of hell while you guys were locked up, but I loved her. She was all I had. Besides, I never sold street drugs. The stuff I dealt with was pure and I always kept it hidden. Caroline was aware of this, so why didn't she explain this to you guys?"

"She tried, but your mother didn't want to hear it. She saw the effects of drugs up close when she was in prison, so she vowed to do whatever she could to help those who wanted to kick the habit, but when it came to dealers…well you know. She hated them. In her eyes they were monsters, because they preyed on the weak…"

"So now I'm a monster?" I started to cry even more. "I tried to support me and Caroline the best I could, and I get chastised because of how I did it. Well you tell my mother I don't care if she never speaks to me again. I was left alone for years to raise and support myself. I had no help, and besides that, I was stuck taking care of Caroline, who, by the way, wasn't just battling a drug problem, she was coping with her rape as well, and you know who had to deal with all of that? Me! So, no…I'm not proud of what I did, but it happened, and if she can't forgive me then fine. I'll stay dead to her, because I'm done apologizing."

"Rhonda, you don't mean that."

"Like hell I don't? For you guys to think that I could be so cold as to give drugs to my own sister, then you're sick! I bet you never once thought about how we were going to make it while you guys were locked up. Did you honestly think that Caroline would take care of everything? Well she didn't, and I had to pick up the slack. So, I'm sorry if I'm not the perfect daughter you wanted, but at least I tried to bring us together as a family again."

"I know you did, and that's why I love you. I'm not proud of what you did, but I love you anyway. You're my child, Rhonda. Don't you get that? I love you no matter what. So, don't think for one minute that I'm not grateful for what you did for us. You went to jail, just so we could be free. It takes a lot of self-sacrifice to do something like that. So, no matter what. If no one else loves you, your father does." I fell into my father's chest and I wept like a baby. With everything that was going on around me, I really needed to hear that. "It's okay."

"I'm sorry. I didn't mean to." I tried to stop crying, but I couldn't.

"You're fine." My father continued to console me. "So, I want you guys to have a safe trip and take care of my grandbaby."

"Your grandbaby? You know?"

"Yes. Caroline told me about her when I came over. I know you probably wanted to tell us yourself, but we didn't make it easy for you to do that."

"No. You didn't." We both started to laugh. It felt good having my father back in my life. As for my mother. Well time would surely tell. "I'll make sure to send you some pictures of her when we get back." I got up and walked into the kitchen. Prez and Caroline were sitting around the kitchen table drinking coffee. I reached out for Olivia and she started smiling.

"Hey, are you alright?" Prez stood up and wiped away my tears.

"Yes. I'm fine. Hey come with me." I walked into the living room with Olivia in my arms, and Prez by my side. "Well, Dad, as you know this is Olivia, and this is my husband, Prez…which…I guess you know him from my case as Detective Castillo."

My father was playing with Olivia, and as soon as I said husband, he stopped.

"Your husband?" He then turned to face Prez. "You never told me you were married to my daughter."

"I know and I'm sorry, but Rhonda wanted to be the one to tell you."

"So, you're married and you have a child. You've been quite busy, haven't you?"

"Not really." My father and I smiled at other.

"So, Detective, let me ask you something. Do you really love my daughter?"

"With all my heart, sir."

"Awe." I gave Prez a kiss on the cheek. I loved him too, and I promised myself I wouldn't allow what happened between me and Damien to ever happen again.

We said our goodbyes and headed to the airport. Once we arrived back home, I tried my best to get back into the swing of things, but it was hard. My thoughts were scattered and I couldn't think straight. The only thing on my mind was Olivia's paternity test. Prez and I were in the bedroom unpacking, and out of nowhere I saw a hand waving back and forth in front of me. I must have spaced out again.

"Hey. Are you okay?"

"Yeah, I'm sorry. I just have a lot on my mind, that's all."

"Well, you've been in a daze all morning. So, is everything okay?"

"Yeah, everything's fine. I just have a lot to do. Nothing to worry about."

"Okay, but if you need to talk, let me know."

"Wait…I do have one thing to ask you."

"Sure, what is it?"

"Have you ever heard of a Mr. Parcel?"

Prez looked as though he had seen a ghost. I had him. Now all I had to do was figure out what role he played in all of this.

"A Mr. Parcel. No. I never heard of him."

"Really…because I was told he was hired by Gregory Fletcher to represent me when I was locked up."

"Gregory Fletcher? So, is he any relation to Damien Fletcher?"

"You know he is, and don't pretend as if you don't. So, tell me Prez, why are you lying to me?"

"I'm not lying to you Rhonda. I don't know a Mr. Parcel, and I didn't know he was hired by Gregory Fletcher to help you."

"Come on Prez. We're going to start playing this game now. Let's continue to lie to Rhonda. You know I can't stand it when people lie to me. So, don't." Prez got upset, and walked out of the bedroom. "What's wrong? Did I hit a nerve?"

"No, but you're about to."

"Oh really. So, I must be getting closer to the truth? Someone else offered to come to my defense, but you couldn't allow that, could you? You kept Mr. Parcel away from me—why?" Prez continued to walk in silence. "What happened Prez? Tell me!"

"Nothing happened, Rhonda. Nothing. Now I told you I didn't know a Mr. Parcel, so drop it."

"And if I don't…then what?"

"Don't take it there."

"Really. You're going to play this game with me? A lawyer was sent to help me that I never met, yet he was told I refused counsel every time he came to visit me. Now what part of that makes any sense to you?"

Prez stopped walking.

"Look. I don't know where you're getting your information from and quite frankly, I don't care, but I never met nor do I know of a Mr. Parcel. So, let it go."

"But what if I can't?"

"Then we're going to have a problem. Aren't we?" Prez headed downstairs. "I have to go."

Prez words were upsetting, his tone was disrespectful, and I was becoming irate. Something was definitely up.

"Problems! Really…and where are you going?"

"Out."

"Out. Now?"

"Yes. I'll be back later."

"But we just got home and now you're leaving?" I was frustrated. "You know what, fine. Do whatever you want."

Prez looked like he wanted to say something else, but he didn't. He grabbed his coat and walked out of the house. I was livid. Not only was Prez lying to me, but he had the nerve to walk out on our conversation as well. I was about to head upstairs, but then I thought about Olivia's paternity test. I walked into the kitchen, grabbed a couple of Ziploc bags, and headed back upstairs. I went into the bathroom, took some hair out of Prez's hairbrush, and then some out of Olivia's brush. I bagged the hairs and hid them in my purse. One way or another, I was going to figure out the truth, because if Prez wanted to keep secrets from me then fine, keep them. Because as it turned out, I had a few secrets of my own.

# Chapter 23

### 🦅

# Let the Battles Begin

It had been over a week and Prez still hadn't returned home. I didn't know what to think. I checked his job, the hospitals, everywhere, but he was nowhere to be found. It was bad enough I was all alone, but to make matters worse, a letter arrived in the mail from Damien's lawyer contesting a paternity test to be performed on Olivia. I felt like I was about to lose it. I rushed to Mr. Wyatt, and I asked him if he would run a DNA test on the hairs, I collected from Prez and Olivia's hairbrushes. I then asked him to mail me the results, and to make sure that he signed off as the processor. As for Prez, I packed up all of his belongings, and I had them waiting for him by the front door. So, whenever he returned home, he could take all of his crap with him and leave for good. I loved him true enough, but you just don't up and leave your family without a care in the world. He didn't call. He didn't write. He didn't do anything to let me know that he was okay. So, if he chose not to care, then why should I?

A couple of days later, I received the results from Olivia's paternity test in the mail. My heart was racing. I was so afraid of the truth. I went upstairs and I watched Olivia as she slept. She was so innocent in all of this, and I didn't want to complicate her life, but I needed to know the truth. As I was about to open the envelope, I heard the front door close downstairs.

"Rhonda." It was Prez. I took the envelope and I placed it in my purse. I sat in the rocking chair beside Olivia's crib, and I was determined to stay strong. She was my only concern, and I had nothing else to say to Prez. "You didn't hear me calling you?" Prez walked into Olivia's bedroom, and I pretended not to see him. I was so angry with him, that if I was a guy, I would've stomped him out. "Rhonda!" I kept quiet. All I wanted was for him to leave. "Look, I'm sorry…"

Sorry? That was the straw that broke the camel's back. I snapped.

"You're sorry. You left me and your child alone here for almost two weeks. No phone calls. No, 'hey, I'm okay,' but you're sorry. Well, you can keep all of your "*sorries*", because I'm done."

"Look, you don't understand; my boss sent—"

"No! Don't even try and put this on your job, because I went by there and your supervisor didn't know where you were either."

"You went by my job?"

"Yeah. Surprised? But don't worry. I didn't tell anyone who I was. I didn't want to embarrass you, considering no one knew who I was anyway."

"Look, it's not what you think."

"No. It's exactly what I think. I was just a pet project for you. Your dirty little secret, but none of that matters anymore, and you know why? Because you no longer live here, and I want you out of my house. Now!"

"Wait a minute, Rhonda. I know you're upset, but just give me a chance to explain."

"What is there to explain? You left!"

"You're right I left, but hear me out. The other night when I left, I drove around to clear my head, and that's when I noticed that one of the marks, I was investigating was following me. If I came home, then my cover would've been blown, and I would've led them straight to you guys. I couldn't risk it. So, I went back undercover until an arrest was made. I know it's a lot to take in, but it's the truth."

"You're joking, right? You've been undercover this entire time… do I look stupid to you?"

"It's the truth, Rhonda…and what's up with all my stuff downstairs?"

"It's down there because you left! Come on, Prez. What was I supposed to think? You've been gone for almost two weeks now. So, I packed up your things so you can take them with you when you leave, because honestly, I don't have time for this. I have a lot of stuff on my mind right now, and your disappearance isn't one of them."

"Wait a minute, Rhonda. You're not putting me out of my house. This is my home and—"

"Your home, really? Because I can't tell. A man doesn't up and leave his family, but then again, I forget you're FBI, so you guys tend do that. No courtesy. No regard for your loved ones. Nothing."

"Look, Rhonda. I explained to you what happened, and you can choose to believe me or not, but I'm done arguing about this." Olivia woke up and saw Prez. She was so excited to see him. "I'm going spend some quality time with my daughter, and you can do whatever you want." Prez reached passed me and picked Oliva up from her crib.

"Your daughter…" I let out a sarcastic laugh.

"And what is that supposed to mean?"

"Nothing. Do what you want."

I tried to walk off, but Prez grabbed me by the arm.

"Don't play games with me, Rhonda. What are you talking about?"

I quickly pulled away.

"Don't touch me! I don't know where you've been or what you've been up to, but a lot has happened since you've been gone, and if you would've been here then I wouldn't have to explain it to you. So please...just leave me alone."

Prez released my arm, and then he placed Olivia back in her crib. I may have gone too far. As I walked off, Prez tried to stop me, but I pulled away. He tried again, and before I knew it, he had me pinned me up against the wall.

"Look at me." I rolled my eyes at him. I wasn't in the mood for any more of his lies.

"Damn it, Rhonda! I'm serious. Look at me." I turned and stared into his eyes. I missed those eyes, but I had to be strong. "Okay, I get that you're mad at me, but this? This has to stop now."

"Really? You want this to stop...if that's the case then you shouldn't have left. You could've called me. It wouldn't have taken you but a minute to pick up a phone and let me know that you were alright. But guess what...you didn't. And now you want to come home and play the loving husband and father as if nothing has happened. Get real, Prez. You don't get the right to come in here and demand anything from me. You left us, remember?"

"You're right. I left; but I explained to you why I wasn't able to come back. Now I get that you're mad, and you have every right to be, and for that I'm sorry, but that still doesn't explain why you keep trying to push me out of our home."

"Our home! Whatever. I don't have the energy to deal with you right now." I tried to walk away, but Prez stopped me.

"No. It's not whatever. You and Olivia mean the world to me. I wouldn't do anything to hurt you, and that includes bringing danger into your world. I love you. Don't you get that? There's nothing I wouldn't do for you, and I will not allow you to push me away." My eyes started to tear up due to the anger, frustration, and the fact that I did miss Prez; but I wasn't about to give in. "Now I get that you're hurting, but don't. Don't do this to me." Prez pulled me closer to him. I tried to brush his hands away, but he wouldn't let go of me. He began to kiss me along the line of my neck, and I fought to stay strong.

"No. Come on, Prez. Stop." His lips felt good on my neck, and even though he was turning me on, I needed for him to stop. I couldn't allow him to break me.

"No. I won't stop." Prez tried to kiss me, but I pushed him away. I was hurt and upset and the last thing I wanted to do was to pretend as if everything was okay when it wasn't, but Prez was persistent and he kissed me anyway. I started to crack. I hated the fact that I loved him so much, and it drove me crazy that he wasn't around when I needed him the most. "I'm sorry...I'm so sorry that I hurt you." I tried to wipe away my tears. Prez saw that I was hurting, and I hated it. Before I could gather my thoughts, he picked me up and carried me towards our bedroom.

"Wait. What are you doing?"

"Making it up to you."

"No. You're not..." Prez laid me on the bed, and his mouth and hands were all over my body. I tried to fight against my emotions, but my heart wouldn't let me. I began to break down, and before long, I had completely caved in. "Wait...we can't. Olivia. She's up."

"Yeah, but do you hear her crying?"

"No."

"Exactly."

"You're still not off the hook. You know that, right?"

"Yeah. I know."

Prez made love to me and it was so intense. It was like my body craved his. I hated how he made me feel. I'd never been in such an addictive relationship before. In the midst of our love making, Prez whispered in my ear.

"You're the only one I'll ever love."

"I love you too."

Olivia started to cry, and eventually we had to get up. Prez took care of her, while I jumped in the shower. The heat from the water relaxed me, and a lot of the stress I felt throughout the day started to evaporate with the steam. After I was done, I was in the process of getting dressed when I heard my cell phone ring. I looked around the room, and I was able to detect the ringing coming from my purse. By the time I reached my cell, the ringing had stopped. It was Caroline. I was in the process of calling her back, but then I noticed the envelope from the lab sitting in my purse. I placed the phone on the dresser, and I picked up the envelope. I kept going back and forth with myself about opening it. I needed to know the truth, so I took a deep breath and ripped it open. My hands were shaking as I read through the results. My worst fears had come true. Prez wasn't Olivia's father. All I could do was cry. Damien was her father, but how? The timing didn't add up. I sat in the room and continued to cry. I could hear Prez calling for me, but I couldn't move. Finally, he made his way up the stairs. I was sitting on the floor crying, gripping the letter in my hand.

"Hey, what's wrong?" I took the paper and balled it up in my hands. Prez leaned down and released the letter from my grip. "What is this?" I didn't answer. Prez started to read over the results. "Rhonda, what is this?"

"She's not yours."

"Who's not mine? What are you talking about? You're not making any sense."

I tried to pull myself together.

"Olivia. She's not your daughter."

"What do you mean she's not my daughter? What is this, Rhonda?"

"It's a paternity test…"

"You ran another test on Olivia? But why?"

"Because the first one was flawed and I needed to know the truth."

"What do you mean 'flawed'?"

"There were errors all over the test that didn't add up, so I decided to have it redone, and to make matters worse, Damien ordered a paternity test to be performed on Olivia as well."

"But why?"

"For some reason he felt as though Olivia was his daughter, so I had Mr. Wyatt run a test for me a couple days ago, so I would know the truth for myself."

"But this can't be right!"

"But it is, and once Damien discovers the truth, he's going after Olivia. His father's a judge, Prez, which means this could only get worse. What am I going to do?"

I started to get upset. How was this happening? It didn't make any sense.

"Are you doing this just to get back at me?"

"Are you serious? You think I would stoop this low just to get back at you? I didn't ask for this to happen. All I was looking for was the truth. When I discovered Olivia's paternity test was wrong, I figured it was probably just a glitch, and that I would check into it later, but during our visit to Florida, Damien saw Olivia and that's when the problems started. He kept insisting that Olivia favored his father, and I kept reassuring him that you were her father. So, a couple of days ago, I received a letter from Damien's lawyer requesting a paternity test to be performed on Olivia as soon as possible. He's coming up here within a couple of days and..." I started to break down. "I can't lose my baby. I can't."

Prez took the test and tore it up. He dropped the pieces of paper onto the floor, and walked out of the room. What was I doing? I was allowing myself to look weak and pathetic, so I got up and I tried to pull myself together. Prez, on the other hand, grabbed Olivia from her crib, and he headed downstairs towards the living room. He sat with her on the couch, and all he could do was stare at her. I eased down the stairs, and Prez patted the couch for me to come and sit next to him. I sat down and I watched as Prez kissed Olivia on her forehead.

"You see this little miracle here?"

"Yes."

"We're not going to lose her. No matter what. She's *our* daughter."

I wanted to cry but I held it in. I had to be strong for Olivia's sake. Damien had the means to tear my world apart, but I wasn't going down without a fight. Olivia was my daughter, and I loved her, and I wasn't about to hand her over to anyone—including Damien. He may prove to be Olivia's biological father, but in my heart, it'll always be Prez. My life was supposed to get better, but for the most part it was going in the opposite direction. Damien was on his way up to prove Olivia was his daughter, and there was nothing I could do to stop him. I loved Prez, and I would do anything for him, but I prayed that in the end he would be willing to do the same.

# Chapter 24

### ⚜

# Time to Play Dirty

I hated what was happening to my family. Prez took on another case, and I felt as though he did it just so he wouldn't be around when Damien came up. If I wasn't already depressed, then I was halfway there. I didn't know if Prez's story about being followed was true or not, so just to be safe, I started back carrying around my glock. I wanted to make sure I was able to protect me and Olivia, in case something unexpected was to happen.

The house was always lonely whenever Prez was away, and the fact that I was a homebody didn't help my case any. Then one day while I was sitting at home watching television, I heard the doorbell ring. I got up to answer and to my surprise it was Caroline.

"Caroline. What are you doing here?"

"I needed to see you."

"Why, what's up?" I pulled Caroline into the house as I closed the door.

"I've been calling and calling. You don't know how to answer your phone?"

"I'm sorry. I meant to call you back but I kept forgetting to. Why? Has something happened?"

"A lot has happened. Have you seen Damien yet?"

"Yeah, I saw him a couple of days ago, and how do you know he's up here?"

"That's why I'm here. To give you heads up about Olivia's paternity test."

"Olivia's paternity test…how do you know about that?" I hadn't mentioned her test to anyone"

"I'll get to that in a minute, but first let me ask you something. Has Damien done the test yet?"

"Yes. The results should be back today. Why?"

"I screwed up, Rhonda."

I started to feel uneasy. Whenever Caroline would screw up, it would always lead to something bad.

"What did you do?"

"Stacy. She found out about me and Jacob."

"She what! But how? And what does that have to do with my paternity test?"

"Hold on, I'm getting around to that. Okay. What I didn't know was that Stacy was keeping tabs on the visitation log at the prison. She caught wind of all of my visits, and somehow she talked Jacob into telling her the truth about us, and now she's pissed."

"Okay, but you still haven't told me what that has to do with me?"

"She's dating Gregory, remember?"

"Yeah and..."

"Well she figured the only way to hurt me is to hurt you. She told me herself that she spoke with Gregory about the custody hearing, and that she somehow convinced him to get Damien to apply for full instead of joint custody of Olivia."

"She what! He wouldn't."

"Oh, but she did, and if your paternity test comes back saying that Damien is Olivia's father, then it's on. You guys are heading straight to court, and guess who's representing him?"

"Stacy."

"You got it. She's going to be sitting second-chair to some guy named Mr. Parcel."

My world was crashing right before my eyes. I couldn't see Damien taking me to court. He wouldn't.

"Mr. Parcel. Are you serious? I can't fight against him. I don't have that kind of money."

"I know, and that's why I'm here."

"What are you talking about?"

"I took some money from one of Brad's investment accounts to help you."

Caroline showed me stacks of cash that she had hidden away in one of her suitcases.

"Oh my God, Caroline...Brad is going to kill you."

"Yeah, but it won't be over money. Once Stacy blabs to Brad about me and Jacob, then our relationship is over."

"Wait a minute. Where's JJ?"

"He's in school. I didn't want to take him out, so I left him there. He's better off with Brad anyway."

"How can you say that? That's your son..."

"And you think I don't know that, but pulling him out of school and dragging him God-knows-where isn't in his best interest. Besides, if I would have taken him, Brad would have had every cop in Florida looking for me. I don't need that kind of drama right now...but enough about me...what are you going to do?"

"I don't know. Prez isn't here. He's out on assignment, and I can't do this by myself."

"Well if you want me to, I can stay here and help you out. It's not like I have anywhere to go."

"You'll do that for me?"

"I brought you the money, didn't I?"

"Yes, you did and thank you."

I hugged Caroline. It was about time she offered to take care of me, instead of it being the other way around.

"Anytime. So, where's my niece?"

"She's upstairs sleeping."

Caroline was about to head upstairs to check on Olivia when the doorbell rang. I had no clue who it could be. When I answered the door, some guy handed me a letter stating that I had been served. In the letter was a copy of the paternity test and a summons to appear in family court.

"I see he's not wasting any time."

"What is it?"

"It's a subpoena. I'm to appear in family court in the next three days. Why is he rushing this?"

"Does he know Prez is out of town?"

"No. Not that I know of."

"Well if he does then he can use that against you. Stating how Olivia needs stable parents in her life and that Prez's job somehow prevents that." I gave Caroline an inquisitive look. "What? I watch a lot of court TV."

"Okay, so say you're right. Then how would that work in Damien's favor? He's single, so he has no room to talk."

"Well, all I'm saying is watch your back. From what I know about Gregory, he's good at getting what he wants, and right now he wants Damien back in his life. So, he'll be willing to do anything to make that happen—even if that means taking Olivia away from you."

"I can't see Damien agreeing to that. It's not him."

"Of course, it's not him. It's his father. This has Gregory written all over it, and with Stacy in his ear, there's no telling what will happen next."

I needed to talk with Damien. There was no way I could allow this case to go to court.

"Hey, can you do me a favor?"

"Sure. What is it?"

"Can you watch Olivia for me? I need to run an errand."

"Yeah. I can do that, and, Rhonda…"

"Yeah."

"I'm sorry about this. I didn't mean for you to get caught up in my drama."

"I know you didn't. You were just following your heart— regardless of the consequences."

"Rhonda…"

"I didn't mean it like that. I'm sorry. I'm just…you understand."

"Yeah I do."

"Okay. So, I'll be back soon, and don't let anyone in while I'm out."

"I won't, and by the way—"

"Yeah?"

"Love the house."

I smiled at Caroline as I walked out the door to look for Damien. I was eager to end this. I didn't know what I was going to say, but I needed to find a way to convince him not to file for full custody. I finally made it to his hotel room, and began to bang on the door.

"Rhonda. What are you doing here?"

"You know why I'm here. How could you?"

"What are you talking about?"

"Don't play crazy with me, Damien." I pulled out the summons and the paternity test. "Full custody. Really. You think I'm going to just give you my daughter!"

"See…that's exactly why I'm doing this."

"What are you talking about?"

"She's not just your child, Rhonda. She's my daughter as well. But you; you kept her from me. Granted, I hurt you in the past, but that didn't give you the right to keep my daughter away from me."

"I didn't know she was yours."

"Like hell you didn't know. One look at her and I knew she was mine. Her resemblance to my father…."

"No! Stop right there…she favors Prez as well, so don't. Don't pretend as if I did this to you on purpose, because I didn't."

"And you expect me to believe that you didn't know?"

"Yes. Come on, Damien, I may be a lot of things, but I'm not cold. You know I wouldn't hurt you—not deliberately."

"I don't know what you would or wouldn't do. You've proven to me and everyone else that you can't be trusted."

"I can't be trusted. Really…and why would you say that?"

"Because, you sold drugs, Rhonda, and then you had the nerve to keep it a secret from everyone, including me. I never thought I would feel this way, but in my eyes you're capable of anything. So, let's be honest. Do I trust you? No, I don't. Do I believe you intentionally lied to me? Yes, I do."

"Why are you doing this? I'm not proud of my past, but it's just that…the past. Now, regardless of what your father may have put in your head, I'm not heartless. If I would've known that you were Olivia's father, then I would have told you, and that's the truth."

"Well you have your truth and I have mine, but I'm not dropping the case. I will get custody of my daughter, and then you'll know how it feels to have someone you love taken away from you."

Without thinking, I slapped Damien in the face. I was so angry with him. I couldn't believe the things he was saying to me.

"That's right! Take it out on me, but it won't change anything."

"You're right. It won't change a thing, because it's apparent who the cold one is in this situation, and it's not me. So, you do what you have to do, and I'll do the same."

"And what is that supposed to mean?"

"Whatever you want it to mean."

"Don't even think about doing anything crazy."

"Why? Because I'm not a rational person? Because I'm so heartless that I would keep your child away from you? No. It's because I moved on, right? No, that can't be it. So, what is it, Damien? What's the real reason behind all of this?"

"Come on, Rhonda. I'm not playing this game with you. I'm done talking and I'll see you in court."

"Like hell you will."

Damien grabbed me by the arm as I was walking towards the door.

"Listen to me…I can tell by your tone that you're thinking about doing something crazy, and I'm warning you right now that if you even think about leaving town with my daughter, then I promise you, Rhonda, you'll never see her again."

"Let go of me." I pulled away from Damien. "You know on paper it may say that Olivia is your daughter, but one thing is certain; you'll never be her father."

Damien flinched at me, and I thought he was going to hit me, but instead he became very emotional.

"Do you know how it feels to have a child out there and not even know it? All this time another man has been raising my child. My child Rhonda! So, you're right. She doesn't know me as her father, but that's about to change."

"Well, you're right about one thing. A lot of things are about to change. I'll see my way out."

"Rhonda…"

I left Damien's room with only one thing on my mind, and that was leaving town. I had no intentions of handing Olivia over to him or anyone else. If Damien thought I was crazy, then I was going to show him just how crazy I could be.

I started walking and I didn't stop until I made it to the bank. Not once since I've been out of jail have, I had the urge to touch the money I had hidden away in my offshore account, but now my circumstances had changed, and I needed that money and fast. I went into the bank to make a large withdrawal, and the teller informed me that my account was closed, and that all the money had been withdrawn. There was over 10 million dollars in my offshore account, and now it was gone. My mind was racing and I didn't know what to do. No one knew about my account, so who could've withdrawn the money? I demanded answers from the teller, but she didn't have any. I requested to speak to her supervisor, but he had no explanation as well. My money was just gone. Upon stepping

outside the bank, my emotions took over, and I broke down in tears.
I couldn't lose my daughter. There had to be something I could do.
Then I remembered the extra money I had stashed away back home.
Granted, it was in the house my parents sold, but that wasn't about
to stop me from taking it. Damien could threaten me all he wanted,
but there was no way I was going to allow him to take away my child.
Not if I could help it.

# Chapter 25

And the Hits Keep Coming

My court date was approaching, and I needed to make a move and fast. Flying to Florida was out of the question, due to the amount of cash I planned on bringing back with me. So, I asked Caroline if she would watch Olivia while I took a road trip back home, and she agreed.

I didn't know what I was thinking. The drive alone was about to kill me, but before long my journey was complete, and I was finally back in Florida. I drove to the house I grew up in, and I wrestled with the thought of what I had to do next, but I put my fears aside, and I proceeded ahead with my plan. I couldn't risk being seen, so I stayed hidden in the car until the owners were away. Once they left, I got out the car and headed towards the house. There was a side window off the kitchen that Caroline and I use to sneak in and out of when we were kids. I just prayed that the new owners hadn't fixed it. As I approached the back of the house, I was able to check the side window and to my surprise it opened. I crawled through the window, and headed upstairs towards my old bedroom. As I entered the room, I noticed there was an old antique desk positioned in the middle of the floor where my bed used to sit. I moved the desk, and underneath the floor boards were large stacks of cash. With so much happening in my life, it made sense that I almost forgot about it. I took the money, and I loaded up my car and left. Once I arrived back home, I was so tired and sleep deprived, that I almost passed out. I needed to rest. I peeped in on Olivia and she was asleep in her crib. I took Olivia from her crib, and I placed her in the bed next to me. There was something calming about watching her sleep, and before long, I was asleep as well.

When morning arrived, I woke up and began to pack. My mind was so focused on leaving, that I didn't notice Caroline when she entered the room.

"Morning sis. So…" Caroline was shocked to see the suitcases lying on the bed. "You plan on going somewhere?"

"Hey. Yeah, I was going to talk to you about that."

"Okay then. Talk."

"Look, I tried to be rational with Damien, but he wasn't hearing it. So, I have to do what's best for me and Olivia, and that means leaving town."

"And what about Prez? You plan on telling him what you're up to?"

"I'll explain it to him after I'm gone, but right now I can't risk sitting around waiting on him to get back just to let him know what's going on."

"So, will I ever see you again?"

I stopped packing. I didn't think of how leaving would affect the people in my life.

"I'm sorry, Caroline. Of course, you'll see me again. It's just…"

My hands were shaking. I was running off of fear and nothing else.

"It's going to be okay. Just breathe."

"I'm scared. I'm so scared. I can't lose her. I love her so much."

"And you won't. How about this. How about I come along with you guys? I know it can get lonely out there on the run by yourself. So, what do you say?"

"I don't know what to say. It's a nice gesture, but I couldn't ask you to do that. I can't risk you getting into any more trouble."

"And how would I get into trouble? All I'm doing is watching over my baby sister. There's no crime in that."

I hugged Caroline. I was so happy she understood why I had to leave town. As we were in the process of packing, the doorbell began to ring. I ignored it and continued packing. As I grabbed all of my important papers and passports, the doorbell continued to ring.

"I wonder who's at the door." Caroline looked outside the window.

"I don't know. Do you see anybody?"

"No. I don't see anyone."

The doorbell continued to ring. Finally, I decided to answer the door.

"Damien."

"Surprised to see me?"

"What do you want? Shouldn't you be out preparing for your hearing tomorrow?"

"If memory serves me right, *we* have a hearing tomorrow, and that's why I'm here. You see, I figured you were probably up to no good, so I hired someone to keep an eye on you."

"You what! You have someone watching me?" I tried to peep around Damien as he stood on the front porch.

"Of course, I do. You know I don't trust you." Damien smiled, and then he walked into the house.

"Wait! What are you doing? I didn't invite you in."

"Well, I thought you would've wanted me to come in considering the things I had to say to you." Damien gazed around the room. "By the way…nice house."

"Whatever. What do you want?"

"Well, I came by to talk to you about your most recent trip to Florida. I take it you had a good time, but I don't know how you could have possibly enjoyed yourself, considering you weren't there for very long."

"And what are you getting at?"

"I'm not getting at anything, but I do know that if you even think about leaving town with my daughter, then I'll have every cop in DC after you. Besides, I know they would love to see the pictures of you breaking and entering." Damien pulled out some photos of me breaking into my old Florida home. "So, you think long and hard about what you plan on doing next, because any move you make—trust me, I'll know about it."

"So, that's how you want to play it?"

"I'm sorry, Rhonda, but you left me no other choice."

"Really! So first you make it impossible for me to do anything by wiping out my bank account, and then you have the nerve to have me followed; why? I mean you've already taken everything away me."

"I don't know what you're talking about. I admit to having you followed, that much is true, but I had nothing to do with your bank account."

"Yeah sure, and I'm supposed to believe you…but anyway, there is one thing you can do for me."

"And what's that?"

"You can tell whoever it is you have watching me, that I hope they can keep up, because this time I'm not giving them an inch. Now if you'll excuse me. I have a child to take care of."

"Don't make this harder on yourself. I love you true enough, but if you even try and take Olivia away from me, then I'll turn you over to the cops."

"Well, Damien, you do what you have to. Now get out of my house."

"Not until I see Olivia first. I need to know for certain that she's here."

"She's here; now leave. I'm surprised your little watchman didn't inform you of that."

"I'm not going anywhere, Rhonda; not until I see Olivia."

I thought about it, and I couldn't risk Damien seeing Caroline, because she was going to play a vital role in my new plan.

"You stay here and I'll go and get her."

I went upstairs into Olivia's bedroom, and Caroline was sitting in the rocking chair playing with her.

"Look, it's Damien. He wants to see Olivia. Now I don't know if he knows you're here or not, but to play it safe, I need you to stay in this room. If Damien asks about your car, I'll say it's a rental. Besides, he has some guy watching me, and I can't risk them knowing that you're here. So, no matter what happens, don't leave this room."

"Okay. I can do that."

"Alright." I took a deep breath. "So here we go."

I picked up Olivia and I took her downstairs.

"You see? She's here. Now leave."

Damien seemed anxious about seeing Olivia.

"I want to hold her."

"I don't think so. It's bad enough you got some creep following me, so there's no way I'm about to give you the opportunity to just walk out of the door with my baby in your arms."

"See Rhonda, unlike you, I wouldn't do that. Now come on. I want to hold my daughter."

I looked at Olivia, and I prayed Damien wouldn't try anything funny.

"Fine."

I handed Olivia over to Damien, and I could tell he was happy to see her. As they played together, my heart broke at the thought of losing her.

"Okay. That's enough. It's time for her to get dressed." I reached out for Olivia, but Damien wouldn't give her back. "Come on, Damien. What are you doing? Give me my baby."

"I'm sorry, Rhonda, but I can't."

"What do you mean, you can't? Give me my daughter." Damien held Olivia in his arms and walked towards the front door, and then he knocked on it. "What are you doing? Give me Olivia." I looked up, and a cop and a woman in a suit came walking through the door. "What's going on here?" The woman reached out for Olivia, and that's when I lost it. "Get away from my daughter. Olivia!" Before I knew it, Caroline came running down the stairs, and there went my plan.

"Rhonda, what's going on?"

"Give me my baby!" I was in tears fighting to get to Olivia, and the more I fought, the harder it was for the cop to restrain me.

"Damien, what's going on? What are they doing with Olivia?" Caroline tried to go after Olivia, but Damien held her back. "Let go of me!" Caroline tried to break free, but Damien made it impossible for her to move. "Why are you doing this to Rhonda?"

"It's for her own good."

I was absolutely devastated, but that quickly turned to rage. I was furious with Damien. I watched as my baby was carried out the door, and that's when I lost it. I broke free from the cop, and I went after Olivia. There was no way I was allowing anyone to take my baby away from me. Olivia was screaming and crying. I took her out of the woman's arms, and I refused to let her go. As Damien and the cop approached me, I immediately went into defense mode.

"Get away from me! All of you! Get off of my property, and stay the hell away from me and my daughter."

"Rhonda, don't make this harder on yourself. Hand Olivia over to the social worker, and we'll try and work something out."

"Like hell I will. You told me to trust you and then you pull this. Well, you don't ever have to worry about me trusting you again." I started to walk backwards towards the house. "Now leave."

Damien walked towards the social worker and the cop. He spoke with them, and they left. He then made his way towards me and Olivia, and Caroline stood between the two of us as a mediator.

"Are you crazy? You're lucky you weren't arrested; but at least now you know."

"I know what?"

"That if you even consider running away with Olivia, then I won't have to worry about going to the courts for custody, because you'll lose all consent over her, and it won't be anyone's fault but your own."

"And if you win full custody then I still won't have her, so what do I have to lose?"

"Well, you've been warned."

Damien walked towards his car, and I rushed into the house holding Olivia with all of my might. Caroline followed behind me and closed the door.

"I can't believe him. How could he do something like that?"

"He did it to scare me. He wants to make sure I don't run. What am I going to do?" I picked up my cell phone, and I tried to call Prez, but I kept going to voicemail.

"It's going to be okay. We're going to figure something out."

I didn't know what to think. Damien had me under surveillance, and now he was willing to bring social services into the picture just to scare me. The thought of Olivia being put into the system scared the hell out of me. There was no way I could lose her. I had to be strong. I needed a plan and I needed a good one. I looked at Olivia, and I knew I couldn't let her down. So, if Damien wanted to play dirty, then I was willing to play along. I pulled myself together, and I began to think of different things I could do in order to keep Olivia with me. I stared into her eyes, and I immediately came up with a plan. I didn't know how good of a plan it was, but I prayed that it would work.

"Okay, this is what we're going to do. During the trial, I want you to keep Olivia for me. Chances are, Damien has someone watching me, and I'm sure he'll have them watching you as well. So, instead of packing our suitcases, I want you to take our things and mail them for me. Once I figure out where I'm going, I'll give you the address. I'll go to court day in and day out, and pretend as if nothing has changed. Then on the day before the verdict, we're going to have a party."

"A party?"

"Yes. A big party. I want so many people here that it'll be hard for them to keep track of both of us. During that time, we'll sneak away. I'll have a rental car waiting for us, and then we're leaving town. Damien is not taking my baby away from me."

"Now what happens when they figure out that we're gone, and they decide to send the cops after us?"

"Then we'll give them the ride of their life. Like I've said before, I'm not turning over my daughter to anyone."

I knew it was a long shot to think we could actually get away with it, but I didn't see any other way. I knew that even with a good lawyer, I would lose against Damien. I needed Prez but he wasn't around. It was time I took matters into my own hands. If Damien wanted a fight, then I was ready. He was about to discover that he wasn't the only one with a few tricks up his sleeve.

# Chapter 26

## One Shot to The Heart

I was nervous about going to court. First impressions meant everything, so I arrived at the courthouse dressed to kill. I needed to show the judge that I was capable of taking care of Olivia, but most importantly, that I was a good mother. Caroline wanted to accompany me to court, but I didn't trust Olivia alone with anyone else, so Caroline agreed to stay at the house and watch over Olivia while I was away. Mentally, I wasn't ready to face off against Damien, but somehow, I made my way to the courthouse, and I convinced myself to go in. I tried to prepare myself for Damien's lawyer, because I knew he was going to come after me with everything he had. I went inside the courtroom, and I sat at the table, staring at the empty chair that sat beside me. Where was my husband when I needed him? I watched as Damien entered the courtroom, and surprisingly, I saw a familiar face. Rachel. I couldn't believe it. I was so excited to see her. I hopped up out of my chair, and ran over to her.

"Rachel." I leaned in for a hug, but she brushed me off. "What's wrong? What are you doing here?"

"I'm here to support my friend." Rachel looked over at Damien.

"Your friend. What are you talking about? I'm your friend."

"Are you really? During my treatment in rehab, I started seeing things a little bit differently."

"In what way?"

"Well, for starters, I was able to see that during our friendship you did nothing but use me. That's all I was good for, right? To provide a cover for you? And if that's the case, then we were never really friends to begin with. Now were we?"

"Rachel, what are you talking about? We've been friends since junior high. What do you mean I was never really your friend?"

"My friend..." Rachel laughed. "After the incident with Damien, I felt so guilty because of what I had done to you that I even blamed myself for you being arrested. But then I came to realize that it had nothing to do with me or Damien, because the reality of the situation is, the only person you ever cared about was yourself..."

"Really. So that's the excuse you're going to use for stabbing me in the back. If I didn't care about you then I would've never taken you to rehab. You would still be alone in your apartment high as a kite, and no one would've cared. So, don't talk to me about friendship, because it's obvious you never knew the definition of it."

Rachel's eyes started to tear up. The court's bailiff then called the room to order.

"I'm sorry, Rhonda."

"That's an understatement."

I headed to my seat, and I watched as Rachel went and sat down beside Damien. My heart broke in two. Not only was Damien going after my daughter, but he was using my best friend to help him do it. I couldn't allow my emotions to get the best of me. I had to remain strong for Olivia's sake. Stacy looked over at me and gave me a sinister smiled. There was a time and a place for everything, and she had her day coming. I sat in my chair in a daze. I could hear my lawyer, Mr. Crenshaw, speaking, but it was all just a bunch of mumble jumble to me. Then I heard something that snapped me out of my trance. Damien's lawyer stated that the motion was filed under Mr. and Mrs. Fletcher. Was he *serious*? I looked over at Damien and Rachel and they couldn't even look my way. I was so hurt that I couldn't even think straight. The trial was passing me by, and all I could do was sit in my chair and stare into outer space. I was at a loss. I felt numb. My best friend and my ex were both betraying me, yet again.

Judge Callahan called for a recess, and I couldn't get out of the courtroom fast enough. I headed straight for the restroom. I felt sick. I went into the stall, and I tried my best to hold it in, but I couldn't. I began to vomit. I felt like I was stuck in a nightmare that wouldn't end. As I came out of my stall, Stacy walked into the restroom. I couldn't risk going to jail, so it was best if I left as quickly as I could.

"In a rush?" I didn't say anything. I didn't want to give her the satisfaction. "Well, I wouldn't have too much to say either if I saw my best friend married to my ex, now would I? It leaves a nasty taste in your mouth. Doesn't it?"

"Yeah the same way it does when your husband is screwing around with your best friend. Nasty indeed." I couldn't help myself. I walked out of the bathroom and I bumped into Rachel. She had proven to me where her loyalties lied, so I ignored her and continued walking.

"Rhonda."

I had nothing else to say to her. Sleeping with my ex was bad enough, but marrying him to gain custody of my child was just downright low. The compassion I had for Rachel was gone, and our friendship was definitely over. I continued to walk away, and I saw Damien and his father talking in the lobby. There were no words for him either. Damien saw me, and he started to walk my way.

"Rhonda." I continued to walk away. "Rhonda." Damien cut me off from entering the courtroom.

"What, do you want Damien? You come to gloat?"

"No. I just…"

"You what? First you go after Olivia, but that wasn't enough. No…you had to go and turn my best friend against me as well. You make me sick." I could see Gregory heading our way. I certainly didn't have anything to say to him. "I have to go."

"Look, you pushed me into doing this."

I felt as though I had turned in slow motion.

"I pushed you! Really. So, I'm the one who pushed you into filing for full custody of our daughter? I'm the one who pushed you into marrying my best friend. No. I didn't push you into any of that. That was all you. You made those decisions all on your own."

"Like you did when you sold drugs instead of coming to me for help. Those type decisions?"

Gregory walked pass us.

"Damien, let's go."

"That's right. Listen to your daddy. You've been doing such a great job of that so far."

I began to walk back towards my seat.

"Rhonda."

I continued walking. I could hear Gregory telling Damien to let me go. His father was definitely the mastermind behind all of this. He probably was in cahoots with the judge as well. I sat in my chair waiting patiently for the trial to resume, when out of nowhere Stacy decided to stop by my table.

"And, Rhonda, just so you know. I did look into the matter we discussed in Florida, and you were right. Someone did screw with your paternity test. Can you say FBI?"

Stacy thought she was hilarious. I could see Damien looking my way. I was so ready for this day to be over with. I didn't know how much more I could take. During the proceeding all I could think about was why the FBI would tamper with my paternity test. Mr. Crenshaw was trying his best to counteract against Mr. Parcel, but Mr. Parcel was too good. Since everyone wanted to screw me over, and put my past out in the open, then it was only fair that I returned the favor. I whispered to Mr. Crenshaw, and I told him about Rachel's drug addiction, and I made sure to inform him of her supplier. If they wanted to play dirty, then let's. Mr. Crenshaw made sure it went on record that Mrs. Fletcher was a recovering addict, and that her supplier was none other than her co-counsel Stacy Jones. It was the only good moment I had the entire day. The look on Stacy's face when Judge Callahan called her to his podium was priceless. Rachel looked over towards me, and I pretended as if I didn't see her. The judge then called Mr. Crenshaw to the podium, and the next thing I knew I was being called into the judge's chambers. No one knew what was happening. I entered Judge Callahan's chambers and he told me to have a seat.

"So, Mrs. Castillo, you stated that Mrs. Fletcher was a recovering addict, and that Ms. Jones was her supplier."

"Yes, Your Honor."

"You do know those are some serious allegations you're making regarding Ms. Jones."

"I know, Your Honor."

"Now Ms. Jones swears me up and down that she never gave Mrs. Fletcher any drugs."

"Your Honor, I can only go by what was told to me. Rachel..." I had to stop and correct myself. "I mean, Mrs. Fletcher, was strung out really bad, and I asked her who her supplier was, and she told me it was Ms. Jones. I wouldn't lie to you about this."

"Okay, I understand that, but I was also informed that you, my dear, once sold drugs yourself. Now you and I both know that this knowledge can't be used in court, because your record was expunged, but we both know that it happened. So how would I look taking your word over a respectable lawyer such as Ms. Jones?"

I knew that was coming.

"Well, Your Honor, all I can say is that you'll be amazed at what people do behind closed doors. I'm not a saint and I'm not claiming to be one either, but I am telling you the truth. I was there when Mrs. Fletcher was admitted into rehab. I listened to my used-to-be best friend tell me out of her own mouth that Ms. Jones was the one who gave her drugs. Now you're a judge, and you can do whatever

*Catherine M. Clifton*

you want with that information, or not, but right now I don't have the luxury to lie."

"Alright, Mrs. Castillo. You can return back to the courtroom."

As I headed back to my seat, the bailiff called the court back to order, and Judge Callahan resumed his position.

"Upon recent allegations made by the defendant, I have no choice but to remove Ms. Jones from co-counsel, until an investigation can be done."

Stacy was livid! That wiped the smile right off of her face. They may win the trial, but this was without a doubt a win in my book. I couldn't help but smile, but with every action comes a reaction. As Stacy was packing up her belongings, I saw her hand Mr. Parcel an envelope. The bailiff then escorted Stacy out of the courtroom, and as she was leaving, she had this evil smirk plastered all over her face. Whatever she gave Mr. Parcel couldn't be good. Mr. Parcel advised the judge that he had new evidence he wanted to submit on the record. The bailiff took the envelope over to the judge, and then Mr. Parcel went on to explain how, even though Rachel was a recovering drug addict, that her and Damien were still more suitable parents for Olivia then I was, especially since I was a single parent.

Single parent. Why would he call me a single parent? Mr. Crenshaw objected on my behalf stating that I was married to Detective Castillo, and that we had been together for over two years, and that's when the bomb dropped. Mr. Parcel went on to explain why.

"Your Honor, if it pleases the court, I would like to show that Mr. Perez Santiago a.k.a. Mr. Ramirez, a.k.a. Mr. Castillo or whatever name he goes by these days is legally married to a Maria Santiago, and not to Miss Rhonda Brown. Their marriage is a sham and it's not real in the eyes of the court." I think for a few minutes I actually blacked out. The bailiff brought over documentation of their marriage and pictures of Maria and Prez together. I glanced at the pictures and then I pushed them away. "They have no children together. Mr. Santiago works for the FBI and Mrs. Santiago works for the Washington Post. They live in Maryland in the outskirts of DC and they have been married for the past four years."

Everything was a blur after that. I couldn't remember anything else that was said after that moment. I took one of the pictures of Prez and Maria together, and I placed it in my purse. The judge stated that he needed some time to review everything, and that we were to return back to court the following day. I got up and I walked out of the courtroom in a daze. Damien approached me, and I pushed past him and continued walking. Stacy was sitting out in the lobby as if she was waiting for me to exit the courtroom.

"So, tell me, Miss Brown. How does it feel to be screwed over?"

Damien tried to be the median between the two of us. "Come on, Stacy, now isn't the time." Damien said, as if he actually cared. I continued to walk away. I was trying my best to ignore Stacy, but I had so much anger boiling inside of me, I snapped. I jumped on Stacy, and Damien had to pull us apart.

"Arrest her! Someone arrest her. You saw what she did to me." Stacy tried to compose herself.

"Let me go! Get your hands off of me!" Damien was holding me, and I was trying my best to pull away from him. "You satisfied? Are you truly happy now? You destroyed everything in my life!"

"Rhonda. Listen."

"No. I've heard enough from all of you!" Rachel was walking by, and the sight of her enraged me even more. "You and your cracked-out whore make me sick! You never loved me, and you were never my friend." I wiped the tears from my eyes. I was beyond livid. "There's no way in hell I would ever allow my daughter to be raised by people like you."

Rachel was crying and Damien appeared perplexed.

"Rhonda, I'm sorry. I didn't mean for things to go this far." Damien seemed sympathetic, but I wasn't hearing it.

"Really. So, you thought once I found out that my marriage was a sham, that I would feel what? All warm and fuzzy inside? Is that it? How did you think this was going to turn out, Damien? You and your father play with people's lives with no regard to what it may do to them, and then you wonder why I don't trust anyone—and that's why. Because the people you trust the most are the ones who seem to cause you the most pain."

"Rhonda."

I stormed to my car and I headed straight for the FBI headquarters. I had to calm down. I couldn't let on that something was wrong. I went in, and I explained how I needed to speak with Prez's supervisor, Mr. Robertson. I was then escorted upstairs to Mr. Robertson's office. On my way there, I walked by what I assumed to be Prez's work desk, and, low and behold, on top of it was a picture of him and Maria together. No wonder he never wanted me to come by his job. I froze in my footsteps. I then advised the guard I would leave Mr. Robertson a note instead. I took a pen off of Prez's desk, and when the guard wasn't looking, I took the picture of him and Maria, and I placed it in my purse. I then asked the guard if he would just inform Mr. Robertson that Mrs. Castillo came by, and I left.

It was official. I was leaving town. I couldn't take any more lies. The only truth I had was my daughter. I had enough money to skip town and to start over. There was no reason to include Caroline in my scheme. She had her own life to live without having to be on the run with me. Everyone I had ever loved had betrayed me, which made leaving town that much easier. I didn't know what life had in store for me, but I was determined to make a new one for me and Olivia, even if I had to do it alone.

# Chapter 27

## Let's Be Honest

When I made it back to the house, Caroline was sitting on the couch waiting for me in the living room. I couldn't even think straight. I had so much to do. I needed to pack my things, and get out of town as soon as possible.

"Hey. So how did everything go?"

"It was a nightmare. Everything just fell apart."

"How? What happened?"

"Well let's see. For starters, Rachel showed up and…"

"Rachel...well that's good. At least you had someone there to support you, since I couldn't be there with you."

"Oh no. She wasn't there to support me. No. She was there was to support Damien…as his wife!"

"She what! Stop playing, Rhonda. Are you serious?"

"Oh yes, but it gets even better. I thought I had made some headway by exposing Stacy as Rachel's supplier, but…"

"You what? What did she say?"

"Oh, she denied it of course, but the judge removed her from the case, and placed her under investigation, and that's when she decided to go for the jugular."

"So, what did she do?"

"She had Mr. Parcel inform everyone, including me, that I wasn't legally married. That my marriage to Prez was nothing but a lie, and that he had been playing me for the past three years."

"Wait a minute. This is too much. So, you're telling me that you're not married?"

"Nope...but he is."

"What do you mean?"

"Prez. He's married to some chick named Maria." I pulled out the photo of Prez and Maria that I had taken from courtroom. "They live in Maryland and they have been married for the past four years. Anyway, I have to get away from here. I'm taking Olivia, and we're leaving tonight."

Caroline stared at the picture in shock. "So. You're really going to do this?"

"I don't have a choice. Besides, I can't take anymore."

I had so many emotions running through me that I felt as though I was going to hyperventilate. I tried to calm myself down, but I couldn't, and before I knew it, I was on the floor in tears. It was too much to deal with. Caroline walked over and hugged me, and all the hurt and pain I was holding inside come pouring out. I had never felt this way before. I couldn't stop my heart from hurting. My heartache was so intense that it even brought Caroline to tears.

"Alright. Let's pull ourselves together. We're stronger than this. I'm going to get our things together, and then we can leave."

"No. You're not going with us."

"What do you mean I'm not going with you?"

"I love you, but you can't. You have been through enough, and I don't want to get you into any more trouble."

"What I plan on doing with my life is my choice, and I choose to come with you. Now hush up and let's do this."

Knowing that Caroline was coming with me made things seem a lot less stressful. We went upstairs and started packing. Olivia was asleep, and that helped out a lot.

"Hey. I'm going to head out and gas up. You finish up here and I'll be back soon."

"Okay. Hurry back."

"I will."

Caroline left and I grabbed everything that was important to me. All of my necessary documents, birth certificates, and valuables. I had papers flying everywhere. I was almost done, but then my fingers came to a standstill. I had stumbled upon my marriage certificate. All I could do was stare at it. My anger took over and I ripped it into small pieces. It took a minute for me to regain my composure, and after that, I cleared my head, and I was back to business. I took the tote I had filled with money, and I began to cut small openings into the linings of my luggage. After that, I began to fill the empty spaces with cash. I preformed the same procedure on Olivia's bag as well. I took my glock and I placed it in my purse. I wasn't about to travel without it. Once I was done, I sat and waited on Caroline to return.

Time passed and it was getting late. Where was she? I was starting to worry. I didn't want to go out looking for her, because then I would have to pack up everything, including Olivia, just to head out. I waited and waited and still no Caroline. Finally, I decided I had no choice but to go out and look for her. I grabbed my purse, and time I was about to pick up Olivia, I heard the front door open and close. I raced downstairs.

"Hey. Where have you been? I've been waiting..." I looked up, and, to my surprise, it was Prez and not Caroline. He had some nerve. I placed my purse on the coffee table, and all I could do was stare at him. Why was he here?

"Going somewhere?"

"What I do and where I go is none of your concern. Anyway... why are you even here?"

"Mr. Robertson called and informed me that he got wind of my real name being mentioned today in court. He also explained to me that a Mrs. Castillo stopped by the office today looking for me. So, I knew then that my cover had been blown."

"Your cover...so, you were still playing me as a mark? Why?"

"Because having you wasn't enough. The Bureau wanted your supplier."

"My supplier." I started to laugh. "If you wanted to know who my supplier was then why didn't you just ask?"

"Because I knew you wouldn't have told me the truth."

"So, you thought by pretending to love and care about me, that I would one day open up and tell you who it was?"

"Yes. I needed to gain your trust. I mean think about it. If you would've known that Damien was Olivia's real father, then you would've probably gone back to him. So, I had the doctors at the hospital lie to you about how far along you really were. That way you would've thought I was Olivia's father, and not Damien."

"So, you had the doctors lie to me?" My blood was starting to boil.

"I had to. It was the only way to ensure my plan would work. See, when it comes to you, I learned very quickly just how sneaky you really are. You're very crafty at what you do. I'll give you that. I knew right then that there was no way you were going to just come straight out and tell me who your supplier was. So, I had to break you. Slowly. Until I was able to take everything away from you and you were left with no other option but to go back and do what you do best. Sell dope."

I was listening to Prez explain himself, and I couldn't believe the things he was saying to me. How could he be so cold? No emotions. No love for me; just hate.

"So, you wanted me to resort back to selling drugs, just so you could try and catch my supplier? The hell with me and Livy. We didn't mean anything to you. I mean why should we? She's not your daughter and, as for me, I was just your average, low-life dope dealer. Right?"

"That's right." Tears fell from my eyes. Prez was the only guy I had ever truly given my whole heart to, and it had become apparent that I meant absolutely nothing to him. "You were just a means to an end, 'Hahn'."

"Hahn?" I was shocked.

"You know it took me forever to figure that out. Otto Hahn. Really?"

"You have to be a true science geek to appreciate it, but now I get it...my father. That's why you kept in contact with him. It wasn't to keep him informed; it was so you could learn more about me. It was you! You took all of my money. Why?"

"What money? As far as the Bureau is concerned, that money is property of the United States Government."

Prez had officially lost his mind. It was bad enough he played me, but now he was openly admitting to stealing my money. He had gone too far.

"The United States Government? Yeah, right. I think you kept my money for yourself, so you could spend it on you and your wife..."

"Don't talk about my wife."

"And why not? Does she know that her loving and faithful husband would go to any length just to convict a criminal? Even if that included having sex and playing house with another woman?"

"Shut up. Don't."

"Don't what? Speak the truth? I can't believe I allowed myself to be played by someone like you."

"Well it wasn't hard. You wanted so badly to start over that you were willing to believe anything I had to say."

Prez was right. It was easy for him to deceive me, because I loved him.

"You're right. I played the fool. I now get why you were gone so much. You were never out on assignment, because I was the assignment. You were just at home playing house with your wife."

"I told you not to talk about her."

"Why? Is that a sensitive area for you? Because as far as I'm concerned, she was a bigger fool than me..."

"I told you to shut up. My wife is nothing like you. She's loving and caring, and she doesn't believe in hurting people like you do by selling dope. She's smart. She's beautiful, and she puts other people's needs above her own. As for you—you couldn't even image how hard it was for me to just be with you. It took everything in me to even touch you whenever we had sex..."

"Shut up!"

Prez just kept going on and on. The more he talked, the angrier I became. Even though he was yelling at me, his eyes were tearing up right along with mine. I didn't understand why he was so emotional. *He* was bashing *me*. Not the other way around.

"Her family isn't surrounded by drama. Her parents have never been to jail...her brother and sisters aren't cracked out...but as for you. You'll never be like her."

And that's when I absolutely lost it. I reached into my purse and I pulled out my glock, and without even thinking I shot Prez twice in the upper chest. It happened so fast that I was left in shock. I dropped the gun and I walked over towards him. I became an emotional wreck. I couldn't believe what I had done. Prez was lying on the floor bleeding out. I kneeled down to check his pulse. I caressed his cheek with one hand and clutched my chest with the other. No one told me that it would feel like this. I stroked his hair like I always did, but this time, he wasn't smiling back at me. The pain was so unbearable that I could barely breathe. I didn't know what to do. I stood alone in silence. My face was burning hot. My hands were shaking, and for the life of me, I couldn't stop crying.

"What did I do? What did I do?"

So much had happened so fast that none of it seemed real. I tried to move but I couldn't. My thoughts had me paralyzed.

"What did I do? Oh God what did I do?"

All I could do was stare at the blood on the floor. There was no way I could fix this. I allowed my emotions to overcome me, and now my life was spinning out of control. I could hear Olivia upstairs crying, but I couldn't move. I knew she needed me, but fear and shock had a hold of me, which made it impossible for me to think straight.

"I'm coming, baby, I'm coming." I mumbled to myself. With every blink, a tear fell. At that moment nothing seemed real. All I could think about was how was I going to fix this…but I knew I couldn't. The situation was no longer in my control. I thought my life was getting better, but then Karma had a way of rearing its ugly head. The distress in Olivia's cries grew louder and louder. She knew something was wrong. With all of the yelling and screaming that had taken place, she had a right to be alarmed.

"Mommy's coming."

I looked down. There was blood on my hands. I began to wipe it on my shirt, as I slowly stepped over Prez's body, and headed upstairs. I walked into Olivia's room, and as soon as she saw me, she stopped crying. She knew her mother and I loved her with all of my heart. I picked her up and positioned myself in the rocking chair that sat beside her crib. I sat in denial, trying my best to phase out everything that was going on around me, but nothing worked. I held back my tears as I tried to rock Olivia to sleep. What was I going to do? I couldn't go back to jail. I couldn't go on the run. Not with a baby. I had no idea what my next move would be. I sat and prayed that these events were nothing more than a bad dream, but the sirens outside my window brought that dream to a reality. Love can make or break anyone, and as for me it took me to my breaking point.

I heard the cops as they kicked in my front door. I didn't move. I continued to rock Olivia to sleep. Within seconds, they made their way into her bedroom.

"Don't move."

It wasn't like I was going anywhere. One of the officers tried to take Olivia away from me, but I wouldn't let go of her.

"No. She's scared."

"I know… Let me take her. She's going to be alright."

I knew I had to let her go. I handed her over to one of the officers while another one handcuffed and escorted me downstairs. I looked as they placed Prez onto a stretcher, and carried him out towards the ambulance. As they were moving him, he was up and yelling in pain. He saw me as one of the officers were escorting me out. He was mumbling something, and then he signaled for my escort to bring me over towards him.

"You shot me." Prez whispered to me.

I looked at him and I didn't know what to think.

"If it hurts, then we're even." The officer then placed me inside of his squad car.

My life was ruined yet again. I allowed my emotions to get the best of me. I was all alone. I no longer had anyone in my life I could turn to. Olivia was taken away from me. Caroline was in the wind. Damien and Rachel were dead to me, and I didn't know what was going on with my parents. As for Prez, his lie was the ultimate betrayal. There were no second chances this time. The life of Rhonda Castillo was officially over and the life of Rhonda Brown had recommenced.

# Chapter 28

# The Unexpected Visitor

It felt like a nightmare that wouldn't stop. My life was once again repeating itself. I was taken to booking where I was processed back into the system. Then I was escorted to my cell, and for the life of me, I couldn't figure out how or why I allowed myself back into this type of situation. Olivia was gone and the guards refused to tell me where she was. I was wrecked with grief. I just wanted to know she was safe. I continued to badger the officers until they walked out of the room, unable to listen to my cries anymore. I tried to focus on something else, anything else, but Olivia was all I could think about. She was scared, in a strange place, and around a bunch of people she didn't know.

A couple of days had passed and I hadn't heard from anyone. Finally, the guard came and informed me that I had a visitor. I was hoping it was Caroline, but it wasn't. I walked out and, to my surprise, saw Maria. I recognized her from the photo I stole from Prez's desk. However, the bags I noticed under her eyes made me wonder if this whole ordeal had caused her as much grief as it had me. In some ways, I hoped it had. But what did she want and why was she here? It wasn't like I had anywhere to go, so I decided to stay and hear her out. I was curious to hear what she had to say. I sat and waited for her to say something. It wasn't like I was going to start off the conversation. She came to see me; I didn't ask to see her.

"So, you're the one." All I could do was stare. Her entire facade sent a flicker of jealousy through me. From her thin petite frame, to her long brown hair, and her freakishly large doey eyes. I could see why Prez was so protective over her. "You shot my husband. Why?"

"Because he pretended to be mine."

"What do you mean he pretended to be your husband? Perez Santiago has only one wife; and that's me."

"Okay."

"Don't be coy with me. You could've killed him."

"I know how to use a gun. I didn't shoot to kill him. I only wanted to wound him so that he could feel the same pain he had inflicted on me."

"Why are you lying to me? No offense, but my husband wouldn't be caught with someone like you. You're not even his type."

Little Miss Prissy was starting to get on my last nerve.

"Why are you here?"

"Because I want the truth."

"No, you don't. You want me to lie to you about what really happened, but I won't. Your husband was a lying, manipulative, hypocritical bastard, and he played me. He fooled me into thinking he was the father of my child, and I was dumb enough to believe him. I actually thought he loved and cared about me, but he didn't. It was all an act. Noting but a bunch of lies."

Maria became uneasy. I could tell my words were making her uncomfortable.

"So, you guys lived together?"

"Yes! He lived with me. I thought we were married. We were raising a child together…and I actually loved him. So, what else do you want to know?"

Maria sat in silence. I could see she was hurting, but I didn't care. I wasn't the creator of her pain. Prez was.

"You know…every time Perez would leave out on an assignment, I hated it. I felt as though his job was taking too much out of him. Whenever he would return home, it was as if there was this distance between us. I figured his cases were becoming too stressful, and because of that, I left him alone. But then I found out about you, and that's when everything started to make sense."

"What do you want from me? You want me to apologize for being in love with a man who I thought was my husband? Well I won't. So, are we done here?"

"You're upset because you feel like Perez lied to you, but it's obvious to me now that…he wasn't playing you…he played me."

I didn't know what Maria's intentions were and I didn't care. I was just ready for her to leave.

"Look, I don't know if Prez—"

"His name is Perez."

"Like I was saying…I don't know if Prez put you up to this, and I don't care, but you can take your sad sob story and bounce. The only person I care about right now is my daughter. That's it. You and your problems with Prez are the least of my concern."

"So, Olivia, she really is your daughter?"

"What did you say?"

"Olivia. That's her name, right? She's your daughter…"

"How do you know her name?"

"Because I met her."

"You met her? When? Where?"

"The night you shot Perez. His squad called and informed me of what happened. I didn't know what was going on. All I knew was that my husband had been shot and—"

"No offense, but what does that have to do with my baby."

"Everything. When I got to the hospital, I saw the paramedics wheeling Perez into the emergency room, and moments later there was this cop who showed up holding a crying baby in his arms." My heart broke. I hated I had put my daughter through so much pain. "I was trying to figure out what was going on with Perez, but the doctors wouldn't let me near him. I kept trying to talk to him, but all he would say to me was 'take care of Olivia', but I didn't know who 'Olivia' was. I continued to hear crying off in the distance, and when I turned, around, all I could see was this baby reaching out for my husband. Perez continued to yell out to me to take care of Olivia, and then they wheeled him off into surgery. His squad leader asked me if I could watch over the baby until either social service, or her next of kin showed up."

I gave Maria a unsettling look.

"Don't worry, I wasn't allowed out of their sight. I took her and I didn't know what to think. She's a cute baby. The officer then informed me that her name was Olivia, and that's when my heart dropped. We wanted kids but the timing was never right, and here it was, Perez had this little person in his life. It wasn't fair."

Tears fell from my eyes, and I quickly wiped them away.

"So, what happened to her? Where's my baby?"

"A social worker came and got her, and then later on, this guy showed up and took her away."

"Who? Did they say who he was?"

"Her father is what I overheard."

I hated that I wasn't with her, but at least she was with Damien and not in the system.

"That's good to know."

"Look, I don't know how to feel about all of this. I know Perez isn't going to be completely honest with me about everything that has happened, but the fact remains...he cared about you, and that doesn't sit very well with me."

"Look at me. As you so politely put it, I was never really a threat to begin with, so what are you so worried about? I'm the one who's locked up behind bars. Not you."

"I'm not worried. I'm just tired of being lied to."

"Well join the club. Look, Maria, I'm not trying to disrespect you in any way, but I don't know you, and for that reason alone, I don't feel any sympathy towards you. I'm not saying that to be mean, but it's the truth. Your husband pretended to love and care about me, and that's what I have a problem with. So, I can't say that it was nice to meet you, but thank you for watching over my daughter." I was done speaking to Maria. "Guard."

I got up to leave, but Maria stopped me.

"Wait."

"What do you want?"

"I'm just curious. How long were you guys together?"

"For almost three years, why?"

"I just wanted to know. That's all."

I turned to face the guard and waited on my escort. My heart was heavy. All I wanted was to see my baby. I went back to my cell and it felt like I was losing my mind. I decided to try and sleep away my problems. I used to do it when I was younger. It worked then, and I prayed that it worked now. I was about to close my eyes when the guard approached my cell stating that I had another visitor. She said it was my lawyer, but I didn't have a lawyer. I walked into the visitation room and it was Stacy.

"Guard, take me back. She's not my lawyer."

"Rhonda, wait. I really need to talk to you."

"Why? So, you can keep trying to stick it to me? I don't have time for this. Guard."

"It's about Rachel."

Rachel was no longer my friend, but if Stacy was here, then it had to be something serious. So, I sat down to hear her out.

"What about Rachel?"

"She's missing, and no one seems to know where to find her."

"Trust me, Rachel's not missing. Wherever she's at, it's where she wants to be."

"I don't know. On the night you shot Prez, Caroline went out looking for Rachel and..."

"Caroline? Wait. Why would she be looking for Rachel?"

"Maybe, because Rachel lied about who gave her the drugs?"

"But why would Caroline care unless…" My sister, my sister. Why couldn't she get anything right? "She wouldn't have. Not Caroline."

"That's what I'm trying to tell you. Damien told me Caroline went off on Rachel for marrying him, and then she ripped into her for saying that I gave her the drugs."

"So, you really didn't do it?"

"No. I may be a lot of things, but I'm not that heartless, and I'm not saying that Caroline is, but she doesn't see things the same way as we do. I learned about what she had done some time back. I'm not proud of it, but Brad had me keeping tabs on Caroline every time she came down to visit."

"He what?"

"Don't flip. He wasn't doing it for the wrong reasons, he just didn't want Caroline to relapse, but what Brad failed to realize was that no one could watch her every minute of every day, but I soon discovered her routine. It was the same every time she came down. She would stop by and visit with me for a while, and then she would go by the prison and visit with Jacob. But what threw me for a loop was the fact that she was spending so much time with Rachel. I followed her one day, and that's when I was able to bust them both. Caroline begged me not to tell Brad that she had relapsed, and Rachel was quick to point the finger at Caroline for getting her hooked."

"Caroline wouldn't do that. She knew what Rachel meant to me."

"Rhonda. Rachel was hurting and Caroline sympathized with her. They both were in pain, and before long, they grew dependent on each other to keep one another's secret. Their plan was going fine until Caroline almost overdosed, and that's when her secret was exposed."

"So, Caroline almost died, and yet that wasn't enough to stop Rachel from using."

"She was hurting, Rhonda. I don't know what was tormenting her, but she was in a lot of pain."

"Okay…so why are you here? To prove that it was my sister who hooked Rachel on drugs, and not you? Well mission accomplished. So, what do you want from me? I don't know where Caroline is if that's what you're hoping for."

"No. That's not why I'm here."

"Then why, because from what you've just told me, Caroline would put an end to your investigation."

"My investigation ended the day you shot Prez. By the way, thank you for that. But no, I'm only here because we really don't know where Rachel is."

"And I'm supposed to know? My best friend betrayed me not once, but twice with Damien. She tried to help him take away my child. Now I get that she's dealing with some issues regarding the choices she's made in her life, but when it comes to Rachel, I don't know her anymore."

"Well, I know this isn't the right time to tell you, but you might as well know."

"Know what?"

"Caroline and I did talk with each other on the night of the shooting. We got into it after I told her about the deal I had made with Jacob in return for his cooperation."

"What deal?"

"I promised his release if he told me the truth about everything that happened."

"So, you expect me to believe that you helped Jacob to be released from prison, even though he lied to you about everything, including messing around with Caroline."

"Yes. I've moved on, but I still wanted to know the truth, and as for Caroline, I haven't seen or heard from her since that day. No one has. Have you?"

I wanted to lie, but I didn't see the point.

"No. I haven't heard from her either."

"Well that goes to show you. Caroline doesn't care about me, you, or anyone else for that matter, including JJ. The only person she seems to care about is herself."

Stacy was right. Caroline had promised to leave with me on the night of the shooting, but as soon as she found out about Jacob's release, she left me high and dry. I couldn't believe it. I actually thought Caroline had changed, but I was wrong.

"You're right. Nothing has changed. Caroline is still the same selfish person she has always been."

Stacy was about to leave, but I stopped her.

"Wait. How's Olivia?"

"She's fine. Damien is taking her back to Tallahassee this weekend."

"He's what…"

"I'm sorry, Rhonda."

Stacy left and I was escorted back to my cell. My heart was aching for my daughter. I longed to see her face. I had no one in my life. Friends didn't exist. There was no one there to comfort me. My world had completely fallen apart. Returning home had become the worst mistake of my life. Why did I ever go back?

# Chapter 29

### Time to Move On

M y arraignment date had finally arrived, and mentally I wasn't even fazed by it. Whatever the judge's decision was it wouldn't have mattered, considering there was, no one in my life who would've been willing to bail me out anyway. I made my way to the courtroom, and, low and behold, Prez and Maria were sitting out in the gallery. I guess they wanted to ensure I stayed locked up. I looked around the courtroom and I didn't see anyone I knew. I would've given anything to catch a glimpse of Caroline's face, but she wasn't there either. I was truly alone. The bailiff called the court to session, and I stood in defeat. I listened as my lawyer struggled to get his words out. I sat in a daze waiting for the guard to escort me back to my cell, but then I heard something unbelievable. The judge stated that due to the mistreatment I had endured from Prez, I had suffered an emotional breakdown and that my actions couldn't be held against me. He then declared that I was free to go. I couldn't believe it. I was free. I looked over as Maria got up and walked out of the courtroom, and all Prez could do was stare at me as I walked away in content. I was so happy. All I could do was smile.

After processing, I was taken to retrieve the rest of my things, and after that, I walked out of jail as a free woman. I didn't have anyone to call, so I went outside to try and catch a cab. The moment I looked up I was stunned to see my father standing across the street waiting for me. It felt like a dream. He began to walk towards me, and as soon as he hugged me, I broke down in tears.

"You came."

"Of course, I came. I received the news the other day about what happened. So why didn't you call me?"

"I don't know. I guess I was ashamed."

"You're my daughter. If anything, I should've heard the news from you, not Stacy."

"Stacy." I couldn't believe she called my parents.

"Yeah, she told me you were arrested for shooting your husband."

"He's not my husband! Never was. Did she tell you that?"

"Look, Rhonda, I don't know what happened, but I do know that if my baby had to shoot anyone, then it was for her own protection."

"No, it wasn't. I shot him because he lied to me, and I couldn't deal with it. I actually thought he loved me, but I was wrong. I was so wrong."

"It's okay, baby."

"So why did you come?"

"I'm here to take you home."

"Home? You know mom isn't going to allow that to happen, but it was a nice gesture anyway."

"No. I've spoken with your mother, and she understands that you need us right now, and that you're coming home with me."

I started to cry even more. I needed them more than they realized.

"Can you take me by my place first? I need to pick up a few things, and then I'll be ready to go."

"Sure, baby. Let's go."

My father drove me to the house. Everything was as it was when they arrested me. I went upstairs to my bedroom and my luggage was still intact. I looked into the slots and the money was still there. I guess the cops didn't think to search anything, since they had me in custody. I sat on the bed and I looked around the room. Everything I knew to be true was a lie. I was angry with my life. It wasn't fair. I looked on my dresser at the picture of me and Prez, and I became enraged. I went downstairs to the kitchen and I grabbed a couple of trash bags. Any pictures I saw of me and Prez, I threw away. My father tried to calm me down, but I was furious.

"Rhonda. Stop. Please, baby, calm down."

"It's not fair. Olivia is gone and I have no one. He lied to me and I hate him. I hate him!"

"What he did to you was wrong, but you've got to move on."

"How? When it hurts? I don't know how to make the pain stop."

"We're going to get through this. You hear me? What he did to you isn't the end of the world, and once you see that you'll be able to move on."

My father was right. I needed to find a way to move on. I went upstairs to finish packing. I took Olivia's suitcase as well. She was going to need her clothes and toys, and hopefully Damien would allow me to give them to her. As I walked downstairs carrying my luggage, I looked up, and there stood Prez, standing in the foyer.

"So, you're really leaving?"

"Where's my father?"

"I asked him to give us some privacy. I really need to talk to you." I looked at Prez and his right arm was in a sling.

"Well I'm sorry, but I have nothing else to say to you. Now if you'll excuse me...I have to go."

I tried to walk past Prez, but he grabbed me by the arm.

"Don't touch me! Don't ever touch me again!"

Prez released my arm. He tried to follow after me, but instead, he bumped into the trash bag that was sitting on the floor. He reached down to pick it up, and I could tell he was in a lot of pain as he tried to lift the bag. He struggled to open it. He tried to pull the straps back and that's when he saw all the pictures I just tossed.

"You're throwing all of these away? Why?".

I turned around and Prez was holding our wedding picture in his hand.

"Because they represent a lie. So, there's no need for them."

Prez took the pictures out of the trash bag and began to place them on the table, one by one. I was outraged. He just wouldn't stop. I took my suitcases and placed them by the door. I went outside and got the lighter fluid and a trashcan. I took the pictures off of the table, and squeezed lighter fluid all over them.

"What are you doing?"

"Putting an end to this game."

I tried to locate a match but I couldn't find one. I rummaged through the kitchen drawers, cabinets, and even the junk basket. Finally, I found a lighter. I tried to light a piece of paper, but Prez slapped it out of my hand.

"You need to stop. Olivia is in those pictures."

"And you think I don't know that? But she's not yours, so why do you even care?"

"She's right. Why do you care?"

We both turned around and Maria was standing in the doorway. What was she doing here? Dealing with Prez was hard enough, but I sure as hell didn't feel like dealing with his wife as well.

"What are you doing here?" Prez walked over to Maria.

"I could ask you the same question."

"Look, Maria." Prez reached out for Maria's hand but she pulled back.

"Don't. I saw you when you left the courthouse and I followed you here. On the ride over, I passed through all these beautiful neighborhoods, and it amazed me that you were actually living here. I tried for years to get you to buy us a house, but you wouldn't. Telling me the timing was never right, but as I look around, it's become apparent who you seem to have time for, and it sure as hell wasn't me."

Maria looked at me with tears in her eyes.

"Look, Maria, it was just part of the job. A cover. That's all."

Maria looked around the house.

"A cover."

She walked over towards the trashcan, and picked up one of the pictures out of it. I wasn't in the mood for their marital spat, so I decided to walk off.

"And where are you going?" Was this chick serious? Was she really questioning me?

"Wait a minute. I know you didn't just ask me that. What I do is none of your business—at all. Now when it comes to you and Prez, the two of you can discuss whatever you want, but don't you ever question me about anything I do. Ever."

"I didn't mean it like that. I…"

"Maria, word of advice. Just let it go." As I was walking towards the door, I stopped and turned around to hand Maria what represented the biggest lie of all. My wedding and promise ring. "You're his real wife, so I think these belong to you."

Maria looked at the rings and began to cry. With tears in her eyes, she turned to face Prez.

"Are you kidding me? Look at these. I can only image how much they cost. We live in an apartment, and you bought her a house. You pretended to be a father to her child, and now this." Maria continued to look at the rings. "You know what? I don't think this was an act at all. You really did love her, didn't you? And the only person you ended up fooling was yourself."

I didn't have time for their lover's quarrel. I grabbed my luggage and headed out the door. My father placed my suitcases in the trunk of his car, and I gazed at my house one last time, before we drove off. As we headed towards the airport, nothing seemed real. On the plane ride back to Florida, all I could think about was my life with Prez, and how it was nothing but a lie. I couldn't stop the tears from flowing. My father tried to comfort me, but there was nothing he could say to make the pain go away.

Once our flight landed, my father drove us home, and all I could think about was the life I left and the one I was returning to. As we pulled into the driveway, I sat in the car, too ashamed to move, but my father finally convinced me to get out. I walked into the house and it smelled like my mother was preparing dinner. It felt like home again. I placed my bags by the door and I walked towards the kitchen. I stood and watched my mother as she worked in her element. I didn't know what to say, so I walked over and hugged her.

"I'm sorry. For everything. I'm so sorry."

I held on to my mother. I didn't care how she felt about me. I just wanted her to know that I loved and needed her. As soon as I released her, she grabbed hold of me and hugged me back. All I could do was cry. I had my parents back. Both of them.

"No. I'm the one who's sorry. I'm your mother and I wasn't there for you. I had all of this hate inside my heart, and I ended up blaming everyone else for my pain, even you, and for that I'm sorry." I looked at my mother, and smiled. "Now go and freshen up. Dinner will be ready soon."

My father carried my luggage upstairs to my bedroom. As I looked around the room, part of me felt like a kid again. I felt fortunate to have my parents back in my life which made starting over a little bit easier.

As I washed up for dinner, I began to feel dizzy. I figured it was due to all of the craziness I had experienced throughout the day, but then the nausea came, and I knew it had to be something more. This feeling was familiar. I had only felt it one other time and that was when…no, it couldn't be. I asked my father if I could borrow his car to run to the store. When I made it back to the house, I hurried upstairs and took out two pregnancy tests. As I sat on the bed, I could hear my father calling for me to come down for dinner, but I wasn't budging until I was able to read my test results. I went into the bathroom to check the first test. My heart sank. My suspicion was confirmed: I was pregnant. Again. I glanced at the other test just to be sure, and they were both positive. What was I going to do? I had already lost Olivia to Damien, and there was no way I could lose this baby to Prez and Maria. I became apprehensive. I didn't know how to feel. I was happy about the pregnancy, but disappointed with my current situation.

I made my way downstairs, and it felt nice having dinner with my parents again. I looked at them, and I figured they should at least know the truth about the baby, since I was going to be living with them for a while.

"This is nice." My father seemed genuinely happy.

"Yes…it is, but Mom and Dad there's something you should know."

"What is it? Is everything okay?" I could hear the anxiety in my mother's voice.

"Yes. Everything's fine, but…" I didn't know if I could tell them the truth. I had disappointed them once before, and I didn't know if I could do it again.

"But what? What is it, Rhonda?" I could see the concern on my father's face, so I decided to tell them about the baby.

"I'm pregnant. I promise once I'm out of my first trimester—I'll start looking for a job, and…"

"You're pregnant?" I was trying to read my mother's expression, but I couldn't tell if she was excited or just shocked.

"Yes, but understand, when this baby was conceived, I thought it was with my husband, and…"

"No. We understand, and we'll do whatever we can to help you. Besides, it'll be nice to hear some pitter-patter around the house again."

I couldn't believe my mother was being so understanding. I sat and enjoyed my parents' company, and as long as Prez stayed out of the picture, then everything would be okay. I was tired of playing the fool. When it came to him or any other man, my heart had grown cold. It was time I started to get what I wanted out of life. Things were going to change, and this time they were going to happen on my terms.

# Chapter 30

### ⚜

## The Compromise

I sat in my room thinking about the baby growing inside me, and as much as I hated Prez, I missed him. I needed to clear my head, so I decided I would go out for a ride. When I reached for my purse, I noticed I still had the picture frame I had swiped from Prez's office desk sitting in my bag. Seeing the picture of him and Maria together only reinforced my decision to follow through with my current plans. I decided to keep the picture as a reminder of why I was keeping the baby a secret. As I was removing the picture from the frame, the unexpected happened. A family photo of me, Prez, and Olivia fell out from behind the picture of Prez and Maria. I saw the picture and I broke down in tears. I truly loved Prez, but I no longer cared if he really loved me or not; I just needed to move on. I rubbed my belly and I began to think about the baby. There was no way I was allowing anyone to take anything else away from me again. I got dressed, borrowed my parent's car, and I went out to see Damien. I didn't know if he was going to allow me to see Olivia or not, but one way or another, I was going to see my daughter.

I made my way to Tallahassee, and all I could think about was seeing Olivia. I pulled up to Damien's house and rang the doorbell. As the door opened, I could hear Olivia crying in the distance.

"Rhonda? What are you doing here? I thought you were still locked up."

"I was, but the judge decided to let me go." I tried to peep around Damien to see why Olivia was crying. All I wanted to do was to hold my baby. "Is she alright?"

"She's fine. So, what do you want?"

"What do you think I want? I want to see my daughter."

"Rhonda…"

"Don't. Don't shut me out of my daughter's life. Like I told you before, I didn't know you were her father. Stacy admitted to me in court that Prez tampered with the test. So, come on. Don't try and hold this against me."

Damien seemed hesitant about letting me in, but then he stepped aside and waved me on through. As I entered the house, I headed for Olivia, and once she saw me, it was as if nothing had changed. The moment I embraced her in my arms, she stopped crying. I sat down with her on the couch, and it felt nice to talk and play with her again. I looked over at Damien, and even though it felt like he was supervising my time with Olivia, I didn't care. I was just happy to have my baby in my arms again. Olivia became fussy, and I knew she was due for a nap. As I rocked her to sleep, I picked up her right hand, and began to play with her fingers. Even after Olivia had fallen asleep, I continued to hold her. I missed her so much. Damien made an attempt to move Olivia, but I wouldn't let her go.

"Come on, Rhonda. I need to lay her down."

"No. Not yet. Just let me hold her for a little while longer."

Damien caved in and walked away. Time passed and before long, I had fallen asleep with Olivia on my chest. When I woke up, I started to panic when I noticed Olivia wasn't in my arms. I assumed Damien must've taken her and put her down. As I began to move around, I looked down and saw that he had given me a blanket while

I slept. I turned over and let out a yelp because Damien's face lay inches from mine. I stared at him for a moment, slightly amazed that he didn't wake up from that. I had to give it to him—he was trying, but shutting me out of my daughter's life wasn't an option. I pulled back the blanket and tried to ease off the couch, but his eyes opened.

"Hey, you're leaving?"

"Yeah. I booked a room downtown, and if it's okay with you, I would like to come by tomorrow and spend more time with Olivia. I really miss her."

"Rhonda. Even though the judge gave me full custody of Olivia, I would never keep her away from you. I didn't go after Olivia to hurt you. I did it to ensure she became a part of my life."

I began to sympathize with Damien, but I shut those emotions down immediately. The only ones I would truly give my heart to were going to be my kids, and no one else. I had endured enough pain and I wasn't about to allow anyone else to hurt me...ever again.

"For the past two years, I thought Olivia was Prez's daughter. So, you weren't the only one who was duped in this situation. The person you loved didn't lie to you every waking moment about who they really were, and how they truly felt about you..."

I had to stop myself. I was allowing my anger to surface. I was there for one reason and one reason only, and that was to see my daughter.

"No, I understand."

"No. You don't understand. You don't know how it feels to have everything taken away from you. To have the people you love turn their backs on you. To have your friends betray you. Hell...even you had the nerve to betray me..."

I was doing it again. I was allowing my emotions to get the best of me. I knew how to shut them down, but then I began to think, and it clicked. The only way to ensure Olivia stayed a part of my life was to incorporate Damien back into mine. I was willing to do anything to keep my daughter with me. I wasn't proud of the person I was becoming, but I had to do what needed to be done.

"I didn't want to hurt you, but you left me no other choice."

"No. You were weak! You allowed your father to come in and take over, and make my life a living hell. You could've filed for joint custody, but you didn't. You knew how much I loved my daughter, and you knew how I felt about Prez, and yet you allowed your hurt to guide you. You decided to take away the one person I loved the most, my daughter."

"I wasn't weak! I was hurt. When I look at Olivia, the first thing I see is us. I watched as Prez lived the life I was supposed to be living. He had my daughter and, most importantly, he had you. I wasn't trying to hurt you, but it was hard trying to come to terms with the truth—that you really were in love with Prez, and for me, that hurt like hell."

"Well, if it makes you feel any better, I discovered I was in a one-sided relationship. I loved Prez. He didn't love me."

"I find that tough to believe. It's hard not to love you."

Damien was saying everything I needed to hear. He still cared about me, and that was going to be my way back into Olivia's life.

"You didn't love me. If you did, you would've never slept with Rachel."

"Rachel. Rachel was the biggest mistake of my life. Hell, the only reason I slept with her was to get back at you. Five years we were together, and you allowed this guy to come in, and take you away from me. I was hurt, and I wanted you to hurt as well."

"Well you succeeded in that, because the two of you hurt me deeply. Now if you'll excuse me, I have to go."

I started to walk off.

"Rhonda, wait. You don't have to leave."

"No. I do. It's getting dark, and I need to check into the hotel, before it gets too late."

"You can stay here."

I thought my ears were deceiving me.

"You want me to stay here, but why?"

"Because, I have a spare bedroom that no one is using. So, if you want it, then it's yours. Besides, it'll keep you from having to go out and pay for a hotel room. You came all this way just to spend time with Olivia, and I'm not about to stop you from doing that."

I didn't want it to show, but I was so excited. I looked at Damien and hesitated before extending my hand to him.

"Seriously?" Damien smirked.

"Come on, Damien." He took the peace offering and shook my hand. See? We can be mature, I almost wanted to say, but decided against it. "Thank you," I said.

Damien set me up in his spare bedroom, but it didn't do any good, because I stayed in Olivia's room the entire time. I was sitting in the rocking chair watching her sleep when Damien walked into the room.

"She's so beautiful."

"Yes, she is."

"Rhonda, there's something you need to know."

Damien seemed nervous about what he had to say.

"Okay. So, what is it?"

"My job offered me a position in London, and I took it."

"You what! And how am I supposed to see Olivia? London. Really, Damien?"

My world was crashing again. While I was trying to process what I had just heard, my cell was going off repeatedly. I glanced at the screen and saw it was Prez. I hit 'ignore'. I had nothing else to say to him.

"Who was that?"

"No one. I just need to change my number, that's all. But anyway, don't try and change the subject. London. Come on, Damien. How does London fit in with me trying to spend time with Olivia? How am I supposed to make that work?"

"Easy. I want you to come with us."

I was trying to hatch out a plan but going to London wasn't even a consideration. I looked over at Olivia, and I thought about the baby I was carrying. London would be a good way to hide my pregnancy from Prez, because by no means did, I ever want him to find out about the baby I was carrying.

"You want me to come to London with you...why?"

"Because nothing has changed. You know how I feel about you...and besides, Olivia is going to need her mother there with her."

I was grateful for what Damien was trying to do, but I was still in love with Prez, and as much as I loved him, I knew that in order for me to move on, I had to figure out a way to let him go.

"If I'm to go to London with you, then there's something about me you should know."

"And what's that?"

"I'm pregnant, and, yes, it's Prez's baby. Now I don't expect you to be cool about this in any way, but I'm putting it out there so you'll know."

"You're pregnant?"

"Yes."

"So does Prez know?"

"No, and that's the way I would like to keep it. I know I'm wrong for wanting to do this, but that's just how I feel right now. Prez lied to me and the truth was hidden away from you. So, my question to you is, knowing that Prez willfully lied to the both of us, are you capable of doing the same thing in return?"

Damien stood in deep thought. I knew I was asking a lot from him, but I was hurting, and I felt as though it was only fair if I was able to capitalize on my pain.

"If I was to say yes, would you come to London with me?"

"Only if you're serious."

"But as my wife."

I was shocked. I didn't know what to say. "Your what? But that wasn't part of the deal."

"I know, but those are my terms."

"But you're still married to Rachel. Remember that?"

"No. I *was* married to Rachel, but not anymore. We only agreed to a fake marriage just for the court's sake."

"Okay, but I still can't marry you."

"And why not? Your marriage to Prez was a sham. So, what's stopping you?"

Even though my marriage to Prez wasn't real on paper, it was nonetheless real to me, and the reality of that situation still hurt like hell.

"Well, for starters, I'm not in love with you, so why would I marry you?"

"Consider it for show. When I go to London, I want to make a respectable first impression, and showing up as a single parent isn't the way to go. So, what do you say?"

"I don't know."

"Come on, Rhonda. My marriage to Rachel is null and void. So, marry me."

I thought about what Damien was asking, and I began to think to myself. *Who was really playing who?*

"Fine. I'll marry you, but under one condition. Kill the custody ruling. I'm Olivia's mother and there's no way around that. If you want me to agree to this, then the court ruling has to be out."

"Deal." I felt as though I was making a deal with the devil. Damien wanted me back in his life, and I guess he was willing to do whatever he had to in order to make that happen, even if that meant using our daughter as leverage. I looked at Olivia and I just prayed I was making the right decision. "Come on, it's not going to be that bad. At one point in time you did love me."

"You're right, I did."

"And you know I'll always love you right?"

"Yeah. I know, but in order for me to do this, I'm going to need your help with something."

"And what's that?"

"I need you to help me free myself of Prez. I need him out of my system."

I walked over to Damien and I stood before him broken. Against my better judgment, I forced myself to kiss him. The entire time I was kissing him, I was thinking about Prez. How do you rid yourself of someone who was once a part of you?

"Rhonda…"

"Hush. Just shut up and go along with it."

Damien stopped kissing me and pushed me away.

"I can't. Right now, you're not even here with me. I can feel it in your kiss. You're a million miles away. Now I get that you're hurting, but you can't use me to get over your pain."

"And why not?" I went back to kissing on Damien. "This is what you wanted right?"

"Yes, but not like this. I want you to want me and right now I know that isn't a possibility. You're broken here." Damien placed his hand over my heart. "And it's affecting you here." And he started to caress my head. "Now I don't know what this guy did to you, but you need time to heal."

Slowly, I began to break down and, before long, I was in tears. Damien was right. I was hurting, and I willing to do anything to suppress my pain. I knew Damien was probably uncomfortable with trying to console me when my heart was breaking over another man, but he hugged me and I just broke down in his arms. I cried and cried. I was hurting, and all I wanted was for the pain to stop, and I didn't know what to do in order to make that happen. Damien picked me up, and he took me to my room, and he laid me down on the bed. What surprised me was the fact that he decided to get in the bed with me. He didn't say anything, nor did he try to make a move on me; he just held me in his arms as I cried like a baby.

When I woke up the next morning, I was still in Damien's arms. He stayed in the room with me the entire night. I knew he loved me, but how was I to find the love I once had for him? Prez was the only guy who I had willingly given all of myself to. I stared at Damien as he slept. I knew he truly love me, and for Olivia's sake I needed to find my way back to him. I didn't know what I was thinking, but I kissed Damien on the lips while he was sleeping, and he woke up.

"Rhonda."

"Yes…"

I continued to kiss Damien on the lips.

"What are you doing?"

"I'm trying to find my way back to you."

"But you're not ready to go there and you know it."

"I know, but I'm willing to try. If I'm going to marry you, then I at least owe it to myself to get to know you again."

I continued to kiss Damien until he finally gave in. Even though we didn't make love, his kisses alone were enough to make me feel loved.

"Don't ever leave me again."

My heart felt torn. I could easily tell I had hurt Damien by leaving him for Prez.

"As long as you promise not to hurt me again."

"Promise."

I fulfilled my promise to Damien and we were married. My parents came out to the ceremony, and, as strange as it was, Gregory and Stacy even showed up. Damien kept his end of the bargain as well, and the full custody ruling in regards to Olivia was overturned. I packed up all of my belongings, and I prepared myself for the new life that awaited me in London. My relationship with my parents had been renewed. Caroline was still in the wind with Jacob. Rachel had literally disappeared and no one knew of her whereabouts, and as for Prez, I was slowly allowing myself to get over him. I was a new woman. Ready to start on a new adventure. Rhonda Castillo may have been a fabrication, but Rhonda Fletcher was my new reality, and she was here to stay.

# Part III

Discovering Self-Love

In life we can pretend to be happy
We can try and mask our pain
We'll go as far as living in denial
We'll do anything to sustain

We'll fight off our true feelings
We'll bury all our emotions
We'll ignore our desires
We'll lie under any notion

But know that in the end
The truth will reveal
How the power of love
Has the amazing power to heal.

# Prologue

I tried to get up but I couldn't move. What was I thinking? Why was I continuously hurting myself? My heart was racing, my thoughts were scattered, and it felt as though I couldn't breathe. All I could do was lie on the floor in pain. Every time my eyes closed, I would feel a rocking motion as if someone was shaking me back and forth.

"Rhonda. Can you hear me?"

A voice echoed in my head, but no matter how hard I tried, I couldn't respond.

"Rhonda! Come on!"

I could no longer feel the pain that use to saturate my heart. My body became relaxed. I could feel the pulsating of my heart as it beat in my chest. My heartbeat was no longer erratic. It had taken on a slow and steady pace. What was happening to me? I could feel the tears as they ran down my face, but no matter how hard I tried, I wasn't able to move my hands in order to wipe them away.

"Don't do this to me! Come on. Wake up."

I could hear screaming all around me, but I couldn't move. I was so tired, and all I wanted to do was to sleep.

"Rhonda! Wake up. Baby, please wake up!"

I tried to open my eyes, but my eyelids were way too heavy. I was trying to remember what had just happened, but I couldn't. Then, out of nowhere, I felt a slap across my face. The intensity of the blow allowed me to open my eyes, and when I looked up, the only person I could see was Damien.

"Damien?"

"Yes. It's me, baby. Come on. Wake up."

"But I'm so tired…just let me sleep." My eyes started to close and that's when Damien started to freak out.

"No. Come on, Rhonda…don't close your eyes. You have to stay awake for me. Open your eyes. Come on, baby. Open your eyes. I'm sorry. I'm so sorry. Please wake up."

I tried to open my eyes, but I couldn't. All I wanted to do was sleep. I had been through enough heartache in my life, and for once, I couldn't feel any pain. My heart wasn't breaking. I wasn't lying to anyone and no one was lying to me. I no longer had to choose. There was no reason for me to wake up. I continued to feel my heartbeat as it grew slower and slower. I could no longer hear the voices all around me. I finally felt at peace.

# Chapter 31

❧

# Living the Life

I was running late. Shoes were scatted across the floor, dresses were flying in the air, and my head was covered in countless rollers. I was trying to pace myself but time wasn't on my side. Damien was picking me up within the hour, the babysitter was running late, and dinner wasn't close to being ready. Dominick was aggravating Olivia by pulling her hair and she was having a fit for him to stop. I didn't have time to deal with either one of them. I needed to get dressed and finish preparing dinner. I rushed around the house, and before long, I was half way dressed and dinner was finally ready. I placed Dominick in his booster seat, and Olivia eventually made her way to the table. I fixed their plates and then headed towards the bedroom. While they were eating, I needed to finish getting dressed, and hopefully do something with my hair. I looked at the clock and time was quickly passing me by. My babysitter, Julie, was running late and Damien was on his way. Finally, I heard the doorbell ring. I raced downstairs, and it was none other than, Julie.

"Mrs. Fletcher, I'm so sorry. My dad's car broke down, and I had to wait until I was able to get a jump."

"Don't worry about it. I'm just glad you're here. The munchkins are in the kitchen eating dinner, and watch out for Dominick tonight. He's doing everything he can to irritate Livy and it's working, because, as you can hear, she's in a crabby mood tonight."

I didn't know what to do with the two of them. I felt like putting them outside in the cold. Now that Julie had arrived, I could finish getting dressed. I was so excited about getting out of the house. Damien got us tickets to a stage play in the city, and I didn't care what the play was about, as long as it got me out of the house and away from Frit and Frat.

I heard the car horn. Damien was outside. I bundled up and headed out. Florida and London were like night and day. I missed my sunshine state. Anyone who craved the cold weather could have it. I ran out to the car, and Damien was sitting on the driver's side looking quite striking. He had on his black and white attire and it looked rather good on him.

"Oh, I like. So, where did you get the outfit?" I said smiling.

"I stopped by and picked up a rental after work. You look pretty good yourself."

I just had on a simple black dress and some red pumps. It was the only two things I could put together at the last minute that seemed to match.

"Whatever. You don't have to lie to me, but it was the best I could do in such a short time."

"And yet it works. In my eyes you will always be the most beautiful woman in the world. So, it doesn't matter what you wear, you'll always look good to me."

"Awe...you are so sweet. I love you."

"I love you too."

Damien and I enjoyed the show, and it felt good to be out of the house and to partake in some adult conversation. The only time I was ever separated from the kids was when I was away at work. I worked part time at the Milford Medical Laboratory in London. I loved my job, and I enjoyed motherhood as well, but I needed a life outside the home and away from the kids. No matter how much I loved them, they could easily become a handful at any time.

As we were returning home, I noticed we were heading back in the wrong direction.

"Hey. Where are you going? Home isn't this way."

"I know, but I have a surprise for you."

"Really? A surprise for me?"

"Yes. So, enjoy the ride and we'll be there soon."

I couldn't wait to see what it was. I needed some excitement in my life. The everyday norm was starting to take its toll on me. Before long, we had arrived at a hotel located on the outskirts of town.

"What are we doing here?"

"This is your surprise. We are going to enjoy a weekend retreat together."

"Are you serious? Just me and you, and no kids for the entire weekend?"

"Yes. Just me and you. No kids. So, are you excited?"

"Of course, I'm excited. You don't know how badly I needed this break."

"Well that's good to hear because this weekend is all about you."

As we got out of the car, it dawned on me that I didn't have an overnight bag.

"Wait. This isn't going to work."

"Why? What's wrong?"

"I don't have any change of clothing."

"Stop worrying. I told you, this weekend is all about you. I took care of everything. So, come on."

All I could do was smile. I always felt as though Damien enjoyed being a family man. He was such a great father and a wonderful husband. He was very committed to his family, but I, on the other hand, couldn't say the same, because no matter how good Damien was to me, there was always this void in my heart that I could never explain.

Damien booked the penthouse suite and the ambiance was so romantic. Soft-toned furniture, candles, a fireplace, and champagne chilling on the table. Damien tipped the bellboy, and then he walked over and gave me a kiss. I felt so relaxed. I flopped down on the sofa and closed my eyes.

"Hey. There will be none of that."

"What are you talking about? All I'm doing is relaxing. You know how to do that right?"

"I do."

Damien walked into the bathroom and drew us a bath. We sat in the tub together, and I began to unwind.

"Thank you. I really needed this."

"I figured that much."

"Why would you say that?"

"Remember the other day when the kids were playing around the house together? Dominick accidently pulled Olivia's hair, and she started crying, and you almost bit his head off. I didn't know what was going on with you, but I figured you needed a break."

I thought about that day, and I did mistreat my baby. I knew he was only playing around with his sister, but I was so tired of all the back and forth with the both of them that I just snapped.

"You caught that, huh?"

"Yes. So, what's going on with you? Is there something I should know about?"

"No. There's nothing going on. I was just tired, that's all. They had been at each other's throats all day, and I couldn't take it anymore. I didn't mean to yell at my baby; I just wanted to noise to stop."

"Okay. I realize you're tired, and being stuck at home all day with two kids it can be stressful at times, but if you need some extra help, then let me know. I could easily hire you a permanent sitter if that would help."

"No…I'm good. I can take care of my own kids."

"You know that's not what I meant. Look. I get that we're a long way from home, but I don't want you to ever feel overwhelmed or trapped by the kids."

"And I don't. Yes, they can be a handful at times, but we're good."

"Rhonda..."

"I'm serious, Damien. I'm okay."

"Alright, I'm not going to fight you on this, but if it ever becomes too much for you, then I want you to let me know. Okay?"

"Okay."

I became irritated by the entire conversation. As I made a move to get out of the tub, Damien pulled me back in. He could tell I was upset.

"And where are you going?"

"To get dressed for bed if that's okay with you."

"No. It's not."

"And why not?"

"Look, tonight was supposed to be special, and all I did was upset you, and for that, I'm sorry."

"I know you didn't mean to. I just..."

And before I could say anything else Damien leaned over and kissed me. He continued to kiss me until I forgot what I was mad about. We made our way from the bathroom into the bedroom. Being with Damien was definitely what my body needed. I had so much built-up tension inside me that I released it all out onto Damien, and he enjoyed every minute of it.

"What's gotten into you?"

"Nothing. I just missed you. That's all."

Damien took over and he tried to control the moment, but I wouldn't let him. I wanted him and it showed with every kiss, touch, and position I placed him in. It felt as though we made love the entire night.

Marrying Damien was probably the best thing I could've done for me and the kids. He was such a good father. No matter what I needed help with, he was always there. It was hard in the beginning to find the love I once had for him, considering Prez took it all away and destroyed it. But over the course of the three years we had been married, Damien showed me just how much he truly loved me, and I knew then that I had made the right decision. He always treated Dominick as his own, and that made me love him even more, considering Dominick was a spitting image of Prez. As for Prez, I hadn't spoken to him since the day I left him in DC. There were times when I wanted to call and let him know about Dominick, but then I would always think back to how he made a fool of me, and that would kill any notion I had of telling him the truth. My life had truly changed for the better, and I was so grateful with each and every day that Damien was a part of my life.

# Chapter 32

·⁂·

# A Distressed Heart

M y weekend was perfect. I came home feeling renewed and relaxed. I checked the answering machine, and there was a message on there from my parents. They had called to check on me and the kids. When it came to my parents, I was always in constant contact with them. They would even fly out to visit during the holidays. I felt so blessed to have them back in my life. As for Caroline, she waited until I moved away to London, before she finally got up the nerve to call me. She claimed she was too ashamed to face me, after she had the nerve to ditch me in DC for Jacob. I fussed her out, but when it was all said and done, I ended up forgiving her anyway. What else could I do? After all, we were sisters. As for Rachel, I finally got a letter from her about two years ago. She apologized for stabbing me in the back with Damien, and even though it was hard for me to forgive her, I did. I didn't want to be the reason for her relapsing, so I wrote her back accepting her apology and I even invited her out to visit me in London, but she never came. Stacy ended up marrying Gregory, and she became my mother-in-law. That's something I still haven't grown accustomed to, but for once in my life everything seemed pretty normal, and I was enjoying every minute of it. Another message played. It was from Caroline. She sounded upset, and she begged for me to call her as soon as possible. The distress in her voice scared me because I didn't know what was wrong. I called her phone and it rang for what seemed like forever before she finally picked up.

"Hey, it's me. What's going on? I got your message and you sounded upset. What's wrong?"

"Rhonda. Thank God. I've been trying to reach you all weekend."

"I was away with Damien. You're scaring me. What's wrong?"

"Okay, you may have to sit down for this."

"Caroline, what's going on?" Caroline let out a muffled cry. "Caroline. Tell me what's wrong."

"It's Rachel."

"Okay. What about Rachel? What happened?"

"She's dead, Rhonda."

The phone fell from my hand. I stood in shock and I couldn't move. I could hear Caroline calling out to me over the phone, but I couldn't respond. Rachel was dead. It was like my mind couldn't register the concept of Rachel being gone. All I could do was cry. It felt as though someone was playing a cruel joke on me, and it wasn't funny. I was trying to hide my emotions, but Olivia could sense I was upset.

"Mommy, are you okay?" I looked at Olivia and all I could do was cry. "Mommy…"

I knew my crying was starting to upset her. I had to snap out of my trance and take care of my daughter.

"Mommy's fine. I'm sorry. Mommy didn't mean to scare you. Now go back in the living room and watch TV with Dominick. Okay."

"Okay."

I needed answers. I forced myself to pick up the phone and continue my conversation with Caroline.

"Caroline."

"Yes. Rhonda, are you okay?"

"No. What happened? Are you sure Rachel's dead?"

"Yes. Justine called Mom and Dad last night crying her eyes out. I couldn't believe it when I heard the news myself."

"Oh my God. How did this happen?"

"She overdosed. Justine found her dead in her apartment last night."

"No...No..." I became overrun with grief. I tried to control myself to keep from upsetting the kids, but nothing was working. I decided to go into the bedroom to try and finish my conversation with Caroline.

"But I don't understand. I thought Rachel was clean. So, what happened?"

"I don't know. She must have relapsed. I'm so sorry, Rhonda."

"I have to come home. I need to see my friend. Has anyone mentioned anything about a service?"

"No, not yet, but knowing Justine it'll probably be on Saturday."

I continued to break down over the phone.

"I can't believe this. This is all my fault. I should've been there for her. She needed me, and I wasn't there."

"Come on, Rhonda, you can't do this to yourself. There was nothing you could've done to stop this from happening. Rachel was hurting and now she's at peace."

Why did Caroline say that? I began to brawl like a baby. My friend was gone. All we shared were a few phone calls over the course of the three years I was away. It was bad enough I missed her, but now she was gone forever. My heart couldn't take it.

"Call Mom and Dad for me, and let them know that I'm coming home as soon as possible."

"I'll call them, but, Rhonda, there's something else you should know before you return home."

"And what's that?"

"Justine blames you for Rachel's addiction...so you might want to stay clear of her when you return home."

"Me…but why would she blame me? I didn't hook Rachel on drugs; that was you."

"But Justine doesn't know that. All she knows is that you sold drugs out of the shop. So, when you come home, just remember, no Justine. Okay?"

"Fine…bye."

I hung up the phone, and I didn't know how to feel. Rachel was gone. I knew she was hurting, but I underestimated the amount of pain she was really in. I tried to call Damien, but I couldn't pull myself together to dial the numbers. I was too upset. Moments later, Olivia walked into my bedroom, and she saw me crying on the bed. I picked her up, and I hugged her with all my might. Dominick walked into the room, and I hugged him as well. I knew my children were frightened, but I couldn't stop the tears from flowing. My best friend was gone and I couldn't change that.

Time passed, and I finally put the kids down for a nap. I grabbed a couple of suitcases, and I began to pack for my trip back home. I heard the front door close. Damien was home. He walked into the bedroom and he saw the suitcases on the bed.

"Hey, baby. What's going on?"

"I have to go home." I continued to pack. It was like I was possessed. I could hear and see Damien, but I couldn't stop myself.

"Go home for what?"

"Rachel. I have to go and see Rachel."

Damien tried to get my attention by grabbing hold of my hands, but I pushed him away, and I continued to pack.

"Rhonda. What's wrong with you?" Damien grabbed hold of me, but I fought against him. "Rhonda! Stop." But I couldn't stop. I was so angry and upset. "Rhonda! What's wrong with you?" I was so overrun with grief that it finally brought me to tears. I couldn't stop crying. I was in so much pain. "Rhonda, talk to me. I can't help you unless you tell me what's wrong."

"Rachel's dead." I continued to cry. I couldn't stop blaming myself for Rachel's death.

"Rachel's what?"

"She's dead! She overdosed over the weekend. I told her to call me whenever things got too rough. Why didn't she call me? Why didn't she call?"

Damien tried to comfort me, but I was a wreck. I kept thinking if I would have done this or if I would have done that, then maybe things would've turned out differently. I kept beating myself up over the situation, knowing that no matter what I would've done, it wouldn't have changed anything.

"Rhonda, I need you to calm down." I tried, but it was too hard. "Come on. Calm down. Now listen to me. Rachel loved you, and you loved her as well. So, don't beat yourself up over this. This is not your fault."

"Yes, it is…I was her best friend. I was supposed to have been there for her, but I wasn't, and now she's dead."

"This is not on you. You hear me? You could only do so much…"

"No! I could've done more. I should've never moved here. I was too far away from home, and Rachel needed me, and I…"

"Stop. Let's not go there. You're grieving and I understand that, but you will not blame yourself or anyone else for Rachel's death. Understood?"

I nodded my head. I couldn't stop crying. Rachel was gone. She never had a chance to meet Dominick. There was so much we needed to catch up on, and now that would never happen. I missed her so much.

Damien, the kids and I packed up and headed to Florida, and my parents had us stay with them. I wanted to go and see Justine, but I didn't want to upset her, so I never went. I sat in my room thinking about everything that had happened. Noting seemed real. I heard a noise at my door and it was my mother.

"Hey…so how are you feeling?"

"Okay, I guess. I still can't believe she's gone."

"I know, but it's going to be okay. You have to believe that."

"How? She was my best friend. We just started back talking to each other, and now this. Not once did she mention to me that anything was wrong. Why?"

I started to cry. I was so tired of crying. My eyes were sore, and my heart couldn't take any more.

"Sometimes when people are in pain, they don't know how to express themselves. She held on to her pain, and in the end, it cost her everything."

"But why? I don't get why this had to happen to her."

"We may never know why, but you have to be strong. You have two beautiful children who love and need you, and what you can't do is allow your grief to get in the way of their wellbeing."

"I know, and I'm trying."

"Well I need you to try harder. Damien told me you're not eating and you're barely sleeping. I need you to do better. You can't fall apart on your family because you're grieving. They need you as well."

"I know Mom and I'm trying." My mother hugged me, and then she kissed me on the forehead.

I got up and looked out of the window. Damien was outside playing with the kids. I loved them, and for their sake I needed to do better.

"Rhonda." I looked in the doorway and it was Caroline. She walked over to hug me, but I pushed her away. "Rhonda…"

"Don't. This is all your fault. Rachel would still be alive if you would've never hooked her on drugs. She was my best friend, Caroline, and you took her away from me."

"No…"

"Yes. This is all your fault and there's no way around it. You hooked Rachel on something she couldn't control, and it killed her. Now I accept the part I played in causing her pain, but you…there are no words for what you've done."

"You think I enjoyed giving Rachel drugs, no…but I was high, and it felt good to have someone else to get high with. I didn't feel alone. She may have been your best friend, but she was my friend as well. She understood my pain and I understood hers."

Caroline was in tears, and in one way or another, we both played a role in Rachel's downfall.

"I can't do this with you."

"Do what? You think you're the only one in pain? Well wake up, Rhonda. There are other people hurting besides you. You're so quick to judge, but until you have walked in my shoes, you'll never understand my pain."

"I don't understand your pain? Are you serious? You were beaten and raped; well, guess what? So was I. You've had failed relationships. Same here. You've been in and out of jail. Well, guess what? Me too. I've been through the same kind of hell as you, but you don't see me out shooting up or getting high."

"Well maybe you're just stronger than me. How about that? Everyone can't be a robot like you. Some of us actually have feelings."

"So now I'm a robot, because I choose to not let my failures run my life. I have feelings. There are days I feel as though I'm about to explode, but guess what, I have to think about how that would affect me in the long run, so I press on. Some of us don't have the luxury of getting high whenever things don't go our way."

"You...pressed on. What a bunch of bull. So why didn't you just press on when Prez lied to you, instead of shooting him? You can't control your emotions any better than I can. I chose to get high. Not my proudest moments, but I've accepted my flaws. But you...you live in denial. You act upon your hurt, and you're willing to destroy anyone who gets in your way. Your problems are more deadly than any drug I could ever shoot up."

Caroline was right. I didn't know how to control my emotions, but one thing was certain; I didn't allow them to run my life.

"You keep telling yourself that. Meanwhile, I'm going to visit my friend who happens to be dead, because of all the dope she shot up in her veins. The same stuff you claim isn't deadly. Remember?"

I put on my black shades that coordinated with my black dress, and I walked out of the room. I didn't know how I was going to react at Rachel's homegoing service, but I knew I had to hold it together.

"Wait. I'm riding with you."

"Why won't you leave me alone? Isn't it obvious I don't want you anywhere near me today?"

"And that's the main reason why I won't leave you alone. You can hate me all you want, but I'm your sister, and we both need each other right now."

"You're wrong. I don't need anything from you. Not even your sympathy."

I walked out to the car, and everyone was loading up in their vehicles getting ready to head out to Tallahassee. Caroline decided to ride with our parents. I didn't have anything else to say to her. I knew that eventually I would have to forgive her, but today wasn't the day for forgiveness.

Once we arrived at the church, my heart started to race. I tried to pull myself together, but I couldn't. Just seeing the hearse made it harder for me to get out of the car. Damien had to help me pull myself together. My parents took the kids as we slowly walked towards the church. Rachel's family had already arrived, and they were lined up outside the church. My parents led the way, but as soon as Justine saw me, she stopped me dead in my tracks.

"You…" I didn't know what to do. Justine looked as though she wanted to say something else, but couldn't get it out. Her body language was all over the place, eyes were bloodshot red, and she looked like she was barely holding it together. "Your parents are the only reason you're allowed here today. If it was up to me, you wouldn't be here."

Tears continued to fall from my eyes. I was so hurt, and I was sick and tired of everyone blaming me for something I didn't do, but Justine was grieving, and she was allowed to think whatever she wanted to think about me.

"I'm so sorry…"

"Don't. Not today, Rhonda. Not today." Justine didn't want to hear anything I had to say.

Damien escorted me into the church. Everyone was walking by viewing the body, and the closer I got the more emotional I became. I didn't want to show my weakness, but Rachel was my friend. My best friend.

"Damien. I don't think I can do this."

"Yes, you can. You're stronger than you think."

As we made our way towards the front, I just prayed that it was someone else other than Rachel lying in the casket. Once we approached the front I broke down in tears when I saw Rachel's body. I couldn't believe it was her. Rachel was really gone.

"Why didn't you call me? I would've came." I took a picture from my purse and I placed it in Rachel's hand. "Now you'll never be alone."

It was a picture of JJ. I knew how much she loved him, and now they'll always be together. I walked over to my seat, and I watched as Rachel's family was escorted into the church. Justine made her way over to view Rachel's body. She kissed her on the forehead, and right when she was about to walk away, she stopped. She must have noticed the picture I placed in Rachel's hand. I just prayed Justine wouldn't take it out. She picked it up, and then she let out a small cry. With tears in her eyes, she placed the picture back into Rachel's hand. At that moment, my heart broke into a million pieces. Everyone knew how much Rachel loved JJ, and I hated how she put herself through so much hell—because of love. During the service, Pastor Virgil stated how Justine was going to sing a song in remembrance of her daughter. Justine walked up to the podium and began to sing. Her voice was shaky, and before long, she broke down in tears. I couldn't stop crying. She tried once again to do the song, but she was too emotional. Eventually, she gave up, and told Pastor Virgil that she couldn't go on. Pastor Virgil then went on to do a very moving eulogy, and there wasn't a dry eye in the house.

After the service was over, we headed out to the grave site. The entire day felt surreal. I felt as though I was in a daze. As I was walking towards the burial plot, I felt a hand come by and grab hold of mine. I looked up and it was Caroline. I squeezed her hand and didn't let go. Pastor Virgil said a prayer as they lowered Rachel's body to the ground. I tried my best to hold it together. Damien held my right hand and Caroline held my left. I was so glad they were there with me. Even though I was very angry with Caroline, I needed her at that moment, and I knew I was going to need the love and support of my entire family in order to make it through this heartbreaking ordeal. Damien wiped away my tears, and then he kissed me on the cheek. Rachel was right about one thing. Damien did love me, and her wanting us to be together was spot-on. Through all the good times, the heartaches, and all the fights we had endured, one thing would never change: Rachel was my best friend, and she was truly missed.

# Chapter 33

### A Familiar Face

We said our good-byes, and Damien and I headed back to London. During the plane ride home, I thought about all the great moments Rachel and I shared together. We had our ups and downs, but at the end of the day we loved each other, and that was the only thing that mattered. Once we arrived back home, I took a few days off from work to try and wrap my head around everything that had happened. I decided to take the kids out to the park, just so I was able to get some fresh air. I didn't feel like being cooped up in the house with two energetic kids, especially when I didn't have any energy to chase after them. I watched the kids as they played in the park, and I marveled at the life that was all around me. Sometimes I take a lot of things for granted—even something simple as having healthy kids. I took joy in watching them play. I vowed to become a better mother and wife. As we were about to leave the park, I saw a suspicious car drive by the playground. It was a luxury car, one too fancy for our neighborhood, but I remember seeing it once before. As it turned the corner, I glanced inside, and my heart stopped. I prayed my eyes were deceiving me, but they weren't. It was Dabula, my old supplier. Why was he in London? I took the kids and hid, hoping that he didn't see me. Dabula was one of those guys who was good for business, but if you ever crossed him then he would make your entire family pay for your mistake. After the car was out of sight, I took the kids back to the house, locked all the windows and doors, and awaited Damien's return from work. Once he opened the door, I ran over and hugged him.

"Okay, what was that for?"

"I'm just glad you're home."

"Is that all?"

"No. But we'll talk later."

"Talk about what?"

"A part of my past I still haven't told you about."

Damien grabbed my hand and led me to the bedroom.

"Okay, so tell me. What's going on?"

I took a deep breath.

"Back in the day, when I used to sell drugs, I got so good at it, I ended up cutting out the middleman, and I started buying directly from the cartel."

"You what! You bought drugs from the cartel?"

"Yes, but back then I didn't care. I needed the money, and before long I had made us all rich."

"Rich? But you don't have any money."

"At one time, I did. I had over 10 million dollars saved up in an offshore bank account, but Prez seized my money and turned it over to the FBI, and there went my small fortune."

"So, you're telling me, you were a big player in the drug game."

"Yes, and no one could touch me, because of who my supplier was."

"Your supplier. This is too much."

"I know…but that's why Prez played me. He wanted my supplier, but I wouldn't give him up."

"And why not?"

"Because there are some people you just don't cross, and he's one of them."

"Okay. So why are you telling me this now?"

"Because I saw him today when I was leaving the park with the kids."

"You saw him! Here? In London!"

"Yes."

"This can't be happening."

"I know. I can't believe he's in London either. I don't know why he's here, but whatever his reasons are, I know they can't be good."

"Did he see you?"

"I don't know, but this guy suffers from paranoia, and the last thing I need is for him to think that I sold him out."

"So, you think he'll come after you?"

"I don't see why he would? I've been out of the drug game for some time now. I never mentioned who he was to anyone, so I don't see why he would want to come after me."

"Do we need to go to the cops?"

"No. This guy is dangerous. I say we continue on as if nothing has happened, and hopefully he'll leave town soon."

"And what if he doesn't? I can't allow you and the kids to be put at risk while this guy is running around London."

"And if you go to the cops, then you might as well sign our death certificates. Please. Just allow this to play itself out, and hopefully he'll leave town soon."

"I don't know, Rhonda."

"He's dangerous, Damien. If you don't want anything to happen to us, then I beg you not to ever mention this again—to anyone. For the sake of our family, just let it go."

"Then you need to quit your job."

"What are you talking about? Why would I quit my job?"

"Because I don't want you leaving this house. If he's out there, then you're staying in here. I'm not losing my family to some paranoid kingpin."

"But, Damien, you can't confine me to this house. I'll go crazy."

"Then what do you suggest, because I'm all out of ideas."

"I don't know! I still can't believe this is happening. I'm sorry. I'm so sorry. I thought this was all behind me."

Damien grabbed my hand.

"We're going to get through this, okay?"

"Okay."

Then it became official. I took a leave of absence from work until the matter with Dubula was under control. Weeks passed and nothing had happened. I was starting to go crazy. I felt like a prisoner in my own home. I missed my freedom. I missed the outdoors; I missed anything that wasn't associated with the inside of my house. There were only so many television shows I could watch before I would eventually lose my mind. Then one day, out of the blue, I heard the doorbell ring. "Company." I didn't care who it was. I needed to speak with someone other than a five and a three-year-old. I opened the door and was immediately knocked unconscious. The next thing I knew, water was being splashed in my face.

"Awe. What's going on?"

There were three guys standing around me and not one of them said a word. I could hear traffic on the other side of the walls, so I must have been in a warehouse somewhere downtown. I was tied up to a chair and there were dim lights all around me. I could barely make out where I was. I was so afraid. I didn't know what was going on, but finally, I saw a figure walking towards the light. It was Dabula.

"Rhonda. Long time, no see."

"Dabula. What the hell is going on?"

"I don't know. You tell me."

"What are you talking about? I've done nothing wrong. I'm no longer in the drug game…"

"And I'm aware of that. You know, at one point in time I was actually happy for you until—"

"Until what? I haven't done anything wrong."

"I used to think that, until I found out you were married to the FBI agent who's been following me all around the world. You see, when I saw you the other day, I thought it was strange seeing you all the way over here in London, but just recently, I saw your husband downtown as well. So, tell me, Rhonda. Are you trying to set me up?"

"I don't know what you're talking about. My husband is an architect. He designs buildings. He doesn't work for the FBI." My anxiety was building up. I didn't know if my kids were safe or not, my arms were sore from being tied behind my back, and the sweat dripping from my hair was constantly burning my eyes.

"Why are you lying to me, Rhonda?"

"I'm not lying to you. Check it out if you want to. My marriage to the cop wasn't real. He lied to me in order to get to you, but I never gave you up. Just look into it. My husband is an architect. That's why we're over here in London. Come on, Dabula. You know I wouldn't betray you."

Dabula signaled for one of his guys to come his way.

"Okay, just to be safe, I'll check into your story, but until then, let's see if you're really telling me the truth." One of Dabula's guys pulled out a bag that held some heroin and a syringe in it.

"Wait! What are you doing? I told you the truth."

"Well my little friend here, he's good at letting me know if you're really telling me the truth or not."

"But I am telling you the truth. Dabula, please, don't put that poison inside of me. Just wait until your guy comes back, and he'll confirm that I'm telling you the truth."

Dabula wasn't listening to anything I had to say. He prepped my arm as if he was a doctor getting ready to draw blood.

"Oh! So now it's poison, but it wasn't back in the day when you were selling it."

"Dabula, please!"

"You're truly terrified. Aren't you? So, tell me Rhonda. A girl like you, in a business like this; you're telling me, you were never once tempted to sample your own supply?"

"No. I just sold it. That's all. My plan wasn't to get high; it was to get paid. So, come on Dabula. Please...don't do this."

"I'm sorry, Rhonda. You know I like you, but I need to know the truth." I kicked and screamed as they approached me with the syringe. I was in tears begging Dabula not to shoot me up, and before I knew it, it was done. I didn't know how I was going to react to the heroin. "Don't fight it. Just let it take over."

I didn't want to give in. I tried to fight it, but I couldn't. I felt so free. It was an indescribable feeling. I was so relaxed. I fought to keep my eyes open, but I couldn't. Then out of nowhere I felt a slap go across my face.

"Rhonda. Can you hear me?"

"Dabula."

"Yes. Now tell me. Did you tell anyone about me?"

"I like you, Dabula. I could never tell on you." I kept smiling. I was high as kite. My eyes closed again and I received another slap. I started laughing. The slap actually felt good.

"Rhonda. Does the FBI know who I am?"

"I don't know, but they know me." I started laughing. I couldn't sense fear, only pleasure.

"Get her up."

The guys untied me, and then they stood me up.

"If you're telling me the truth then you have nothing to worry about, because I'm getting ready to leave the country, and you, my dear, are going to ensure that I make it out untouched."

"Okay." I laughed.

"Bring him in." I looked up and one of the guys came walking in holding Dominick in his arms. "You see, when we picked you up, there were two little kids playing around in the living room. I looked at the little girl and she favored you, but not the cop, but this little guy here is a spitting image of Detective Santiago. Now if you want to ever see him alive again, then you'll ensure that the FBI backs off.

"Dominick. My baby."

"Take her away, and give her one more boost for the road."

"Wait. We can't leave Dominick."

"Say, bye-bye to Mommy."

Dabula took Dominick's hand and waved good-bye to me. The guys took me out back, and shot me up one last time, and that was the last thing I remembered.

My life had come full circle. The poison I once sold was now flowing through my veins. I was impaired. I couldn't think straight. I couldn't even move. I couldn't do anything but slip into a cataleptic state of mind. My son's life was in danger, and there was nothing I could do to help to him. I thought I was done paying for all my wrongdoings, but maybe I'll never be done. Karma.

# Chapter 34

⁂

# Save My Son

When I woke up, I was in a hospital room, and Damien was by my side. I looked around the room, waiting for my mind to catch up with my vision. Then suddenly, I remembered Dabula and I went into a panic. I remembered he had Dominick.

"Rhonda...are you okay?"

"Damien. Dominick. Where's Dominick?"

"Rhonda. Calm down."

"My baby. They have my baby."

"Who?"

I thought about what Dabula had told me and I kept quiet. I needed to play this safe, or they were going to kill my son.

"No one. No one at all."

"Come on, Rhonda. If you know something then tell me."

"I can't. Trust me." I looked around the hospital, and I had no clue as to how I got there. "How long have I been here?" I had tubes running in and out of me. "And what's with all the tubes?"

"You've been out for two days. Someone found you drugged up in an alley not too far from the hospital. The doctors have been trying to flush all of the drugs out of your system since the day you arrived." Damien looked around the room. "Look, Rhonda...I know you're scared, but Dominick is missing and we need to find him. So, if you can remember anything, please tell me."

"I can't. If I say anything, they'll kill him. I'm sorry."

"So, what are we supposed to do?"

"Wait."

"Wait and do what? Nothing?"

"Wait for them to call us. They won't hurt Dominick unless they feel like the cops are on to them." I started to look around the room and I noticed Damien was alone. "Wait a minute. Where's Olivia?"

"She's at home with Julie."

"Julie...alone?"

"No. She's not alone. She's there with a couple of FBI agents."

"The FBI. Why the FBI and not Interpol? Shouldn't they be handling this?"

"Evidently the FBI followed your supplier all the way to London, and Interpol is allowing them to take over. They placed all of us under police protection after you were taken...and, Rhonda. There's something else you should know."

"What?"

"Prez is the one heading up the FBI detail."

"Prez?"

My heart started to race. Prez didn't know anything about Dominick, and this certainly wasn't the way I wanted him to find out about his son.

"Yes. He's been working the case and he wants to come in and talk with you...but, Rhonda. Listen to me. I know you may not want to hear this, but you may have to tell Prez the truth about Dominick. If you tell him Dominick is his son, he may be more likely to prioritize this and to work with us to help us find Dominick alive."

"But Damien. Prez is liable to kill me if he finds out that I've kept Dominick away from him after all these years. I don't think I can tell him."

"You have to. From what you've told me, if the cops go after your supplier, then Dominick is dead. So come on, Rhonda. Let's play it safe and try and save our son, and remember, no matter what happens…I love you."

"I love you too."

I had to put my feelings aside and work with Prez for the sake of our son. I looked outside my room door, and I saw Prez standing in the hallway talking with another agent. From the looks of things, he allowed both his hair and his bread to grow out. It actually looked good on him. He looked at me and then made his way to my room.

"Rhonda." Prez slowly walked into the room.

"Detective."

"Look. I know this may be hard for you right now, but I need to ask you some questions."

I reached out for Damien, and he grabbed hold of my hand, then he kissed me on the forehead.

"You can do this." Damien whispered in my ear, then he walked out of the room. I didn't want him to leave. I was afraid of how Prez would react once I told him the truth about Dominick.

"So, what do you want to know?"

"What I've always wanted to know. Who's your supplier?"

"You know I can't tell you that. So, what else do you want to know?"

"Come on, Rhonda. You were found doped up in an alley, and your son is missing. So, do you really wanna play this game with me?"

"I know this game, and I'm not telling you anything."

"So, I take it you don't love your son."

"Don't, Prez! Don't go there!"

"Then help me. The cartel has your son, and no matter what you may want me to believe, I know you're not this reckless."

"You're right. I'm not, but I know how this works. You go after my supplier, and my son turns up dead. If you just allow them to leave the country, then they won't hurt him. That's all I'm asking."

"Come on, Rhonda. You know I can't do that. I came here to make an arrest, and I will make one. So, I'm not leaving this room until I get a name."

"Then you better get comfortable, because I'm not telling you anything."

"Why are you doing this? Why are you protecting this guy?"

"I'm not protecting anyone but my son."

"How? By keeping your mouth closed. Work with me, Rhonda. Give me a name, and we'll go out and bring your son home safely."

I felt as though I could barely breathe. I knew I had to tell Prez the truth, but I was afraid to. Somehow, I had to put my fears aside and do what was best for Dominick.

"If he was your son, what would you do?"

"Come on, Rhonda. I don't have time to play these games with you. Your supplier is out there and…"

"And if Dominick was your son, what would you do? Would you put his life in danger just to catch a criminal?"

"I don't know what I would do, but one thing is certain. There's a dangerous man running around London, and he has your son. So why are you doing everything within your power to hinder me from catching him?"

"I'm not. I'm just protecting my son. Why can't you understand that?"

"How? By keeping silent? This guy is dangerous, Rhonda…"

"And you think I don't know that, but he has our son, and…" I tried to catch myself, but it was too late.

"Wait! What did you say?"

I was afraid to say anything else, but deep in my heart I knew Prez deserved to know the truth.

"I said he has *our* son." I didn't know how Prez was going to react. I was trying to hold back my tears, but I couldn't.

"What do you mean, our son? Don't play games with me, Rhonda. I want the truth."

"And that's the truth...Damien isn't Dominick's biological father. You are."

Prez went silent. He looked at me, and then he began to pace back and forth around the room.

"No. You're lying. You're just making this up to get me to back off."

"I wouldn't lie to you about this. Dominick is your son, and if you don't believe me, then look at his picture, and tell me if I'm still lying."

"See, I know you, and you don't have it in you to do something like this. You're not that cold. You wouldn't have hidden a child from me."

"But I did, and if you think I'm cold, then it's only because you made me that way. You hurt me, and I couldn't risk losing another child, so I kept Dominick a secret."

"You're lying. I don't believe you."

"Then don't, but pictures don't lie. Dominick is your son."

"Okay. We'll see about that."

Prez walked out of the room, and went over to talk with one of the guys from his squad. I observed as he passed Prez a picture of Dominick, and I watched Prez's facial expression change like the wind. He kept running his hand through his hair in disbelief. Prez then made his way back into my room, and he looked as though he was about to snap.

"So, you're serious? You're telling me, this little boy is my son." Prez became very emotional as he held up the picture of Dominick.

"Yes. So now you have to choose between catching the bad guys, and saving your son. It's not so easy anymore, is it?"

Prez began to walk towards me with tears in his eyes. He leaned over me, and I felt trapped. I didn't know what he was going to do to me.

"Hate couldn't describe what I'm feeling for you right now." Prez was so close to me that his tears fell upon my face, and I wiped them away along with mine.

"Feel what you want for me, but if you go after my supplier then you will ensure the death of our son. So please. Tell your squad to step down and back off."

"Damn it, Rhonda!" Prez was all over the place. I could see the hurt all over his face, but there was no room in my heart for his pain. Damien peeped inside the room, and then he walked off. Prez leaned over me again as if he was about to say something else, but instead he broke down in tears.

"How could you?"

"Really. This coming from Detective Santiago. The gatekeeper of lies."

"Rhonda…"

"No. I want you to listen to me. Now you can hate me all you want, but right now I need you to go out, do your job, and save our son. Man up, and tell your squad to back down."

Prez was speechless. He tried to compose himself and then he left. I could see him talking with some more agents in the hall, and then Damien walked back into the room.

"Hey. Are you alright?"

"Yeah. I'm fine."

"So how did it go?"

"I told him the truth, if that's what you're asking."

"And how did he take it?"

"How you think he took it? I just told him that he had a son, who's being held captured by the drug cartel. So, he's pretty livid right now."

"Well, hopefully they'll back off now."

"If Prez has anything to do with it, they will. Now that he knows Dominick is his son, he's not going to jeopardize his life for a drug bust."

"Well let's just pray that he doesn't."

Time passed and we heard nothing. I began to feel sick. I didn't know if it was due to the drugs in my system or just worry. My cell phone sat by my side as I waited for Dabula to send word of

Dominick's whereabouts. Two more days passed, and I was about
to lose my mind. The doctors were releasing me to go home, and
Prez and Damien were both by my side. I felt so uncomfortable. By
the time, I walked out of the hospital my cell went off. I grabbed the
phone, and it was a text stating where I could find Dominick. Prez
took the phone, and passed it off to one of his guys.

"Come on, Damien, let's go."

"And where do you think you're going?" Prez stopped us from
leaving.

"I'm going to get my son."

"No, you're not."

"What do you mean I'm not? He's my son and I'm going to
get him."

"Damien. Help me out here." Was Prez seriously asking Damien
for help? I looked over at Damien, and he didn't know what to do.
So, I grabbed him by the hand and we started to walk off.

"Take me to my son."

"Let's allow the police to handle this matter. They'll bring
Dominick to us. Okay?"

"No. It's not okay. They texted me; not the police." I was getting
upset. "You know what…just forget it. I'll go and get Dominick
myself."

I tried to wave down a cab, but Prez stopped me.

"You're not doing this. Now I told you, me and my guys would
handle this. Let me bring Dominick home…safely. Okay?"

"But I need to make sure he's alright."

"And I'll do that for you, but right now I need you to let me
take care of this."

Prez waved for Damien to come and get me, and then Damien
drove me home. I had so many thoughts running through my head.
What if Prez decided to skip town with Dominick, or even worse,
he challenged me in court for custody? My mind was racing, and
I didn't know what to do. When we arrived at the house, I was so
thrilled to see Olivia.

"Mommy!"

"Livy! I missed you."

"I missed you too, Mommy. Look, I made this for you."

Olivia gave me a get-well card that she drew by hand.

"Oh, it's so beautiful." I showed Damien the card. Olivia was too cute. She always knew how to brighten my day.

"Mommy when is Dominick coming home? I miss him too. Look I made this for him." Olivia showed me another card she had made for Dominick, and it brought me to tears. There was still no word from the FBI, and I didn't know if my son was dead or alive. "Mommy."

"She's okay, Olivia. Take the cards to your room, and I'll be there in a minute. Okay?"

"Okay Daddy."

Olivia walked away and I tried to pull myself together. Damien took me to our bedroom and sat me down on the bed.

"Rhonda, it's going to be okay. They're going to bring Dominick home, and everything is going to be fine."

"But you don't know that."

"But we have to believe that. If not…" I continued to cry and Damien hugged me. "They're going to bring him home. Okay?"

"Okay."

I felt sick. I went into the bathroom and threw up. I felt horrible. I took some aspirin, but nothing was working.

"Rhonda. Are you okay?"

"Yeah I'm fine. I feel a little sick, that's all."

"You may still be going through some forms of withdrawal. Just give it some time. The doctors gave me these to help you out." Damien pulled out some pills.

"What are these?"

"Methadone. They're supposed to help you cope with the side effects from the drugs."

Damien gave me two pills, and I sat and waited for Prez to call. An hour passed, and finally we heard the doorbell ring. I raced to the door and it was Prez holding Dominick in his arms. They were truly father and son.

"Mommy!"

"My baby! You brought him back."

"I told you I would."

I gave Dominick a big hug and kiss, then I began to examine him all over.

"You don't have to do that. We just left the hospital. He's fine."

"Thank you."

"Don't thank me just yet. Can we talk in private?"

I looked at Dominick and I didn't want to let him go. Damien reached out for him but I held him tightly in my arms. "I can't."

"Yes, you can. Go and talk to Prez and I'll take care of Dominick."

"Fine." I was hesitant in handing Dominick over to Damien. I wanted to hold on to him and never let go, but I knew I needed to hear Prez out, so I escorted him to my home office so we could talk in private. "So, what's on your mind?"

"Now that you have Dominick back, are you willing to tell me who your supplier is?"

"Look. I'm grateful for what you've done, but I can't tell you who he is, and you know that."

"And why not? What's stopping you now?"

"My family. If I was to tell you who my supplier was, then he could order a hit on my entire family."

"You wouldn't have to worry about that. I wouldn't allow anyone to hurt you…"

"No, because you're the only one who can do that, right?"

"Rhonda…"

"No. I'm sorry. Reliving the past. So, was that all you wanted to talk to me about?"

"No. There's another matter we need to discuss."

"Dominick."

"Yeah. I get that I hurt you, but to keep my son away from me… that was foul and you know it."

"No. The way you played me. Now that was foul. I was hurt, and Damien had already taken away Olivia, and I couldn't risk losing another child."

"I get you were hurt, but come on, Rhonda. You knew how I felt about kids. You and Olivia were my life and—"

"Don't. Don't pretend as if we mattered to you, because we didn't. You used me for the same reason you're trying to use me now, and that was to get information about my supplier, but I'm not stupid Prez. I didn't fall for it then and I'm not about to fall for it now."

"You're wrong. I did love you. Maria was right. I played myself. I started believing in the lie that I had created. I didn't want to hurt you, but I couldn't tell you the truth either."

"So, allowing me to believe in something that wasn't real was your version of loving me. I was in love with you. Do you know how long it took for me to get over you? I had never experienced that kind of pain before in my life. What you did was low down, and I hated you for it."

"So, keeping Dominick away from me was your form of payback?"

"No. It was my way to ensure Dominick stayed a part of my life, and not yours."

"So how are we going to do this?"

"Do what?"

"Dominick, Rhonda! He's my son too. Now I'm not going to do you like Damien and drag you through the courts, because I feel like we're two civilized people, and we can come up with a plan that works. But we *will* come up with a plan, because I'm not walking away from my son."

I was willing to work with Prez, even if I didn't trust him.

"You're right. We can come up with a plan, but how do you expect it to work when you're in DC and I'm in London?"

"I thought about that, and that's why I'm willing to stay here in London for a while. I want to get to know my son."

I didn't know if I could handle Prez being that close to me. He hurt me and he knows this. He could easily manipulate a situation, and I don't want to play his victim, ever again.

"You're going to stay here…in London?"

"Yes. Is that going to be a problem for you?"

"No, but what about your job? How will that work with you being over here? Never mind that. What about your wife? How is she going to react to your decision?"

"Well when it comes to my job, they'll understand, and as for my wife…we're divorced."

"So, what happened? She got tired of being lied to as well?"

"No. She realized I really did love you, and she left me."

I felt my heart flutter, but I was stronger now. I was with Damien and there was no room in my heart for Prez—not anymore.

"Sorry to hear that."

"No, you're not."

"Whatever. So…where will you be staying?"

"I found a rental downtown."

"Already?"

"Yes. After you told me about Dominick, I made plans to stay. I want him to know who I am. I still can't believe I have a son. I have a son, Rhonda."

"Yes. You have a son. So, what about your case? Are you going to let it go?"

"No. My squad will take it over. They will find your boy, and when they do, he's going down."

"Well, good luck with that, but just so you know. You may not know who he is, but he very well knows who you are. That's why he took Dominick and not Olivia. So be careful. They'll do anything to ensure that you'll back off, and when I say anything, I mean anything."

"Don't worry about it. I won't allow anything to happen to you guys. I love you too much…"

"Okay. I think you should be going now."

"Alright." Prez reached into his pocket and pulled out a piece of paper. "Here's the address where I'll be staying, and my cell number. Call me."

"Okay. Bye."

I walked Prez out. I headed towards the living room, and I looked at my family. I didn't want anything else to happen to them, yet I didn't know how to protect them. I looked at Damien and the danger I didn't want to bring into his world, I brought anyway. My future was up in the air. Dabula was running the show and I had no idea where he was. When we first met, he told me he would never hurt me as long as I didn't betray him. Not once did I mention his name to anyone, yet he chose to shoot me up with heroin. Dabula was way too paranoid, and I was starting to think he may have been sampling his own supply, which was a scary thing. Now that Prez was in town, part of me felt safe because I expected him to protect his son. But who was going to protect me, Damien, and Olivia? I had got us into this mess, and I didn't have the slightest clue as to how I was going to get us out.

# Chapter 35

❧

# Medicating the Pain

I needed to get my life together, so I begged Damien to allow me to go back to work. I was going crazy sitting around the house all day doing absolutely nothing. I was popping pills like they were candy. The methadone worked, but I was becoming addicted to it. I kept thinking back to the day when Dabula drugged me. The feeling I had was like no other. The grief I felt for Rachel, the hate I carried around for Prez, and any other emotions I tried to suppress were gone. I finally understood why it was so hard for Rachel to kick her habit. The methadone helped to numb my pain, but I was running low, and there were no more refills to be made. I needed to figure something out, because my medication was the only thing allowing me to cope with reality.

As for Prez, he kept his word and moved into an apartment downtown. He was so excited, because I was finally bringing Dominick over for his first visit. I didn't know how they would react to each other, but I was willing to give it a shot. I rang the doorbell and Prez answered.

"Hi."

"Hi. Come on in."

The apartment was nice. It was way better than his first place back in Tallahassee. It must have come fully furnished, because Prez didn't have a decorative bone in his body.

"Nice."

"Thanks. The Bureau arranged it for me."

"Really."

"Yeah. They set it up like I'm still working a case. That way I would be able to stay in London, and spend more time with Dominick. My supervisor was real understanding about the whole ordeal."

"Your supervisor only wants one thing, and that's to know who my supplier is, but tell him I'm not talking. Anyway, here are all of Dominick's things." I handed Prez Dominick's tote bag. "There's a change of clothing in there just in case you guys decide to go out anywhere, and a couple of his toys for him to play with. If you allow him to take them out all at once, then he'll have them all over the place." I looked up, and Prez was fixated on Dominick. I could've been talking to myself. "Hey. Are you listening to me?"

"Yeah, I hear you...its crazy how he looks so much like me."

"I know. Crazy, right? Anyway, don't give him too much sugar. He's already a hyper child, so beware, and I'll be back after work to pick him up."

"Thank you for this. I know you may not believe me, but I am sorry. For everything."

"I know you are. So, I have to go. Bye, baby." I waved good-bye to Dominick.

"Bye." Prez said smiling.

"I was talking to Dominick."

"I know."

I tried to walk away, but Dominick held onto my leg.

"Wait a minute, buddy. You can't go with me. You're going to stay here with Prez. He's going to watch you today. Okay?" Dominick wasn't hearing it. I had to peel him off of me and hand him over to Prez. "There's a movie in his bag. Put it on and you should be good to go."

"Okay. Come on, buddy. We're going to have a good time. Alright."

I eased out of the apartment and headed for work. While I was driving, I started digging through my purse in search of my medication, but when I found the bottle, it was empty. What was I going to do? They had become my coping mechanism. I needed them. I tried psyching myself up. Telling myself that I didn't need them, but as soon as I got to work my head started spinning. I knew right then that it was going to be a long day.

Time was progressing at work and I couldn't cope. I was barely making it through the day. I went to drop off some documents at the pharmacy lab, and it was like I had walked into prescription heaven. The shelves were lined up with bottles and bottles of medication. I felt like all of my prayers had been answered, but knowing where they were, and being able to get my hands on them was a totally different story. An access card was required to enter the room with the pills and once inside you had to know what shelf and level each medication was on. So, I waited, and when one of the technicians wasn't looking, I swiped their badge from the table and stuck it in my pocket. I waited until everyone had left for lunch, and then I made my way back into the lab. I had to hurry and find what I was looking for before I got caught. I kept searching until I was able to find some methadone. I took a supply bag from the closet and I filled it up with pills. I had more than enough to last me for a while. I didn't want to cause any suspicion so I counted the pills as fast as I could, and then I found the log journal and changed the pill count. If I was caught then that was my job, and maybe some jail time too. So, I needed to move fast. I placed the badge back on the table where I found it, then left. I needed a pill badly. I decided not to take one until I was safely hidden away in my car. I took an aspirin bottle out of my purse, poured out all of the pills in it, and replaced them with methadone. I decided to stash the remaining pills away in my car.

I had truly turned into an addict. I was stealing from my job and I was self-medicating at work. I needed to stop, but I didn't know how. As long as I was able to take a pill then I was able to function, but without them I felt like a nervous wreck. I did well at hiding my addiction, but that ruse wasn't going to last too much longer. I knew I needed help, but I wasn't ready to inform anyone of my current failures. I hated myself, and I didn't know of any other way to cope with all of the pain and guilt I was feeling, so I allowed methadone to be my way out.

After work I felt so guilty by what I had done that I ended up taking several more pills. I was a thief. Stealing from my job. Who was this person I was becoming? I needed some serious help. I called Damien and informed him that I was stopping by to pick up Dominick, and then I was heading home. Once I arrived at Prez's apartment I rang the doorbell. He answered the door with his finger over his lips, shushing me.

"Hey. I'm here to get Dominick."

"He's asleep in my room."

"So how did he do?"

"He cried a lot in the beginning, but I put the movie on for him, and he was good to go after that. We had pizza and I took him to the park. He's a good kid."

"He's the best. Well let me get him and we'll be on our way. It's getting late."

"I know this might be too soon, but can I keep Dominick overnight?"

"Prez, I don't know about that. He's just getting to know you. I don't want it to be too much, too quick; you know what I'm saying? If he wakes up, and he doesn't see me or Damien, then he's liable to flip out on you."

"No. I understand. It's just…he's so innocent in all of this, and when I look at him, I see myself. I still can't believe he's my son."

"I know… but he'll be back tomorrow, and you guys can do this all over again, but right now we have to go."

"Rhonda."

"Yeah."

"There's something else I wanted to ask you."

"Sure. What is it?"

"Tell me. Why did you marry Damien? After everything he put you through. Why would you marry him?"

"Why did I marry Damien? Well, for starters he allowed me to be honest with him. I explained to him everything that had happened between the two of us, and I even informed him of my pregnancy with Dominick, and after all of that he still accepted me. So that's why I married him."

"But you didn't love him."

"I didn't at the time, but I grew to love him again."

"So…what we had for each other…you're telling me it's gone?"

"Yes. I love Damien now, and we have a family together, and it's been good."

"Okay, that may be the case, but I can't figure out how to stop loving you. You may have moved on, but I haven't. I know that I hurt you deeply, and that's why I didn't come after you in the beginning."

"Come on, Prez. Let's not do this. I'm only here so you can see your son, but if you keep this up, then I'll have Damien dropping off Dominick instead of me."

"So, you're serious."

"Yes. So, bring me Dominick. It's getting late."

Prez brought me Dominick and he was out like a light. He placed him in my arms, and then he placed his tote bag on my shoulder.

"Here you go. So. Same time tomorrow?"

"Yes…and can you do me a favor? Can you get the door for me?"

"Sure."

Prez leaned over as if he was about to open the door, but then out of nowhere he turned and gave me a kiss. I was so shocked that I almost dropped Dominick. I was no stranger to Prez's lips, and oh, did they feel nice, but I needed to snap out of my trance and pull away even though part of me didn't want to.

"Why are you doing this?" I whispered to Prez because I didn't want to wake up Dominick.

"I don't know." I turned to leave. "Look. Hear me out. I don't want to mess up what I have going with Dominick, but I couldn't help myself. I miss you and nothing is going to change that."

"Okay. I get where you are coming from, but don't ever do that again. Now I have to get home—to my husband. Okay?"

"Okay."

I couldn't get to my car fast enough. By the time, I got inside I popped a pill. Why was Prez messing with my head? I didn't need this. Not now. I drove home thinking about the kiss. Why was I allowing it to fester in my head? I needed to forget about what had just happened. I finally made it home, and I put Dominick to bed. I walked into my bedroom, and Damien was up reading a book.

"Hey. You're still up."

"Yeah. I was waiting up for you."

"Thanks."

I got ready for bed, and when I came out of the bathroom Damien was asleep. I got in bed and I cuddled up under him. He held onto me and I needed that. No matter what I may have felt for Prez in the past, I needed to let it go. I was allowing him to get to me, and I needed my thoughts to cease. I eased out of bed and I took another pill. After I was done, I slipped back into bed. I was becoming way too dependent upon my medication. Even though they numbed my pain, the underlining cause was still there. I didn't want to destroy my family, so I needed to get a grip on life and get my act together. I needed to wean myself off of methadone and learn how to deal with my problems the correct way—through therapy.

# Chapter 36

※

# Crossing the Line

Months passed, and I was trying my best to deal with my addiction, but I was running out of ways to stay busy. I was cleaning my house like a madwoman, but I was determined to stay strong. By the time Damien had come down for breakfast, I had cleaned the house, made breakfast, and finished my morning jog. I was hyped.

"Morning."

"And good morning to you too. What's all of this?"

I didn't know what to cook, so I cooked a variety of things. Pancakes, waffles, bacon and sausage. Eggs and Toast. Juice, coffee, and sliced fruit. I was on a roll.

"It's breakfast. So, are you hungry?"

"Sure." Damien looked at the array of food on the table. "So, you think you cooked enough food?"

"You're funny." I pulled a chair out from the table, and I motioned for Damien to sit down. "Come on. Sit down and eat."

"Well, I guess I have time to grab a bite before I leave. So where are the kids?"

"Getting dressed. I'm dropping Dominick off, and then Olivia and I are heading to the shops.

I was all over the place. I was jittery. I didn't know what was wrong with me.

"Rhonda. Are you okay?"

"Yeah I'm fine. Why?"

"You seem a little jumpy, that's all."

"No. I'm good. So, eat up, and I'm going to finish helping the kids get dressed."

I needed to calm down. I ran and took a quick cold shower before Damien left for work. The shower actually helped. I kissed Damien good-bye and then I headed out to drop off Dominick. I had Olivia with me since it was one of my days off. We arrived at Prez's apartment and I took the kids inside.

"Okay, Dominick, be good for Mommy, and I'll be back to get you later. Okay."

Dominick nodded his head.

"Olivia. Hey honey, and, how are you?" Prez tried to shake Olivia's hand.

"Good." Olivia was acting shy.

"Do you remember me?" Olivia shook her head. "Well that's okay. It was a long time ago."

"So, Olivia and I are about to head out, and I want you guys to have some fun together, okay?"

"We can certainly do that. Can't we, buddy?" Prez and Dominick gave each other high fives. "So where are you guys heading off to?"

"We're going to hit up the shops and then we're off to the park."

"That sounds fun. So, do you mind if Dominick and I join you guys?" Prez suggested.

"No, because you're supposed to be bonding with Dominick— not me and Olivia."

"And we'll be bonding together except you guys will be with us. So, come on. Stop being so serious. It'll be fun.

"I don't know..."

Prez turned to Olivia. "Do you mind if me and Dominick join you and your Mommy today?"

"No."

"See. Then it's settled. We're coming with you guys."

"Olivia! How are you going to sell us out like that?" Olivia laughed. "Fine. You guys can come along."

Prez and I spent the entire day together with the kids. We shopped, ate, and played our hearts out. By the end of the day the kids couldn't keep up. We wore them out. They ended up crashing on Prez's bed. I peeped in on them and they were fast asleep. I closed the door and decided to let them enjoy their nap.

"And they are out." I flopped down on Prez's sofa.

"Well they had a good time, and so did I."

"Me too. I actually had fun."

Prez walked over and sat down beside me on the sofa.

"See? Aren't you glad we came along? It wouldn't have been the same without us." Prez smiled. It felt nice hanging out with him again.

"Whatever."

I glanced over at Prez and I noticed the top button on his shirt had popped off, and the chain around his neck was exposed. I looked up and I saw something familiar hanging onto it. I reached over and pulled the chain completely out of his shirt. Attached were my wedding and engagement rings.

"You kept them. Why?"

"To you they may have represented a lie, but to me they represented the only time I was truly happy."

I released the chain. I stood up and went into the kitchen to get a drink of water. Seeing my rings brought back so many memories.

"Are you okay?"

"Yes. I'm fine. Memories. That's all."

"And we had some good ones together, didn't we?"

"Yes, we did. I can admit that I was happy when we were together, but now things have changed. I'm married to Damien and…"

"And what?"

"I love him."

"The same way you loved me?"

Prez slowly cornered me up against the kitchen sink.

"Our love was different, you know that; and what are you doing?"

"I'm not doing anything."

"Then move back."

Prez had me trapped between the kitchen sink and the fridge.

"I'm sorry. I didn't mean to get too close."

As soon as Prez moved out of the way, I tried to walk off, but then he grabbed me by the arm, and he pulled me into a kiss. There were so many thoughts running through my mind, and I knew I needed to break away, but I didn't. Prez continued to kiss me, and the longer we kissed, the harder it was for me to deny him. I couldn't control myself. Was I really allowing this to happen? The next thing I knew Prez had me up against the wall, and his hands were all over my body. Everything was happening so fast, and before I knew it, I had allowed Prez to sex me up in his kitchen, while the kids were asleep in another room. I had truly lost it. My commitment to Damien had gone straight out the window. Prez held me in his arms and I didn't know what to say. In actuality, what could I say? There was no explanation for what I had allowed to happen. I tried to compose myself, as I eased out of his arms. The realization of what I had done began to sink in really fast. I couldn't risk losing Damien, but I was still emotionally attached to Prez. I didn't know what to do.

"Rhonda…"

"Don't. I shouldn't have allowed this to happen. It was a mistake and I need to go."

I tried to gather up the kid's belongings, but Prez stopped me.

"Don't pretend as if you didn't want this to happen. You wanted me, the same way I wanted you."

"What I did was wrong and it won't happen again."

"Why? All you're doing is lying to yourself. You still love me. You've just proven that."

"No. The only thing I've proven is that I need help."

"You hate me that much, that you can't allow yourself to love me. I get that I hurt you, but come on, Rhonda. Let's not play these games with each other. Now I don't know what you may feel for Damien, and I don't care. All I know is that I'm in love with you, and I'm not willing to let you go."

I was sitting on the sofa in tears. I was no longer in control. I was allowing myself to act upon my feelings instead of thinking about the consequences. I was throwing my marriage away, and for what? A man who's proven that his job was more important than me. What was I thinking?

"You don't love me. The only thing you love is your job. You were willing to submit me to any form of hell just so you could close your case. No regard for what it would do to me, or how it would make me feel. I hated you, and yet I allowed this to happen." I reached into my purse, took out two pills, and I swallowed them.

"What I did was wrong. I can't lie about that, but my love for you was never an act. It took everything in me to say those hurtful things to you, but I had no choice and..."

"You had no choice. My heart broke with every hateful word that came out of your mouth. I had never reached that type of rage before in my life, and what hurt me the most was the fact that you were the person who took me there."

"I didn't want to hurt you but my job..."

"Damn your job! What about me? Did you ever think about what your job was subjecting me to? I gave you all of me. Do you know how hard that was for me? I had never done anything like that before in my life, and when I finally did, the one person who I thought truly loved and cared about me ended up being a manipulative backstabbing bastard."

I could see the tears as they fell from Prez's eyes, but I had carried around that hurt inside of me for over three years and it needed to come out. The FBI wanted Dabula so bad that they were willing to put me through any form of hell just to catch him. I hated them for that, and for that reason alone, I never gave them Dabula's name.

Prez walked over and hugged me, but I didn't want him to touch me. I quickly went from wanting him to hating him. My emotions were way beyond erratic.

"I love you. That's all I know. My life hasn't been the same without you in it. I need you, Rhonda."

Prez squeezed me in his arms and I broke down crying. I didn't want to love him. I wasn't allowed to love him, and yet I did. He wiped away my tears, then started kissing me all over my face.

"I…" Prez wouldn't stop kissing me. First on my cheeks, and then on my forehead, and around my eyes. His kisses were breaking me down slowly. "I…" I knew I was wrong for what I was feeling, but I couldn't control my emotions.

"Say it."

"I can't…"

"And why not? Come on, Rhonda. Say it." Even though it was in me to say it, I knew that I couldn't, and without warning Prez gave me the most passionate kiss, and I began to feel at home in his arms. "Say it, Rhonda. You don't have to be afraid to."

"I love you." I said the words out loud and it broke my heart. How could I be in love with two men at the same time? I loved Damien, but it was nowhere near the level of intensity that I had for Prez, but nevertheless I loved them both.

"And I love you too."

Prez peeped in on the kids, and then he escorted me to his guest room. As we made love, I tried to control the flow like I would when I would make love to Damien, but Prez wouldn't allow it. He was always aggressive, and maybe that was the one thing my body kept missing. The reality of going home didn't even register in my mind. Being with Prez was the only thing that mattered.

I knew I was going to regret what I was allowing to happen between me and Prez, but I didn't care. The only thing I cared about was how I felt. I knew I was being selfish, but I was willing to take that gamble. I didn't know what was going to happen between me and Damien, but at that moment it was the least of my worries. I was addicted to prescription medication, I was in love with another man, and the most daunting part about the entire situation was the fact that I didn't care. Karma.

# Chapter 37

❧

# Facing Reality

Months passed, and my affair with Prez was still going strong. I knew I was wrong for what I was allowing to happen, but for once in a long time the void I used to feel was gone. I considered that maybe I felt that way because I didn't have to choose anymore between Prez and Damien. I had them both in my own way. I never knew if Damien was aware of the affair or not. If he was, he never let on that he knew, but regardless if he knew or not, I had to learn how to play the situation before I got myself caught. Once I almost slipped and said Prez name while I was making love to Damien. I had become reckless, and I needed to take control of the situation—if that was even possible.

Even though the affair was difficult to handle, my drug addiction was becoming way out of hand, and it was starting to take over my life. I had become a full-blown drug addict and I no intentions of giving up methadone. It was no longer a coping mechanism; it had become a defensive one as well. I had become numb to everything around me. My marriage, kids, and even the affair. They all meant something to me, but it became more about what I wanted verses what I needed, and for that reason, I grew to hate myself. I couldn't face what I was allowing myself to do, yet I couldn't stop. If I sought out help, then I would have to come clean about everything I had done, and I wasn't ready to face that type of criticism, not just yet, but I knew I needed help. Once, I caught myself kissing Prez in public. What would've happened if Damien had caught us? I needed to suck it up, and do what needed to be done, before I lost everything that meant something to me. Even though it was hard for me to do, I called Caroline, and I asked her if she would come out and visit with me for a while. There was no way I could go home and face my parents. Not in my current state. So, I figured it was in my best interest if Caroline came out to visit me instead.

I drove to the airport to pick up Caroline and I was so happy to see her. It felt nice to see a familiar face again. She walked over to me and I gave her the biggest hug imaginable. I kissed her on the cheek and told her that I missed her. I could tell Caroline could sense something was off, but I didn't want to talk to her about anything until I made it home safely. Once I got her settled in, I figured it was time I told her the truth about everything.

"So. What have you been up to? You look good."

"Nothing much. Just learning how to take things slow."

"Slow? What are you talking about? Slow how?"

"Rhonda, there's something you should know."

I thought I was going to be the one dropping secrets; not the other way around.

"What's going on?"

"I left Jacob."

"You what? But why?"

"The entire time we were together I was happy, but I felt like something was missing, and then I came to realize that no matter how much I loved Jacob, I missed my family and I wanted them back."

Caroline's words were hitting home, and for once in my life I knew exactly where she was coming from.

"So, what happened?"

"I told Brad I wanted to come back home, but he wasn't hearing it. He told me he had moved on, and that I should go back to Jacob."

I could tell Caroline was hurting, but I had no words of encouragement for her. I was a walking contradiction, and I was facing the same dilemma.

"I'm sorry to hear that. So, what's your plan?"

"I'm going to fight for my family and somehow find a way to win Brad back. I don't know what I was thinking. I remember you tried to warn me once, but I wouldn't listen. You asked me what was more important: the love I had or the one I craved. I never forgot that, and now I'm regretting that I didn't listen to you."

Caroline was in tears. I wanted to help her, but I didn't know how. If I would have taken my own advice, then maybe I wouldn't have been in the same predicament.

"I'm sorry. I'm so sorry, but things are going to work out. Just be patient; you'll see."

"I know you must think I'm such a failure. I look at you and I'm so jealous. You seem to have it all together, while my life is slowing falling apart. I mean look at you. You have a husband who loves you, two beautiful kids who adore you, and you seem so happy. I wish I could've been more like you."

I felt like an impostor, and the life I was living was one big charade. I was a fake, and there was nothing good about what I was doing. Caroline may have felt as though her life was falling apart, but mine was about to blow up in my face.

"Don't say that. Don't ever say that!"

I was upset—but with myself.

"Rhonda…what's wrong? What did I say?"

"You don't ever want to be like me. I'm not who I pretend to be."

"What are you talking about? You don't have to be modest. You got it right. No need to defend that."

"Modest." I laughed. "You know…there's something about me you should know as well, and once you hear it, you'll be quick to change your tone."

"Okay, Rhonda. You're scaring me. What's wrong?"

"Well for starters…I'm an addict. And I've been having an affair with Prez for months. Feel better now?"

Tears were falling from my eyes. I was such a hypocrite, and now the tables were truly turned. Karma was in full swing.

"You're what?" Caroline was in shock.

"An addict. I became addicted to my pain pills."

"But how? And why is Prez back in the picture? After what he did to you. Come on, Rhonda."

"I know, but a lot has happened that you don't know about."

"Like what?"

I went into graphic details regarding the kidnapping and the affair I was having with Prez. I was so ashamed of myself. I couldn't believe what I had allowed to take place in my life. I had abandoned my responsibilities as a wife and a mother, and worst of all, I was an addict.

"So does Damien know about any of this?"

"No. No one knows but you. I'm just tired of pretending. I thought I could control my addiction, but I can't, and then Prez came back into the picture, and that only made matters worse."

"I don't get it. How could you fall for him again? After everything he did to you. He played you, Rhonda."

"I know…but regardless of what he did to me, I never stopped loving him. Besides…it's not like I meant for any of this to happen. One thing led to another, and before I knew it, we were bed buddies again."

"Rhonda! Really! And you're the smart one. What do you think is going to happen once Damien figures out the truth? He's crazy about you, and he's liable to kill Prez if he was to ever suspect the two of you were fooling around behind his back."

"And you think I don't know this."

"So, what's your plan? Because you need a plan. The last thing I want is for you to end up like me."

"I know, and that's why I'm going away to rehab. I can't do this alone, and that's why I called you."

"So out of all the people you could have called, you chose to call me; why?"

"Who else would I call? You're my big sister."

Caroline walked over and gave me a hug. I knew it meant a lot to her that I turned to her for help.

"I love you, Rhonda, and I'm glad you called."

"I love you too."

I didn't know how I was going to do it, but I had to tell Damien the truth about my addiction. I wanted to tell him about Prez as well but I couldn't. I didn't want to risk losing him, so I decided to keep the affair a secret. As soon as Damien walked through the door fear ran though me. I didn't know how he was going to react to my news, but I knew I had to tell him anyway. Caroline decided to take the kids outside to play so I was able to talk with Damien in private.

"Hi, babe. So how was your day?"

"It was good; and guess who's here?"

"Who?"

"Caroline."

"Caroline? So, she finally decided to come out and see you. Why?"

"What do you mean why? She's my sister."

"Come on, Rhonda. This is Caroline we're talking about. So, what's going on? Why is she here?"

"She's here because I invited her to be here."

"Really..."

"Yes. I have to go away for a while, and Caroline agreed to stay here and help out with the kids while I'm away."

"You have to go away? Okay, and where are you supposed to be going?"

"To rehab."

"Rehab? Rhonda, what are you talking about? You're not making any sense."

"I know it's complicated, but long story short...I'm an addict."

"An addict! Come on, Rhonda; stop playing. You're not an addict..."

"But I am. After the kidnapping, I became addicted to my pain pills, and now my addiction has grown much worse. I actually stole pills from my job. That's how out of control this has all become. I tried to stop but I couldn't. That's why I need help. I don't know how to quit."

"Rhonda." Damien seemed upset. "Why did you keep this from me? I could've helped you."

"Because I was ashamed. I thought I could control it, but somehow it ended up controlling me. You know I can't stand not being in control and that's why I have to go away to rehab." Tears fell from my eyes and I quickly wiped them away. I felt like such a failure. "I'm so sorry. I never meant to let you down."

"You didn't let me down and I'm glad you told me. We're going to get through this—together."

"Together?"

"Yes. Together. For better or for worse. Remember?"

"Yeah. I remember. I love you so much."

Guilt was eating away at me. Damien loved me through all my faults, and yet I cheated on him with Prez. I craved a pill, but I knew I had to stop. I could no longer depend on them to take the pain away. Not anymore. I needed time to heal, and going away to rehab seemed like the right thing to do.

"I love you too. So, tell me. Where were you keeping your pills?"

"In my purse. Why?" Damien went looking through my purse. "Where are they?"

"They're in the aspirin bottle."

"Are you serious? Come on, Rhonda. What if someone would've taken one of these by mistake? This is reckless..."

"I know. I told you I needed help."

Damien took the pills out of my purse and flushed them down the toilet.

"Do you have any more?"

"No."

"Don't lie to me, Rhonda. In order for you to get better, you have to rid yourself of them completely. So, do you have any more that I should know about?"

"No. That's it. I don't have any more." I was lying. I still had a stash locked away in my car. I didn't know why I was afraid to rid myself of them. Even though I knew I needed help, my mindset was still that of an addict.

I knew the journey ahead was going to be hard, but I needed help, and I was willing to do whatever it took to get better. My life was spiraling out of control, and maybe now with the help of rehab I could get it back on track. My true testament was yet to come. Going away to rehab one thing, but breaking things off with Prez was going to be my biggest challenge yet.

# Chapter 38

❧

# Letting Go

Rehab was one of the hardest things I ever had to do in my life. You don't know how dependent your body becomes to something until you have to give it up. I was sick all of the time, and I was forced to face the pain I was trying to mask with medication. Therapy sessions were the hardest. I struggled with opening up. I didn't want to talk about my past, nor did I want to discuss Rachel's death. I didn't know how to cope with her being gone. I always felt as though I was the blame for her self-destruction. My therapist tried to explain to me that Rachel's death wasn't my fault, and that I shouldn't blame myself for happened, but I did.

During my stint in rehab, I discovered a lot about myself. I realized that I buried a lot of my feelings, which in the end only caused me more pain. I had to learn how to release all of the hurt and pain that I carried around inside, and to move forward with my life.

During my sessions, I talked about everything. My rape, my family: I even discussed the affair I was having with Prez. My therapist tried to explain how I needed to make a decision about who I really wanted to be with, and to commit myself to just that person. It was easy for her to say, but harder for me to do. I was in love with Damien and Prez, but the doctor was right. I needed to make a choice. So, I weighed my options both ways, but in the end, I was still confused. Damien was a good provider, and he loved me, and I knew he would do anything for me. Prez on the other hand was a good provider and he loved me as well, but the love we shared was on a different level than what I shared with Damien, and I needed to figure out why. Why did I love him more? When I would weigh the options out loud, they were always the same. So, what was the underlining cause of my infatuation with Prez? Something was keeping me bound to him, but I didn't know what it was. My therapist kept pushing and pushing, until one day I finally admitted how I felt like Prez was my soul mate. During the course of our marriage, I felt complete when I was with him. There was no void in my heart like there was now. My therapist expressed that Prez might have been the cause of the void I felt. I longed for him when he wasn't in my life. If I wanted my marriage with Damien to work, then I had to let Prez go. If not, then I had to let go of Damien, but I couldn't be with them both. It sounded easy enough, but I didn't know how I was going to do it. I needed a plan. I didn't want end up like Caroline by making the wrong decision and lose my family in the process. So, I decided I was going to have to end things with Prez; and for good this time. I would always love him, but I loved my family more.

It was my release date, and Damien was right on time to pick me up. As we were driving home, I looked over at him, and it felt like it used to when we were dating. I leaned over, and I gave him a kiss on the cheek.

"What was that for?"

"For loving me."

Damien grabbed my hand and he held it the entire ride home. We pulled up to the house and I was so anxious to see the kids. I missed them so much.

"Now the kids have been waiting for this moment all day. So, are you ready?'

"Yes. I'm ready to see them."

I walked inside the house, and there was a welcome home banner and balloons hanging on the wall. The kids ran towards me, and I gave them the biggest hug imaginable. I was so happy to see them. I looked at my family, and I knew that I had made the right decision to cut Prez out of my life. Caroline walked over and gave me a hug as well.

"You look good. So how do you feel?"

"I feel good. I'm clean in the mind, body, and spirit."

"Well okay. I'm glad to see that you're doing better. We really missed you, and the one who missed you the most is sitting right over there."

I looked up and Caroline was pointing at Olivia.

"Why do you say that?"

"Because your daughter is really attached to you. Poor Olivia couldn't comprehend why you were gone. Damien tried his best to explain it to her, but she didn't understand. Then one day we noticed Olivia wasn't in the house. We looked everywhere. We didn't know where she had wandered off to."

"Are you serious? She left the house?"

"Yes. We pulled out the driveway to go and look for her, but we didn't have to go too far. She was walking down the street with her backpack, and a picture of you in her hand. Damien put her in the car and he asked her where she was going. She said that she was going to get you, and to bring you home. It was so precious, I wanted to cry."

I looked at Olivia, and even though she seemed happy I could see the sadness in her eyes. I never knew how much I was hurting my kids until that moment. Throughout the day, it didn't matter where I went, I noticed Olivia was right there behind me. She wasn't letting me out of her sight. Wherever I went, she followed.

I enjoyed the rest of the day with my family. It was nice to spend time with them and not have to stress about things that weren't in my control. Before long, it was the kid's bedtime. I had missed tucking them in at night, and watching their faces as they slept gave me the confidence, I needed in order to do better. It was late, and I decided to turn in as well. Damien looked at me and smiled as I tried to get comfortable in bed.

"What are you grinning about?"

"Nothing. I'm just glad you're home. That's all."

"Well, I'm glad to be home. I really missed you guys."

I leaned over and gave Damien a kiss. I had truly missed the simplicity of the life we shared together.

"Let's make a pact."

"Okay."

"No more lies. No more secrets. No more anything. No matter what we're going through, we're going to always be honest with each other. Okay?"

"Okay."

I thought about Prez, and how our affair would destroy my family. There was no way I could tell Damien the truth. He would leave me, and I didn't want to lose what we had together. So, the affair would remain a secret. Damien gave me another kiss, and we talked the night away. I eventually fell asleep in his arms.

The next morning when I woke up, I rolled over to notice Olivia lying next to me in bed. Seeing her underneath me brought tears to my eyes. I was hurting my baby, and she didn't deserve the way I was treating her. Damien woke up, and he saw me wiping away my tears. He looked over, and he saw Olivia lying down beside me.

"I never knew how strong the bond was between the two of you until the day you left. She loves you so much."

"And I love her too. Olivia and Dominick mean the world to me. I never meant to hurt my kids. You know I would do anything for them."

"I know you would, and staying clean is the best thing you can do for them now."

"And I will."

Olivia woke up and she saw me in bed. A big smile came across her face.

"Mommy."

"Morning, baby."

Olivia hugged me, and gave me a kiss on the cheek. I pulled Damien over towards me, and I hugged them both. I loved my family so much. Before long, I heard little feet running towards the room. It was Dominick. He came into the room and jumped onto the bed. I had my entire family with me, and everything about that moment felt right.

A week passed, and I was trying my best to avoid facing Prez. I hadn't seen him in a couple of months, and I knew it was time I confronted him head on. Caroline had flown back home, and now it was up to me to fall back into my regular routines. She told me she never informed Prez of my whereabouts whenever she would drop off Dominick for his weekly visits. She explained to him that I was out of town, and that I would return home soon. I loved the fact that Caroline never felt obligated to tell Prez about my addiction.

I gathered up Dominick's belongings, and I had Julie watch Olivia while I dropped off Dominick. I was so nervous about seeing Prez again, but I was much stronger than I used to be. I needed to do what had to be done, and that was to end things between the two of us. Prez opened the door and he was surprised to see me.

"Rhonda. You're back."

"Yes. I'm back."

Prez tried to kiss me but I pulled away.

"Okay...am I missing something?"

"Yeah. We need to talk."

"Alright. So, what do you want to talk about?"

"Us and what we've been doing. I can't do it anymore."

"What do you mean you can't do it anymore? Why? What's changed?"

"I've changed. I can't keep hurting my family, so…I have to let you go."

"Okay. So…where did you go? You've been gone for a while, and now that you're back, you're telling me that things are over between the two of us? What's going on, Rhonda?"

"There's nothing going on. All you need to know is that what we had is over. I can't do this anymore."

Prez seemed confused about what I was saying. He took Dominick to his room to watch television, and then he made his way back towards me.

"What happened? Why are you all of a sudden pushing me away? We love each other, and now you're telling me that it's over? What's going on, Rhonda?"

I struggled with whether or not I should tell Prez the truth about rehab, but I figured he deserved to know what was really going on.

"When I went away…it was to receive help. I was in rehab."

"Rehab? But why?"

"I was addicted to pain pills. While I was using, I wasn't able to think clearly, but now I can. What we were doing was wrong, and it needs to stop."

"Pain pills! Are you serious? Why didn't you tell me?"

"Because, as long as I was medicated, I was able to keep the affair going, but now I know better. I love you, and you know that, but what we had is over. I choose my family."

"Rhonda…I love you. Come on. Don't do this to me."

"No. Our love is toxic. You're killing me and I can't take it."

"So, I'm supposed to just let you go, regardless of how I feel about you."

"Yes. For me and my family, you have to let me go."

"I knew this day would come but I'm not ready to let you go."

"I know, but you have to."

Prez walked towards me and gave me a hug. I was really doing this. I was letting him go.

"I love you, but this is going to be hard for me to do."

"It's hard for me too, but it's for the best. So, friends."

"Friends."

Prez tried to kiss me, and I pulled away, but that didn't stop him from getting what he wanted. He continued to kiss me, which only made it harder for me to let him go. This crazy attraction between the two of us was the one thing that got us in so much trouble. I struggled to break away but Prez wouldn't let up.

"Stop. We can't do this. I told you. I'm done."

"I know, but I can't help it. How am I supposed to stop loving you?"

"I'm not asking you to stop loving me. All I'm asking you to do is to respect my boundaries. We have to stop."

"I know, and I promise to work at it, but you have to understand that this is going to be hard for me to do."

"I know it is, but we can do this. Okay?"

"Okay."

Prez gave me a kiss on the cheek and I walked away. I loved Prez true enough, but my heart was at home. My family was the most important thing to me. Was it going to be hard to be around Prez? Yes. It was going to be a struggle, but I knew that in the end I was making the right decision. The love we shared for each other would always be there, but for the most part, I knew I had to let him go. Getting my life together was the only thing that mattered. I had been to hell and back and I was determined to prove that it wasn't for nothing. Keeping my family together was the only thing on my mind, because if the affair between me and Prez ever came to light, then my efforts for keeping my family together would've all been in vain.

# Chapter 39

# Karma

Weeks passed and Prez and I had finally found a system that worked. He kept his word and he never once over stepped his boundaries. Things between Damien and I were going well, and I found myself falling in love with my husband all over again. Life was good—maybe too good to be true.

Prez finally headed back to the States. He caught a lead on one of his cases, and just like that, he was gone. It felt weird not having him around, but I knew that it was for the best. My life soon returned back to normal. I went back to work, and Damien and I fell back into our normal routine. Life was as it used to be and I was loving it. I didn't mind the routines. They reassured me everything was okay, but then one day out of the blue, I got a surprise visit from Prez. Luckily, the kids were down for a nap. It would only confuse them if they saw Prez inside the house.

"Hey. What are you doing here?"

"Well, I decided to stop by and deliver the good news myself."

"What are you talking about? What good news?"

"We caught your guy! We have Dabula behind bars as we speak."

"Are you serious? You caught him?"

"Yep. He tried to throw us off, but we realized he never left London to begin with. He has been here the entire time. Go figure, right?"

"Dabula. Has been here?"

"Yes. Why?"

I began to worry. If Dabula never left London, then that can only mean one thing. Him and his thugs never stopped spying on me.

"No reason. I'm just glad that it's over. So, are you satisfied now?"

"Yes, I am."

"Well good. It took some time, but now you can finally close your case. So, what's next for you?"

"I'm going home. While I'm there, I'm going to put in for a request to come back to London, so I can continue to spend more time with Dominick. Being a good father to my son is all I care about."

"And what about Dabula?"

"I'm transferring him back to the States tomorrow, and then it will be officially over."

Prez was so happy and I was happy for him.

"Well, I wish you the best of luck, and don't forget to call me and let me know when your transfer goes through."

"I will."

Prez picked me up and gave me a kiss.

"Hey. Boundaries, remember?"

"I know and I'm sorry. I got caught up in the excitement, that's all."

Damien came walking through the door. I turned around and I didn't know if he saw the kiss or not.

"Hey. So, what's going on in here?"

"Nothing. Prez just stopped by to inform me of Dabula's arrest. It's over. It's finally over."

"Dabula?"

"Yeah. I'm sorry. I forgot I've never mentioned his name before. Dabula Mendoza, he was my old supplier. It feels so weird being able to say his name out loud without being afraid for my life."

"So, you caught him?" Damien glanced between me and Prez, then narrowed his eyes.

"Yes. It's done. Dabula is finally behind bars."

"So, what was the kiss about?"

"What are you talking about?" I tried to play it off, but I couldn't. Evidently, Damien saw the kiss between me and Prez.

"Don't play crazy with me, Rhonda. I just saw him kiss you. So, what's up with that Prez? You come in here and you disrespect me in my own home?"

"No. It wasn't like that. I just got caught up in the moment. That's all."

"Do I look crazy to you?" Damien was getting upset and he started approaching Prez. "Is there something I should know about? Tell me, Rhonda. Is there something still going on between the two of you?"

"No. It's like he said. It was in the heat of the moment. Nothing more. Okay?"

Damien looked like he was about to snap. Then he turned his attention towards Prez.

"Leave! Get out of my house now before I end up in jail."

Prez started to walk out.

"So, I'll call you later."

Why did he say that? Damien rushed Prez and I tried my best to stop him, but instead, I caught a punch in the face that was intended for Prez. Once Damien realized what he had done, he dropped to his knees in horror.

"Rhonda! I'm sorry. I'm so sorry. Are you okay?" Damien was trying to check my face.

"Yes. I'm fine." Prez was trying to compose himself, but I just needed him out of my house. "Prez just go. Please."

Prez hesitated. I could tell he wanted to comfort me, but decided against it. He motioned as if to say something, but instead took my advice, and decided to leave. I went into the bathroom to examine my face. I could see a bruise starting to form on my right cheek.

"I'm sorry. You know I would never hit you."

"I know. It was an accident."

Damien was sympathetic, but he was angry as well. I didn't know how to play the situation. He was all over the place. I touched my face and it hurt.

"Let me see." Damien tried to examine the bruising around my right cheek. I didn't know how to react. I knew it bothered him that he had accidently hit me in the face, and I for one was about to jump out of my skin.

"I said it was okay." I tried to walk out of the bathroom and Damien followed after me.

"Be honest with me, Rhonda. Am I reading too much into what happened, or is there something still going on between you and Prez?"

Damien deserved to know the truth, but I was afraid to tell him.

"There's nothing going on between us."

"But was there something going on between the two of you? And don't lie to me. Not now."

My hands were shaking. I didn't know what to say.

"Damien, please. Let's not do this."

"No lets. Was there something going on between you and Prez? I want the truth, Rhonda."

Tears fell from my eyes because I was truly afraid of telling Damien the truth. There was no telling how he would react, but I knew it had to be done. I had to look past my fears and expose the truth.

"Yes, but it didn't mean anything. It was a mistake and now it's over."

Damien grabbed hold of me and he slammed me up against the wall. He was gripping me tightly, and I didn't know what to think. He had never man handled me like that before.

"Why? Why would you do this to me? I did everything for you, and you betray me like this?"

"I'm sorry. I'm so sorry."

"You're sorry! Are you serious?"

Damien kept squeezing and it began to hurt.

"Stop! You're hurting me."

"You're hurting! Really? So how in the hell do you think I feel right now? I just found out that my wife has been screwing around with her ex. What did I do? Tell me, Rhonda! What did I do to deserve this?"

I couldn't stop crying. There was no excuse for what I had done. My husband was hurting, and it was no one's fault but my own.

"Nothing! I was weak. That's all. I messed up and I'm sorry."

"Weak!" Damien began to laugh. He picked me up and he began to carry me out of the house.

"Stop! Come on, Damien. Put me down."

Damien threw me to the ground in the front yard.

"You're not welcome here anymore."

I couldn't believe it. Damien was throwing me out.

"Damien! Wait! What are you doing?"

"I'll have your things ready for you tomorrow, but you can't stay here, not anymore."

"Damien, don't do this. Please! I was self-medicating when it happened. I didn't know what I was doing. Please. Don't do this to me."

"So, it's been going on that long. Nice."

Damien walked inside the house and locked me out. What did I do? I had nowhere to go. Prez was leaving London. I was all alone. I sat on the porch and all I could do was cry. I didn't know what to do. Damien opened the door and I tried to force my way in.

"Stop. You're not coming in here." Damien pushed me back and threw my purse onto the porch. "I figured you were going to need some money to get a room. Now leave."

"Damien, please don't do this. Please. I love you."

Damien became enraged. He grabbed my purse, picked me up off of the porch, and he took me to my car kicking and screaming. He opened the door but I wouldn't let go of him. He had to peel me off of him. He put me in the car and closed the door.

"Leave. Now."

I couldn't move. I knew I was wrong for what I had done, but I didn't want to lose my family. As soon as Damien stepped out of the way, I jumped out of the car, and I took off running towards the house. I wasn't giving up without a fight.

"Damn it, Rhonda! Don't make this any harder than it has to be."

I stood in the living room determined to reconcile with Damien, even though he wanted nothing more to do with me.

"I'm not going anywhere. This is my home and I'm not leaving. You and the kids are my family. So please. Don't do this."

"Your family. Were you thinking about us when you were out screwing around with Prez? You knew how I felt about you being around him, and then you go off and do this behind my back. I can't stand the sight of you right now. I want you out of this house, now!"

"Come on, Damien don't do this to me. I messed up and I get that, but please, please don't push me away. I need you guys."

"And what I needed was a wife who was faithful, and you—well you're not that woman. So please. Just go."

I couldn't move. This was my home. Where was I to go? Damien was so angry that he began breaking things around the house.

"Stop! Don't do this."

"Then get out. Just the sight of you makes me sick right now. So please leave, before I do something I'll regret."

I was about to speak, but then I saw Olivia peeping around the corner. Our arguing must have woken her up.

"Mommy. What's wrong?"

My heart was breaking. I had destroyed my marriage, and now my kids were caught in the crossfire.

"It's okay, Livy. Let's go back to your room, and once Daddy and I finish talking, then you can come out. Okay?"

"Okay."

I walked Olivia to her room and I turned on the television. Children are not stupid. Olivia could sense something was wrong, and I didn't want to upset her any more than I had already done. I walked out of her room and I looked at Damien. He was hurting and I hated it.

"I refuse to argue in front of the kids. So, you win. I'm leaving, and for what it's worth...I am sorry."

I walked out of the house and Damien closed and locked the door behind me. I got into my car and I drove down the street. I sat at the stop sign and all I could do was cry. The one thing I didn't want to happen was happening. I had nowhere to go and no one to turn to. I went and got a room at a local hotel. I tried calling Damien several times, but he never picked up. I was so hurt. I laid in bed and cried all night long. I had time to think about all the choices I made over time, and then I realized all I could do was welcome this day into my life. I was the creator of all my pain, and I had no choice but to face the consequences.

The next day, my eyes were sore from crying. I drove back home and Damien kept his word. All of my things were boxed up and sitting on the front porch. I was done crying. I took as much as I could and left. I found a hotel I could rent by the week, and I sat in the room trying to come to terms with everything that was happening in my life. My cell rang and I answered. It was a guard from the prison. Dabula had requested to see me. I didn't know why he wanted to see me, but I was at a low point, and I decided to entertain his request. I drove to the prison and I met up with Dabula.

"You asked to see me?"

"Yes. Rhonda. I'm glad you came."

"Like I had a choice in the matter. So, what do you want?"

"I just wanted to see an old friend. That's all."

"Okay. You've seen me and now I have to go."

"No. Not just yet."

"And why not? I'm going through something right now and I don't have time for this."

"Then I'll be quick. Over the course of time I've been here in London, I've had time to observe you on a regular basis and—"

"And what? Because you and I both know that I didn't have anything to do with your arrest. I've never mentioned your name to anyone."

"And I'm aware of that. Your loyalty was never a question."

"Really. So why did you drug me? What did I ever do to you to make you hate me so much? I made you rich, but that wasn't enough. You drugged me after I begged you not to. And…"

"And after that, you became an addict." I gave Dabula a surprised look. "Oh yes. I know all about your addiction."

"So why did you do it? What was the point of shooting me up if you knew I wasn't a threat?"

"I needed a decoy, and you were it. I never planned on leaving London, but I needed the cops to think otherwise. I knew your boyfriend would listen to you, and once he saw how serious I was, I knew you could convince him to back off…and you did."

"So, this was all just a game to you."

"Yes, and you played it perfectly."

"Wow! So, my life meant absolutely nothing to you. You could have killed me with the amount of drugs you pumped into my system, but you didn't care. I was just a pawn in your stupid game. I regret the day we ever met."

"Really? Because I distinctly remember back in the day you searched me out, not the other way around."

"And not once did I ever cross you, but you could've cared less about me. You drugged me, and for what? You destroyed my life."

"Your life was nothing until you met me. I supplied you when no one else would. So, don't come at me like you didn't have any part in this. Anyway, let's get back to the real reason I called you down here. Since I'm in such a generous mood, I wanted to be the one to give you the head's up."

"Heads up about what?"

"Well, I promised you a long time ago that I wouldn't ever harm you or anyone in your family, and I've kept my word, but as for your FBI friend. Well I hope you said all of your good-byes, because your little boyfriend is history."

"What are you talking about? You said that you wouldn't hurt anyone."

"No. I promised not to harm anyone in your family. Detective Santiago isn't your family. He's a cop and I've had enough of him; but this." Dabula held up his shackled hands. "This was the last straw. So, I wish you well, and give my regards to Santiago, if he's still alive."

"Dabula, please. Don't do this."

"It's already done."

The guards came to take Dabula away and my heart was racing. I needed to find Prez. Dabula ordered a hit on him, and I needed to find a way to warn him. I raced out of the prison, and I tried calling Prez, but he never picked up. I was so afraid. I could barely drive because of my shaking hands. I tried to rush to Prez's apartment, and as soon as I approached his turn, I could see him leaving his complex. I looked up and I saw a van sitting across the street. I knew I wouldn't get to him in time, so I got out of the car, and I raced towards him. I was yelling out his name and before long, he saw me. By the time Prez looked my way, the van took off. I was running and screaming, and out of nowhere, I heard gunshots. Prez turned as soon as he heard the first shot. He tried to draw his weapon, but he never had a chance. I screamed in terror as I watched Prez's body fall to the ground. I was clipped in the shoulder from the gun fire. I could hear sirens in the distance. I got up and I continued to run towards Prez. When I got to him, he was lying on the ground bleeding out.

"Prez! Baby! Come on…stay with me. Come on. Stay with me."

Prez had tears in his eyes as he fought to hold on, and I was a wreck. I saw the chain around his neck and I ripped it off. I took the chain and rings and I placed them in his hand.

"Hold on to these. Think about us. Come on. Don't leave me. Please don't leave me."

Prez was coughing up blood, but through all of his pain, he was able to mutter out one thing.

"I love you."

I became hysterical. The paramedics arrived to rush Prez to the hospital. They wouldn't allow me to ride with him, because I had been shot as well. As soon as I arrived at the hospital, I insisted on speaking with someone regarding Prez's condition, but no one would tell me anything. I became irate, and the doctors had to sedate me in order to remove the bullet from my shoulder. When I woke up, I forced myself out of bed, and I went out looking for Prez. One of the nurses saw me, and she tried her best to escort me back to my room, but I wasn't hearing it. I demanded someone tell me what was going on with Prez. I lied and told them that I was his wife. Finally, one of the doctors notified me that Prez had died upon arrival…

My heart felt as though it had stopped beating. He couldn't be gone. Not Prez. He was stronger than that. He was a fighter. He couldn't be dead. I asked to see the body, and one of the doctors escorted me to a room where Prez's body was waiting to be moved. I walked into the room, and once I saw the sheet over Prez's body, I broke down. I pulled the sheet back and I immediately fell apart. He was really gone. I ran my hand through his hair and then I gave him one last kiss good-bye. I tried to walk away, but I couldn't. The doctors had to help me out of the room. Later on, one of them handed me the chain Prez had been holding onto. The pain had become too much to bear, and the doctor had to sedate me once again.

My life had been a lot of things, but "fair" wasn't one of them. I had truly loved Prez and now he was gone. I didn't know what to do, and worst of all, I had no home to return to. What was I going to do? I had endured so much loss in my life, but Prez's death was the ultimate bombshell. I couldn't handle it. The doctors called Damien, because he was listed on record as my point of contact, but he never came. My arm was placed in sling to try and relieve some of the pain from my shoulder, but it didn't work. My emotional pain was greater than my physical pain, and I didn't know how to manage it.

Upon my release, the cops gave me the keys to my car, and I tried my best to drive back to the hotel. During the ride back, all I could do was stare out of the window in a constant daze. Prez was all I could think about. I couldn't believe he was gone. Once I made it back to the hotel, I sat in the car, and I tried to rationalize everything that had happened. None of it seemed real. I tried to manage my pain, but I couldn't. Prez was gone. I began to think about the pills I had stashed away in my glove compartment, and I took them out. I went inside my room, and I stared at them contemplating on what I should do next. I was clean. I had written off methadone, but I was in so much pain, and self-medicating was the only way I knew how to cope. I needed the pain to stop, and I debated on whether or not I should take a pill. I needed to be strong, but the pain was so overwhelming. How did I get to this point? My family was gone, and now I had lost Prez forever. All I could do was scream. Why was this happening to me? I tried calling Damien, but just like before, he never picked up. I knew he was hurting, but it broke my heart to know that he didn't show up at the hospital after hearing that I had been shot. To hate me was one thing, but to not care about my well-being was just downright cold. I began to break down. I couldn't take it anymore. I placed a pill in my mouth and I chased it with a glass of wine. After that I took another one. All I could do was cry. I felt as though I was paying for all of the wrong, I had done in my life, but when were the payments going to stop? I could only endure so much. I was truly at my lowest, and I didn't know if I was going to make it. I had lost everything. This was once again my well-earned *karma*.

# Chapter 40

## Saying Good-bye

I didn't know how I was going to do it, but I needed to pull myself together in order to attend Prez's funeral. I booked two plane tickets back to DC. One for Dominick and one for myself. Regardless of what Damien may have thought about me, I was taking Dominick with me to DC, so that he could say good-bye to his father.

My shoulder made it hard for me to drive, but eventually I made it to the house. I rang the doorbell, and to my surprise Damien answered the door.

"What do you want?"

Damien was so cold but I had to be strong.

"I've come to get Dominick."

"Well, that didn't take long."

"What are you talking about?"

"I figured you would've come for him sooner or later. So, let me guess. Prez is leaving town and you're going with him."

"No. That's not it."

"Then what is it? Why do you want Dominick?"

"Because he's my son. Why else?"

"And what about Olivia? She's your daughter, but I don't hear you asking for her."

"Don't try and play me as if I don't love my daughter, but I need Dominick to come with me, so he's able to say good-bye to his father."

"So, Prez *is* leaving town. You're sure you're not going with him? I mean the two of you just can't seem to get enough of each other."

"You're a real ass, you know that…but I don't have time to play these games with you. I have a flight to catch, and I need Dominick now, along with his passport."

"His passport? Why do you need his passport?"

"I've already explained this to you."

"No, you didn't. What's going on, Rhonda? What are you up to?"

"I'm not up to anything. I just need for Dominick to come with me. That's all."

Tears fell from my eyes.

"Rhonda. What's going on? Are you seriously planning on leaving town with Prez?"

"No."

"And why should I believe you?"

"Because Prez is dead." There was only silence.

"He's what?"

"You heard me. He's dead! Now I don't care what you may have thought about him, but Dominick is his son, and I'm taking him with me."

"No, you're not. When the hospital called me the other day, I didn't think it was this serious, but if Prez is dead, then how do I know it's safe for Dominick to be out and about with you?"

"Because I'm his mother, and I would never put him in any danger."

"Really! You're standing here with your arm in a sling, your ex is dead, and yet you're trying to convince me that it's okay for the kids to be around you right now? Get real, Rhonda."

"I'm not reckless, Damien. I would never…"

"You would never what? Put your kids in danger? Please! Do I look stupid to you?" Damien was livid. "I take it you were shot at, but that doesn't seem to register in your head. You could've been killed don't you get that? When are you going to wake up and realize that you're a hazard to yourself and everyone around you?"

My heart continued to break.

"You're right. I'm a walking train wreck, but what do you care? The doctors called and notified you that I had been shot, and you didn't even show up. You could've cared less if I was dead or alive. So, let's not pretend as if you give a damn about me, because you don't."

I started to tear up but I held them back. I needed to be strong.

"Look, Rhonda. I don't have time for this. Now I've made up my mind, and you're not taking Dominick anywhere. So just leave."

"No! I will not leave. Any other day I would argue with you about this, but not today. Prez was his father, and I'm taking him with me so he can say good-bye. Now move out of my way." Damien wouldn't move. "Come on, Damien, move! I'm tired and I've been through enough. So just give me my son."

Olivia came running to the door.

"Mommy!"

She ran over to me, and I tried my best to pick her up. I gave her a kiss and then I put her down. My shoulder was in a lot of pain.

"Hey Livy…how's momma's baby?"

"Good. So, when are you coming home?"

"I don't know, baby, but you look so cute."

Through all my grief, I almost broke out in laughter. I looked at Olivia's head and I could easily tell that Damien was struggling with trying to do her hair, but it was so cute, because Olivia was none the wiser of how her head really looked. I tried to stop the tears from falling, but I couldn't. I had to pull myself together, because I didn't want to upset the kids. I was hurting and I missed my family.

"You need to go before you upset her."

"I'm not leaving without Dominick."

"Think about what you're asking."

"I know what I'm asking and I want my son. You have no rights in this situation, so hand him over now."

"Fine. I guess you won't be satisfied until you ruin his life as well."

I was so hurt. I couldn't believe Damien allowed those words to come out of his mouth.

"Nice. Real nice. Just bring me my son."

Damien went inside to gather up Dominick belongings, and I followed in after him. I went and sat on the sofa, so that I was able to talk with Olivia.

"So, have you been a good girl while Mommy's been away?"

"Yes, but I heard Daddy say that you're not coming back. What's wrong, Mommy? You don't love us anymore?"

Tears fell from my eyes. I loved my kids, and I didn't want them to think otherwise. I needed to find a way to make things right.

"Olivia. Don't ever think that. You know I love you. No matter what Daddy says, I'm coming back. I couldn't leave you if I wanted to. You're my baby. Remember that."

"I love you, Mommy."

"I love you too."

I had to wipe away my tears. I was becoming too emotional in front of Olivia.

"And Mommy."

"Yes, baby."

"Can I go with you and Dominick?"

"No, baby. You can't go. If you leave with me then who's going to be here with Daddy? You don't want him to be alone, now do you?"

"No, but I want to go too."

Damien bought Dominick into the room, and he ran over and I gave him a big hug.

"Mommy!"

"Hey, buddy. So, are you ready to go?"

"Yes."

I grabbed Dominick's suitcase, and I could see Olivia starting to tear up. My heart began to break. I didn't want to leave her, but I knew Damien wouldn't allow me to take her with me.

"Be good for Mommy. Okay, and I'll be back soon. I promise."

"Mommy, I want to go too."

As I began to walk out of the house, I could hear Olivia crying. My heart was breaking. I buckled Dominick in his car seat, and I took two more pills and drove off. My nerves were bad, and I needed the extra help just to make it through the day.

I headed to the airport and once I arrived, there were two officers waiting for me in the terminal. I had done nothing wrong, and I didn't know why they wanted to see me.

"Mrs. Fletcher?"

"Yes."

"Can you come with us please?"

The officers escorted me to a different terminal, and I sat there and awaited instructions. Before long, an airline attendant approached me, and she escorted me aboard a private plane. I asked her what was happening, and why was I being placed on a different flight, and that's when she informed me that I was requested to escort Prez's body back to the States. I almost broke down in tears, but I didn't want to frighten Dominick. It took everything in me to hold it together.

The flight was long, and I wanted nothing more than for it to come to an end. I watched Dominick as he slept, and he was genuinely his father's son. From his curly hair to his facial expression. Dominick and Prez were truly one in the same. I was so glad Prez was able to spend so quality time with Dominick. He loved his son, and guilt was eating away at me for keeping them apart. Regardless of how Prez may have treated me in the past, I shouldn't have kept him away from his son. I stole moments away from him that he'll never get a chance to experience, all because I was selfish. I had allowed my pain to provoke me to make some questionable decisions in my life that I would forever regret.

Once we landed, I escorted Prez's body to the funeral home, and then I left him in the care of his family. I didn't know any of them, which made the entire experience for me that much harder. They all wondered who I was, and I continued to tell them that I was close friend of Prez, but as soon as they saw Dominick, they became very emotional. It was all too much. I tried to be strong, but the entire experience had proven to be too much.

I rushed to the car, and I began to head towards the hotel, but on my way there, I decided to take a detour. I drove by the colonial Prez and I use to own, and I just sat there as I began to reminisce about the past. Even though our marriage was a fake, we shared some happy times together. My heart began to ache, and I had to force myself to drive away. I checked into a hotel and I stayed there until the day of the funeral.

The day had finally arrived and I was dressed and ready to go, and yet I couldn't force myself to move. I knew I had to be strong. Prez would've wanted me to be there. I had to pull myself together in order to say good-bye. Once we arrived at the church, I walked inside holding Dominick's hand, and everyone's attention was drawn towards us.

They all were staring at Dominick. I looked up and I saw Maria. She was sitting with the family. I slowly walked towards the casket, and all I could do was stare at Prez. He looked so handsome. I took the wedding rings that were attached to the chain, and I placed them in his hand, and then I gave him a final kiss good-bye. I picked up Dominick in order for him to say good-bye as well. Dominick began to lean over, and I couldn't figure out what he was trying to do. He was heavy and my arm was beginning to hurt, but as I watched him, I immediately saw what he was up to. He was trying to give Prez a kiss as well. I leaned him over, and I watched as he gave Prez a good-bye kiss on the cheek. I could hear the family as they broke down in tears. It took everything I had within me to walk over to my seat. I sat in a daze as the service commenced. As we were escorted to the burial plot, memories of my life with Prez started to flood my head. I thought back to the day when we first met at the doll shop, and how from that day forth, we were immediately drawn to each another. I never intended to fall in love with him, but it happened anyway. I thought back to when I was in prison, and how Prez came out to visit with me every day, up until the day of my release. Regardless of his intentions, he was always there. I even recalled the day when we were married, or so I thought, and it was one of the happiest days of my life. We both cried during the entire ceremony, and Prez promised that we would always be a family. He made sure he was there for the birth of Olivia, and despite what he may have told me in the past, I knew he truly loved me. We had a good life together even though it was short lived, and through all of the drama and the sea of lies, I still loved him. We both shared a bond that was indescribable, and for that reason alone, I would always love, Perez Santiago.

My nerves were bad, and I didn't know if was going to make through the entire ceremony. The Bureau gave Prez a true departmental service. Everyone from the Bureau was there, along with local police department. It was all surreal. I wasn't ready to let him go. Then they performed the 21-gun salute, and I almost passed out. The ringing of the gunshots started to tear away at my heart. I tried to be strong but it was hard. After the service was over, I went to say my final good-bye.

"Hey. I just wanted to let you know that everyone came out to say their good-byes, and it was so beautiful. Even Dominick moved everyone to tears. He gave you a kiss on the cheek, and it was so sweet. He misses you. I miss you. I still can't believe you're gone. I'm so sorry for any part I may have played in this. You know I love you. I'll always love you, and I miss you so much."

I broke down crying and felt as though I was going to faint, but to my surprise Maria was there to catch me. I turned to her and I continued to cry. I couldn't control myself. Maria didn't say anything. She just allowed me to weep in her arms. I could feel Dominick pulling on my hands. I tried to compose myself, but my heart was in pieces.

"I'm so sorry. I didn't mean to..."

"No. Trust me. I understand." Maria wiped away her tears, and then she looked over at Dominick. "So, who is this handsome fellow?"

"This is Dominick. Say hi."

Dominick was pretending to be shy.

"Hi." Maria extended her hand to him, and he shook it.

"Hi." He was so adorable.

"Well, don't you look just like your father." Maria then turned her attention back towards me. "So how old is he?"

"He's three."

"Three. So, you were pregnant when we first met."

"I guess I was."

"You know. For the life in me I never knew what Perez saw in you." I bit my tongue, and I didn't respond. "But it had to be something special, because he loved you in the way that I loved him. When I look at you, it hurts, because you had what I always wanted—a family with Perez."

"I'm so sorry. I never meant to cause you any pain." I grabbed hold of Dominick's hand. "But if you'll excuse me, we have to go."

"When are you leaving?"

"Tomorrow, why?"

"Because the reading of the will is tomorrow morning, and they have you down to be there."

"Me? But why?"

"Because, Perez listed you in his will."

Maria gave me the location information, and then I left with Dominick. The next day arrived and I made sure I was packed and ready to go. I went to the lawyer's office and Maria was already there. There were other people there along with Mr. Dawes who was presiding over the will. Before long, Mr. Dawes began the reading of the will, and he started out with Maria. He stated how Prez had left her his insurance policy, and he went on to mention how Prez wanted to apologize to her for all the hurt he had caused her throughout their marriage. Mr. Dawes also mentioned how there was a letter intended for her as well, and once he handed it to her, Maria broke down in tears. I looked over at Dominick, and I had no clue as to why we were there. Before long, Mr. Dawes mentioned my name. He stated that there were letters for both Olivia and Dominick. Mr. Dawes approached me, and handed me the letters along with a badge. He mentioned how Prez wanted Dominick to have his FBI badge. Mr. Dawes went on to explain how the Bureau had agreed to release Prez's badge, but they had to file off his serial numbers before releasing it. Mr. Dawes continued on with the reading of the will and to, my surprise, Prez had also written a letter for me as well. I decided to wait until later to read it. I said good-bye to Maria, and then I headed out towards the airport.

I boarded the plane, and it felt as though I was leaving a part of myself behind. I didn't know what I was going back to England for. Damien had made it clear that our marriage was over. I was probably going to have to fight for custody yet again, just in order to see Olivia. I had made my bed and now I had to lie in it, and it wasn't comfortable at all. I was hurting all over. My heart was broken, and I had no way of fixing anything anymore. I decided to do the only thing that made any sense to me, and that was to pack up my life in England and move back home to Florida.

# Chapter 41

## The Black Hole

On the plane ride back to England, I decided to go ahead and read Prez's letter. I was nervous about reading it, only because there was no telling what he had to say in it. When it came to Prez, our relationship was complicated, and I felt as though my letter could've gone either way. He could've loved or hated me. I took the letter out of the envelope and a piece of paper fell into my lap. I picked it up and I stared at it in shock. It was a check for 10 million dollars. The same money Prez had claimed to have turned over to the Bureau. I couldn't believe it. He had my money all along. I began to read the letter.

Dear Rhonda,

If you're reading this letter then I'm no longer with you and for that I'm sorry. Throughout my life I've had the chance to meet a lot of people, and never before have I met anyone like you. From the day we met, I knew there was something special about you, and you made me question every decision I had ever made in my life. Loving you was probably one of the easiest things I could've ever done, and lying to you was one of the hardest. I regret how our lives turned out. I never meant to hurt you, and I miss you. My life hasn't been the same since the day you left. I lost a part of me when you walked away, and I would've given anything to have you back in my life. I miss Olivia as well. She was my little girl, and I hate that I won't get a chance to see her grow up. I thought of so many ways to get you back into my life, but I hurt you deeply and for that I'm sorry.

I kept a lot of secrets from you, and one of the biggest ones involved your money. The government was never informed of your offshore account. I knew you had changed, so I couldn't see taking your money away from you, but I had to hide it from the Bureau. Enclosed is the check from your account. You no longer have to hide it in offshore accounts. It's clean. I made sure of it. I'd always planned on giving it back to you, and if you're just now receiving it then it's only because I never got around to doing it myself. I love you so much. I miss my family, and most of all I miss you, and regardless of what the courts may have said, you were always my wife. My happiest moments were when I was with you.

I love you always,
Perez Santiago

I took the letter and I placed it back inside the envelope. I was so glad Dominick was asleep, because all I could do was cry. I missed Prez, and I hated the fact that he was taken away from us. We had a bond that was like no other, and even though he was gone, he would always have a place in my heart.

Once we landed, I headed back to the hotel. I began to pack up my belongings, and even though it was hard for me to do, I called Caroline, and I explained to her everything that had happened leading up to Prez's death. I sat in silence as she scolded me over the phone. I knew I had it coming, so I took it, and buried it along with all my other feelings. I had been popping pills all morning long. I was unaware of how many pills I had actually taken, but all I wanted was for the pain to stop.

I decided to take Dominick to the park to play before heading over to Damien's to pick up the rest of his belongings. I sat on the bench in a daze. Nothing seemed real. I could see things happening all around me, but nothing seemed to have registered in my head. Out of nowhere, Olivia was racing towards me.

"Mommy."

Even though I was happy to see her, I could barely move. I tried to hug her, but I couldn't. Olivia jumped into my lap and gave me the biggest hug possible. I missed her so much, but it didn't show. I was numb to everything around me.

"Hey...what are you doing here, pooh?"

"Denise brought me to the park."

"Denise?"

I looked up and a strange woman came walking over towards me and Olivia. She was very pretty, and she seemed familiar, but I had no idea as to who she was.

"Okay, Olivia, it's time to go."

I got up, because I didn't know what was going on. Who was this strange woman, and what was she doing with my daughter?

"Excuse me, but who are you?"

"I'm Denise and you are?"

"I'm Rhonda. Olivia's mother...and why is she with you and not Julie?"

"I'm sorry, but I don't know of any Julie. I only have Olivia because Damien asked me to watch her for a while."

"He did? Well tell Damien that Olivia is staying with me, and that I'll drop her off later."

"I'm sorry, but I can't do that. Damien left me in charge of Olivia, and I can't leave her with you, even if you are her mother."

Regardless of how I felt, I had to force myself to get it together. I didn't know this woman, and she wasn't about to go anywhere else with my daughter.

"Oh, but you will, and if you have a problem with that, then I suggest you take it up with Damien, because Olivia is leaving with me." Denise tried to reach out for Olivia and that's when I snapped. "And if you ever touch my child again, I swear before God, I'll break your hands. Now, I'm nowhere in the mood to deal with you or Damien and his dumb ass decisions, so if you think I'm playing, then try me."

I was livid. I didn't know who this Denise was and I didn't care, but one thing was certain. She wasn't taking my daughter anywhere. I grabbed Dominick and Olivia, and we left the park. I didn't want to go back to the hotel, because I knew that would be the first place Damien would check. So, I drove around and I enjoyed the rest of the day with the kids. They were just the medicine my body needed.

It was getting late, so I decided to drop Olivia off at Damien's and pick up the rest of Dominick's belongings. I pulled up in the yard, and I got the kids out of the car. I was about to ring the doorbell, when I noticed the front door was cracked open. Without thinking I decided to let myself in, and that's when I interrupted a kiss between Damien and Denise. The strange part was that it didn't even faze me. I had taken so many pills that I was void of emotion. Damien looked like a deer in headlights, but I, on the other hand, had no reaction at all.

"Rhonda. Where have you been and where's Olivia?"

"She's right here, but if you weren't so busy lip-locking then you would've seen her." I looked over at Denise.

"Don't go there."

"And why not?" I stopped myself, because there was no point in me getting upset. We were over, and it was time for me to accept that, and to move on. "You know what? Don't answer that. What you do is your business. Not mine."

"You're right, and you would be wise to remember that."

"Whatever."

"Don't 'whatever me' and another thing, if I leave Olivia in the care of someone else, then you are not to interfere. Denise was freaking out because you took off with Olivia, and she didn't know what to do."

"And what were you doing? Comforting her?" The entire situation was laughable to me. "Anyway, I'm here to get the rest of Dominick's things."

"Why?"

"Because he's my son, and he's moving back to Florida with me. It's apparent there's nothing else left for me here, so I'm moving back home. I'll have my lawyer get in touch with you regarding a visitation schedule for Olivia." I looked over at Denise. "And don't worry. Your divorce papers are in the mail as we speak. So, you're free to do whoever or whatever you like."

"You're moving back to Florida…and when did you decide this?"

"Who cares when I decided it? It was my decision."

"So, what about Olivia? The hell with her, huh? As long as you have Dominick, right? Considering he's the only one you seem to care about these days."

"You would think that, but no. I just don't have it in me to fight with you anymore. I love Olivia, and I would do anything for her, but for once in my life I'm thinking about her feelings, and not mine. All I want is for her to be happy. Regardless of who she's with. So, when my lawyer sends you the paperwork, just agree to the visitations, because I don't have it in me to fight with you in court again. I won't."

I walked into the kitchen, fixed a glass of water, and then I went into the bathroom and closed the door. I had lost my family, and Damien had made it obvious that he had moved on. The grief had returned. I took three more pills to try and numb the pain. As I walked out of the bathroom it became apparent that Damien was watching my every move. I had to think fast. I headed to Dominick's bedroom, and began to pack.

"What were you doing in there?"

"Nothing. So, go and entertain your friend and I'll be done in a minute."

"Rhonda! What were you doing?"

"I said nothing. Now leave me alone."

I tried to pack as fast as I could. I could feel my heartbeat racing. I didn't know what was going on. My hands began to shake. I wasn't sure of how many pills I had actually taken throughout the day, and I may have taken one too many.

"What's wrong with you?"

"Nothing. Now get out. Let me finish packing and I'll be on my way."

Damien wasn't hearing it. He grabbed my purse and started to dig through it.

"Give it back!"

I tried to snatch it away, but Damien had found what he was looking for. He opened the aspirin bottle and poured out the methadone.

"You're using again?"

"No. Now give them back."

"Do I look stupid to you?" Damien took the pills and flushed them down the toilet. "If you think for one minute, I would ever leave Olivia alone in your care, then you are sadly mistaken. You're spaced out right now. Aren't you?"

"No. I'm not. Come on, Damien. You know me."

"No. I used to know you."

"Please. Don't do this. Don't try and hold this against me. You know I love my kids, and I wouldn't do anything to hurt them."

"Then why are you using again?"

"I'm not using. You talk as if I'm shooting up or something. They're just pain pills. That's all."

"The same pills you became addicted to, or did you forget that? You're an addict, Rhonda, and you'll never change."

"And you're a hypocrite."

"I'm a hypocrite?"

"Yes. You kick me out of my home because of Prez, and yet you have another woman over here, and around my daughter. It's only been a few weeks, and you've already moved on."

"Denise and I are just friends, and besides, it's none of your business who I choose to be with. You and I are no longer together. Remember?"

"And how could I forget? Especially when I see the two of you lip-locking in the living room. 'Friends' my ass. Anyway. You know, now that I think about it, Denise does seem familiar. I couldn't put my finger on it earlier, but now I remember. She's a contractor at your job. You're around this woman every day, and you have the nerve to judge me. So how long has this little affair been going on?"

"I'm not doing this with you."

"And why not? You know, now it's becoming apparent why you really kicked me out. You were never hurt by my betrayal; you just needed me out of the way. You've been playing this situation to your advantage from the very beginning. You hypocritical bastard. That's why you didn't come and see me after I was shot. You were probably hoping I was dead. You make me sick."

I went back to packing, and my hands began to shake even more. My heartbeat had intensified. I needed to leave, and fast. Whatever I couldn't pack up, I would leave behind, because my heart couldn't take anymore.

"For you to even think that I could do something like that lets me know that you never really knew me at all. I loved you, Rhonda. You get that? I would've given my life for you, but you threw that away, and for what? Prez. So, don't come at me like you're the victim in this. You sabotaged our marriage. Not me."

"You're right. I screwed up everything. So just go back to Denise and leave me the hell alone."

"Rhonda."

"No. I get it. I truly get it. So, go and say good-bye to Dominick, and I'll be on my way."

"You're not leaving until we finish our conversation."

"Our conversation is over, just like we are, remember? So just go." Then out of nowhere we heard something break. It sounded like one of the kids had knocked over something in the living room. "You might want to go and check on that."

"Don't you go anywhere, because we're not done talking."

"Oh, we're done."

Damien went to check on the kids. My heart was aching, and I couldn't make it stop. Then all of the sudden I blacked out. What was happening to me? I had fallen to the floor. I tried to get up but I couldn't move. Why was I continuously hurting myself? My heart was racing, my thoughts were scattered, and it felt as though I couldn't breathe. All I could do was lie on the floor in pain. Every time my eyes closed, I would feel a rocking motion as if someone was shaking me back and forth.

"Rhonda. Can you hear me?"

A voice echoed in my head, but no matter how hard I tried, I couldn't respond.

"Rhonda! Come on!"

I could no longer feel the pain that use to saturate my heart. My body became relaxed. I could feel the pulsating of my heart as it beat in my chest. My heartbeat was no longer erratic. It had taken on a slow and steady pace. What was happening to me? I could feel the tears as they ran down my face, but no matter how hard I tried, I wasn't able to move my hands in order to wipe them away.

"Don't do this to me! Come on. Wake up."

I could hear screaming all around me, but I couldn't move. I was so tired, and all I wanted to do was to sleep.

"Rhonda! Wake up. Baby, please wake up!"

I tried to open my eyes, but my eyelids were way too heavy. I was trying to remember what had just happened, but I couldn't. Then, out of nowhere, I felt a slap across my face. The intensity of the blow allowed me to open my eyes, and when I looked up, the only person I could see was Damien.

"Damien?"

"Yes. It's me, baby. Come on. Wake up."

"But I'm so tired…just let me sleep." My eyes started to close and that's when Damien started to freak out.

"No. Come on, Rhonda…don't close your eyes. You have to stay awake for me. Open your eyes. Come on, baby. Open your eyes. I'm sorry. I'm so sorry. Please wake up."

I tried to open my eyes, but I couldn't. All I wanted to do was sleep. I had been through enough heartache in my life, and for once, I couldn't feel any pain. My heart wasn't breaking. I wasn't lying to anyone and no one was lying to me. I no longer had to choose. There was no reason for me to wake up. I continued to feel my heartbeat as it grew slower and slower. I could no longer hear the voices all around me. I finally felt at peace.

# Chapter 42

❧

# Exposed

When I finally woke up, I realized I was in a hospital room, and that I was confined to my bed. I didn't know what was going on. I tried to call out but my throat was sore. I looked around the room and I didn't see anyone. I tried to lift up my arms, but I couldn't move them. I tried to move my feet, and they were restrained as well. Before long, a nurse entered the room and noticed I was awake.

"Well, look who's finally up. So how do you feel?"

"I'm fine...and what's going on? Why am I here?"

"You're here because you overdosed last night. The doctor had to pump your stomach, and then he placed you on suicide watch. That's why they have you restrained."

"Overdose? But I didn't overdose. I would never do that."

"Well, that's not for me to decide. When Dr. Strickland comes in, you can tell him all about it. Okay?"

The nurse checked my IV bags, and then she left. I was angry and I wanted to go home. I would never try to kill myself. I began to cry. Before long, Dr. Strickland entered the room, and Damien followed in after him.

"Mrs. Fletcher...I was told you were awake. So how do you feel?"

"I'm fine. So, can someone please take these off of me?" I looked over at the restraints that were binding me to the bed.

"I can't do that right now. Once I determine you're not a threat to yourself, then I'll have them removed."

I looked over at Damien, and I couldn't believe he was allowing this to happen.

"Come on, Damien. Tell him. I would never try to kill myself. You know this isn't right. So why won't you get me out of here?"

"Because, you need help, Rhonda. Dr. Strickland knows what he's doing, and he'll be able to help you, because I can't."

"I don't need help. I'm fine. Come on. Let me out of here."

"Mrs. Fletcher you're here because you overdosed on methadone. You could've died if your husband wouldn't have brought you in when he did. So, tell me. Why were you taking methadone?"

"I'm sorry. I have nothing to say." I didn't know Dr. Strickland, and I wasn't in the mood to share with him. I turned around and looked at Damien. "I'm not doing this, now get me out of here."

"Come on, Rhonda. Answer his questions." I was shocked. Damien knew I didn't want to go there. Especially in front of him.

"I can't."

"Yes, you can. You can do this. Dr. Strickland is only here for your benefit. You're sick, Rhonda and you need help."

My heart was hurting and I didn't want to share, but I knew Dr. Strickland wasn't going to release me unless I was willing to play along.

"Fine. If you must know. I took the pills because they took the pain away; now let me out of here."

"What kind of pain?"

"What kind do you think? Emotional pain. I've been through a lot and I couldn't cope. So. I took the pills...okay?"

I looked over at Damien and I felt so ashamed. I couldn't stand for him to see me like this. I looked weak and it wasn't fair.

"So, when you took the pills, how did they make you feel?"

"Numb."

"Numb? In what way?"

"I don't know. My heart didn't hurt anymore. The methadone enabled me to function as if everything was okay."

"So, you thought by taking methadone, it would cure your problems?"

"No. It just made the pain stop. That's all."

"Have you seen a therapist before?"

"Yes. I saw one when I was in rehab."

"So, you've been to rehab before?"

"Yes."

"And by going to rehab and speaking with a therapist, did it seem to help?"

"Yes. In a way."

"So, what went wrong? Why did you relapse?"

"Because…"

I looked over at Damien and I struggled with the thought of telling them the truth.

"Because what? What happened Mrs. Fletcher?"

"Because my life fell apart. I had to bury two of my closest friends, I missed my kids, and to make matters worse, my husband kicked me out of our home…"

"Because you had an affair." Damien was quick to defend his actions.

"An affair I had ended months ago. What I did was wrong and that's why I went away to rehab. I wanted to make things right, but you… you had already moved on. You used my affair as ammunition to kick me out, just so you could move on with someone else."

"Why do you keep saying that? I told you, Denise and I are just friends."

"Yeah, and so were me and Prez."

"But you had an affair with him, Rhonda. You were sleeping with him for months, and you expect me not to be upset."

"Okay Mr. Fletcher you've expressed your concerns, but beating up on your wife while she's down isn't going to help the situation. Now from what I've just heard, it appears as though this 'Prez' seems to be the root cause to a lot of your problems. So, tell me, Mrs. Fletcher, what drove you to have an affair?"

My affair with Prez was not up for discussion.

"I'd rather not say."

"Come on, Rhonda. I deserve an explanation. What were your reasons for screwing around behind my back?"

"Mr. Fletcher. Please."

"I'm just saying. I would like to know."

"So, tell me, Mrs. Fletcher. Are you willing to talk about the affair?"

"No."

"Well, I think if you were able to talk about it, then maybe, just maybe, it could help save your marriage."

"My marriage is over. My husband has moved on and I'm fine with that. So, can we please talk about something else?"

"Mrs. Fletcher, you're avoiding the question. I think if you were truthful with yourself, then maybe it could help you to heal."

"Truthful...you know what I've learned about the truth? I've learned that the truth is an ugly bastard that no one wants to deal with. So, here's the truth for you. I was in love with two men at the same time. I didn't want to lose my family so I went away to rehab to get help, but once that truth was exposed, my husband kicked me to the curb. So, was that the truth you were looking for?"

"So, you were still in love with him?" Damien was crushed.

"I don't know. I thought I was, but it doesn't matter anymore, now does it? My life is what it is, and I've come to terms with that." I then turned to face Dr. Strickland. "Now can you release me?"

"As soon as I run a couple more tests, then I can release you back into your husband's care."

*"Damien?* No. He's made it very clear how he feels about me. So, I'll be taking care of myself."

"I'm sorry, Mrs. Fletcher, but I can't allow that. I'm releasing you into your husband's care, only because he's to escort you over to rehab by the end of the day."

"Rehab! But I don't want to go back to rehab. I just need to go home."

I began to cry. I didn't want to face my problems. All I wanted to do was to run away and hide.

"You can't go home. You're not well, Rhonda. You need help." Damien said in a sympathetic voice, but I wasn't hearing it. Rehab was out of the question.

"There will be no need for any of that." I looked up, and there stood my parents. I began to bawl like a baby. I didn't want them to see me like this. I felt so ashamed.

"Mom. Dad. What are you doing here?"

"Damien called and told us what happened. So, we're here to take you home."

"But she needs rehab." Dr. Strickland tried to explain to my parents.

"Then I'll take her myself." My mother claimed as she walked over and kissed me on my forehead. "I'll take care of you. I promise."

My father demanded the removal of my restraints, and as soon as they were removed, I hugged my mother and then my father. I watched as Damien slowly slipped out of the room. My parents wanted to know what went wrong, and I tried my best to walk them through everything that had happened. It sounded like something out of a movie when I explained it out loud. My father reassured me that everything was going to be okay, and then he went over to speak with Dr. Strickland.

Once I was released, I took my parents to the hotel where I was staying to get the rest of my belongings, and then I had to face my hardest obstacle yet: going over to Damien's to retrieve the rest of my things. I didn't know how I was going to face my kids. When we arrived at the house, Damien opened the door and the kids rushed me the moment I walked in. It felt so good to see them. I sat and talked with them as my parents set up moving instructions with Damien. I glanced over at him, and he seemed flustered by everything that was happening.

"And make sure they pack up Dominick's things as well."

"So, you're still planning on taking Dominick with you?" The possibility of me leaving Dominick with Damien had never crossed my mind.

"And why wouldn't I? He's not your son, and we're no longer together, so why wouldn't I take him with me?"

"Because it wouldn't be fair to the kids. That's why."

"But Dominick needs to be with me."

"And I get that, but splitting the kids up right now isn't in their best interest, and you know it."

"Then what would you suggest, because I'm not moving back to Florida without him."

"And I'm not asking you to, but you're going away to rehab, and you're not going to be there with him anyway. So just leave him here with me, and I'll take care of him until you get better."

Even though what Damien was suggesting made sense, I didn't want to leave my kids knowing that I was going to be thousands of miles away from them. The mere thought of leaving them broke my heart.

"Come on, Rhonda. Listen to him. Leave Dominick, and then when you're better you can get him back. Okay?" My mother was trying to reason with me, but I wasn't hearing it. I didn't want to leave either one of my kids.

"But I don't want to leave them. I'm their mother. I'm supposed to be here for them. How can I do that when I'm millions of miles away?"

"And how can you do it if you're not well? Work with us, Rhonda. Come home and get better, and then after that you can see your kids again. Okay?" My father was right. I couldn't see about them if I wasn't well. I had to suck it up and realize that I had no choice but to leave my kids in London with Damien—at least until I was better.

I took the kids into another room and I tried to explain to them why I had to go away for a while, but Olivia wasn't hearing it. She wanted to come with me. I tried to explain to her that kids weren't allowed to go where I was going, and that I had to go alone. I gave them both a kiss, and I tried to leave the house as fast as I could. I sat in the car and I watched as Damien fought to get Olivia back into the house. I tried to convince myself that what I was doing was for the best, but no matter what I told myself, it didn't stop my heart from breaking.

During the plane ride home, my mother sat next to me and held my hand the entire trip. When we pulled up to my parents' house, Caroline walked out with JJ. He was so big. He had to be what, ten-years-old now? Eleven? I couldn't believe it. I was so excited to see them. I got out of the car and ran over to hug them.

"So how do you feel?"

"I don't know. I miss my kids, so…I don't know how to feel right about now."

"Well, you have a true prayer warrior right there, and she's going to help you pull through this." Caroline hugged Mom. She was right. My mother loved me, and I knew that she was going to do everything within her power to help me beat this and help me get my kids back.

Caroline walked with me to my room.

"So, what's up with JJ? I see he's here with you."

"Yes. Brad finally granted me shared custody."

"So, what's up with the two of you? Are you guys getting back together?"

"We're not making any decisions right now. Our plans are to take things slow and see where they lead."

"That's smart…"

"And what's not smart is you overdosing on methadone. What were you thinking?"

"That's the problem. I wasn't thinking. I just wanted the pain to stop. I took one pill too many, and my body just shut down."

"But you were clean, so what happened?"

"A lot happened. Damien kicked me out, I couldn't see my kids, and then Prez..." I started to tear up. "It was just a lot to deal with."

"And I understand that, but..."

"No! You don't know...how hard...it was..."

I tried to hold it together, but I couldn't, and eventually I broke down in tears. Caroline tried to console me, but I was overcome with grief. I had lost my family, my parents were now aware of my addiction, and to make matters worse, I had to go back to rehab. My life was in shambles, and I wasn't sure if I was mentally capable of putting it all back together again.

"You're going to be okay. You'll always have me." I continued to hug Caroline as she repeated to me over and over again that everything was going to be okay.

Finally, the big day had arrived and I was off to rehab. My parents drove me to the clinic, and my father dropped me and my mother off at the registration office. She helped me through processing, and when it was time for her to leave, she didn't.

"You're not leaving?"

"No. Not until you're better."

I hugged my mother and then I was escorted to my room. The doctor explained to me how, even though my mother was staying, I could only visit with her whenever I showed signs of progress. My mother would be like a reward for each step I completed.

Rehab was hard yet again because there were times when I didn't want to share. There were days at a time when I didn't get to see my mother because I wouldn't participate in therapy. I knew I had to come to terms with my problems, but the pain was unbearable. I had lost Rachel, and now I had to somehow face Prez's death as well. I loved him, and even though he was gone I was still finding ways to hold onto him. I didn't know how to let him go. I had to also face the hurt I had caused Damien and the kids. Having to come to terms with how I treated them almost tore me apart. I was aware of Damien's love for me, but that didn't stop me from hurting him. I thought about Olivia, and all the hell I put her through. My love for her was so intense that I ended up shutting down. It was days before I decided to speak again. How could I have been so selfish? Olivia and Dominick were innocent in all of this, and yet they were the ones who were suffering the most. I began to realize that I had to stop lying to myself, and that I needed to get better; if for no one else, then for my kids. So, I stopped fighting progress, and I decided to truly embrace rehab. I wanted to get better. I needed to get better, and I didn't want to be the one to block my own recovery. I knew it was going to be hard, and no matter how many demons I had to face, I was determined to get better.

After I decided to stop fighting myself, rehab became a breeze. I couldn't allow my pain to run my life, so I had to learn how to face my problems head on, and not mask them just because I didn't want to face them.

Before long, it was my release date and I was going home. My mother stood by me every step of the way, and that made me love her even more. Just having her there with me made the experience that less stressful. I had to rediscover self-love, and I had to remember that, regardless of my actions, I was worth loving too. I deserved to be loved. I deserved to be taken care of. I even deserved to be treated like a queen. Knowing how to love yourself will open your eyes to the fact that, yes, it feels nice to have someone else to love and take care of you, but you have to first know how to love and take care of yourself. Karma.

# Chapter 43

### ❧

# The Breakthrough

It was the day of my release, and my father was there to pick up me and my mother. I was so excited to be going home, and the only thing I could think about was seeing my kids again. Later on, that evening, my father surprised my mother and I by taking us out to dinner. Caroline and JJ were already at the restaurant, and it felt good to have my family together again.

After dinner was over, we made our way back home, and Caroline and I stayed up and talked the night away. It felt like old times again. It was getting late and we decided to call it a night. I was getting ready for bed when I, surprisingly, saw my mother was still up. She made her way into my room and sat down next to me on the bed.

"Mom. You're still up."

"Yes. I wanted to talk with you before you went to bed."

"Okay. So, what do you want to talk about?"

"I wanted to know if you'll be willing to go to church with me tomorrow."

"Church?"

"Yes. See, I've noticed that you can go to rehab a thousand times over, and you'll never be able to fully heal like you should. Not if you don't have God in the picture."

"Mom..."

"No. Hear me out. I know you're looking at me and you're going, 'yeah, yeah,' but trust me on this. When I was locked up, I saw something that shook my soul. Like most women in prison, I was lost, so I started to attend the Sunday morning worship. The services were typical. A lot of praying and soul searching, but over the course of time I started to really listen, and I watched as women who had lost everything, and those who seemed to have had nothing else to live for, were able to rediscover God's love, and it was so amazing to see how they were able to transform their lives. I truly believe that God can heal all things, and I know that he can heal you as well."

"And I know he can, but I'm good. I don't need church to know that God loves me."

"Don't fool yourself, Rhonda. You need him more than you realize."

I didn't know what my mother was getting at, but I decided to entertain her proposition by attending church with her the next day. Morning arrived and everyone was dressed and ready to go, and to my surprise, Caroline and JJ were dressed as well.

"So, I see she talked you guys into going as well."

"No. I've been going for the past two years now, and I'm telling you, Rhonda, if you allow God to come into your heart, then you'll see firsthand that there's nothing in the world that you can't handle, and as long as you trust in him, then you'll never be alone."

"Okay. You're starting to sound just like mom, but we'll see."

I attended service with my family, and I sat there, and I tried to be open, but there was nothing. No aha moment. No breakthrough or anything. Maybe I was missing something, but my mother was determined. So, the following Sunday I decided to be a little more open. I wanted to be healed. I needed to be healed, but I didn't know what I was doing wrong. Maybe I didn't believe enough, but I was willing to try harder. I sat through the service, and then halfway through the pastor made a short announcement that the choir would be performing a special selection. While I was looking down over my program, I started to hear a voice. It was a familiar voice. I looked up and it was Justine. She was singing. I couldn't believe it was her. My parents looked over at me, and they smiled. Justine continued to sing and I noticed the lyrics related not only to me, but her as well.

*"He was there always to protect me*
*For He's kept me in the midst of it all…"*

Her words were hitting home. They felt like an ice pick chipping away at my heart. She praised God for helping her through her darkest of days, but I could barely stand it. I knew she was only there to help me, but I was starting to feel overwhelmed with emotions. I began to think back to all the trials I endured in my life, and it felt like I couldn't breathe. It was when Justine came to the bridge of the song that all of my past memories started to flood my head, fighting with Caroline, Damien being there for me, meeting Prez, pulling a gun on Damien and Rachel, being raped, my parents turning their backs on me, fighting with Damien in court over Oliva, shooting Prez, marrying Damien, losing Rachel, being kidnapped, becoming addicted to methadone, having an affair with Prez, going to rehab, Damien throwing me out, Prez dying, and then overdosing. So many thoughts were running through my head, but Justine kept right on singing.

*"Jesus kept me, Jesus kept me, and Jesus kept me in the midst of it*
*all yeah…"*

Then all of a sudden, I stood up. Everyone went to clapping and praying, but I didn't get up to go to the altar, I got up because I wanted to leave out. It was all too much. I made my way to the end of the pew, and when I turned to walk out, I couldn't move. Something had a hold on me and it wouldn't let go. Justine made her way down from the choir stand as she continued to sing. It was as if she was singing the song just for me. Tears were running down my face as I tried to take another step, but I couldn't. I felt like I was going to fall, but the ushers rushed over and they held onto me as Justine continued to sing on. I kept thinking about how she blamed me for Rachel's death, and yet she was in church singing just for me. It was a feeling I had never felt before. I became overwhelmed in the spirit. Though the ushers held me up, I felt weighed down. It was like the song Justine was singing was written just for me. My family was in tears. They watched as all the hurt and the pain I was secretly holding in came pouring out. The next thing I knew Justine extended her hand out to me and I grabbed onto it. She was still singing, and now she was singing directly to me. It was all too much. I knew of forgiveness but it was hard for me to forgive myself. I held on to pain for so long that my heart didn't know how to let it go, but I knew it was time to forgive myself.

My mother rushed over and held my hand, and then I felt her remove her hand and replace it with another. I looked up to see it belonged to Damien. As soon as I looked in his eyes, I knew we both had regrets of the way we acted. I gave him a small smile and he nodded knowingly as if to say all was forgiven. Justine escorted us to the altar while she was still singing. I stood before the alter holding Damien's hand—not broken, but renewed. My mother was right. The type of healing I was experiencing at that moment was like nothing I had ever felt before.

I stood at the altar as the pastor spoke words of encouragement over me and Damien. I had never cried so hard in my life. I looked over at Damien and he was in tears as well. The pastor's voice came over the speakers.

"This is a true testament of God's everlasting love. It doesn't matter who you are or what you've been through, God forgives all things. There's nothing too big for God that he can't fix it. He is the Alpha and the Omega, the beginning and the end. He made you and he knows what you're going through. He doesn't care about your past; he forgave you for that a long time ago. All God wants you to do is to trust in him, to love him, and to do his will. There's nothing too big. Remember that. There's nothing too big. Trust in God and he'll never lead you wrong. Amen…Amen."

I tried to compose myself, but it was hard. My heart felt as though it had been elevated. Damien squeezed my hand, and I was so grateful he was with me at that moment. He escorted me back to my seat, and sat down beside me. I saw the kids and I was so happy. I knew right then that things had to change. I needed to get my life together before I was able to get my house in order.

After the service Damien drove me back to my parent's house. I didn't say anything. I rode in the back seat with the kids the entire ride home. Later on, that evening my mother was inside cooking dinner, and the kids were running around playing outside. I looked up, and I saw Justine walking towards me. I got up, and hugged her.

"Thank you."

"It was my pleasure."

Justine sat down next to me on the porch.

"So why did you do it? I mean, I heard you blamed me for Rachel's death, so why would you come and sing for me?"

"Because deep down I knew it wasn't your fault, and I would be a hypocrite to try and hold Rachel's death against you."

"So, I take it my mother called you?"

"Yes. She told me you had been through a lot lately. While she was explaining everything to me, I kept thinking about Rachel. She had been down the same road, and no one was there to steer her in the opposite direction. I felt like I had failed her in so many ways, and I didn't want the same thing to happen to you. Regardless of our past, we shouldn't be denied a second chance."

I was so grateful to Justine for what she had done for me. I wiped away my tears, and I gave her another hug.

"Thank you so much."

"Anytime. Now cheer up. It's a beautiful day. So, enjoy it."

"I will."

Justine got up and walked into the house. I sat on the porch, and I felt the sun as it warmed my face. The entire day had felt like a dream, but I knew things were going to get better. While I was sitting on the steps, Damien walked over and sat down beside me.

"So, are you okay?"

"I am now."

"Well, you seem a whole lot better."

"Because I am. I know I have a lot of work ahead of me, but this time I'm not going to run away from it. I'm going to do what needs to be done, and get my life back on track."

"And you will."

"You're right. I will, but enough about me; how are you holding up?"

"I'm good. Trying my best to get a handle on the kids. They had been counting down for the past couple of days…ready to see their mom. They really missed you."

"And I missed them as well. I'm going to do better. I promise."

"I know you will."

Damien gave me a kiss on the forehead, and then he walked off. I loved him, but through the grace of God, I realized I didn't need his love in order to survive. I had been relying too much on others and not enough on the Word, and that needed to change.

I stayed home for a while, and decided to get back into the church. I wanted to get more and more into the Word, and to rediscover myself. I met a young lady during bible study by name of Alicia who turned out to be a great friend. She reminded me so much of Rachel, and we became friends instantly. I was loving where the Word was taking me, and I was determined to become the woman that God wanted me to be, and not who I thought I should be. I was going to be there for my kids and I was going to get my life together one step at a time. I had been through the storm, and now I was ready to come out of it—for good this time.

# Chapter 44

### The Road Home

The day had come for me to decide what I was going to do next. I thought long and hard about it, and I decided to go back to England. I wanted to be near my kids, so I booked the next flight out, and I headed back to London. There was so much I needed to do, but the first thing on my list was to find a new place of worship. So, I searched around town until I was able to find a church home that shared my religious background, and thanks to Prez I had more than enough money to survive on my own, so I went out and bought a condo in the heart of downtown London.

My condo was new and upscale, but I didn't want it to feel cold; I wanted it to feel more like home, so I hired a designer to come in and decorate the kid's rooms. They did such a great job that I had them redecorate the entire condo. The final touches were made, and I was ready to show off my new place. I was so excited, that I forgot to call Damien to let him know I was back in town. I decided to let it be a surprise. I was so nervous about seeing the kids again. I kept telling myself that it was going to be okay as I drove to Damien's. I didn't know how they were going to react to me being back in London or to my new place. I rang the doorbell, and Damien answered.

"Rhonda. OMG, you're here." Damien seemed a little surprised.

"Yes, I'm back."

"Come in." I walked into the house, and Denise was sitting in the living room on the couch. "You remember Denise?"

"Yes. I remember her. Hi."

Denise seemed shocked when I spoke to her.

"Hi."

"So where are the kids? I came to see them."

"They're out with Julie. They should be back soon if you want to stick around and wait."

"Sure, I don't mind." We all sat around looking at each other. So, I decided to be the one to break the silence. I opted to spark up a conversation with Denise. I was curious to hear what she had to say regarding her relationship with Damien. "So how are things going with you and Damien?"

"No…there's nothing going on between us. We're just friends." Denise looked uncomfortable.

"Well, it's okay if there is. We're no longer together, so there's no need to hide your relationship."

"There's nothing to hide. We're only friends. She helps out with the kids every now and then, nothing more." Damien looked at Denise and she seemed embarrassed.

"You two aren't fooling anyone, but I'm willing to play along."

"I'm serious. There's nothing going on between the two of us."

"He's right. Damien's a nice guy, but I don't date married men." Was she serious? I had to refrain myself before I said something out of character.

"Then why are you here?" My question had left Denise speechless.

"Rhonda!"

"What? I'm just stating the obvious. If she's not into you, then why is she here? I mean we're no longer together, so if she wanted to make a move, then she should've done it by now. It's been months and you two are still using the, 'we're just friends' line. Give me a break."

"But we are. I'm not going to lie. When Damien first showed me his divorce papers, I did try to a make a move, but he turned me down. Now, I get that's he's going through a lot, and I'm trying my best not to overstep, but I don't know what it's going to take in order for him to move on."

"She's right, Damien. You owe it to yourself to move on."

"And once our divorce is final then I'll think about it."

"What are you talking about? I signed the divorce papers months ago, so why isn't our divorce final?" Damien remained quiet. "Come on, Damien. What's going on?"

"I haven't signed the papers yet."

I was shocked.

"And why not?"

"Because…I don't know."

"You don't know? So, what I am supposed to do? Sit in limbo while you decide on whether or not you want to be married? Well I can't do that. I won't. So, just sign the divorce papers and get it over with."

"And why are you so eager to be divorced?"

"I'm not, but I signed the papers so that you could move on with your life. So, what happened?"

"Nothing happened."

"So why didn't you sign the papers?"

Denise stood up. "Look. The two of you need to talk and right now I'm just in the middle of things. So, if you'll excuse me." Denise got up to leave. She looked over at Damien. "I'll call you later. Okay?"

I thought back to the day when Prez said almost the exact same words and Damien went ballistic. I started to laugh to myself. The hypocrisy of it all.

"Sure." Damien then turned to face me. "And what's so funny?"

"Noting. Just memories. That's all." Denise left, and I was determined to figure out why Damien didn't sign the divorce papers. "So, are you going to tell me?"

"Tell you what?"

"Why didn't you sign the papers? Look, I know how you feel about me, and it's not fair to keep me trapped in a marriage that isn't going anywhere."

"You're wrong. You don't know how I feel. I sat in this house day after day, and I watched as my daughter would cry in secret and pray to God to bring her mother home. Do you know how it feels to see your child in pain, and to know that there's nothing you can do to take that pain away?"

I began to tear up. My daughter was still hurting, and this time I was determined to get it right. The only way I was leaving my kids again would be in a casket. There was no way I was walking out of their lives—ever again.

"And I'm sorry for that. I never meant to hurt my babies. They are my life and I would do anything for them, but for one brief moment in my life I was sick, and it was no one's fault but my own, but I'm better now and there's no way I'm ever leaving them again."

"Well that's good to hear, because they truly need you. They miss you. I miss you."

I thought my ears were deceiving me.

"You miss me; but why? You threw me out. Remember?"

"Because I was hurt and angry..."

"And you had every right to be..."

"No let me finish. I was in love with you, Rhonda. I've always been in love with you, and then Prez came along and took your love away from me. I thought I had lost you forever, until the day you agreed to marry me. I had you back in my life and everything was as it should've been. I knew in the beginning you weren't in love with me because of Prez, but then you started to come around. I could see the love in your eyes again, and I knew it was genuine, and for a while we had a good thing."

"Yeah, until I messed it up. You were right to kick me out. I was only good for one thing, and that was destroying people's lives. That's why I signed the divorce papers. I want you to have a good life. I want you to be happy and I know you can't accomplish that as long as you're married to me."

"You're wrong. The only time I was truly happy, was when we were together."

"I want to believe that, but I can't. Denise has been around too long for me to believe there's nothing going on between the two of you. What you said was nice, but I need you to sign the divorce papers. I need to move on with my life, and you need to do the same."

"See you're doing it again."

"Doing what?"

"You're pushing me away when it's obvious I don't want to go."

"And what am I supposed to do? I'm trying here. I moved back to London to be a part of the kid's lives and…"

"You moved back?"

"Yes. It was supposed to be a surprise. I bought a condo downtown, and that's why I came over here today. I wanted to show the kids my new place. They have their own rooms, and I know they're going to love it."

"So why didn't you call me? You could've stayed here with us…"

"No, I couldn't. I needed my own space. I need time for myself."

"So, you're really doing this."

"Yes, and before I forget, I wanted to thank you for taking care of the kids. Especially Dominick. You didn't have to take care of him, but you did anyway, and so…thank you."

"He's my son, Rhonda. So why wouldn't I take care of him?"

I started to tear up. It meant a lot to me that Damien never treated Dominick differently.

"Your son…"

Damien got up from the couch to sit next to me. I was trying to hold back my tears, but they came anyway, and Damien gently wiped them away.

"I get that a lot has happened, but when it comes to the kids, they're my kids. I've raised them, and I love them, and nothing is going to change that. Now Dominick and I may not share the same blood type, but he's my son in every way that counts."

"I'm so glad they have you in their lives, and I'm so sorry for all of the hell I've put you through. I hurt you, I hurt the kids, but I promise to do better."

"And you will, and when times get too hard, just remember I'm always here for you."

"You're something else. You know that?" I hugged Damien. That fact that he was so understanding made me smile on the inside. Most men would have called it quits, but for some reason Damien always stuck around. "So, can I ask you a question?"

"Sure."

"Why didn't you move on? I mean after everything I did to you, how could you not?"

"Because I was determined to be a better man than my father. When my mother abandoned us years ago, I grew up hating him, because I felt like he didn't fight for her. He didn't fight for us. He just let her go."

"But sometimes it's better to let go."

"And sometimes you have to fight and hold on. Back in college I knew you were the one, and even now you're still the one. Unlike my father, I'm willing to fight for my family."

"But am I truly worth fighting for? I've messed up so many times and…"

"Stop right there. Let me ask you a question. Do you love me?"

"I'll always love you. You know that."

"No. That's not what I asked. Do you love me? I mean truly love me."

I thought back to the teachings I had learned in church about knowing the difference between lust and love, and true love and real love.

"You know, I used to put so much of myself into feelings. It was always about what I wanted and how I felt. Feelings. But when it came to love, I never really knew love because I didn't have God guiding my heart, but when I broke down at the alter, and you stood there with me before God—broken, damaged, and not fully healed—that's when I discovered real love. You've been with me through the storm, and I never really saw you, because I was walking in a fog. I was letting time pass me by while I was sleepwalking through life, but when I woke up you were there. You've always been there, and that's why I'll always love you."

Damien started to tear up, then he leaned over and kissed me. There was something different about this kiss compared to any other kiss I had ever had with Damien. This one was the real deal. This kiss signified the birth of something new between the two of us. Damien called Julie and asked her to keep the kids for a little while longer. Damien and I made love to each other and it was as if we were making love for the first time. There was no void. I wasn't trying to lead. I was allowing my husband to make love to me and not let my past interfere. I discovered that when you allow God to enter your marriage, things will change. The love you have for each other changes, the respect you have for each other changes, and most of all the understanding that through Christ we can do anything together...saved my marriage—and it saved me.

Over the course of time, Damien and I grew together in the church and in love. I sold my condo and I moved back in with him and the kids where I belonged. I became more aware of the decisions I made in life, and I became more aware of me. Rediscovering myself and molding myself in God's love.

Throughout my life I was always looking for someone to love me, when in the end I had to learn how to love myself. God will always give you what you need, but if you walk through life in a fog, you'll never see it. Understanding God's love and recognizing my own self-worth redefined who I am, shaped me as a person, and taught me how to truly *love me*.

The End

Dear Olivia,

Before you can remember, I was your father. I did some very bad things to ensure that I became your father, and for that I'm sorry. I was wrong to lie to you and your mother, but for once in my life I had a real family, and I didn't want to let that go. You were my daughter and I loved you. I was there for your birth, your first word, and I could never forget your smile. I don't know if your mother told you, but you were named after my mother. Olivia Santiago. I lost her to a car crash, but she was given back to me in you. I loved her and I love you. No matter what happens in the future, just know that the choices I made in life were out of love and nothing else. I know you'll grow up to be a beautiful young woman and you will break many hearts, but whatever you do, don't be in a rush to grow up. Enjoy your childhood and enjoy your family, but most importantly please take care of your mother. She loves you deeply. I love you as well, and no matter what, you'll always be my daughter in spirit.

Your dad in every way that matters,
Perez Santiago

Dear Dominick,

My son. I still can't believe I'm your father. I've only had a short time to get to know you, but the love I have for you was instant. I look at you and I see myself. There are days when I hold you, and I don't want to ever let you go. There's so much I want to tell you, but just in case something was to happen to me, here are some little-known facts about your father. I was born and raised in Brooklyn, New York, and my parents died in a car crash when I was 10 years old. I was taken in by my grandmother, Sue, and you would have loved her. She could cook the best Latin dishes in the world, and even though I grew up without my parents, Grandma Sue always made me feel loved.

I also grew up watching cop shows, and I knew at a young age I wanted to be a cop. So, I went off to the academy, and then later on I joined the FBI. I love my job and I wouldn't trade it for any other job in the world. When you get older you can ask your mom about how we met, and it'll be up to her to explain it to you. There's a bond that your mother and I share, and nothing in the world would ever change that. When you came into my life, for the first time in a long time, the world felt right again. I know that the world can be a big and scary place, but know that nothing comes without sacrifice. Love and respect your mother because she's a blessing to have, and do what you're told. Never lie about what's important. Always be truthful when it comes to the heart, and know that I'll always love you. I pray that you grow up to be a respectable young man, and that you learn the value of a good woman, and remember that a real man always takes care of his family. I love you always.

Your father,
Perez Santiago

Sanity is considered a state of mind
Thoughts can be regarded as preparation
Anger can appear as an action
Love can alter your perception.
Remember that in life
there are no mistakes
-Just lessons.

- Catherine Clifton

Feedback is welcomed at: Catalystic2002@Yahoo.Com

Printed in the United States
By Bookmasters